"This anthology is a moving collection of voices from all sides of the complex, often tumultuous mosaic of relationships created by adoption, and the love, loss, deep feeling and struggles that come with them."

   —Laura Ingram, board member, PACER (Post Adoption Center for Education and Research), San Francisco Bay Area

"Far from being a narrowly focused anthology, this book is about the core issues for humans everywhere: how we came to be here, in what company, how to shape our lives and love each other in the midst of luck and fate, choice and will."

   —Kim Addonizio, author of *In the Box Called Pleasure, Jimmy and Rita: Poems* and *The Philosopher's Club*

"This wonderful collection resonates some of the deepest truths of the adoption experience from the points of view of all who are affected; adopted people, birthparents and adoptive parents."

   —Beth Hall, director, PACT: An Adoption Alliance

A Ghost at Heart's Edge

*Stories and Poems
of Adoption*

edited by Susan Ito *and* Tina Cervin

NORTH ATLANTIC BOOKS
BERKELEY, CALIFORNIA

Published by
North Atlantic Books
P.O. Box 12327
Berkeley, California 94712

Cover and book design by Ayelet Maida, A/M Studios
Printed in the United States of America

This is issue number 61 in the *Io* series.

A Ghost at Heart's Edge is sponsored by the Society for the Study of Native Arts and Sciences, a nonprofit educational corporation whose goals are to develop an educational and crosscultural perspective linking various scientific, social, and artistic fields; to nurture a holistic view of arts, sciences, humanities, and healing; and to publish and distribute literature on the relationship of mind, body, and nature.

Library of Congress Cataloging-in-Publication Data
A ghost at heart's edge : stories and poems of adoption / edited by Susan Ito and Tina Cervin.
    p.   cm.
ISBN 1-55643-323-9 (alk. paper)
1. Adoption Literary collections. 2. American literature—20th century. 3. Adoptees Literary collections. I. Ito, Susan, 1959–   .
II. Cervin, Tina, 1960–   .
PS509.A28G48   1999
810.8'0355—dc21   99-29299
                                             CIP

1 2 3 4 5 6 7 8 9 / 03 02 01 00 99

To my mother and stepfather, two points in the triad—T.C.
To the memory of my grandmother, Asano Inouye—S.I.

Acknowledgments

Putting together this book was an endeavor of the heart, not only of ours, but of each of the writers, poets, and behind-the-scenes people who contributed to this collection. We would like to express our deepest gratitude to all of the contributors—we have been truly inspired and moved by their words while preparing this anthology.

Thanks to Susan Bumps of North Atlantic Books, who said yes to the idea we had begun working on seven years ago. Her friendship and patience have made the steep learning curve of preparing a manuscript for publication a smooth ride upward. We also wish to thank Jacquelyn Mitchard for her willingness to embrace more work in the midst of a busy schedule and blooming family life. We would never have made our various deadlines without the invaluable help of Sasha Hom, our editorial intern. We thank Alison Lee—her gentle prodding, outright support, and grace toward the creative spirit and the challenges of juggling motherhood and working are deeply appreciated. We are indebted to Jill Aldrich for her generosity and editorial expertise.

We want to thank our husbands, David Gavrich and John Roark, for their love and emotional anchoring throughout this long journey. And we acknowledge our children—Max, Noah, Mollie, and Emma—for their patience while their mothers were inextricably attached to computers and phones.

Finally, we thank you, the reader, for picking up this book, for adding more life to its stories and emotions, for opening a door to the heart.

Contents

(III)

GROWING

(IV)

IDENTITY

(V)

RELATIONS

Foreword

Stories about the loyalties and losses, the conflict and redemption basic to family life are presumed to be "soft stuff," not the big-shouldered subjects that inspire real literature. The serious writer tackles war, urban violence, politics. Serious writers, usually men, writing for the movers and shakers of the world, not the dancers and dreamers of dreams.

What a myth. What a shame.

In fact, most great books are, in the end, about family, family and identity, family and crisis, family and destiny. From *Wuthering Heights* to *Cold Mountain* to *A Thousand Acres,* the landscape changes, but not the locus. Stories spring from our center, where we try to understand the things our families teach us and deny us, what they do to us and for us. The nature of our families comprises the answers to the intractable social questions of our times: Why do politicians philander? Why do the young sing songs of violent death? Why were we in Vietnam?

We are the flowers of the garden from which we spring. Given this, I've often felt bewildered by how little respect we give stories about homegrown topics. After all, these are the matters that occupy most of our attention for most of our lives.

My children came to me through birth, through adoption, through marriage. They came to us as seeds, as buds, as stripling plants, and as they grew, our roots entangled and merged into one system, a garden shaped and colored by our genetic personalities and the heritage of our love. As it says on the pennies in our pockets, out of many, we are one.

So given my roots I would be expected to respond with empathy to a collection of fiction and poetry about adoptive families, and, in fact, when I began to read *A Ghost at Heart's Edge,* I did. But not because these tales and songs are personally and socially close to my marrow, but because they are worthy of the telling.

They beam straight down the hallways of the house that is the birth family of us all. The human one.

Jacquelyn Mitchard
Author, *The Deep End of the Ocean*

Preface

This is not just another book about adoption. Bookshelves are over-
flowing with how-to books, memoirs, advice, information, and aca-
demic studies on the topic. This, however, is a collection of literature,
which goes to the heart of adoption through poetry, song, and story.
This anthology—a reflection of reality told by many voices—explores
the myriad themes of adoption and their pull upon us.

We chose to travel this complex, emotional, and sometimes poignant
terrain through literature because we believe that truth often is found
in a tale. Some of the authors in this collection have not had personal
experiences with adoption, yet the stories they tell are real, if not "true."
All, however, have chosen adoption as a vehicle through which to tell
compelling stories of people who are deeply, openly human.

Thirty million Americans are directly touched by adoption. It res-
onates throughout our collective mind, bound up in how we think
about family, identity, longing, loss, and hope. The word itself provokes
many questions: *Who am I? To whom do I belong? What is family? What
is a name?* Given these essential questions, one cannot help but be
moved by the stories and poetry in these pages.

In response to a call for submissions for this project, we were inun-
dated with manuscripts. Astounded, we began to sift through the hun-
dreds of pieces we received. As we read, a theme began to rise to the
surface: that of phantoms or ghosts hovering around the lives of many
of the characters and narratives. One line of poetry, "a ghost at heart's
edge" (in "My Stone is Sardonyx," by Katharyn Howd Machan), made
palpable the presence that seemed to filter through the collection, and
gave us the title of our book.

It is our goal, through these poems and stories, to deconstruct many
of the adoption myths that permeate our culture and to show each of
the adoption triad characters—adoptees, adoptive parents, birth par-
ents—in all their complexity.

Adoptive parents often are portrayed as grateful recipients of a gift
given only after they have failed to become "real parents." After adopt-
ing, their wish finally fulfilled, they are supposed to live happily. Yet

adoptive families have their share of ghosts: children never conceived, children conceived and lost, and the often invisible members of the family from which their son or daughter came. The voices of adoptive parents in this volume, both fictional and poetic, convey anxiety on many levels: over being judged "good enough" during the long uncertain waiting; at the joy of welcoming their child; and throughout the complex process of becoming parents.

The voices of birth parents have frequently been silenced, particularly those who relinquished children prior to this decade. Birth parents were supposed to disappear gracefully, forget, and go on with their lives. They often are the ghosts that haunt adoptive families: fearsome kidnappers or fantasy rescuers, sources of hidden genetic defects, holders of the ever-elusive key to history and identity. The birth parents here are as real as flesh, each carrying a differently shaped scar. Some are overwhelmingly tender in their love for their child; others are marked by guilt, violence, regret—the many faces of loss.

Adoptees, frequently perceived as objects of exchange rather than as active participants, are all too often expected to be grateful, to integrate seamlessly into their new families, to let the past slip away. Here, we let them all, grateful and bitter alike, speak their own truths. We see them grow from bundled infants, transferred from one family to another, to children and adults grappling with identity and belonging, wrestling with their own phantom histories.

Adoption does not take place in a bubble, but in a widening circle that touches all levels of family and society. In addition to the primary characters in the adoption triad, we have represented the voices of others affected by it—lovers, siblings, grandparents and grandchildren.

We have divided the book into parts that represent stages in the adoption process. The first, "Waiting," chronicles the lives of individuals before adoption occurs. It includes the voices of pre-adoptive parents as they make the decision to adopt and struggle to prove themselves worthy. Other stories reflect the pregnancy experience. We hear the perspectives of double sets of parents, and we witness the sometimes fragile, tentative bonding that occurs between them during the wait.

The second section, "Passage," depicts the period of transition when a child moves from one family to another, a time that is both ecstatic and heartbreaking. For adoptive families, this is the moment when a long-held wish comes true. Often there is a communication between families, an attempt to bridge the space between them. Other times there is simply a relinquishing and turning away—out of fear, sadness, determination.

We follow this with a section called "Growing." These pieces reflect the many ways in which adoption affects children, from their perspective as well as that of their parents.

The fourth section, "Identity," addresses the question that ticks inside each member of the adoption triad: *Who am I?* This question, inevitable for most youths, is especially pressing for the adopted child who is moving into adolescence and adulthood. The stories and poems here speak of the complex task of taking up the strands of Self and weaving them into a complementary whole. Adoptees are not the only ones who grapple with issues of identity; parents also question their roles as their children come of age.

The final section, "Relations," illuminates the reverberations that occur in all directions when separated blood relatives unite, when people who have been concealed are brought into the light, when individuals struggle to understand the meaning of family. Tales of search and reunion are powerful and mythical. They may relate devastating rejection or deep connection. No matter the outcome, individuals come away with more pieces to fit into the puzzle of their identities.

Although we cover a lot of ground in this book, we recognize that infinite tales remain untold. Much as we tried to represent everyone in this collection, we would like to have had more stories that reflected the voices of gays and lesbians, families who are not white and middle class, and open adoption and single-parent adoption. We hope that in future editions we will be able to include even more voices. This collection is a beginning, and by no means closed or definitive.

Pain, questioning, and joy are as intrinsic to adoption as they are to life itself. Our common experience teaches us that these tales and poems belong to each of us. Adoption, and the stories that surround it, is a crucible. It tests by fire our ideas about identity, loss, family, belonging or not—questions that burn in us all.

Tina Cervin and Susan Ito
Summer 1999

(I)

WAITING

Ten-Thousand-Foot Blue Sky

GAIL FORD

Over his right shoulder, a small cloud appears,
from nothing to something.

We talk
about easy things.

The cloud doubles in size.

I pass him the water,
watch it glisten on his lip.

The cloud billows at its edges,
blows, changes shape.

We don't talk about the children
we cannot have.

Amoeba-like, the cloud divides.

With the back of his hand he wipes his mouth,
tells a joke, grins white.

The cloud thins, fades, returns to blue.

I brush my fingertips against his cheek.

A patch of blue breathes white.
Out of nothing, something.

The Seed

JACKIE KAY

Serif italic typeface: birth mother
San serif typeface: adoptive mother

I never thought it would be quicker
than walking down the mainstreet

I want to stand in front of the mirror
swollen bellied so swollen bellied

The time, the exact time
for that particular seed to be singled out

I want to lie on my back at night
I want to pee all the time

amongst all others
like choosing a dancing partner

I crave discomfort like some women
crave chocolate or earth or liver

Now these slow weeks on
I can't stop going over and over

I can't believe I've tried for five years
for something that could take five minutes

It only took a split second
not a minute or more.

I want the pain
the tearing searing pain

I want my waters to break
like Noah's flood

I want to push and push
and scream and scream.

When I was sure I wrote a short note
six weeks later—a short letter

He was sorry; we should have known better
He couldn't leave Nigeria.

I missed him, silly things
his sudden high laugh,

His eyes intense as whirlwind
the music he played me

Anything

PAMELA GROSS

Yossi Farber leaned against the screen door and stared into the back-yard, where empty seed packets braced by Popsicle sticks guarded each row of newly planted carrots, lettuce, green beans, and asparagus. His wife, Miriam, had caught spring fever and spent the last three Sundays digging out the garden. Yossi breathed in the heavy scent of lilacs and peonies that grew along the back fence. *Flowers and vegetables,* he thought. *All that is needed to sustain a human being.* A door slammed, followed by a small dog's bark and sixteen-year-old Anna Levenson dashed into her yard, blond hair flying, a pair of scissors catching the dwindling Friday evening light. Yossi looked at his watch. It was almost time for *shul.*

Anna smiled at him over the fence as she clipped an armful of lilacs. "My mom said to tell Miriam that she'll be over later."

"I'll tell her," Yossi said.

He lingered in the doorway then moved inside to the dining room, where Miriam prepared to light Sabbath candles. But he didn't want to see that her eyes were puffy and red so he looked away. They had argued the entire afternoon about adoption and her shoulders curved with exhaustion. They were both exhausted, seven years exhausted from fertility specialists, temperature charts, tests, drugs, surgery. And now the panacea, adoption. Her voice, excited, had come through the shower water later that evening, "There's this baby . . ." and Yossi had stepped under the faucet and pressed the heels of his hands hard against his eyes until a low whining sound filled his ears.

Miriam struck a match.

"I have to go," he said.

He glanced at the two solitary place settings on the table. Normally, he would have been thrilled that they were eating alone. Yossi worked long days in his drugstore, and the hours, coupled with a heavy Sabbath meal, made him logy. When company stayed late, Yossi often embar-rassed himself by sitting at the table with his eyes closed, startled awake by a snore and polite laughter. But tonight he wished for a party, any-thing so he wouldn't have to face Miriam.

Robert Levenson, Anna's father, knocked lightly and peeked in the front door. "Ready?"

"Sure," Yossi said. He turned toward Miriam. "Anna said to tell you that Nessie's coming by."

Miriam's lips already moved in prayer. Robert waited for him on the sidewalk. "I love you," Yossi said before he closed the door.

Miriam checked the soup on the stove. Through the kitchen window, she saw Nessie wave as she opened the gate between their yards.

Nessie was older by ten years, but because of Anna she belonged to the neighborhood conversations about childbirth and nursing. Yet the distance Miriam assumed with her other friends was absent with Nessie. There seemed to be a sense of sterility about having only one child.

Nessie stood looking in through the back door, where a few minutes ago Yossi had stood looking out. She wore an ankle-length white skirt with an emerald green blouse. Aside from long earrings and her wedding ring, she wore no jewelry. The spicy scent of Opium perfume drifted across the kitchen.

Miriam spoke unconsciously, as if Nessie had appeared in the middle of a dream. "I envy you," she said.

Nessie's smile faded and she touched Miriam's hand. "Don't. Don't do that. Don't envy anyone."

Miriam blinked and withdrew her hand. She moved back toward the pot of soup. "How is the new book coming?" she asked as if she hadn't previously spoken.

Nessie moved to the other side of the counter. "It comes in spurts. And there never seems to be enough time. Sometimes I hate *Shabbos*. Here are twenty-four hours of virginal time and I think of all the ways I could use it. All the work I could get done. But then again I'm grateful to be able to shut down for a while. Catch up on a little reading."

"But if you were working, it would just be more of the same. You'd never manage to stash time away."

"Don't we have this conversation every week?" Nessie rubbed the back of her neck. "Etta invited me to Matthew's birthday party."

Miriam nodded. Etta had invited Nessie for Miriam. So she would have someone to talk to. She thought about the park overrun with three-and four-year-olds, about her friends' bellies in various stages of pregnancy, of Etta, ready to drop her eighth child. "Are you going?"

Nessie shrugged. "It'll give me a chance to get some sketching done."

"Thank you," Miriam said.

In the dining room, Nessie sat in Yossi's chair, picked up the cloth napkin and spread it across the plate. She turned down one corner then the other. "I can't be there all the time."

Miriam lowered her eyes and, flushed with an anger she'd never experienced toward Nessie before, stopped herself from saying that Nessie wasn't there a fraction of the time. She wasn't in the kitchen when Yossi kissed the back of her neck, expecting her to melt toward him with a passion that excluded the pressure of making a child. Nessie was in her sunroom painting when Miriam lay on the bed with her legs in the air so Yossi's sperm would have better access to her womb. She was across the yard baking bread that afternoon when the lawyer called about the baby and Miriam thought her heart was going to explode in her chest. She had been setting her own table when Yossi came out of his shower and said, "I just can't talk about this now."

Nessie turned the napkin over and continued to fold. She tucked up the napkin's edges and produced a rose. She centered it on Yossi's plate.

Miriam took her napkin. "Will you teach me how to do that?"

"This I can teach you. What I can't teach you is how to stand up for yourself—to politely change the subject when your friends get caught up in talking about strained apricots or to decline invitations where you know you'll be uncomfortable."

"No, I guess you can't." Miriam bit her lip and concentrated on the napkin. None of this was Nessie's fault. The candlelight added a softness to the room as the sky darkened. Nessie pulled back the curtain exposing a purple sky. "I have to help Anna with the salad," she said.

"Thanks for coming over," Miriam said.

Miriam kissed Nessie's cheek and Nessie's perfume enveloped her and she suddenly wanted to be Anna so she could lean against Nessie and be held and have her hair stroked, but she just stood and watched as Nessie faded into the shadows of the yard. She heard the gate click. Children argued over some toy in the family room of the house next door. In all the other houses on the block—except for the Weisses, whose children were grown and no longer lived at home—children blossomed like bouquets of wildflowers. She turned her attention toward her garden, where the soil was moist from recent watering and where the carrot leaf shot straight out of the soil, angling toward an invisible sun.

"You're rather quiet tonight," Robert said to Yossi as they walked home from *shul*.

Yossi raised his *kipah* from his head and ran his fingers through his hair.

"Miriam found a baby."

Robert appeared surprised.

Yossi kicked at a pebble and sent it skittering down the sidewalk. "I'm surprised Nessie didn't tell you. Miriam usually tells her everything." He waited for a rebuttal, but Robert's face spread into the calm he had when he dealt with children. His sandy-blond hair and soft brown eyes seemed to hold the patience of the world, a prerequisite for a pediatrician. Yossi bristled, but realized he was angry in general. The last hour in *shul* had faded to a blur, and Yossi couldn't remember if he had prayed. And then for a brief moment he wondered if he even believed in prayer. But he knew it wasn't the strength of his belief that he doubted, it was disbelief in the prayer. He wanted to pray: a prayer to make Miriam forget she wanted children, or a prayer for something worse.

"What are you going to do?" Robert was asking. Robert's voice was pleasant, "sexy" he'd heard some of Miriam's friends say, and sometimes when he saw him and Nessie talking softly in their yard and heard Nessie's laugh, he knew that Robert had said something suggestive, and he'd wait breathlessly for Nessie to touch Robert's thigh or for Robert to press his palm to the side of Nessie's breast. Their talk seemed effortless. His conversations with Miriam weighed so much that the words took up space in the room for hours and days, and it was often difficult to find a place to move around in.

"I don't know," Yossi said.

Two months ago he'd agreed to go with Miriam to a lawyer that a friend had recommended. "Just to know all the facts," Miriam had said. Yossi went just as he had gone to the Home Show to look at sinks they never purchased or on a Sunday ride to Wayzata to look at homes they couldn't afford. And then there was this phone call. Some girl, six months pregnant, wanting to give up her baby. Yossi thought it took years to adopt a baby. Years of lists and forms.

The house smelled of soup and lilacs. He noticed the two napkins folded like roses in the center of their plates. Miriam was in the back-yard staring at her new garden, probably willing everything to grow, he thought. She wore a long silky skirt with a flowered blouse, a thick black belt that made her middle disappear in the dark as if there were two separate parts of her. Her scarf was tied in an arty way that Nessie had taught her, and she wore long dangly earrings that tinkled slightly in the evening breeze.

Yossi was visible in the kitchen, and if Miriam turned she'd see him. He felt mournfully alone. Miriam had Nessie and Etta and an entire community of women with whom to share and sympathize. They gath-ered around her like protective armor. He had no one and trusted no one with his thoughts. Fear raged through him and sweat prickled his spine even though he stood under the air-conditioning vent. The lawyer's call had shifted everything, had changed the theoretical into reality. He could deny Miriam nothing. So he prayed for the baby to die.

Miriam no longer expected to give birth to a child. She'd prayed for one, but her prayers seemed diminished, as if she'd prayed for a new refrigerator or new tile for the hall. Somewhere in her rational mind she knew there was something lacking inside of her, something trun-cated. She did the right things, obeyed the laws, but knew in her heart that she fell short. It was as if she functioned only on a horizontal plane, while her friends and neighbors had some depth of faith that she lacked. There was a time when she was innocent with joy in God. Which had come first? Her infertility or her lack of belief?

Yossi was in the kitchen. She felt his eyes on her. Adopting this baby was not something she was ready to do alone. She could not give up her husband. For the first time, she realized he held her life in his hands.

Miriam ladled the soup and sprinkled in soup nuts. They had decided on silence for the meal, and the room filled with the sounds of eating and silverware and ice settling in glasses. In between courses, Yossi closed his eyes and sang Shabbos songs. Miriam was grateful that it was near summer, that the meal was late and there were fewer hours until bed.

Yossi started to eat a piece of bread but put it down, laying his hand on hers. "Miriam . . ."

"I better get dessert," she said and stood up.

There was a knock at the door. Miriam paused in the kitchen doorway, Yossi pushed his chair back to get up, their eyes joined in irritation and relief. "I'll get it," he said.

From the kitchen she heard Adele Weiss's whispery voice. She'd moved to Minneapolis from Atlanta almost twenty years ago, but her Southern accent remained distinct. "We were just out for a walk," she said, "and thought you two might not mind some company."

Adele poked her head in the kitchen. She was in her mid-fifties. Her hair was dyed a diminished shade of red and styled in curls on top of her head as if she were going to a dance. "Doesn't that look gorgeous," she said, eyeing the chocolate cake. Then in a none too quiet voice, said, "I'm sorry about bustin' in, but I need to ask Yossi about some medication they want to put Herb on."

"It's fine," Miriam whispered back and then in her normal voice said, "I was wondering what we were going to do with this big old cake." She found it irresistible to mimic Adele's accent and Adele accepted it as a mark of friendship.

"One Southern belle in this community . . . ," Herb hesitated slightly.

". . . is enough," Adele finished for him. Herb had been diagnosed recently with Parkinson's disease, and while his hands had been helped by medication, his speech still was unsteady. Adele had taken on the habit of completing his sentences. Herb smiled up at her, then at Miriam as she placed a large slice of cake in front of him. He seemed so frail and Adele so substantial next to him. They had three children and five grandchildren. Their oldest son had, ironically, taken a job in Atlanta. The other son lived in St. Paul, while their daughter Susan had moved to Sioux City. Miriam had been friendly with Susan from college, and it was through Susan that they'd moved to Saroyan and onto the Weiss's block.

"Yossi, will you get the tea?" Miriam asked.

Adele rose quickly. "Let me help," she said.

Herb concentrated on the even movement of the fork from the cake to his mouth. He smiled at Miriam and she smiled back. "The cake's delicious," he said, and Miriam didn't know if he was more satisfied with successfully maneuvering the cake or finishing his own sentence. She pressed the crumbs of cake with the back of her fork. Despite three children, Adele and Herb were alone. The children came on holidays and Susan sent her kids up in the summer for a week or two, but the Weisses were alone basically. She wondered what hurt more, the silence of childless rooms or going from a full to an empty house.

Yossi sat on the edge of the bed and kicked off his shoes. The bedroom was dark except for a dim triangle of light from the bathroom. From the bed he could see Miriam's reflection in the mirror as she unwound her scarf. Her thick auburn hair tumbled down her back and a lust for her surged in the pit of his stomach. Her hair, perfume-sweet and lush, and covered during the daytime, was for him alone: for him to weigh in the palms of his hands, to bury his face and lose himself in. She picked up the brush, and he watched the rise and fall of her breasts as she stroked her hair, feeling for knots with her fingers. He remembered years and years ago watching her like this, and imagining her soft and round with pregnancy. Every month he would shudder with a mixture of sadness and relief at her flat, taut stomach while also being pierced through when she'd bleed and separate herself. He felt the bleeding was his fault. And now he was faced with raising another couple's child.

Miriam stood in the doorway, backlit by the light, softening it with her presence, and Yossi remembered that night five years ago: they'd gone to New York to visit college friends, a couple who also was having difficulty conceiving. Those were the years of grasping for every bit of advice, checking the *mezuzahs* and *teffilin* to see if the parchments were intact, Miriam giving *tzedakah* before lighting the candles, Miriam reciting Hannah's prayer. And then they'd heard about this Rabbi who was known to help infertile couples, so they'd gone with their friends, stood in line behind others who had shifted their feet and joked about what had brought them to this cramped house in Brooklyn. Their friends had gone first, and from the entryway Yossi and Miriam watched as the Rabbi closed his eyes and extended his veined and freckled hands over their heads and said loudly so everyone could hear that within a year they would give birth to a boy, and he would be invited to the *bris*.

For Yossi and Miriam there was no great pronouncement, but a voice of lilting advice to go home and change the beds so the heads faced south and say *tehilim* before they made love. How they had giggled that night, turning the beds in their friends' upstairs bedroom carefully so as not to scratch the wood floor and not to draw attention to what they were doing even though half of Brooklyn had heard the Rabbi's advice. Yossi had stood by the window and said *tehilim* while Miriam smoothed the sheets. Before they made love Yossi brushed her hair and they'd listened to the crackle of the static, afraid to break the balance by talking.

When they returned home, they changed their own beds and made love every night with a renewed passion and promise that this time their lovemaking would set off some spark inside of her. A week and a half later Miriam got her period. They kept the beds facing south for another month, but Yossi gradually stopped saying *tehilim* and after three nights of falling asleep without making love, Miriam turned the beds back against the wall. Their friends called to say they were expecting. Just as Miriam was about to plunge into a desperate sadness, they explained that they'd been pregnant before they went to the Rabbi, they just hadn't known yet.

Robert had once asked Yossi if he knew what women went through to conceive, and Yossi thought that it was a ridiculous question coming from a man with a child. Who else but Yossi understood the longing and despair that sometimes filled up their lives and pushed aside love? But tonight, seeing his naked wife embraced by light, her hair burning around her shoulders, he realized he had no concept. He had turned beds and muttered prayers to please her, but his acquiescence had belied the core of his selfishness. She was the only thing he wanted. There was no room inside him for anything else. Now this adoption, this unborn child, would reveal the truth. Up until now everything had been remote, theoretical. He could afford to turn beds and pray because he didn't believe it would make a difference.

The bathroom tile was cold under Miriam's feet, and she shivered. She realized that her scalp and her skin, even her fingertips, tingled as if she were tuned to something about to happen, as if her body's surface was charged with those electrons she'd learned about in junior high, skittering along the wires faster and faster until they would generate electricity. She heard the rustle of Yossi's shirt and the thump of his shoes on the carpet. He was clothed by pitch dark, but she knew his secrets because they were her secrets. Their initial pulsing desire for a child had dulled to a throb. They had arrived at this complex balance between fear of admitting they had failed at tests and prayer and the fear of losing their lingering love. But with the impending reality of the child, that balance shifted. She wanted more than Yossi could give her, and Yossi wanted more than she could give him.

She moved forward into the shadows of the room. Every inch of her vibrated. Momentarily, she thought, she'd begin to glow. "I love you," she said when she touched his skin. He raised his eyes and squinted as if the light from her were too much to bear.

The moon had risen and its reflection played across the bed. There was a softness to her body that Yossi hadn't noticed before. He raised her hand to his lips and thought he could still smell the garden earth and the heat of the sun. "I'd do anything for you, give you anything," he said.

She slipped her arms around him and stroked the back of his neck. "Then let me have the baby," she said.

They had moved beyond the point of discussing motivation or need or wants or desires. Out there was this child preparing to be born, and in here they were on this brink. His eyelashes brushed her skin, and sensation rushed through his body as he clung to her and closed his eyes.

A Couple of Kooks

CYNTHIA RYLANT

> *We've bought a lot of things*
> *To keep you warm and dry*
> *And a funny old crib*
> *On which the paint won't dry.*
> *I've bought you a pair of shoes,*
> *A trumpet you can blow,*
> *And a book of rules*
> *Of what to say to people*
> *When they pick on you.*
> *'Cause if you stay with us*
> *You're gonna be pretty kooky, too . . .*
> —David Bowie, "Kooks," *Hunky Dory*

They hadn't meant it to happen. Suzy and Dennis were such careful people in so many important ways. They flossed. They wore their seatbelts. Both gave up drinking when three of their good friends went away to detox in the same month. He took vitamin C, she took iron.

So when this pregnancy did happen to these careful people, when Suzy confronted Dennis in the lobby of the free clinic with hot tears of distress running down her face, each was so shaken that for several days after, neither could be careful about anything and they came as near to hating each other as ever they had. They regretted everything—particularly the other's existence—and they prayed with all their hearts for miracles and redemption. They made promises. They wished for anything except that which was happening to them.

But, finally, the hate was exhausted, the prayers spent, and there was nothing left but to love each other again and compare. Suzy and Dennis always had compared everything. They had found that rather than try to describe an experience, it was easier to compare it to something else, something concrete, something they had both seen or heard or touched before. They drove to Towner's Woods to sit on top of a picnic table and compare this revelation from the free clinic.

Suzy said it was like the time they took that country road neither of them ever had been on, and they saw the garden full of sunflowers. She had thought the flowers were plastic, that something which looked like that could not be real.

Dennis said it felt like the night they were waiting for the lunar eclipse out on Johnson Road and a little plane had crossed the front of the moon, casting a shadow across its white face like a scene from a Spielberg movie.

They watched the squirrels and the blackbirds of Towner's Woods and they talked. They talked about telling their parents, they talked about telling Suzy's priest, and, eventually, they talked about giving away a baby like a little tree on Arbor Day. At sixteen there were only two real choices, but because Suzy believed most sincerely in a purgatory that harbored the souls of poor decision makers, their choices became just one: to have a child and to give it away all in a breath.

They cried awhile, then they drove back and told their parents, who, after a few days of standing transfixed before open refrigerators, took it well. Suzy's priest also took it well and assured her she wouldn't be a shoo-in to purgatory.

Then while an attorney and a social worker searched for the man and woman who one day would walk this experience of sunflowers and Spielberg movies to its first day of kindergarten, Suzy and Dennis started thinking about time and Zippy the Pinhead.

Dennis had read in a book that a baby in the womb, can hear everything on the outside—music, the purr of a cat, rain. He brought the book to Suzy who, with one hand resting quietly on her stomach, read with interest the page about the fetus being able to hear.

And the first thing they gave it was *Zippy the Pinhead*. One night in her second month, Dennis curled next to Suzy on her bed and opened a comic book.

"No matter who its parents are, you know they'll never read it Zippy," he said to Suzy.

He put his face near her stomach and began to read:

"'I'm glad I remembered to Xerox all my undershirts,' said Zippy."

Like too much water, a giggle spurted from Suzy's mouth.

"'Why is there a waffle in my pajama pocket?'"

Their parenting had begun.

Suzy and Dennis made lists of the people who were important to them, people sacred, people of such value that one generation has no choice but to pass them on to the next: Pee Wee Herman, Curly Howard, John Lennon.

Dennis talked above Suzy's stomach about Albert Einstein one day:

"Einstein said, 'Imagination is more important than Knowledge.' Remember that. It'll help when you flunk math quizzes."

They played their favorite music for the baby—*The White Album, Ziggy Stardust*—and one night they played their favorite creatures.

Whales.

Dennis showed up at Suzy's house with his Walkman and a cassette of humpback whale songs, and while Suzy lay on the couch, he stretched the headphones across her stomach.

"Wow," he said. "You're getting big."

He started the tape, spread himself out on the floor, and, holding Suzy's hand, fell asleep. Suzy slept, too, and the whales emptied their songs into her body.

"The baby will think it came from the sea," Suzy said later, when they woke up.

Dennis rubbed his eyes.

"It did."

They took it to the movies. After watching *Wings of Desire,* they sat on a park bench with ice-cream cones and talked to the baby about listening for angels who would always be with it—and to watch for them, to watch for the quick shadows that are wings flying past the corner of the eye. Dennis told the baby never to worry, that it would never fall too far or too hard, because the angels would bear it up and keep it safe.

"And one of them might even be John Lennon," he added hopefully.

They watched *It's a Wonderful Life* on video, and they told the baby afterward that to be like George Bailey would be a good thing—to help in small ways, to be honest, to believe in miracles. Suzy told it about her own miracle, about the time her cat disappeared and was gone for weeks. Suzy's parents believed the cat was dead and gave up on it. But Suzy wouldn't. She told the baby about cutting a big star out of foil and hanging it in her window one night, believing it would lead the cat home like the Star of Bethlehem. And the next morning, Suzy told the baby, her cat was at the kitchen door.

In the fourth month Suzy told Dennis that the baby was blowing bubbles, that she could feel them floating and popping against the walls of her uterus. And in the sixth month, Dennis was resting his head on the hard mound Suzy's stomach had become, reading aloud *Krazy Kat,* when the baby rearranged itself. Dennis jumped so hard that he fell off the couch.

"What a woil'," he said to Suzy with a grin. "What a woil'."

They fed the baby their favorite foods: barbeques with slaw at Swenson's Drive-In; orange marshmallow peanuts; Moon Pies; fried bologna and mustard on Wonder bread; banana and mayonnaise sandwiches.

"It'll probably have these strange cravings all its life," Dennis told Suzy as they played miniature golf one afternoon. He fixed a stare into space:

"'Gee, I'm hungry, but I just don't know what I want. Is it . . . is it . . . a *Moon Pie?*'"

Dennis told the baby to believe in God but not in religion. And to sing a lot. Suzy told it to feed the starlings, because nobody else does. And they both asked it to try to make friends with the Russians.

However, as the time for saying hello and good-bye drew ever nearer, their lightness faded, and each began to feel a desperation, a sense of flailing, a tight anxiety much like that of a mother whose child is late coming home, who keeps looking out the window for sight of a small figure in a red coat. Suzy and Dennis began to realize how afraid they were, and that it was themselves the angels would have to bear up. It was they who must watch for the wings that might keep them from falling as they passed this child away from their own arms and into those of someone else who must keep it safe, must keep it warm, must be certain to watch long out the window for sight of a small figure in a red coat.

And it was finally in the last month, when the baby was large and awkward in Suzy's body, always trying to get comfortable in the womb it had outgrown, that both Suzy and Dennis understood that they needed to tell it of themselves. They had taught the baby their world. Now they must teach the baby its parents.

They drove back to Towner's Woods, to their favorite spot near the pavilion that looked out over sloping hills and small trees. The sun was warm this day. It was October and the baby would leave them before the month was gone.

Dennis asked Suzy to go first. He wasn't sure how to do it.

Months ago Suzy had stopped feeling sixteen, and with the deep sigh of a wise old woman, she put a hand on her stomach and began.

"If anybody asked me today what's the most important thing in my life, I'd say it was you. Dennis next. And I guess that's as good a family as anybody could want, so I hope you're not too disappointed in us.

"Some other mother's going to be raising you so you've got to pay attention to me now. We don't have much time left. I have to tell you about me because you'll grow up and maybe you'll feel these things you don't understand, or maybe you'll really like giraffes and you won't know why, and if you know deep inside it's because of me, it's because Suzy had those feelings or Suzy really liked giraffes, then you'll rest easier. You'll know it's just your mother in you.

"What I want to tell you about me, first, is that I love you very, very much."

She stopped, her eyes wet. Dennis reached out but she brushed him away, and, taking a strong breath, began again.

"And I'd keep you if I could but I truly can't. We don't have money or a place of our own. I don't know about anything except how to get through physics with a C- and what days are good for hot lunch. I can't keep you. I can't."

Her eyes followed a cardinal in the trees.

"When I was a little girl I had a dollhouse and it had the prettiest things in it: a little flowered couch, a round white bathtub with feet, a shiny black telephone, a canopy bed in the big bedroom, and a little white crib in the little bedroom.

"It had a mom and a dad. But it didn't have a baby for the little white crib. Because I lost the baby that Christmas I got the dollhouse. I was only five or six, and I loved the baby best of all. All Christmas day I put it in and out of its little bed. There was a tiny piece of flannel in the bed, to keep it warm.

"But people came over for dinner, and they had kids, and the kids played with my things, and at bedtime that night I couldn't find the baby to put it in its crib.

"I cried and I cried and my parents searched through all the bags of wrapping paper and behind the tree and under the furniture. But they didn't find the baby.

"They tried to buy me a new one, but I never could find another baby just like the one I lost. So I left the crib empty. And I always worried about that baby. Where it had gone off to. Who it was with. Whether it needed that little piece of flannel lying in its crib.

"I know I'll worry about you that way. I guess there's no way to help that. But you'll be OK. You'll be better than OK. You'll be great."

Suzy stopped to untie her shoes. Her ankles were swollen with the fluid her body seemed to hoard this final month.

"I'll tell you some things about me. I don't drive a car because I'm afraid to try. Everybody but me has their driver's license now, and I'm pretty embarrassed. I still like coloring in coloring books. When I was fourteen I dyed my hair red one night and my parents made me get it stripped and permed and I looked like a Kewpie doll for weeks.

"When I was eleven I was so crazy about John Cougar Mellencamp that I spray-painted his name on the back side of our garage and my folks grounded me for two months.

"I love gray cats. I want to learn how to play acoustic guitar and sing like Tracy Chapman. And I'm scared to death of crows for some reason. But don't you be, it's silly. I think crows are the only thing I'm scared of.

"Someday I'd like to be a newspaper reporter. And I'd like to have ten cats living in my house with me. I want to go to Holland to see all the tulips and the windmills. And I really want to meet God someday."

She stopped, and Dennis waited while she searched her thoughts for the words that were important, the ones she couldn't risk forgetting.

"I'm really sorry I wasn't too thrilled when I found out about you. I hope you understand. When a person's sixteen and pregnant she just doesn't belong anywhere. I can't hang out with my old crowd anymore. Partly because of them (pregnant people give teenagers the jitters), and partly because of me, because I just can't get excited about a football game when I'm wondering whether you and I are going to survive everything.

"I can't hang out with the women who are old enough to have babies. They don't want me and I know I'm too dull for them.

"I was just scared I couldn't handle it. But I have handled it and I swear to God I don't regret a thing. I really don't. You're going to grow up and be better than I ever was. I know it. And you're going to change every single person you meet. You're going to make *everybody* better, the way you've made me and Dennis better before you've even gotten out of here.

"Everything's going to work for you, I know it. And from wherever I am, all my life I'll be sending you angels to hold you up. I promise."

Suzy took a deep breath then, and smiled at Dennis, who had been staring at the ground the whole time.

They sat in silence for several minutes. Then Suzy said with a whisper, "Your turn."

Dennis shook his head.

"I can't."

"What?"

"What you said—I can't do that good. I thought I had some words to tell it, but I lost them all listening to you."

He looked at her.

"I never knew that about your cat. Or that dollhouse."

Suzy smiled and shrugged.

"Funny, the things you remember," she said.

She took Dennis's hand.

"Just talk to it like you talk to me. And give it some secrets to take with it. You can do it. You tell me stories all the time."

Dennis shook his head in doubt. Then he looked down at Suzy's stomach and grinned.

"You think I should tell it about the Fisher-Price schoolteacher?"

Suzy grinned back.

"Absolutely."

Dennis leaned over and tapped her stomach with his finger.

"Hey little dude. Heads up. It's me this time."

"OK, here's a Daddy-Dennis story you probably won't believe, but I'm going to tell you anyway. When I was six I fell madly in love with the Fisher-Price schoolteacher. She was only a couple inches tall, and hard as a rock, but I thought she was the most beautiful woman in the world. Every night I'd pull her out of my Fisher-Price schoolhouse and I'd sit her beside my bed and we'd just smile at each other."

Dennis looked at Suzy.

"That's why I love your mom. She has the same sweet little face. No kidding. She smiles all the time. You'd fall in love with her, too, if you saw her."

He reached out and touched Suzy's hair, then his eyes narrowed with thought as he looked toward the trees.

"My favorite place when I was a kid was my toy box. I used to crawl inside it and close the lid and sit there in the dark. We've got a small house, and with two brothers, I couldn't find a place for myself. So I got in the box. I'd just sit there and think. I think a lot. It's my favorite thing to do besides listening to tapes. It's caused me enough hassles at school, believe me. But I can't seem to help it. My mind just gets up and goes off somewhere else."

He stopped. He thought hard for several seconds.

"There's not much I'm afraid of. Bats (even though Suzy says they're nice). Freddy Krueger movies. I can't sit through Freddy Krueger and don't you even try.

"I wish I'd been a teenager in the sixties because I'd have been so perfect for them. I'm a hippie in my heart but there's no place to be one right now. Everybody at school's into money and how long it'll take them to own their first BMW. I'd love an apple-red pickup, myself.

"Anyway, the sixties. I'd have loved to protest a war or sit in for integration. I'd have worn those psychedelic shirts and beads. And I bet if it was the sixties now, Suzy and I could find a way to keep you. We'd just go to some commune down the road and live. We'd grow our own beans, and I'd learn to build things—chairs, maybe even houses.

"So if you ever get this urge to, like, join up with some group that's still wearing bell-bottoms and listening to The Doors, I figure you'll know where that came from.

"Suzy and me, we're just a couple of kooks. We're the only two people I know who can come out here and stare at the trees for two solid hours without saying a word. Maybe that's why I never liked school much. You're always having to talk.

"The best parts of me are the crazy parts and if you get those, you'll have all the good I've got. Like, I love sneaking out on rainy nights and walking naked in the backyard. I have seriously wondered at times if I wouldn't be better off in a nudist colony. If you get that part of me, I figure it's a pretty OK thing.

"I'd love to work in animation someday. I love old cartoons like the original Popeye, and Bosko, and 'Steamboat Willie.' Most animation today sucks out loud. I sure hope your . . . your . . . the people who raise you have sense enough to make sure you see the good stuff.

"Know what I wanted for Christmas last year? Chairry from *Pee Wee's Playhouse* and a talking Ed Grimley doll."

Dennis laughed.

"'I'm going completely mental, I must say.'"

He rubbed Suzy's stomach.

"You really will be all right, kid. Suzy's sending angels. And I'll send money."

He laughed again.

When it was time to go, when both Suzy and Dennis knew that chances were this would be the last time they talked to their baby in Towner's Woods, they walked to the edge of a hill and looked out at Lake Rockwell, lying still and brown below them.

"Feels like rain," Dennis said quietly.

Suzy looked up at the sky.

"Good," she answered. "It'll like that."

And just as they turned to go, the sound of wings passed through the trees.

The Waiting Lists

JACKIE KAY

San serif typeface: adoptive mother
Roman typeface: adopted daughter

The first agency we went to
didn't want us on their lists,
we didn't live close enough to a church
nor were we church-goers
(though we kept quiet about being communists).
The second told us
we weren't high enough earners.
The third liked us
but they had a five year waiting list.
I spent six months trying not to look
at swings nor the front of supermarket trolleys,
not to think this kid I've wanted could be five.
The fourth agency was full up.
The fifth said yes but again no babies.
Just as we were going out the door
I said oh you know we don't mind the colour.
Just like that, the waiting was over.

This morning a slim manilla envelope arrives
postmarked Edinburgh: one piece of paper
I have now been able to look up your microfiche
(as this is all the records kept nowadays).
From your mother's letters, the following information:
Your mother was nineteen when she had you.
You weighed eight pounds four ounces.
She liked hockey. She worked in Aberdeen
as a waitress. She was five foot eight inches.

I thought I'd hid everything
that there wasnie wan
giveaway sign left

I put Marx Engels Lenin (no Trotsky)
in the airing cupboard—she'll no be
checking out the towels surely

All the copies of the *Daily Worker*
I shoved under the sofa
the dove of peace I took down from the loo

A poster of Paul Robeson
saying give him his passport
I took down from the kitchen

I left a bust of Burns
my detective stories
and the Complete Works of Shelley

She comes at 11:30 exactly.
I pour her coffee
from my new Hungarian set

And foolishly pray she willnae
ask its origins—honestly
this baby is going to my head.

She crosses her legs on the sofa
I fancy I hear the *Daily Workers*
rustle underneath her

Well she says, you have an interesting home
She sees my eyebrows rise.
It's different she qualifies.

Hell and I've spent all morning
trying to look ordinary
—a lovely home for the baby.

She buttons her coat all smiles
I'm thinking
I'm on the home run

But just as we get to the last post
her eye catches at the same time as mine
a red ribbon with twenty world peace badges

Clear as a hammer and sickle
on the wall.
Oh, she says are you against nuclear weapons?

To Hell with this. Baby or no baby.
Yes I says. Yes yes yes.
I'd like this baby to live in a nuclear free world.

Oh. Her eyes light up.
I'm all for peace myself she says,
and sits down for another cup of coffee.

Waiting for the Baby

ALISON LURIE

Here in New Delhi at the end of their long quest, waiting day after day for International Adoption Services to find them a baby, Aster was finally losing heart. At home in America she and her husband Clark had spoken of the coming journey not only as a necessary mission, but a chance to tour the country and learn more about their future child's culture.

But none of the books and articles she had read had prepared Aster for India: its crazy contrasts of beauty and hideousness, luxury and poverty, friendly simplicity and impenetrable evasiveness. Also, nobody had told them that May was intolerably hot, the worst season for travel. Shopping and sightseeing were possible only in the mornings; after lunch, if they didn't have to go to the agency, Aster and Clark stayed in the air-conditioned hotel or, as now, in its big outdoor pool.

One after another, they had canceled their trips to Jaipur, Jodhpur, Agra, and Benares. It wasn't just the heat, it was the economic uncertainty. International Adoption Services still hadn't come up with a final statement of costs or a definite date; they might have to stay far longer than they'd planned, and spend far more. Mrs. Bannerjee and her colleagues were invariably polite, but refused to commit themselves. Perhaps, Aster sometimes thought, the agency was testing them to see if they were patient and even-tempered enough to be good adoptive parents.

But every day she felt less patient and more stressed out—and so, she suspected, did Clark. They didn't admit this to each other, didn't criticize IAS, except once when Clark referred to the organization as the International Asses. (Aster had flicked a smile, but felt a shiver of fear, as if something or someone might have been listening and would report them.) Instead they criticized the damp, leaden heat of the city, the gritty haze of pollution; the riotous, reckless traffic; the overspiced, possibly spoilt food—for days now Aster had felt a little nauseous— and the terrifying poverty. Along Janpath, tall banks and office buildings shimmered in the sun, and satiny tropical flowers poured over their walls; but below, bundles of rags that on second glance were people lay in dust and vomit, coughing and dying.

At first she had found the Red Fort and the other ancient monuments and temples fascinating; but gradually they began to seem dusty and worn, as if their surfaces had been pitted by too many staring tourist eyes. In the narrow soiled alleys of Old Delhi, a dog pissed on her skirt; and when she rinsed out the new silk scarf she had spilt coffee on, its exotic colors ran into a muddy brown.

It was probably because she was in such an exhausted, keyed-up state that a few days ago Aster had made a fool of herself at one of the local sights. She had gone there on impulse late one afternoon, because it was near the public library where Clark was absorbed in back issues of American newspapers.

The Birla Mandir temple hadn't ever been on their must-see list. It dated only from 1938, and Aster knew already from her guidebook that it would be banal rather than beautiful: an oriental film-fantasy edifice, all balconies and galleries and stairs in marble the color and texture of banana ice cream.

As usual, she had to leave her shoes at a stall by the entrance. But this time she hadn't worn socks, and the yellow marble steps were scorching under her bare feet and also filthy: littered with the fading, slimy remnants of orange and yellow garlands of marigolds and sticky pink sweets.

With the help of the guidebook, she had now identified the most popular Hindi deities: the trinity of Brahma, Vishnu, and Shiva; elephant-headed Ganesh, who favored all new enterprises; graceful Saraswati, patroness of the arts; and the frolicsome blue youth, Krishna. It had seemed a benevolent ancient pantheon, and one that acknowledged the power of the female.

But in this bright, modern edifice, which reminded Aster of brochures for the Indian palace hotels they couldn't afford, the gods were not museum-quality statues softened by time, but glaringly new, like Disney figures. They were overdressed, and decorated in the worst of taste with gold leaf and costume jewelry. Some were pretty in the artificial manner of Indian advertisements; others had the heads of animals, necklaces of flowers and skulls, or faces black with rage; they showed pointed teeth and waved extra arms holding the weapons of war. Like the life-size Mickey and Minnie Mice at Disneyland, they suggested vulgar commercial power.

Early evening is the traditional time of worship in India, and these half comic, half sinister deities basked in the light of many candles; thick, odorous, dizzying smoke shrouded them, and an increasing crowd of devotees stood or knelt before the shrines. Several of these worshippers gave Aster hard looks as she tried to maneuver between them for a better view of Lakshmi, to whom (according to her guidebook) the temple was dedicated; and one woman even muttered what sounded like a curse.

"Goddess of fortune and abundance," Aster read in her guidebook, "Lakshmi gives wealth, fertility, and many children." I'll settle for the one we've been promised, she thought. Lakshmi, who had four arms and sat between two elephants, was heavily jeweled and voluptuous of figure, with the swelling breasts and stomach of a woman in the early stages of pregnancy. She had dark-rimmed almond eyes, an ivory complexion, and a little sly smile. "Nyah, nyah," she seemed to be saying to Aster. "I know something you don't know."

The Indian woman next to Aster now knelt facing the shrine, then lowered herself, breathing heavily, until she was prostrate in a puddle of red silk sari, with her heavily ringed and braceleted hands clasped above her head.

How can she do that, how can she lie there in the filth? Aster wondered. The answer sounded inside her head in a thin mosquito tone: Because she wants a baby more than you do.

Nobody wants a baby more than I do, Aster thought angrily, nobody. And suddenly, without willing it, she found herself dropping to the smeared, dirty floor, kneeling, then actually lying prone, with her legs sticking out awkwardly behind her. Noise and incense streamed round her; time seemed to whirl.

"Please, give us our baby now," she heard herself whisper. Then, dizzy and embarrassed, she rose to her feet, glancing round, seeing or imagining the pink shocked and disapproving faces of other Westerners in the crowd of darker and more golden faces.

What a stupid, unsanitary thing to do, she thought as she hastened away from the shrine into the open air, brushing bits of debris from her stained slacks, checking her watch. It was much later than she'd thought, and behind the temple the sun was setting: rose and purple clouds, edged with gold in the worst possible taste, streaked the smoky sky.

Aster didn't tell Clark about what had happened at the Lakshmi temple; instead the incident added itself to the growing list of things they didn't talk about. It had begun two years ago, she thought, after they went to their first adoption agency. When they realized that they not only had to be, but to act, the part of perfect prospective parents. Which was the truth: they were educated, successful, healthy, attractive, decent people.

But by being consciously put forward and waved about for so long, this truth had slowly turned into a lie, at least for Aster. She knew from the start that if one of them were to be found wanting, it would be her. She began to have anxious, uncertain moods. She kept remembering how her mother had remarked with a gentle, dotty smile that "perhaps it wasn't meant to be." But when she told Clark, this he only laughed and said, "New Age thinking."

So Aster set her doubts and questions aside, concealing them first from the social workers, then from her friends and family, and finally from Clark himself. After a while it seemed that if she admitted doubts or questions she hadn't already mentioned, it would be like admitting that she'd been deliberately deceiving everyone.

That's how it was with her insomnia, Aster thought. And her fear of Clark's parents, who once—before they knew she and Clark would have to adopt—said they didn't see how anyone could feel the same about a grandchild that didn't have their genes. Aster never said that she was worried about their attitude; more and more often, she didn't even tell Clark when she was ill or upset.

We're together all day here, more than we've ever been for years, she thought. But we don't really talk anymore; we haven't for a long time.

Lately, for instance, she had stopped speaking about the noises that kept her awake every night. The sullen intermittent rasp and chug of the air conditioner, the monotonous plinking and sawing of Asian music, the creak and clang of the hotel elevator. And sometimes another, fainter, sound—a sort of gasping whine and wail. The first time she woke Clark. "Did you hear that?" she cried.

"Wha?" In the half-light her husband, who slept easily and heavily, half raised his head.

"There's a child crying."

"That's just air in the plumbing." He fell back into unconsciousness.

But the wailing of the ghostly child, or plumbing, continued. Aster heard it almost every night. She did not wake Clark again, because she feared he would say, as he sometimes did, smiling, "Aster's always hearing things other people can't hear." Which was not only a compliment to her aural acuity, but an oblique reference to her southern Californian counterculture background. It was unfair, because she had long ago put all that behind her, along with her embarrassing given name, Astarte.

Indeed it was from all that the name Astarte stood for that Aster was determined to rescue their baby. Their child, Indian though it might be genetically, would not grow up as she had, in a confused, impoverished, unhygienic world of vague spirituality and too many siblings; a world of mantras, meditation, and meaningless hugs; of faded hand-me-down skirts made of old bedspreads, and spiced vegetables left out on the stove until they turned dry and sour; of the good-natured selfishness called "doing one's own thing."

When Aster first complained of the noises at night, she and Clark had discussed moving to a better hotel. Now, as their stack of traveler's checks flattened, she suggested a cheaper one.

"You know that couple from Sweden we met last week at the agency," she began as they lay beside the lukewarm hotel pool, in which exotic dead insects floated.

"You mean the ones with the very dark baby." Clark's voice had the same mix of amusement and dismay as when he had first pointed out the two very tall and fair young people and their tiny, almost black infant. ("You'd think IAS would make more effort to match the child to the parents," he had commented.)

"Yes, well, they're in a three-star hotel, and she told me it's really quite all right. I thought we might call and see if they've got a room."

"I—don't know." Clark spoke in the manner he'd developed recently: short bursts of words interrupted by long pauses. Somehow it was associated in Aster's mind with the explosive sounds of the twenty-four-hour green death he'd had after eating in an outdoor restaurant, as if speech too were a painful kind of evacuation. "We'd have to tell IAS we were moving."

"Well, yes, of course."

"They might think we were——running out of money."

"Well, we are," Aster said. "At least we may be if we have to stay in Delhi much longer."

"The thing is—if they thought—that we'd misrepresented—"

"But we didn't." Aster's answer was almost a question. Clark's income as a planning consultant was more mysterious and variable than hers as an arts administrator. "Did we?"

"No—but I'd rather not take the chance." Clark did not look at his wife as he spoke, but up into the ragged, sun-faded palms.

But I have to move, I have to leave this expensive haunted hotel, Aster thought. She opened her mouth to say so, then shut it. We mustn't quarrel, she told herself, that would ruin everything. No agency will give a baby to mutually hostile, squabbling parents. And if they did have a fight now it could be serious, and the scars might show at their interview later this afternoon.

"All right," she agreed, not agreeing.

Hang in there, she told herself, turning over onto her back under the smoggy sun. It's going to work out. Hadn't Mrs. Fogel back home practically assured them of that? "You shouldn't have any problem with IAS," she had said, emphasizing the pronoun as if she saw a banner over Clark and Aster's heads that read IDEAL ADOPTIVE COUPLE.

Their baby would be a girl, Aster was almost certain of that; it was girl babies who were given away in India, or neglected and allowed to die of fever or malnutrition—or deliberately destroyed before birth once their sex was known. Aster was in favor of a woman's right to choose, but she couldn't help thinking sometimes of the daily waste, the murder of healthy, lovable Indian infants.

And, since Roe v. Wade, American ones. She and Clark were caught in a pocket of history: thirty years ago people like them would have had their choice of babies. One day, perhaps, the Supreme Court might overturn that decision. But they couldn't wait that long; already she was forty and Clark forty-one, too old for any American agency. Because that was how these places worked; they made you wait four years, five, six, and then said you were too old. This was their last chance.

Aster was glad it would be a girl. She didn't say so though, just as Clark didn't say any longer that he wanted a boy, as he had when they assumed it would be with them as with other couples. "Clark Stockwell IV, first, and then whatever you like," he'd joked, when they still joked about such things. Perhaps even now he hoped for a boy.

How awful it was, how unfair, that they should have to sit in offices and beg favors from strangers, submit financial statements, and be inspected and judged. Meanwhile people who were unstable and irresponsible, or even cruel and crazy, had one baby after another. At home she couldn't go to the mall without seeing some angry, unfit mother with several miserable, unkempt children she didn't appear to want. Didn't deserve.

It was the same here: Delhi was full of ragged exhausted-looking women carrying one half-naked baby and dragging another. And then, almost worse, the child beggars: thin, dirty, barefoot, some seeming as young as four or five. Everywhere you went they crowded round you, patted your arm, fumbled at your clothes, crying, "Baksheesh, baksheesh!" You couldn't know which, if any, weren't faking; the only solution was to give nothing at all.

"Remember what the guidebook said, we mustn't give them anything," she had warned Clark on their first day in Delhi, when skinny clamoring urchins surrounded them as they emerged from the airport into the choking heat.

"Sorry," he had said, following her into the taxi and slamming the door. "It was just some of those little tin coins.—No, damn it, that's all." But more and more ragged children appeared as if from nowhere, crying in their shrill voices, reaching out their thin dark hands. Even when Aster rolled up the window the children pressed their dirty faces and hands against the glass and stared at her with their liquid inky eyes until the taxi, accelerating, shook them off.

"What I don't understand is, why doesn't some agency find decent homes for some of those kids?" she had asked Clark that first evening, when they had gone for a walk along Janpath and had to turn into a souvenir shop to escape the beggars: not just children, but wizened grandmothers in threadbare saris; androgynous toothless gnomes with leprosy-melted noses or hands; threatening adolescents with knife-scarred faces.

"It wouldn't be possible," Clark had said. In the harsh light of the shop, surrounded by the glitter of brass trays and bowls and candle-sticks, he looked exhausted. "Children like that, nobody would want them. They have chronic diseases, bad heredity, could be retarded. Besides, most of them probably have parents already, or at least someone they belong to. Someone who teaches them to beg, lives off them."

His face took on an expression it assumed back home when a job went seriously wrong: the compressed mouth, the narrowed eyes. More and more often he wore that mask, Aster thought; he had it on now as he lay in the deck chair by the pool, his canvas cricket hat tilted to shade his eyes, and his long pale legs shielded from the sun by a blue-striped hotel towel.

But it doesn't matter, she told herself. Soon, surely, we will have our baby. We will take her home to the room that is ready for her, with the big white teddy bear, the bird mobile floating over the crib. We will talk to each other again.

"It's going to happen," Aster declared three hours later as they reentered their hotel room. "I'm sure of it."

"I hope you're right." Clark sighed. "God, I need a shower."

"Me too," she said, following him into the bathroom. "Mrs. Bannerjee smiled much more today, didn't you think?"

"She always smiles," Clark said.

"And she promised to call later with definite news." Aster peeled off her damp cotton dress and tight damp bra.

"Mm. You go first."

Clark's so cautious, she thought as she stood naked in the lukewarm spray. But I know we're going to get our baby. One child at least will be rescued from the confusion, squalor, and violence of India: her life changed forever, her future assured.

"Your turn," she said, reaching for a towel.

Though cooler than outside, the room was warm. Not bothering to put on a robe, Aster stretched out on the flower-patterned bedspread.

"That's better." Naked too, Clark sat beside her, then leaned closer. "Aster? How about it?"

"Why not?" She smiled. The one good thing about New Delhi was what it had done for their physical relationship. Six years ago, when they realized that she wasn't going to get pregnant at once, sex had gradually become a matter first of weighted meaning, later of mechanical calculation, of charts and thermometers. By the time it had been proved and proved again that all efforts were ineffectual, they were worn out, reduced to routine gestures of affection modulating occasionally into the release of tension.

But in New Delhi they had had time to rest and recover; time to experiment.

"Oh, darling," Aster whispered twenty minutes later. In spite of the air-conditioning, she was warmly damp again everywhere. "I feel so good."

"Really." Clark smiled.

"It's as if I were, I don't know, tingling all over, especially my breasts."

"Umhm. . . . Oh, hell." The phone had begun to ring beside the other twin bed; he floundered toward it.

"Clark Stockwell here. . . . Yes?" A long pause, during which he dragged the spread across his legs as if to conceal himself from the telephone's gaze. Aster raised herself on one elbow; there was a sick pain in her stomach, as of nausea.

"Yes, but I understood—" Another pause, so long this time that she sat up, then went to kneel beside him.

"No. I thought you had already approved—" Clark's voice was the formal, neutral one he used when a client ignorant of good business manners called him at home. "No, we didn't."

"What is it?" Aster cried as he replaced the receiver.

"I'm so sorry, darling." Clark cleared his throat with a raw, grating sound. "IAS has turned us down."

"No! Why?"

"They won't give any reason. Said it's against their policy." Clark cleared his throat again. "I don't know—it could be what we were worried about before, that they think we're too old."

"But that's so stupid! Mrs. Fogel said it wouldn't matter—Anyway, America isn't India, our average life expectancy is, I don't know, seventy-five? A child born now would be over thirty by then. We have to explain, we have to tell them—"

"I don't think it'll do any good. Mrs. Bannerjee sounded very definite."

"I don't care. I'm going to call back."

Clark said neither yes nor no; he continued to sit there while Aster fought her way through the hotel switchboard and the New Delhi phone system. Unconcerned now that she might seem a hysterical, pushy, imperfect parent, she demanded to speak to everyone they'd met at IAS—protesting, arguing, begging, trying unsuccessfully to get through the screen of polite regret.

"They're all so impossible, so ignorant," she cried after she had hung up. "I hate that fat Mrs. Bannerjee, I hate every one of them." She swallowed a sob. "Listen, Clark. Why don't you call the director. Men count for more than women in this country; maybe he'll listen to you."

Her husband shook his head. "It won't do any good," he repeated.

Clark doesn't understand, she thought. And when we made love just now he didn't say he loved me. And if we don't love each other, we can't stay together after this; nobody could.

All the rest of that evening, while Aster raged and wept, Clark remained frozen. He had two drinks before dinner and most of a bottle of wine, but to no discernible effect. Aster, though she drank less, soon grew unsteady. At ten o'clock she stood weeping with dizzy fury in the shower, which trickled over her as if weeping too.

"I still can't believe it, I still can't bear it," she wailed, collapsing onto her bed.

"I know, darling. I'm so sorry," Clark muttered from the other bed, his voice thick with alcohol and exhaustion. In a few minutes he was breathing heavily, regularly—almost snoring. Aster lay awake, watching the wavering light through the blinds, hearing the ugly mélange of hotel noises: the meaningless, tuneless tinkling and sawing music, the groan and clank of the elevator, the faint, mocking sound like a child crying.

She slept, finally, and woke exhausted and ill. The wobbly look of the fried eggs on her plate at breakfast sickened her. When Clark volunteered to go to the travel desk and ask for plane reservations to America, she staggered back to their room and fell into a defeated daze.

Half an hour later he returned. They were lucky, they could fly home tonight, he reported; but why shouldn't they, instead, delay their departure and see more of India while they were here? Why not travel to some cool, picturesque hill station?

"Look, here's some possibilities." Clark held out a shiny colored fan of brochures. "I think we should go somewhere, so this trip won't be totally wasted."

Aster struck the brochures with the side of her hand so that they fell in disarray on the carpet. "But it is wasted," she cried. "Everything's wasted, everything we've done for years is wasted. I hate India."

"We could try Nepal, then. There's supposed to be a very good hotel in Katmandu, and at this time of year—"

"I don't want to try anywhere." Aster began to cry again, the dry, empty sobs of exhaustion. "I just want to go home."

"Oh, darling. I'm so sorry," Clark said for perhaps the third time in twenty-four hours. "Whatever you like."

Why does he keep apologizing to me? she thought after her husband had returned to the travel desk.

It's because it's worse for you, said the thin voice in her head. Because the truth is that Clark doesn't want a dark-skinned Indian baby girl; he never wanted one. He's like his parents: what he wanted was a child who would look like him.

But Clark could still have what he wants, Aster thought as she began to fold clothes into her suitcase. Forty-one isn't old for a man: he could marry again and have children. She could even see the bride he would choose: one of those bright young legal aides in his office. He was a good-looking man, well mannered, successful, intelligent. Lots of young women would be glad to marry him and produce Clark Stockwell IV.

He could have chosen one of them already, Aster thought, opening another drawer and taking out a stack of T-shirts. But instead he stayed with me, even after he knew there would never be a real Clark Stockwell IV. He went to all those agencies and interviews with me, because I wanted an Indian baby. He came for me, because he loved me.

Yes, and I love him, she thought. But what good is that? She had reached the bottom drawer now, full of the cool-weather clothes she'd never worn since they left home, and odds and ends of toiletries. A first-aid kit, a box of diapers they would never use, an unopened box of pads named Always—Why had she chosen a brand with that mocking name, a name that promised she would never get pregnant, that she would bleed every month, always, until she was too old to bleed?

Unopened? But they must have been in India nearly a month, Aster thought. She should have been off long before now. It must be the heat, the jet shock, the anxiety and misery that had delayed her period— Aster dropped an armful of clothes on the bed and reached for her pocket diary—had delayed it over three weeks.

It couldn't be that, she thought, not even daring to name the possibility. Not after all these years. But the way she'd felt sick every morning the last week or so, the tingling and swelling of her breasts—

In Aster's mind, the Disneyland figure of Lakshmi reappeared. "I know something you don't know," she seemed to say again, but this time her smile was gentle as well as smug.

I won't mention it, Aster promised herself. Not yet, not until we're home and I've seen Dr. Stewart. It can't be true; but suppose it is?

After they had checked out and had supper, there was still nearly an hour before Clark and Aster had to leave for the airport. For the last time, they strolled down the hotel drive and turned onto Janpath, into a mauve haze of evening heat and the usual swarm of beggars.

"No baksheesh!" Clark insisted, pushing through them into a shop that sold leather goods that might make good last-minute presents for people in his office. While he leafed through stacks of tooled and dyed wallets, Aster stood at the entrance watching the passing crowd of Indians and foreigners: all ages, all races, all colors.

Suddenly, under a tree at the far edge of the sidewalk, the figure of the goddess Lakshmi appeared: a dark-eyed young woman with matted waist-length black hair and four bare arms. That couldn't be, of course, but it was: one thin dark arm holding her sari together, one outstretched, and two more smaller arms waving above her shoulders; and the same little knowing smile. Aster felt sick and feverish; maybe she was going mad.

The figure of Lakshmi moved, turned. Aster saw that on her back, wrapped in a shawl, its head previously concealed, was a small child, the owner of the second set of arms. They were real. They were beggars—gypsies perhaps.

The beggar woman saw Aster staring; she moved nearer, stretching out one of her four hands. The child looking over her shoulder stared back with its liquid blackberry eyes and gave a faint thin cry. As if in a trance, Aster walked toward them. She opened her handbag, reached in, and pulled out the wad of paper money she had meant to change at the airport.

"Okay, we'd better get back to the hotel," Clark's voice said behind her; and then, "Aster? What are you doing?" But he was too late. The beggar's thin dirty hands closed over the notes; she turned and hurried off.

Observing their colleague's good fortune, other beggars surged toward Aster, hands clutching her clothing, voices wailing. But Clark, gripping his wife's arm, pulled her back into the shop.

"What's going on?" he asked. "How much did you give that girl?"

"I don't know. Everything," Aster gasped. "She was so thin. And her baby was crying."

"But darling." Clark put his arm around her. "You had over fifty dollars in rupees."

"I don't care. I wanted to do something, to make a difference to someone."

"Well, I guess you did." He laughed. "Fifty dollars, that's a year's income for a girl like that, maybe more."

"I don't care," Aster said again, her voice shaking.

"Oh, darling." Clark's voice shook too now. "I'm so sorry."

"I know," Aster said, leaning closer.

"Are you all right?"

"I'm fine. Really." She smiled.

Through the growing dusk, they started back toward the hotel. Halfway down the block, Aster saw the beggar girl again, making her way through the crowd. Her baby wasn't crying or waving its arms now; it slept heavily against its mother's back in a fold of ragged shawl.

More than a year's income, Aster thought. Even if what I think isn't true, something's happened in India. I've made a difference to that woman and her baby. Maybe I've even changed their lives.

Do you know that? I've changed your life too! The words were so loud in her head that Aster was sure she had spoken. But Lakshmi, unhearing, walked on, disappearing into the noisy, jostling Indian crowd, into the smoky, darkening city.

Ghost Mother

MARLY SWICK

The first night the girl is in the house, I don't sleep. She does. In the morning she's still asleep, still tired from the flight, I assume. Clifford tiptoes around as he shaves and dresses for work. His exaggerated effort not to disturb her irritates me. I want to say, "Knock it off. She's only a knocked-up teenager, not a visiting dignitary." But I know how awful that will sound. When he swoops over our bed for a kiss, I pretend to have drifted off.

As soon as I hear his car back out of the driveway, I haul myself out of bed, down the hall past her closed door, and into the bright, sunny kitchen. Another cloudless day in southern California. The girl is from Wahoo, Nebraska. Too perfect. Our best friends, Buddy and Eleanor, fellow Hollywood hacks, went berserk when we told them and accused Clifford of making it up. "We've got dibs on the option," Clifford said sternly. "After all, it's *our* life."

When the girl answered our ad, she said she had always wanted to live in California. She wanted to know if we had a swimming pool. She wanted to know if we were involved in "show business." She seemed pleased when we answered yes on both counts, but still said she needed a week to decide. By special delivery, we sent snapshots of our kidney-shaped pool, plus two videocassettes—an episode of *The Waltons* I'd worked on and a TV movie about a farm family that Clifford had written. We figured we'd show her we were glamorous *and* wholesome. The whole time she was making up her mind, I agonized. I dreamed about her: long, wheatlike hair and teeth as even as a row of corn kernels. Halfway through the week, she called to ask if she could bring her cat. I hesitated for a moment—Clifford is allergic—and then said sure, we'd be happy to have her cat. The next night she called and said she had reached her decision: yes.

Pouring myself a second cup of coffee, I frown at the clock on the stove: 10:35. It's 12:35 Nebraska time. Clifford and I have always been early risers, overachievers. Now, instead of the sleepless nights everyone warns you about, I picture us standing over the crib of a sluggish, complacent baby. I don't know what's come over me. I have always championed nurture over nature, but from the moment the girl stepped off the plane, I found myself scrutinizing her for possible bad genes: stringy hair, bitten-down nails, poor grammar. During the car ride home from the airport, I sat silent as a judge while Clifford made amiable conversation with the girl. From time to time, he would look over at me and smile encouragingly, probably thinking I was choked up with emotion, while the girl exclaimed over the palm trees and balmy temperature. She stuck her head out the window like a dog. Clifford chuckled, seemingly enchanted, even though his eyes were already starting to water and itch in reaction to the cat.

Everything about the girl annoyed me. After three years of fertility specialists—tests, drugs, inseminations, in-vitro—it had come to this: some gum-chewing, wide-eyed teenager in pink sneakers. "Midwestward ho!" is the cry of all of us prospective baby buyers from the coasts. You go to Hong Kong for silk, Italy for leather, Switzerland for watches, and the prairie for private adoptions. All this talk about crack babies and fetal alcohol syndrome has us running scared from the cities.

"Where's the beach?" the girl asked, and even though we were only a couple of blocks from our house, Clifford indulgently turned the car around and headed for the highway. We drove a couple of miles up the coast and then pulled off into one of the deserted parking lots. It was dark already, but you could see the white ruffle of surf and hear the waves thudding. The girl got out of the car and kicked off her shoes. As she scuffled across the sand toward the water, Clifford reached over and squeezed my hand. "It's going to be fine," he said. "She's not going to back out."

I nodded but didn't squeeze back. For the past month, ever since she had chosen us over other couples, I had been scared to death she would change her mind. I sighed and pulled my hand away. "But what if I change *my* mind?"

He laughed as if I had made a joke. "All sales are final. No refunds or exchanges."

I forced a little laugh, even though it wasn't so funny. We had paid ten thousand dollars to a private adoption broker. "Less than a Honda Accord," Clifford had pointed out philosophically.

As the girl waded in the surf, the cat started yowling and scratching at the upholstery, making Clifford sneeze in violent spasms. I got out and hollered for the girl until she finally heard and sprinted back up the beach. She was wearing a baggy, drop-waist sundress, and you couldn't really see she was pregnant. The baby wasn't due for another ten weeks. That was part of the deal: She wanted a place to stay. She didn't want to stick around Wahoo once she started to show. And we were only too eager to oblige. We wanted, we said, to be involved.

The instant she climbed back into the car, the cat calmed down.

"Your cat was upset," I said.

"Poor baby," she crooned, scratching it behind the ears.

"You got any tissues?" Clifford asked me.

I rummaged in my purse and handed him a wad. He blew his nose and pulled back out onto the highway.

"Look at the ocean," the girl said, holding the cat up to the window and pointing. "Wow, I really love it here."

"Good!" Clifford handed me his soggy tissue to dispose of and beamed at her in the rearview mirror.

"Do you have a cold?" she asked. "Want me to roll up the window?"

"No, no," he shook his head. "I'm fine. Just a touch of hay fever."

The girl leaned forward and gave Clifford a spontaneous hug, then looked at me uncertainly. "This must be hard for you," she said.

I was caught off guard, embarrassed. "Harder on you," I mumbled. Although, somehow, I didn't really believe it. The only thing in my whole life I had ever failed at was getting pregnant, and here was this semiliterate pom-pom girl who had succeeded without even trying.

Down the hall, at last, I hear the water running in the bathroom. It's 10:55. From the clock, my glance shifts to her purse, a gaudy woven thing slumped on the kitchen counter. I can't help myself. What I find is just what you would expect a teenage girl to have in her purse: lipstick, mascara, gum, an old brush with a tangle of hair entwined in the bristles, a couple of packets of peanuts from the airplane—one of which is ripped open. At the bottom of the purse, loose sticky peanuts are glommed onto shreds of tissue and tobacco flakes. When I see the tobacco flakes, I have to restrain myself from marching down the hall and demanding to know whether she has been smoking during pregnancy. The adoption broker assured us repeatedly that the girl did not do drugs, drink, or smoke. If he was wrong about the smoking, who knew what else he was wrong about?

As the shower continues to run, I pull a fat pink wallet out of the

bag and study her driver's license. Giselle Marie Nelson. Height 5'5",
weight 115, eyes blue, hair blonde, birth date 7/5/76. I flip to a picture
of her family, a posed portrait. Straight out of central casting: the par-
ents, Giselle, two younger brothers, and a dog. All blonde, even the
dog.

I hear the shower go off, and flip quickly through the other plastic
windows, thinking maybe there will be a picture of the boy, the father.
But all I find are a couple of girlfriends' class photos. Disappointed and
vaguely relieved, I slide the wallet back into the purse.

An instant later, the girl appears in the doorway wearing an over-
size hot-pink T-shirt and rubber thongs. "Hi," she says. "I thought I'd
lie out by the pool. I mean, if that's okay." Her long hair drips down
the front of her T-shirt, her inflated breasts.

"Great," I nod and smile. "How about some breakfast first?"

She shakes her head. Something brushes against my ankles. The cat
mews. "Looks like *someone* wants breakfast," I say brightly. Glad for
something to do, I walk to the cupboard where I have a supply of
gourmet cat food. "I didn't know what she likes." I start pulling out
cans—"Chicken, liver, seafood . . ."

The girl seems stunned by the selection. "Usually she just eats dry
food."

"I'll pick up some dry food later," I say, vaguely miffed, "but for now,
how about seafood?" I open the can and scoop its smelly contents into
a bowl. The cat lunges for the food before it even touches down.

"Now. How about you? Are you sure you don't want something to
eat? We've got eggs, cereal, English muffins."

The girl looks at the cat greedily smacking away at its bowl. "Maybe
an English muffin," she says meekly. "But I can fix it myself."

"It's your first morning." I pull out a chair and gesture for her to sit.
"Just relax."

As I cut and toast a muffin, the cat, having licked the bowl clean,
starts acting weird, pacing. "Does she need to go out?" I set the muf-
fin on the table along with a jar of marmalade.

"She's an indoor cat. Do you have a litter box?"

I shake my head. Great, I think, I have thirty cans of gourmet cat
food, and it's never even occurred to me to buy kitty litter. But I smile
stoically and say, "No problem. I'll just zip up to the store." Happy for

an excuse to get away, I grab my keys off the counter. "Do you want anything?"

The girl is holding the cat on her lap, nuzzling her face in its fur like a little girl with a stuffed animal. It occurs to me how alone and scared she must feel. I pause on my way out and attempt a reassuring, motherly smile. "How about a matinee later?"

She shrugs and nods. "Sure, if you want to."

"Good. Back soon. There are beach towels in the linen closet."

I head out to the car and then think of something else. When I duck my head back into the kitchen, she is down on her hands and knees with a wad of paper towels, cleaning up a mess the cat made the minute my back was turned. When she sees me, she jumps up guiltily.

"I'm sorry. She never does this," she says. "It's just that she doesn't have her box."

"No problem. It's my fault." I sniff the air and walk over and take a charred muffin out of the toaster oven.

"I'm sorry," she says again. She looks about ready to burst into tears.

"Don't be silly. There's plenty." I hand her the pack of muffins. "I just wanted to tell you to use the suntan lotion in the medicine chest. You don't want to get burned."

My little bit of motherly advice seems to relax her some. "You think maybe you could pick up some diet chocolate soda?" she asks timidly.

"Sure," I say. "Anything else?"

She shakes her head, then says, "Well, maybe some potato chips. I'm sort of addicted."

I fish a little notepad out of my purse and dutifully jot this down, inwardly moaning at such trashy prenatal nutrition.

On the way back out to the car, I sneak a glance in at her through the window. She is eating ravenously.

I take my time coming back from the store, and when I get home, the girl is floating on the raft in the pool. It's hot out. I imagine she's thirsty, so I pour some chocolate soda into a glass of ice. The stuff looks revolting, but when I take a sip, I have to admit it's not bad. The girl has on a tropical-print bikini and is lying on her back, trailing her hands in the water. I watch her through the window, my gaze lingering on her belly, the smooth warm curve of it, and I grip the icy glass so tight it almost breaks in my hand. How weird life is. Some sixteen-year-old girl gets carried away in the backseat of some boy's car and now here she is, floating in my pool, our baby floating inside of her. If our ad had run a couple of months earlier or later, it would be some other girl, some other baby. The thought depresses me. I want to believe that *this* baby was meant for Clifford and me.

"Hi," I say. "Want a drink?" I hold up the glass. "Chocolate."

She paddles herself over to the edge of the pool. "Thanks," she says. "It's so great here I can't believe it. I feel like a movie star."

"Your nose looks pink. Did you use the sunscreen?"

She nods.

"Well, I think you should put some more on soon."

"Okay." She shrugs and drains her soda.

"You hungry?" I glance at my watch. "I can fix a sandwich."

She shakes her head. "I'm fine."

"Tuna? Ham and cheese? Or I could make a salad."

"Okay. Tuna sounds good. Thanks. But I don't want to be any trouble."

"It's no trouble. I'm hungry, too," I assure her, though I'm not.

"You're going to be a good mother," she jokes as I turn toward the house. The joke irritates me. Although I am glad to see that she has some sort of sense of humor, of irony, even: Clifford and I would hate to have a baby with no sense of humor.

The instant I open the can of tuna the cat materializes at my feet. Through the window, I see the girl drift. I mince onion, glancing irritably at my watch. I should be at the computer, working on the revised teleplay due at the end of the month. And the afternoon will be short, too, since I promised to take her to a matinee. Still, it's her first day here, and I can't very well ignore her. It's just typical that somehow Clifford is all booked for the day, so that taking care of the girl is my responsibility. Long ago, when I had first decided to have a baby, I came to terms with the fact that no matter how noble Clifford's intentions, I had better be prepared to take on the bulk of the grunt work. But that was for the baby, not the baby's mother.

The girl looks blissfully peaceful in the pool, her hair shining like silver in the sun. I have to admit she's pretty. And seems to be polite and considerate. There's nothing about her, really, to account for the wave of hostility—so intense I'd actually felt nauseous—that hit me the moment I saw her walk off the plane.

For weeks, I had been waiting impatiently for her arrival. She was all I talked about: "Giselle this, Giselle that . . ." I had called and asked her what her favorite color was—yellow—and redecorated the guest room in various sunny shades. Before falling asleep each night, I would create little scenarios-Giselle and me shopping, going to the gym, giggling in the kitchen. Girl stuff. I'd always wanted a sister. That I was, in fact, old enough to be Giselle's mother, I didn't like to think about.

A couple of times, my friend, Eleanor never known for tact, had asked, "Don't you worry she'll get too attached? What about afterward? Are you going to send her photos? Let her visit?" Eleanor thought the whole transaction should be quick and businesslike, like a drug deal in the middle of the night. But Clifford argued that it was better this way, our getting to know each other. It was more humane and personal. In the long run, he felt, it would be healthier for all of us. Eleanor said she just hoped we knew what we were doing.

Now, as I cut the sandwich in half and dump a handful of potato chips onto the plate, I'm not so sure. When I glance outside, the raft is empty. A quick check reveals that the girl is not in the water or anywhere in the yard. Guiltily, I imagine her in her room packing her suitcase while I look on helplessly.

ME: What are you doing? You aren't leaving?

HER: I can't take this hostility. *[She dumps a handful of underwear into her suitcase.]* I know you're trying to act nice, but I can feel it. It's not my fault you couldn't get pregnant.

ME: I don't know what you mean. Clifford and I are overjoyed to have you here.

HER: Maybe *he* is. But you've got a problem. I may be from Nebraska, but I'm not completely out of it.

As I'm trying to think what to say next, something that will change her mind so that I won't have to explain to Clifford why she suddenly up and left, I hear the thud of her bare feet tromping down the hall toward the kitchen.

"You were right," she says. "My nose is completely fried." She sits down at the table, and I slide the sandwich over to her. "I want to get some postcards when we go out later." She breaks off a little glob of tuna and feeds it to the cat. "Leslie, my best friend, said she was almost jealous. I promised to write to her every day."

Leaning casually against the sink, I tear the foil off a yogurt container and eat a couple of spoonfuls. "What about the boy—you know—the father?"

"Oh him." She shrugs. "Forget him." She continues feeding her sandwich to the cat. If she were my daughter, I'd make her stop. Don't feed the cat from the table, I'd say. And no doubt, my daughter would frown and sigh and keep right on doing what she was doing. Suddenly, the thought of being anyone's mother seems way beyond me, a task for which I am monumentally unprepared and unsuited. "Listen—" I say.

"Wait!" She grabs my hand and places it on her belly. "It's kicking. Feel it?"

I nod solemnly, feeling the tears pushing against my closed eyelids, the tightening in my throat. This whole thing is too weird. Crazy. I snatch my hand away.

"Do you have names picked out?" she asks.

I shake my head and hand her the movie listings. "Choose anything you want. I'm going to put in a load of laundry."

Trembling, I lock myself in our bedroom and fling myself onto the unmade bed. I look at the clock on the night table. Clifford should be home by the time we get back from the matinee. While the girl is changing for dinner—Clifford promised to take her to a real Hollywood restaurant—I will take him aside and say, "This is an impossible situation. It's never going to work, so let's just call it quits right now. She can find someone else. She can keep the money."

Eyes closed, I can see the look on Clifford's face, confused and concerned.

HIM: If you really feel that way, then I guess . . . *[He sighs]* But I don't get it. You couldn't wait for her to get here. Who's going to tell her? Are you sure?

ME: *[Nods]*

HIM: Great. *[He paces the room.]* This is just great. What if you were pregnant? You couldn't change your mind then.

ME: But I'm not. *[I start to cry.]* Don't you see? That's the point. I'm not.

As we pull up to the movie theater, the girl whips out her hairbrush. She bends her neck down, brushes her lank hair vigorously, then shakes it loose. For a glorious moment, until gravity takes its toll, she looks like a Hollywood starlet. "Is your hair naturally curly?" she asks on the crowded escalator. When I nod, she says in an indiscreet tone, "Too bad the baby can't inherit your hair." If the girl were my daughter, I would tell her to lower her voice, but she is just a stranger who will be gone soon.

Once the movie starts, the girl sits quietly in the darkness, rapt. I begin to feel more kindly disposed toward her than I have since the moment I laid eyes on her.

The evening she was due to arrive—it seems longer ago than just yesterday—Clifford and I went out to eat at an Italian place near the airport. I was too excited to eat. We got to the airport way too early, and I bought a bouquet of pink sweetheart roses for her. I had this image in my mind of how it would be. She would straggle off the plane, tired and shy. I would walk up and say, "Giselle?" and when she nodded, I would give her a big welcoming hug. There wouldn't be a dry eye in the house.

In fact, it all went pretty much according to my script, right up until the big welcoming hug. I couldn't do it. Suddenly, there she was in the flesh, the embodiment of my body's failure. A ghost mother hired to create a child under my name. I felt like pounding my fist and stamping my feet. It isn't fair! It isn't fair! Instead, I traipsed along silently to the baggage claim.

After the movie ends, the girl and I drive home without saying much. When we pull into the driveway, she seems almost as relieved as I am to see Clifford's car.

The girl is sleeping again before dinner. Clifford and I drink our vodka tonics out by the pool because, in just one day, the cat dander has permeated the house. "So how was your day?" he asks me.

"Fine, great." I say, giving him a breezy summary. Then I switch the topic to business. The deal at Paramount looks good, he says. "Great. Terrific. I'll have another drink," I say, holding out my empty glass.

Just before it is time to leave for the restaurant, I beg off, pleading a headache. I know Clifford assumes I am just done in from overexcitement. I stand in the doorway and wave until the car has disappeared.

In the aftermath of their departure, I can't think what to do, what it is that I would usually be doing. I go into the kitchen and open a chocolate soda and grab a handful of potato chips, and gravitate down the hall to the girl's room. The door is closed. When I push it open, I am surprised by how neat the room is. The bed is crisply made, and all her clothes are hanging in the closet. It occurs to me that she must be on her best behavior. The cat looks at me suspiciously with narrowed eyes and then beats a hasty retreat under the bed. On the dresser, next to the hairbrush, is a bottle of cologne—a scent from my high school past. I spray my wrists with it and run the girl's brush through my hair.

Suddenly I feel terribly tired, as if I have been dragging around an extra thirty pounds. A little nap, I think. I fold back the covers and sink into her bed. For the first time all day, I begin to relax. There is a soft thud at the food of the bed—the cat. I stretch out my arm to pet her, and she makes her way cautiously closer. Across the room, the gauzy yellow curtains ripple gently in the evening breeze. I think of wheat, miles and miles of golden wheat swaying in the wind. The cat hesitates for a moment and then nestles up against me. I think of autumn. The harvest. I think of my bedroom back home, the brown leaves falling outside, and me inside, warm and snug, playing with my dolls, bundling them up against the cold, kissing and scolding, pretending to be a mommy.

Family Lines

GEORGE RABASA

This lunch has been two weeks in the making.

First, a woman called asking to speak to Mrs. Brunner, and Jill, my daughter, told her she didn't live here anymore but could be reached in Toulouse, France, where she had gone after our divorce to learn to be a pastry chef. A couple of hours later, a Mr. Grant asked for me, and it turned out he was the husband of the woman who had called before. He said he wanted to invite my daughter and me to lunch so the four of us could meet and discuss something important "regarding your daughter's situation," is the way he put it. He suggested neutral territory, The Willows Restaurant.

There's nothing neutral about The Willows on an academic salary. From the moment we get here, I resolve to pay attention to every detail of this lunch: to what we eat, to what we say, and especially to what the Grants say, and what I think about what they say, and how my daughter is taking it all in.

I glance around the restaurant, which is starting to fill up with men and women in the rigid blue suits, the unwrinkled shirts, the swirling ties of corporate drudges. Jill complains about the nice pleated skirt I suggested she wear because it is suddenly too tight around her waist. She says she is sulking because she knows she is not going to like the Grants and would rather not have to be part of this particular lunch. She pinches pieces of brown crust from a roll and chews thoughtfully. "Did you tell them how to recognize us?" she asks.

"I think they'll know us once they see us."

"We're kind of uncool, right?" She takes a long look around the place. "From St. Paul rather than Minneapolis."

"No, honey, we look fine."

"I'm so nervous I could throw up."

"It's a great place for it."

"You're nervous too," she accuses.

"How can you tell?"

"You're doing your nervous laugh. The one that goes *heh heh heh* real quick, like you're clearing your throat."

When the Grants arrive, they look anything but nervous. I stand to shake their hands and try to focus on everything about them at once. They seem to be in their thirties, their skin is rosy and unwrinkled, their hair sits like poufy clouds on top of their heads, their clothes smell of a dizzying mixture of dry-cleaning fluid and cologne.

Martha (she says right away, "Please, call me Martha") leans across the table toward Jill and looks into her eyes. "I'm so glad to finally meet you, Jill," she says in a conspiratorial whisper. "I've heard a lot about you, and you sound like a wonderful young woman."

"We're very close to your friend Jane Hunt's parents," Craig is quick to explain, although we both already know this from our earlier phone conversations. "When word got around about your status, we were naturally interested."

"Bad news travels fast," Jill says with a weak smile.

"Oh, but it doesn't have to be all bad." Martha tilts her head plaintively. "You have no idea. We've been trying for years. Every which way there is to try. Nothing's worked."

"The food is just great here," Craig says earnestly. He points out an item on the menu. "Aha, here they are, Shrimp á la Scampi."

I find my place on the page and notice they go for $16.95. I want to be able to tell Jill that this means it's okay to order anything up to that price. But before I can catch her eye, she says she will have the lobster. A deal at $24.95.

"Craig recommends the shrimp, honey."

"But I've never had lobster."

"Yes, you have." I force a smile. "Three years ago, Cape Cod."

Martha interrupts cheerfully. "I will have lobster, too. It makes this more of a celebration."

"So, tell me, Craig," I start in. "What do you do with yourself during the week, when you're not trying to buy a baby?" Even as I say the words, I'm already forcing a small laugh to show I'm making a joke, a little icebreaker, as it were. But the only laughter at the table is my own, the nervous one that Jill identified earlier.

"I'm in direct marketing," he says blandly. "I sell people's names and addresses. Long, long lists of names." He smiles. He thinks I don't understand what he does.

But I do. And I can't help calculating that even if he only earns a penny a name, he makes a lot of money. On the other hand, my wealth is the kind you find at the old DNA bank: a solid ectomorphic physique, a full head of hair, Ph.D.-level brain cells. "I sell history," is the way I put it.

"I sell condos," Martha puts in cheerfully. "Although once Jill's baby is born and becomes our baby," she adds, "I expect to be a full-time mom."

The waiter, who has been eyeing us morosely since Jill and I arrived, comes over to take our order. He brightens a little after appraising the Grants and learning he's sold two lobsters and a bottle of chardonnay. Jill orders Diet Pepsi. It's all she has ever drunk since the age of two. I think she should switch to milk now.

"Now, about the daddy," Craig begins. "What can you tell us about him?"

"He told you," Jill says. "He's a history professor at Trent."

"That's your dad," Craig says patiently. "I meant the father of the baby."

Jill shrugs off the question. "I really don't want this getting around. He doesn't know yet."

"Is he in college?" Martha asks hopefully.

"No." Jill frowns. "He's in the shipping warehouse at Ward's."

"Do you know his parents?" Craig wants to know.

"I don't see how his parents have anything to do with this," Jill says.

"For what it's worth," I intervene, "I've known the boy for a couple of years. He's apparently bright, apparently healthy."

"Apparently Caucasian?" Craig looks at me for an answer, then at Jill.

Martha makes a helpless shrug. "I wish we didn't have to ask this kind of stuff. I told Craig to take it easy."

"What's Caucasian?" Jill finally speaks. "Is it only White? Or anything except Black? How about the in-betweens, like Italians and Japanese and Spanish?"

"I know the Spanish are considered Hispanics," Martha says. "That's obvious, I guess."

"Well, they look just like Italians and Greeks. Does that mean Italians and Greeks are Hispanics too?"

"Not exactly," Craig snaps.

"So, if they're not Hispanic, they must be Caucasian. Right?"

"You could say that." Craig looks like he's trying to find another way to phrase his question, but Jill pushes on.

"You'd have to lump the Turks in with the Greeks and the Italians. And then you might as well throw in the Iranians because they look just like them, and so do the Afghanis, who look kind of Jewish, so you might as well bunch them in with Palestinians and Jordanians and Iraqis—in fact, all the Arabs can go into one bag except for the Egyptians, who tend to be mostly brown, which means they belong with the Inuit."

Under the weight of my stare, she pauses to take a long sip from her Diet Pepsi. "You can answer Craig's question, honey," I suggest.

"I was just getting to it," she says seriously. "I'm sure I'll have an apparently white baby, if that's what you're asking."

"It is, dear," Craig says. "Thank you."

Jill nods and finishes the last of her drink with a slurp.

Even as we trade low appreciative murmurs about the food, I'm considering the awkward, vaguely illegal kind of deal we're about to make. In truth, I'm less concerned about the murky ethics of the situation than about the simple practical realities of paying good money for the dubious benefits of raising a kid. I can't imagine what the bureaucracies of the world would do with free commerce in babies. We would need many more lawyers, for one thing. There would have to be minimum quality standards such as height and weight, coloring, life expectancy according to genetic background. The investment in the child would really pay off if it lived long enough to take care of its adoptive parents when they reached old age.

There should be warranties—three years or sixty pounds, whichever comes first. Service contracts might cover the gamut from orthodontics to psychotherapy. Consideration should be given to who actually sells the child: the mother as sole owner, a partnership involving both parents, or a privately held corporation that includes the extended families on both sides. Possibly the natural parents would be only the agents of the sale, and the actual funds would be held in trust and paid directly to the kid upon reaching age eighteen, but only if it maintains a B average or better, does not take up any serious vices, and manages to stay out of jail. Otherwise, in compensation for the heartache of raising a difficult, unappreciative child, the whole of the purchase price, held in trust, would go back to the adoptive parents. With interest.

"And how is the lobster, ladies?" Craig asks, looking up from his food for a moment.

"Good." Jill nods vigorously as she tries to dig out a piece from under a mound of goopy white sauce. Not her favorite kind of food, actually.

"The scampi are great." I hold up one pink shrimp impaled on my fork and watch helplessly as Jill turns very pale.

"Oh, damn, I thought I was over this," she says. "I need to be excused." She pushes her chair back and heads toward the back of the restaurant, weaving her way around the tables, only to stop suddenly in the middle of the restaurant.

"Poor child," Martha says. "I'd better go help her find the ladies' room."

"I don't suppose any of this is easy on her," Craig says. He takes a deep breath and leans toward me as if he's about to make an intimate revelation. I try to meet his earnest gaze but become distracted by his silk tie with its design of geometry-gone-haywire falling limply from behind his jacket and hanging just above his plate. I start to warn him, but he suddenly sits back, as if changing his mind about what he was about to say. He then stabs a shrimp with his fork and leans again toward me with new resolve. This time the tie is not so close to the shrimp.

"You know, this baby thing has become an issue for Martha and me. More for Martha, actually," he corrects himself. "And we're damn near at the end of our ropes; first, with the fertility tests that proved inconclusive, then artificial insemination that didn't take, and for the last three years adoption applications that get us some address in Honduras, the name of a doctor in Sri Lanka, or a spot at the bottom of a waiting list for some all-American baby guaranteed to look like it came from us. Can you imagine? They match hair, eyes, complexion. Only thing is you pay through the nose and then wait for some girl who looks like your wife to meet a guy who looks like you, they then agree to have sex, and finally on one precious occasion, lose the condom. The whole thing can take years."

I nod impatiently. "And here's a teenager that ends up pregnant first time around like there's nothing to it. No justice in the world, right?"

"I suppose that's what I'm saying," Craig admits. Then leaning forward, he adds in hushed, conspiratorial tones, "We want to do the right thing by your girl, you can be sure of that." This time the edge of his tie does skim the surface of the oil, but I see it too late to warn him.

"Good," I say with brisk enthusiasm. "She wants a hundred thousand dollars for the kid."

"Get serious," he blurts out while still leaning toward me across the table. Then he forces a deep breath, sits upright, and reaches for the glass of wine before him. I see his hand shake just a little.

"Just kidding." I smile at him. "Really, I just thought I'd say something to get us into the subject at hand."

"I didn't mean to get angry. But there are people out there," he says, vaguely indicating the outer reaches of the restaurant with a tilt of his head. "People who would try to profit from our predicament."

"I personally think Jill should have an abortion and put the whole problem behind her."

Craig purses his lips. "Is that what she wants to do?"

"She keeps putting off going to Planned Parenthood. She has a tendency to procrastinate until she's out of options."

"We will make it worthwhile for her to take the baby to term," Craig emphasizes. "Anything she needs, medical bills, tutoring, special foods, a little money for college."

"Just for argument's sake," I venture in, "How much do you suppose the baby would be worth?"

"You can't put a price on a human life," he shrugs.

"But you can put a price on the humiliation of attending classes big as a blimp, sitting out the prom, the lack of suitable roles in the class play."

Craig looks at me curiously. "Spell out what you're getting at, exactly."

"Exactly? Nothing." I shake my head. "I just wish there were a way to carry on the rest of this really very pleasant lunch."

Craig's face brightens with an idea. "I could have my attorney talk to your attorney."

"To Jill's attorney," I'm quick to correct.

By the time Jill and Martha get back, Craig and I have gone back to our eating of lunch and sipping of wine, but silent now, as if a difficult subject has finally been dealt with, leaving no energy for even the most perfunctory kind of small talk.

"Ah, the ladies are back," Craig says, acting cheerful again. "We were just talking, Jill, about how Martha and I want to be of help to you these next few months."

Jill glances at me suspiciously. "I'm sorry I got sick," she explains. "But for a moment the shrimp on your plates looked like a bunch of little embryos swimming around in olive oil." She looks down at the cold lobster under the thickening white sauce, prods it with her fork, and after a moment folds her napkin and lays it on the table. "Could we just go home?" she asks me.

"There are still some things we should talk about, aren't there?" Martha wants to know.

"Of course, soon," I promise.

Craig gets up to shake my hand. "We'll stay in touch."

She has been asleep for hours since arriving home, while I sit in front of the TV just down the hall from her bedroom. I keep the volume very low, feeling like a guard posted outside the quarters of someone under threat. It's up to me to keep the Grants at bay, to filter out calls from what's-his-name at Montgomery Ward, to seal our windows and doors against the shrill politics of reproduction.

There are other threats too subtle to have a name or a face. In a Pepto Bismol commercial, the chalky pink syrup dissolves from an imaginary tummy onto my daughter's real womb and her resolute shrimp of a fetus, now also coated in the ubiquitous oozes of the nineties—pink goo like a photochemical soup from the holes in the ozone, from the road paved with the living ashes of our dead garbage, and those new diseases with their sticky little viruses.

Children are not safe anymore, not with those roaming bands of kid-napping pornographers, crack packs, the NRA, all Republicans, Saddam, Joe Camel, *Melrose Place*. (Oh, such a long list.) Even the neighbors' sweet Labrador, barking in their yard under cover of night, becomes the leader of a pack of hang-tongued fugitives from the pound, loping through the streets out to capture a human baby and hold it for ransom against the killer needles of the Humane Society. In time, they raise the kid as one of their own, at home in the inner city alleys, teaching him to scavenge in dumpsters, to snap at old men, to maul cats. (Things would turn out OK in the end: *Dog Boy Rescued! Rejoins Family, Barks Way Through Harvard, Marries Vet.*)

A leaden silence startles me awake and I realize the TV has been turned off. Across the dark room I can make out Jill, a large soft mound sitting on the couch with her legs folded beneath a shapeless black dress. Through the stillness, disturbed only by her shallow breathing, I sense the tiny curled worm that glows like an ember, suspended in a deep red universe of buoyant tissue and mysterious fluids, biding its time, waiting to ripen.

"I keep wanting to throw up," she says. "Even when there's nothing inside me, I just keep on heaving."

"Part of you would like to be rid of it," I venture.

"It's the part of me that doesn't want to be rid of it that worries me."

"You can worry about what you want or don't want. It just happens."

"I don't have to sell them the baby, right?"

"Do you want me to tell you what to do?"

"No, I guess not."

"So, for now, don't do anything."

"I feel like little Miss Rent-A-Womb."

One evening, a few weeks after our lunch with the Grants, Martha calls and says she would like to come over for a short visit. She appears with a heavy canvas shoulder bag from which she pulls a box of assorted herbal teas, to get Jill off caffeine, she explains.

"I've been getting ready for this for a long time, you know," she assures Jill. "I know everything there is to know about car seat safety, and what plastics are good, and when's the right age to introduce a child to television and ice cream and guns. That's right, guns. Kids'll find them, so it's up to the parents to put guns in the right context. I intend to tell my child—our child, Jill—that guns are not toys, but tools that can help you solve certain kinds of problems. Then if he still wants to carry one, it's a decision he can take responsibility for."

"At what age do you think that should take place, Martha?" I ask, hoping Jill won't laugh.

"Age five is what I've read. By then a kid has some sense of other creatures' mortality, if not yet people's."

"What if he's a girl?" Jill asks blankly.

"Four and a half," Martha states. "Girls mature faster than boys. I've been studying this stuff for years."

Later, sitting around the kitchen table with our mugs of Red Zinger,

Martha wants to know everything about our family, how many relatives have worn glasses, had diabetes, suffered heart attacks at an early age. She wants to know about baldness and farsightedness and obesity. Jill brings over a couple of dusty family albums started by her mother.

"This is wonderful," Martha exclaims, opening the first book. We pour over the milky Kodachromes and the yellowed black-and-whites of forgotten children frowning in the sun, old men and women sitting stiffly with looks of longing that reach far beyond the camera, grim bridegrooms rubbed the wrong way by their high starched collars. Martha demands information. She wants names, dates, places, events, which she ceremoniously repeats after me: Uncle Harry at Carlsbad, Jill's fifth birthday, Pauline (who looked like Ingrid Bergman), Melissa's graduation from med school, Ambrose and Theodora on their wedding day. I find myself going on with numbing regularity, punctuated only by Martha's occasional interjections of delight or amusement.

"You know," she says finally, as she pushes the last of the photo albums away and reaches into her canvas bag, "I've brought some pictures of my own." She pulls out a black three-ring notebook. "Craig doesn't understand," she explains. "This is my baby book." She starts to hand it to Jill, then pulls it back until we promise not to laugh.

The book is filled with hundreds of pictures of babies, black and white and brown and yellow babies, naked baby bottoms and wriggly baby toes, nursing babies and tumbling babies and crawling babies, all clipped from magazine ads and labels for baby food and diapers and lotions.

"I've been collecting them for years," she smiles. "Ever since it was clear Craig and I wouldn't be able to make a baby of our own."

During the next few months, life for Jill is held at bay. College applications, new clothes for her senior year, the stock boy at Ward's, all are on hold. Mostly, she spends her time complaining of the heat and the humidity and the boredom. The high point of the month is her visit to the clinic. Here her progress meets with enthusiasm, her struggles against excessive weight gain are rewarded, the development of the fetus is applauded. Here we're told Jill will have a boy, something that makes Craig happy. Occasionally, I catch myself thinking about a grandson out there who may never know me. But I dismiss the sharp moment of sadness that comes unexpectedly; I only play a small supporting role in this thing.

One day, a Sunday, as I sit with the paper and the last of the lukewarm coffee, Jill wants to know if she will look normal after she's delivered.

"Sure you will."

"What makes you so sure?"

"Your mom went back to her usual weight."

"But there are these changes, right? Like the breasts hang different, and the stretch marks."

"You won't have any marks, honey." I try to sound convincing. "I used to rub lotion on your mother so she wouldn't get marks. That was my first contact with you." The memory is vivid, of my hands gliding along the creamy surface of my wife's young skin, of feeling the soft curve of a back, the small bump of a foot, the occasional traveling protuberances that swelled and recoiled along the drum-tight belly.

"Would you put some lotion on me, Dad?"

"Sure," I say as I go back to my reading.

"I mean now."

I put the paper away and look up at her. She is wearing her wrinkled pink flannel gown with the small white flowers. Her preference for staying around the house has made maternity clothes unnecessary. When she goes out, she wears one of my shirts and a pair of jeans with an expanding waist. During the past month she has been cutting away at her hair until it's now down to a short blunt length. Her face is coated with a pale, chalky makeup punctuated by bright red lipstick and blue eye shadow. "I don't want anybody to recognize me," she explained one time when I commented on her appearance.

"Come on, Dad," she pleads. "You don't want to be known as a procrastinator, right?" She hands me a bottle of lotion and stretches out on the couch. "First warm the lotion in your hands," she says, unbuttoning the middle of her gown.

"I've done this before, remember?" Still, I'm not prepared for the sight of the big, hard globe that rises from just below her enlarged breasts, peaks at the navel, and abruptly slopes down to her groin. The paleness of her skin, a stark eggshell-white marked by an occasional pink blush and a filigree of faint blue veins, is a foreign, forbidden sight.

I sit on the edge of the couch, holding a dollop of lotion in my hand.

Jill has closed her eyes, and her breathing, usually shallow under the new weight on her chest, relaxes as she lies on her side. I exhale warm air on the lotion, then cup it with my left hand before spreading it on her belly with a smooth circular motion, thinning it out, spreading it gently into her skin. My hand glides along effortlessly, the fingers skating on her skin, spinning whorls that seem to echo the patterns on my own fingertips.

At the first sensation of movement, I stop spreading the lotion and wait, keeping very still, hardly daring to breathe. The small lump that presses against the palm of my hand stirs once more. I imagine a tiny foot, or a hand with its five nubby fingers clenched into fighting readiness, or possibly the head butting impatiently at the walls of its cell. Speculating that some level of communication might be already possible, I draw small spirals on the milky film, circling with my index finger the restless bump that expands and contracts under the skin, thinking the slow punches and kicks are emphatic answers to the secret, wordless code of my touch. Mysteries wait to be revealed: Is there thought before breath, lust before sight, pain before hunger?

The insistent beeping of the phone jars me from my thoughts. "It's Martha Grant." I hand Jill the phone and retreat to the Sunday paper and the last of the cold coffee on the kitchen table. From here, I can see Jill sitting up now on the couch, the large globe of her belly still visible between the edges of the unbuttoned robe. She speaks too softly for me to hear, but I see her nod emphatically, then take the phone and place it on her navel, hold it motionless, then very slowly move it a couple of inches at a time across the stretched skin, suddenly pause and hold still for a moment, then move it on a couple of inches more until it has traveled the whole expanse of her belly.

"She wanted to hear the baby," Jill says later. "I told her the clinic let me hear the heartbeat, and she wanted to hear it, too; I don't think she heard anything over the phone. She said she did."

A few days before Jill is due, Martha calls to say she knows it's going to happen any moment because she herself has been feeling something like contractions and, while there is no explanation for her having those sensations, she wants to know if Jill is feeling anything yet. "It's the weirdest thing," she says. "But I'm not making them up; it feels like a belt is being tightened around my insides. Even if it is all in my mind, it's still kind of remarkable, don't you think? I just know I'm really meant to have this baby."

"She's been really weird," Jill tells me later. "She started getting morning sickness the day we met for lunch, and it stopped when mine stopped. She says she has gained weight, and her breasts are all swollen, and now she's getting ready to deliver. I might as well stay home and let her do the trick."

One evening, several days after Jill was supposed to start labor, Craig Grant calls because Martha is adamant that Jill will be feeling things at any moment. Martha unfortunately can't come to the phone because while sitting on the couch watching TV, a sudden, viselike pain seized her lower back and gripped her insides.

I place my hand over the mouthpiece. "Craig says Martha wants to know what you're feeling exactly."

Jill closes her eyes, as if trying to become more attuned to the sensations inside her. "Nothing," she says, placing both hands on her belly. "Tell them nothing's happening."

"She's sure you must be feeling something."

"I'm always feeling things," she snaps. "I'm just not feeling contractions."

"Well, Craig claims that Martha is," I insist. "They want to know what's holding you up."

"Tell them if they don't fucking quit bugging me, I'll keep the baby myself." She slams shut the door to her bedroom.

"Hello, Craig," I speak reassuringly. "Jill wants you both to know she is paying close attention to her body and all, but that she's not feeling a thing yet. She did say it might be better if you don't call her; she's feeling a little pressured. You know what they say about a watched pot never boiling."

In the course of the next two days, Jill concentrates on sending her body messages that it's time for something to happen. She takes long walks, striding out into the street with even, ducklike steps; she eats enchiladas for the stimulating properties of the hot peppers and the cilantro; she consults the *I Ching,* which corroborates the obvious (Pi: Holding Together).

Martha Grant is having pains exactly twenty minutes apart. Something seems to be working, I catch myself joking. "I swear," she yells at me over the phone, something has to happen, and soon, because this stuff is not in my head. This is real suffering, you know."

"Martha," I try to calm her. "maybe you should see a doctor. I don't know, a psychiatrist with gynecological experience."

I don't tell Jill about the call, but she guesses anyway that there is turmoil in the Grant household. "Do you think Martha is too crazy to get my baby?" Jill asks cautiously.

"She has been under strain."

"She's not the one who's becoming a mom."

"Sure, she is."

"That's up to me still."

After another day passes, Jill still is not in labor; Martha, however, does check into the hospital because nobody can figure out what is happening to her. Craig calls to say they have ruled out pregnancy, of course, but that they're checking into her gallbladder, liver, pancreas, colon, kidneys, appendix. It could be anything. "Please don't tell Jill I called," he asks me. "But let me know what we can do to help."

One evening, Jill has Craig get her front row tickets to a band she likes. She stands close to the speakers and lets the deep bass rumblings bounce on her body, sending tremors up and down her belly. For a moment, she believes that she and the musicians are in effect working together to break through the still amniotic pool with the clash of cymbals and hollow boom of the tom-toms, searing guitar riffs, and pervasive thud of two-chord bass. In the end, she comes out with only a ringing in her ears.

The next afternoon, I drive her to the hospital for one last examination to determine if they should induce labor. The nurses are brisk and unsympathetic. They tell her, "It's time, sweetie." They have seen this all before, and they hint darkly of drugs and procedures that will take over when the natural processes are stymied. Medical science, they assure us, can deal with this situation.

"I don't know why they call it a situation. Don't babies come out when they're ready?" she pleads while we wait for the elevator. When the doors finally open, Jill marches right in. I follow her, even though I realize it's going up instead of down.

"Shoot," Jill says. "It's going up. Maybe I should just stay in this elevator and go up and down and up and down until I start."

The elevator is full of green-and-white medical people. In the middle of this very hot July day, they have a wan, punchy look, as if only in the privacy of the elevator do they allow themselves to visibly fold. When the door opens on the sixth floor, about four stories above the maternity section, we are swept out by some people who scramble from the rear of the box to exit.

"We'll get it on the way back." I stab the down button.

"I have to pee, again," Jill says, heading from the elevator vestibule down a shiny green hallway. She hurries to catch up with a tiny, white-haired woman taking small steps with an aluminum walker. The woman nods and points Jill to the end of the hall.

When the elevator comes again, Jill is not back, so I wave at the group of medical types to go on without me. I venture a few steps down the hallway and notice a sign that welcomes us to the Women's Geriatric Unit. That explains the silence of the place. Missing are the mad dashes of medical people rushing down hallways with carts of steel and black rubber hardware. I sense that nothing is rushed here, that when a tired old heart stops beating or a leathery set of lungs pauses in midbreath, nobody panics much.

Thinking I'll find the restrooms down the hall, I go until I face a set of double doors to the Recreation Lounge. The room that opens up before me is large, with tall vertical windows that allow the sun to come streaming into an indoor garden of blooming planters and potted palms and ficuses and hanging baskets of flowers.

Suddenly, I become aware of soft, guttural voices coming from a corner of the room. A group of old women buzzes with excitement, and a few stragglers make their way to join them.

At the center of the tight circle is Jill, chatting away with a frail woman with wispy white hair and soft, cloudy eyes. The woman reaches out tentatively, and Jill takes the palm of her hand and lays it on the side of her belly. The old woman smiles excitedly, nodding to the others near her.

As word spreads around the geriatric floor, a line of women forms, their thin, angular bodies dressed in white hospital gowns, flannel robes, and faded cotton dresses. Each woman comes to Jill and touches her; from some, it's a caress, while others poke with their fingers or feel her breasts. She puts her arms around the shoulders of two women, tilting her head to listen to one, then the other. A blind woman reaches up to Jill's face with her fingertips. Tears well in Jill's eyes.

The women's voices mingle into a formless murmur that rises from their midst and courses toward the center of the group like the rush of flowing water. The hum seems to stir a deep, silent pool within Jill that pushes its way down, breaking like a thunderclap through the thin membrane. It bursts in a warm pink flood that at first comes in a gush and then thins out to a rivulet that streams down her legs, turning her jeans a deep blue. It puddles around her feet on the shiny linoleum floor.

As soon as I realize what is happening, I weave my way through the crowd of women. One of them rolls a wheelchair toward me. I position it next to Jill, and a woman with wildly flowing white hair helps her sit on it.

"Wait, Daddy," Jill says anxiously.

"We've got to move, honey."

"No!" she shouts, making me stop the chair by a set of phones. "I want to tell Martha it's time. Make her understand that she's not buying the baby. That she'd better get here and do some pushing."

Catholic Charities Home for Unwed Mothers

LORI JAKIELA

She told friends she was off
to study in Paris.
She would buy a white hat and dark glasses,
spend days in cafés along a silk-scarf river,
amuse lovers with her trick
of slipping her tongue through sheathes
of olives bobbing in martinis
strong as memory

of those months in Pittsburgh, the dark room
with the cedar closet and its five blue dresses
designed to deny everything.
Her breasts grew beautiful as eggplants.
Her belly swelled like an eye.
Sometimes she would ask the crucifix
the housemother hung over the door
for help. Sometimes, forgiveness. Sometimes,
mercy.

There were days she would make
lists of names that were not
the names of saints and she would sing
to the child that was not to be thought of
day is done and shadows fall. She would
lift the nightgown in candlelight,
watch the white hill of the body
that had become not her body,
almost believing she could trace
the sharp angle of a chin like her own.

She never saw them take it away.
She remembers a dream of light
so bright everything was dark,
the doctor's eyes, brown, and the way
his lips moved, worms under a green mask.

He asked if she was comfortable.
She doesn't remember what she said.
She took the pills they gave her
to help her forget. She never
opened the bible on her nightstand.
She slept soundly with the hall light off.
The marks on her belly stretched
into a field of dogwoods.

She dipped her fingers in milk
that still fell from her breasts.
There was nothing to be
afraid of now.

The Natural Father

ROBERT LACY

Her name was Laura Goldberg. She had thick black hair and a "bump" in her nose (as she put it), but she dressed well and she had a good figure. She worked as a typist in an abstract office in downtown San Diego, and when Butters first met her in the fall of 1958 they had both just turned nineteen. They met through a boot camp buddy of his who had gone to high school with her up in San Francisco, where she lived before her parents were divorced. Within a week he was taking her out. Butters was still in radio school at the time and didn't have a car, but Laura did, and she began picking him up several afternoons a week in the parking lot across the highway from the Marine base.

They made love on their third date, on the couch in her mother's apartment out in El Cajon, with the late afternoon sunlight casting shadow patterns on the walls. It was hurried and not very satisfactory, and Butters was embarrassed by his performance. He felt he ought to apologize or something.

"It's okay," Laura said. "It's okay."

After that, though, they made love nearly every time they were alone together, often in the front seat of her car parked late at night on suburban side streets, with the fog rolling up off the bay to conceal them. One night they did it on her bed in the apartment, then had to spend frantic minutes picking white bedspread nap out of his trousers before her mother got home. Another time she met him at the front door, fresh from her shower, wearing nothing but a loose kimono, and they did it right there on the living room carpet, with the sound of the running shower in the background.

Butters was from a little town in eastern Oklahoma and hadn't known many Jewish girls before. In fact, he couldn't think of any. However, Laura's being Jewish didn't matter nearly as much to him as it seemed to matter to her. She was forever making jokes about it, and she liked to point out other Jews to him whenever they came across them, in restaurants or on TV. "Members of the Tribe," she called them, or "M.O.T.s." Butters pretended to share in the humor, but he was never quite sure what he was being let in on. Where he came from, tribes meant Indians.

Still, he was amazed at some of the people she identified as Jewish. Jack Benny, for example. And Frankie Laine. Every time they watched TV together in the apartment the list got longer. One night she even tried to convince him Eddie Fisher was a Jew.

"Bull," he said. "I don't believe it."

"He is, though," she insisted. "Ask Mother when she gets here."

"He's Italian or something," Butters said. "I read it somewhere. Fisher's not his real name."

"Nope. He's a genuine M.O.T."

"Uh-uh."

"He is too, Donnie. Bet you a dollar."

"Make it five."

"You don't have five."

"I can get it."

"All right, Mister Sure-of-Yourself, five then. Shake."

They shook hands.

"How about Debbie Reynolds?" he said. "What's she?"

In March Butters was graduated from radio school and promoted to private first class. Then he was transferred to the naval base down at Imperial Beach to begin high-speed radio cryptography school. Imperial Beach was twelve miles due south of San Diego. The base sat out on a narrow point of land. At night you could see the lights of Tijuana across the way.

One night after he had been there about a month Laura picked him up, late, at the main gate, drove back up to a hamburger stand in National City, and told him she was pregnant.

Butters was astounded, of course. This was the sort of thing that happened to other people.

"How do you know?" he said.

"I've missed two periods."

"Jeez. Did you see a doctor?"

"Yes."

"What did he say?"

"He said I was pregnant."

"Yeah, but what did he *say*?"

"He said I was a big, strong, healthy girl, and I was going to have a baby sometime in October. He said I had a good pelvis."

"Is that all?"

"Yes. He gave me some pills."

"For what?"

"One for water retention and one for morning sickness."

"You been sick?"

"Not yet. He says I might be."

"Jeez."

They sat in silence for a while, not looking at each other. Finally he said, "Well, what do you think we should do?"

She spoke slowly and carefully, and he could tell she had given the matter some thought. "I think we ought to get engaged for a month," she said. "Then get married. I know where we can get a deal on a ring."

"What kind of a deal?"

"Forty percent off, two years to pay."

"Where?"

"Nathan's. Downtown."

"You already been there?"

"I go by it every day at lunch."

"They give everybody forty percent off?"

"I know the manager. He's a cousin."

On the way back to the base, Laura spoke of showers, wedding announcements, honeymoons in Ensenada. She said she thought they ought to sit down with her mother that very weekend, to get that part of it out of the way. Butters, who was hoping to get back on base without further discussion, said he thought he might have guard duty.

"You had guard duty last weekend," she reminded him.

"There's a bug going around," he said. "Lots of guys are in sickbay."

"Come Sunday night," she said. "I'll cook dinner. Elvis is on *Ed Sullivan*."

"I'll have to see," he said.

"Sunday night," she said.

Sunday was four days away, which gave him plenty of time to think. And the more he thought, the more he knew he didn't want to marry Laura Goldberg. He didn't love her, for one thing, and he wasn't ready to get married anyway, even to someone he did love. He was only nineteen years old. He had his whole life in front of him. Besides, he couldn't imagine Laura back home in Oklahoma.

That Sunday evening he caught a ride into San Diego with one of the boys from the base, then took a city bus out to the apartment in El Cajon. Laura met him at the door wearing an apron, a mixing spoon in her hand.

"Hi, hon," she said. "Dinner's almost ready."

Laura's mother, Mrs. Lippman, was seated on the living room sofa smoking a cigarette. She had her shoes off and her stockinged feet up on an ottoman. Mrs. Lippman was a short, heavyset woman with springy gray hair and sharp features. She always looked tired.

"Hello, Donald," she said. "What's with Betty Furness in there? Usually I can't get her to boil water."

"Hello, Mrs. Lippman," Butters said. "How's things at the paint store?"

Mrs. Lippman managed a Sherwin-Williams store down on lower Broadway and complained constantly about the help, most of whom were Mexican-American.

"Terrible," she said. "Don't ask. The chilis are stealing me blind."

Laura had fixed beef stroganoff, a favorite of Butters's, and when it was ready they ate it off TV trays in the living room while watching Elvis—from the waist up—on *The Ed Sullivan Show.* The meal was well prepared. Laura had even made little individual salads for each of them, with chopped walnuts on top and her own special dressing. When they were through eating she put the coffee on, then she and Butters scraped and stacked the dishes in the kitchen while Mrs. Lippman watched the last of the Sullivan show alone in the living room.

"You nervous?" Laura said to him in the kitchen. "You've been awfully quiet since you got here."

"I'm all right," Butters said, scraping a plate.

"Is something *wrong?*"

"No. I'm all right, I told you."

"Well, you certainly don't act like it. You haven't smiled once the whole evening."

Butters didn't say anything. He reached for another plate.

"Look at me," Laura said.

He looked at her.

"It's going to be *okay*," she said. "We'll just go in there and tell her. What can she say?"

"Nothing much, I guess."

"Do you want to do the talking, or do you want me to?"

"Either way. You decide."

"All right. You do it. That's more traditional anyway."

"What about the other?"

"What other?"

"You know."

"Oh. We don't mention that. Why upset her if we don't have to?"

When the coffee was ready Laura poured out three cups and she and Butters returned to the living room. The show was just ending. Ed Sullivan was onstage, thanking his guests and announcing next week's performers. Laura stood for a moment watching her mother watch the screen, then she set the coffee on her mother's tray.

"Mother," she said, "Don and I have—"

"*Sh!*" Mrs. Lippman said, shooing her out of her line of sight. "I want to hear this."

On screen, Ed Sullivan was saying that his guests next week would include a Spanish ventriloquist and a rising young comedian. Headlining the show, he said, would be Steve Lawrence and Edie Gorme.

"Oh, goodie," Mrs. Lippman said. "Laura, don't let me make plans."

"All right, Mother." Laura had taken the wingback chair across the room and was sitting forward in it, her cup and saucer balanced on her knees. She was wearing her pleated wool skirt and a gray sweater, damp at the armpits.

When the Sullivan show at last gave way to a commercial she said, "Mother, Don and I have something to tell you—don't we, Don?"

Butters was seated on the sofa with Mrs. Lippman, the center cushion between them. "Yeah," he said.

Mrs. Lippman looked at Laura, then at Butters. She narrowed her eyes. "What is it?" she said.

"Don?" Laura said.

Butters was studying his coffee. At the sound of his name he looked up and took a deep breath. When he opened his mouth to speak he had no idea what he was going to say, but as soon as the words were out he knew they were the right ones.

"Mrs. Lippman," he said, "your daughter is pregnant."

There was a moment of silence, then Mrs. Lippman brought her hand down, very hard, on the armrest of the sofa. The sound was explosive in the small apartment.

"*I knew it!*" she said. "I knew it, I knew it, I knew it!"

She looked at Laura. "How long?" she said.

Laura was looking at Butters.

"*How long?*"

Laura looked at her mother. "Two months," she said softly.

"Who'd you see? Jack Segal?"

"Yes. Last week."

"I knew it. He won't be able to keep his mouth shut, you know. He'll tell Phyllis. God knows who *she'll* tell. *Look at me.*"

"I didn't know what else to do," Laura said, her voice barely above a whisper.

"You've got a mother, you know."

"Oh, Mother."

"Well, you've broken my heart. I want you to know that. You have absolutely broken your mother's heart. And *you,*" she said, turning on Butters, "you've really done it up brown, haven't you, hotshot? And to think, I took you into my home."

"God," Butters said, "I feel so rotten. I can't tell you how—"

"Oh, shut up," Mrs. Lippman said. "I don't care how rotten you feel. I want to know what you're going to do about it. Look at her. She's knocked up. You couldn't keep it in your pants, and now she's knocked up. So tell me: what are you going to do about it?"

Butters didn't say anything.

"Don?" Laura said. "Donnie? Aren't you going to tell her what we decided?"

He looked at Laura. His eyes were round with grief. "I'm sorry, hon," he said. "I really am."

Laura began to cry. Her shoulders shook, and then her whole body, causing her cup and saucer to clatter together in her lap.

"This is going to cost you money, hotshot," Mrs. Lippman said. "You know that, don't you?"

Their first thought was abortion. Mrs. Lippman knew a man there in San Diego who agreed to do it, but after examining Laura he decided it was too risky (something about "enlarged veins"). So Tijuana was suggested; somebody knew a man there. But this time Laura balked. She didn't want any Mexican quack messing around inside her. Then Mrs. Lippman got the idea of hiring a second cousin of Laura's to marry her ("just for the name, you understand"), and she went so far as to get in touch with him—he was a dental student at Stanford—but he turned her down, even at her top price of five hundred dollars. So eventually, as the days slipped away and it became more and more apparent that Laura was going to have to have the baby, they began scouting around for an inexpensive place to send her. What they found was a sort of girls' ranch for unwed mothers over in Arizona. It was Baptist-supported and the lying-in fee was only a hundred dollars a month, meals included.

"What's it like?" Butters asked when Mrs. Lippman told him about it over the phone.

"How do I know?" she said. "It's clean. Jack Segal says it's clean."

"Well, that's good, isn't it?" Butters said. "That it's clean?"

"Listen," Mrs. Lippman said. "Spare me your tender solicitude. I don't have time for it. What I need from you is three hundred dollars—your half."

"Three hundred?"

"*Three* hundred. She'll be there six months, counting the postpartum."

"What's that?"

"You don't even need to know. Just get me the three hundred, okay?"

That was in April. In the meantime Butters had washed out of high-speed school and had been sent back to San Diego to await assignment overseas. He was placed in a casual company, with too little to do and too much time on his hands, and it was there that he met, one afternoon in the supply room, a skinny little buck sergeant named Hawkins, who rather easily convinced him that maybe he was being had. Happened all the time, Hawkins said. Dago was that kind of town. Why, there were women there who knew a million ways to separate you from your money, and it sounded to him like Butters had fallen for one of the oldest ways of all. Then he asked Butters what his blood type was.

"O-positive," Butters said. "Why?"

"Universal donor," Hawkins said. "They can't prove a thing."

The upshot was that two days later, following Hawkins's advice, Butters found himself sitting in the office of one of the two chaplains on base. This chaplain was a freckle-faced young Methodist with captain's bars on his collar and an extremely breezy manner. He tapped his front teeth with a letter opener the whole time Butters was telling his story, and when Butters was done said he thought Butters owed it to himself to ask around a bit, make some inquiries, find out what other boys Laura had been seeing.

"I mean, after all, fella," he said, "if she did it for you, why not someone else?"

And for a few days after that Butters actually considered getting in touch with the boot camp buddy who had introduced him to Laura. He knew where the boy was—up at El Toro, in the NavCad program—all he had to do was call him. In the end, though, he didn't do it. It was just too much trouble. What he did was hole up on base instead. He quit going into town and he quit taking phone calls. He developed the idea that as long as he stayed on base they couldn't touch him. And it worked for a while. He was able to pass several furtive weeks that way, sticking to a tight little universe of barracks, PX, base theater, and beer garden. But then one afternoon while he and Hawkins were folding mattress covers in the supply room a runner came in and said the Catholic chaplain wanted to see him. This chaplain's office was at the far end of the grinder, half a mile away, and as he made his way up there Butters tried to occupy his mind with pleasant thoughts. He didn't bother wondering why he was being summoned, and when he entered the office and saw who was sitting there, he knew he had been right not to.

"Hello, Miz Lippman," he said. "I figured it might be you."

"You quit answering your phone," she said. "So I came calling. You owe me money."

This chaplain wore tinted glasses and had a stern, no-non-sense air about him. He listened impatiently to Butters's side of the story, then he asked Butters how he, "as a Christian," viewed his responsibilities in the matter. He left little doubt how he himself viewed them.

"You *are* a Christian, aren't you, private?" he said.

"Uh, yes, sir," Butters said.

"Well, what's your obligation here then? Or don't you feel you have one?"

"I don't know, sir. I'm confused."

"Call me Father. What do you mean you're 'confused'? Did you agree to pay this woman, or didn't you?"

"Yes, sir. But that was before I talked to the other chaplain."

"What's that got to do with it? Did you agree to pay her? Call me Father."

"Yes, sir. Father."

"Did you have intercourse with her daughter?"

Butters blushed. "Yes, sir."

"More than once?"

"Yes, sir."

"Did her daughter get pregnant as a result?"

"Yes, sir. I guess."

"You guess?"

"I guess it was me. But it could have been someone else."

Mrs. Lippman bristled. "I resent that," she said. "Laura's not a tramp and you know it."

"Do you think it was someone else?" the chaplain said.

"She's no tramp, father," Mrs. Lippman insisted.

"Do you, private?"

"No, sir," Butters said.

"That's what I thought," the chaplain said. "Now let's get down to business."

So once again it was agreed that Butters would pay half of Laura's lying-in expense, or fifty dollars a month for six months. But this time they drew up a little contract right there in the chaplain's office, which the chaplain's secretary typed and the three of them signed, the chaplain as witness. That night, lying in bed waiting for lights out, Butters thought back over the day's events and decided things had worked out about as well as he could expect. At least he could come out of hiding now.

Just before lights out, the charge-of-quarters came in and said there was a phone call for him out in the orderly room. *Jeez,* Butters thought as he got up to follow the CQ, *what now?*

The phone was on the wall just inside the orderly room door. He picked up the dangling receiver and said, "Hello?"

"Hello—Donnie?"

"Laura? Where are you?"

"Arizona. Where do you think?"

"Well. How're you doing?"

"How'm I doing?"

"Yeah. You know: how're you doing?"

"Not too good, Donnie. Not too good."

"You crying?"

"Yeah."

He thought so. "What's the matter, hon?"

"Matter? Oh, nothing. I'm just pregnant, and unmarried, and three hundred miles from home, and scared and lonely. That's all. Nothing to get upset about, right?"

"Don't cry, Laura."

"I can't help it."

"Please?"

"I'm just so miserable, Donnie. You oughta see us. There's about thirty of us, and all we do is sit around all day in our maternity smocks *looking* at each other. Nobody hardly says a word. One of the girls is only fourteen. She sleeps with a big stuffed rabbit."

Butters felt very bad for Laura. She sounded so blue. "Aren't there any horses?" he said.

"What?"

"Horses. Aren't there any horses?"

"*Horses!* God, Donnie, you're worse than a child sometimes. What do you think this is, a dude ranch? You think we sit around a campfire at night singing 'Home on the Range'?"

Butters fingered a place on the back of his neck. "Your mother says it's pretty clean," he ventured.

"Clean?"

"That's what she said."

"When did you talk to her?"

"About that? About a month ago, I guess."

"And she said it was clean?"

"Yeah."

"What else did she say?"

"Nothing. Just that it was clean."

"I see. Well, yes, it's very clean. Spic and span. And the food's good too. We had chicken à la king tonight—my favorite."

"We had meatloaf. It tasted like cardboard."

"Poor you."

"What?"

"I said, 'Poor you.'"

"Oh."

They fell silent, and the silence began to lengthen. Through the orderly room windows Butters could see the movie letting out across the grinder. Guys were coming out stretching, and lighting up cigarettes.

"Listen," Laura said finally, "I'll let you go. I can tell you don't want to talk to me anyway. I just called to tell you that I've decided to go ahead and have this stupid baby. For a while there I was thinking about killing myself, but I've changed my mind. I'm gonna go through with it, Donnie. I'm gonna do it. But my life will never ever be the same again, and I just thought you ought to know that."

Then she hung up.

Two weeks later he was on a boat bound for Okinawa.

That was in mid-May. By the time he reached Okinawa, halfway around the world, it was early June. He had made his May payment to Mrs. Lippman on the day after the meeting in the chaplain's office, and he mailed her his June payment as soon as he got off the boat. The July payment he mailed her too, but late in the month. The August payment he skipped altogether. And sure enough, not long afterward, sometime in early September, the company clerk came looking for him one afternoon in the barracks with word that the company commander wanted to see him.

"Did he say what it was about?" Butters asked.

"No," the clerk said. "He don't confide in me much. I think you better chop chop, though."

It was the same old story. The company commander, a major with a good tan, showed him a letter from Mrs. Lippman and asked him what was going on.

Butters told him.

"She claims you owe her money," the major said. "Do you?"

"Yes, sir," Butters said. He was standing at ease in front of the major's desk, looking at the letter in the major's hands. It was on blue stationery.

"How much?"

"A hundred and fifty dollars, sir."

"Well, what do you plan to do about it?"

"Pay her, sir. I guess."

"You guess?"

"Pay her, sir."

"Do you have it?"

"No, sir."

"Where do you plan to get it?"

"I don't know, sir."

"*You don't know?* You think you might just dig it up out of the *ground,* private? Pick it off a *tree?* What do you mean you don't know?"

"I don't know, sir. I guess I'll have to think of something."

"You 'guess.' You 'don't know.' It strikes me, private, that you're just not very sure about anything—are you?"

Butters didn't say anything. A phone rang somewhere.

The major shook his head. "How old are you, son?" he said.

"Nineteen, sir. I'll be twenty next month."

"I see. Well, here's what I want you to do. There's a Navy Relief office over at Camp Hague. I want you to go over there tomorrow morning and take out a loan."

"A loan, sir?"

"A loan."

"They'd *lend* it to me?"

"That's what they're there for, private."

A loan! Now why hadn't he thought of that? Getting it turned out to be remarkably easy too. Oh, he had to answer a few embarrassing questions, and there was a final interview that had him squirming for a while, but when it was all over, in less than two hours, he had a cashier's check for the full amount in his hand, with a full year to repay it and an interest rate of only three percent. He was so elated at the sight of the check that it was all he could do to keep from dancing the woman who gave it to him around the room. Rather than risk temptation he sent the entire one-fifty off to San Diego that same day by registered mail. He considered sticking a little note in with it—something like, "Bet you thought you'd never see this, didn't you?"—but thought better of it at the last minute.

And it was funny, but in the days that followed he felt like a different person. He bounced around the company area with such energy and good humor that people hardly recognized him. One morning he was first in line for chow.

"Jeez, Butters," said the boy serving him his eggs, "what's got into you? You hardly ever even *eat* breakfast."

"Just feed the troops, lad," Butters said. "Feed the troops."

But then it was October, the month the baby was due. Throughout the spring and summer and into the early days of a rainy Okinawan autumn he had done a pretty good job of shutting it out of his mind. He had simply refused to contemplate the fact that what had happened back in February in foggy San Diego was destined, ever, to result in anything so real as a baby. But as October crept in it got harder. He found he couldn't help wondering, for example, whether it would be a boy or a girl. He hoped it was a boy. Being a boy was easier—girls had it rough. One night he found himself imagining it curled up in Laura's womb, its knees tucked up under its chin, its tiny fingers making tiny fists. And, lying there, he began trying to make out the baby's face. He wanted to know who it looked like, but, try as he might, he couldn't tell. Later that night he dreamed he was swimming underwater somewhere, deep down, and that floating in the water all around him were these large jellyfish, each of which, on closer inspection, appeared to have a baby inside. He couldn't make out these babies' faces either.

But October passed and nothing happened. At least not in his world. Nobody contacted him, by phone or mail or otherwise. Nobody got in touch. And as the days went by and still he heard nothing, slowly he began to believe that maybe it was all over with now, that what had happened was finally history and he could go about his daily business just like everyone else.

He had made friends by then with a boy named Tipton, from Kansas, and the two of them had begun spending their weekends in a tin-roofed shanty outside Chibana with a pair of sisters who worked in a Chibana bar.

One Saturday morning Butters was sitting out on the back steps of the shanty, watching one of the sisters hang laundry in the yard, when Tipton arrived from the base by taxi, bearing beer and groceries and a letter for him.

Butters took the letter and looked at it. There were several cancellations on the envelope, indicating it had been rerouted more than once. He opened it up and took out a single folded sheet of paper. It read:

Dear Don,

The baby is due any day now, they tell me. You should see me. I'm huge. You probably wouldn't even recognize me. I think the baby is a "he." It sure kicks like one anyway. It even keeps me awake some nights with its kicking and rolling around a lot.

The nurses say I don't have to see it if I don't want to. They say it's entirely up to me. Sometimes I think I want to and sometimes I think I don't. Silly me, huh? Guess I had better make up my mind pretty soon, though, and quit all this procastinating (sp?).

Don, since I know now I am never going to see you again I guess this will have to be goodbye. I'm not bitter anymore. I was for a while, I admit, but I'm not now. And I'm still glad I knew you. I just wish things could have turned out better, that's all.

                                    Best always,
                                    Laura

P.S. You owe me $5. (See clipping)

Butters looked inside the envelope again and saw a small folded piece of paper he had missed before. He took it out and unfolded it. It was a photograph clipped from a magazine *Time* or *Newsweek,* it looked like—and it showed Elizabeth Taylor and Eddie Fisher during their recent wedding ceremony in Beverly Hills. They were standing before a robed man with a dark beard. Both Fisher and the robed man had small black caps perched on the back of their heads. An arrow had been drawn, in red ink, pointing to the cap on Fisher's head, and along its shaft had been printed, in big block letters, also red, the initials "M.O.T."

Butters sat looking at the clipping for a while. Then he put it and the letter back in the envelope, folded the envelope in half, and stuffed it in his back pocket.

"Your mom?" Tipton said.

"Huh?"

"The letter. Is it from your mom ?"

"No. A girl I knew."

"Oh," Tipton said. "You want a beer?"

The legal papers didn't arrive until the first week in December. They were from the office of the county clerk of Maricopa County, Arizona, and they consisted of a form letter, a release document, and an enclosed envelope for which no postage was necessary.

They came on a Friday, as Butters and Tipton were preparing to leave for town.

Butters read the form letter first, sitting on his bunk in his civvies. The letter was very short, just two paragraphs. The first paragraph said that a child had been born on such-and-such a date in the public maternity ward of such-and-such a hospital in Phoenix, Arizona, and that, according to the attending physician, it was free of physical and mental defects. The second paragraph merely asked him to read and then sign the accompanying release. The child was identified, the words typed into a blank space in the middle of the first paragraph, as "Baby Boy Butters, 7 lbs, 6 oz."

When he was finished with the letter, Butters set it carefully beside him on the bunk and picked up the release. It was short too, just a single legal-sized page. It asked him to understand what he was doing— waiving all rights and responsibilities in the care and upbringing of the child—and it cited the pertinent sections of Arizona law, which took up most of the rest of the page. Toward the bottom, however, there was a dotted line that caught Butters's eye. He skipped over much of the legal language, but he lingered at the dotted line. "Signature of Natural Father," it was labeled. He looked at it. That was him. He was the natural father. He turned the page over to see if there was anything on the back. There wasn't. It was blank. He turned it back over and looked at the dotted line. Tipton was standing just a few feet away from him, waiting. They had already called their taxi. It was on the way.

He looked up at Tipton. "You got a pen?" he said.

(II)

PASSAGE

Giving Jewel Away

JOY CASTRO

"The jewel of the first water, the face of the sleeping child." I don't know where the lines came from, where I read, "the nipple of the beloved wife, the beatific spine," but they stuck with me, and I wished I knew who had written them, then in my sixth month, when the sonogram promised a girl, I secretly named her Jewel. Swimmer, quiet turtle turning over, guiding and twirling me through a new dance, a fertile glide. I practiced saying good-bye.

What bloodstorms blossom in a womanbelly, in a woman's unsure heart? Of course they looked the best on paper; were the kindest, wisest of all the couples I'd talked to, but to imagine them carrying my bones away? The bindings in the hospital, the pain, and the breasts that are now softer to no purpose.

I learned that mine was not the first illicit product of a love affair so named. My own minister was a braver, better man, but I raved like any Addie in her coffin, drinking and vomiting up the pain for months, the only anesthetic for the treasure I'd set free, leaving my own self the one buried.

Babygirl, little sister, tiny mother who birthed out of your own birth a torn creature left heaving in your wake, rawborn and blood-drenched, but with none of the birth smear to rub into my skin, nothing to protect from the flaying of the air, the mockery of the daily routine, the kindness from my friends who thought they understood. The depths I surged to, the ugly fires I kindled and put out with my wrists, all hunting a little peace of mind.

And always, of course, the stupid, pointless lacerations of wondering. *Are you the Christmas angel on the wheelbarrow of cut grass, a cornflower stabbed into your dark hair? (Is it dark?) Are you the girl cross-legged on the front porch making potholders on a plastic loom, and do you sing to yourself, and once in a while stare off, forgetting to weave, forgetting the song? Can you dial 911 if something happens and nobody's there? Do your bones sing like flutes when there's too much wind? Do you lie awake at night and make the room spin until your mind is dizzy, secretly sure you're magical? How does she hold you and rock you when you get the littlegirl blues?* The wondering about you that does not stop. The longing, the weeping, the surgery of tears.

Chanter, whisperer, there's a brave gaping hole in my chest where you used to live. I was just an apartment for you, a motel on the highway. A lifeboat until you could climb out, haul yourself up the ladder to a worthy ship, one that could carry you and keep carrying you to dry land.

Did Oregon's old-growth heal me? Not on the sweet blue gasp of your umbilical cord it didn't. Released from the weight of you, a helium balloon let go, I should have floated up through pine needles to a sky-blue sky. Still I lumbered down trails, heavy and handicapped like a horse that runs fast for the stakes. Timber-criers sized me up and disdained me as no challenge, I was so eager to fall, to be pulled toward the center again, belly down on hot ground, crushed fern smell in my face and nauseous, blessedly nauseous again with the spinning of the earth.

They say there's no passion like a woman's for her child. Somebody, give me a little hope. Lie to me on this one.

Poem for an Unknown Daughter, 1973

RONDA SLATER

My mother said,
"If you ever get pregnant,
don't come home."
So I did.

Do you think I have forgotten
lying in my tiny room
and wishing you
were dead?

I remember the small
ripple of your first movement
in my womb,
and the way I bit
my tongue to keep
from telling anyone the new
strange secret
of it.

I followed you around
those months.
You tugged at my fat belly
like a puppy
trying to get free.

I talked to you
at night
to keep from screaming,
but never told you
that I had once
seen your father boil a lobster
tail-end first.

We waited out the
hot summer
eating lemons

and picking out a name
you never got.

You flooded me with pain
in your bloody,
persistent departure
from my body.
When I complained, the nurse
told me to shut up,
but instead, I opened,
every pore a wound
gaping wide like mouths
in wonder, horror.

Your tiny hand
lay curled, blue, on my thigh,
and I was too amazed to speak.

Someone carried you
off in laundered blankets
after you were trimmed away
like fat from a steak.
The doctor sewed me with
quick stitches.

They wouldn't let me
see you. Told me
it would make it harder
to let you go.

I signed my name
three times on the black lines,
as I talked about
the weather.

The milk fell from my breasts
to my lap, nourishing
nothing.
Yellow/white tears I thought
would never dry.

I saw you around every
corner.
The thought of you
kicked at my belly
but I suspect not as hard
as I kicked you.

So we will go on
collecting our years,
you and I.
Me not knowing your face.
You thinking I didn't
have time to love you.

If only I could see you
one time, I would tell you
to be proud that you're a
woman
and be strong.

That we are all
the mothers and daughters
of each other,
and even if I had kept you,
you would not be
mine.

Proverbs

TINA CERVIN

I

Women hold up half the sky
   —*Chinese proverb*

with one hand, I hold up sky.
so blue, heavy, resolute,
like sureness of liberty
or bucket of water full
from the dark inky river.

that word we cannot say.
I must shuh, shuh,
and with other hand lay down
my baby girl on the park bench,
walk away. walk away
like I don't even see.
only sky above me
and the tree of blossoms
weeping one petal each moment
now.

II

I look at my mother and my mother
does not look like me.
I look just Chinese, shiny
black patent leather hair, so smooth
and razor-edged.
She has thin, frizzy hair like plants
by the river where ducks swim through.
Her white skin is like apricots in the summer.
Mine like almond milk. Always.

Her eyes are bluish, like a mix of paints
with green. Mine are dark like stones
where tears fell. We see, when we look out
from the river's bridge, the same hungering water,
the same shaking sky with clouds, the same grey fish
huddled in the reeds like a handful of coins.
We feel the ripple and shock of love,
the gratitude of arms opened, unbundling me
in the world. How she gathered me into her own.

When I ask her why, she says she wanted me.
The world between us cannot take that away.
She says this:
> If I give you an apple,
> You will eat it at once.
> If I give you a seed,
> You can grow your own tree.*

So it comes to this: She took seed
and gave it soil not its own.
She took seed and grew shelter. She took
seed and made me a tree where I might have been
a dry and stunted plant clinging to the side
of a dry little house. Or worse.

But what we do not see together
when we look out at the river
is the annotation of aloneness
for the mother I will not know,
for the seed,
for the tree in China.

* Xïe Lihua, women's activist

Little Green

JONI MITCHELL

Born with the moon in Cancer
Choose her a name she will answer to
Call her green and the winters cannot fade her
Call her green for the children who have made her
Little green, be a gypsy dancer

He went to California
Hearing that everything's warmer there
So you write him a letter, say, "Her eyes are blue,"
He sends you a poem and she's lost to you
Little green, he's a non-conformer

Just a little green
Like the color when the spring is born
There'll be crocuses to bring to school tomorrow
Just a little green
Like the nights when the Northern Lights perform
There'll be icicles and birthday clothes
And sometimes there'll be sorrow

Child with a child pretending
Weary of lies you are sending home
So you sign all the papers in the family name
You're sad and you're sorry, but you're not ashamed
Little green, have a happy ending

Just a little green
Like the color when the spring is born
There'll be crocuses to bring to school tomorrow
Just a little green
Like the nights when the Northern Lights perform
There'll be icicles and birthday clothes
And sometimes there'll be sorrow

Letter to the Adoptive Parents from the Birthmother

CARRIE ETTER

Look, I am like this.
It has taken me two years
to garner the strength
to say this so listen.
I love two things most: him and me.
You have him, I have me.
I have no regrets.
I am chasing the moon,
devouring Strand and Milosz and Gregg,
practicing exorcism with words,
learning to like my father,
concealing an honest love,
becoming strikingly earnest,
peeling potatoes lavishly,
spreading the news,
speaking up,
rediscovering stars nightly,
fluttering,
hovering.
Sorrow is a thing I feel,
but don't pursue.

The Welcoming

EDWARD HIRSCH

After the long drought
               and the barren silence,
After seven years of fertility doctors
And medicine men in clinics
                    dreaming of rain,
After the rainfall and the drugs
                       that never engendered a child—

What is for others nature
                 is for us culture:
Social workers and lawyers,
                    home studies and courtrooms,
Passports, interlocutory orders, a birth certificate
          that won't be delivered for a year,
               a haze of injunctions, jurisdictions, handshakes,
Everyone standing around in dark suits
               saying yes, we think so, yes . . .

It has been less than a month and already
I want to bring you
               out of the darkness,
            out of the deep pockets of silence . . .
While you were spending your fifth day
                   under bright lights in a new world,
We were traveling
             from Rome to New Orleans,
Twenty-three hours of anguish and airplanes,
Instructions in two languages,
                music from cream-colored headsets,
          jet lag instead of labor,

And on the other end a rainbow
                  of streamers in the French Quarter,
        a row of fraternity boys celebrating
          in Jackson Square, the trolleys

buzzing up and down St. Charles Avenue,
The stately run-down southern mansions
Winking
                behind the pecan trees and the dark leaved magnolias.

You were out there somewhere,
                blinking, feeding omnivorously
                        from a nurse's arms, sleeping,
But who could sleep anymore
                        besides the innocent and the oblivious,
        who could dream?

How unreal it was to drive
                        through the narrow, twisted streets
                of an unfamiliar American city
        and then arrive at the empty bungalow
                        of a friend of a friend.
Outside, the trees waved slightly
                        under a cradle of moonlight
While, inside, the floorboards sagged
                and creaked, the air conditioner kicked on
                        in the next room, in autumn,
        an invisible cat cried—a baby's cry—
                and roamed through the basement at four a.m.

All night long we were moored
                to the shoreline of the bay windows,
                        to the edge of a bent sky
                where the moon rocked
        and the stars were tiny crescent fish
                swimming through amniotic fluids.
There was a deep rumbling underground,
And our feelings came in and went out, like waves.

By the vague tremors of dawn,
By the first faint pinkish-blue light
                of morning rising in the east,
All we could think about
                was the signing of papers
                        in a neighboring parish,

the black phone that was going to shout
                    at any moment, just once,
        our lawyer's slow drive to the hospital
                with an infant seat
            strapped into her car. You were waiting:
Little swimmer, the nurses at Touro
                didn't want to relinquish you
                        to the afterlife of our arms . . .

But so it was written:

On the sixth day,
After five days and nights on this earth,
You were finally delivered
                    into our keeping,
A wrinkled traveler from a faraway place
                who had journeyed a great distance,
A sweet aboriginal angel
                with your own life,
A throbbing bundle of instincts and nerves—
        perfect fingers, perfect toes,
            shiny skin, blue soulful eyes
                deeply set in your perfectly shaped head—
Oh wailing messenger,
Oh baleful full-bodied crier
                        of the abandoned and the chosen,
Oh trumpet of laughter, oh Gabriel,
                    joy everlasting . . .

Yadira

SUSAN ITO

I have had many mothers during my lifetime, but I will start with the first one. Perla Calderón, at twenty-five, gave birth to me, her eighth child, alone on a canvas cot in Chilagalpa's two-room health post. The front room of that humble Nicaraguan shack had a few rickety shelves stacked with grimy boxes of gauze, a torn poster depicting the nine months of fetal growth, a wooden table and a few chairs that had been nailed together from scraps. The back room held the cot and a white metal cabinet with a thick padlock hanging on its door. This was the storage area for the village's meager supply of medicines, and during the two hours of her labor, she kneeled on the floor in front of the cabinet, silently gripping the lock, nearly pulling the whole thing over. She prayed for relief, for the magic that she believed could transport her elsewhere. But the lock didn't burst open, she didn't cry out, and nobody came. I slithered from her at 4:19 in the morning, and she bit the cord that bound us with her teeth.

I like to think of those dark hours of morning, when the stars glittered over the black-green mountains and the only sound was that of an animal snorting in its sleep. There were also occasional cracks of gunfire, from the soldiers on the hill, firing into the air to keep themselves awake. But she held me then, rocked me in her delicate, bloody hands. She wrapped me tightly in the torn bottom half of her yellow cotton dress, sang me a song about chickens that she remembered her own mother singing. When I cried, she stuck the tip of her smallest finger into my mouth and laughed at the way my tongue swirled and tickled her.

She knew, as the sky lightened into day, that our time together would be brief. She knew that I, as the rest of my seven sisters and brothers had, would be taken away from her.

It had begun for her twelve years prior, when she was thirteen and a young *campesino,* one of the coffee pickers, had tempted her into the back of his pickup with a bottle of Coca-Cola. The dark, sparkling sweetness, the heavy glass in her hand, stayed with her longer than the pain, the stifling pressure of her cheek against the rough, dusty pile of burlap sacks bulging with hard red beans. She took to wandering the streets, talking to herself in the moist humid evenings, following the sputtering diesel vehicles that wobbled down the mountain to the Jinotega market. As she walked, she brushed her long black hair that swung down around her waist. She smiled at the men with her pretty teeth and they would take her by the hand.

The young Sandinista soldiers who lived in the dense green jungle came into the village at night to whisper revolution to the *campesinos*. In the faint grey hours of daybreak, before they crept back into the shadows of the damp, dark mountain, they led her into storage sheds, into stables, and behind the large rocks by the river. They, too, drank in the sweetness of her slim brown body and repaid her with soda.

Her own mother barely noticed her absence, so immersed was she in the care of eleven children. Perla was the third daughter, known as the slow one, and her older sisters bore the greatest weight of gathering firewood, hauling water to the house in buckets, patting endless rounds of maize into tortillas. At nighttime when the girl disappeared, following the long trail of beaten-down grasses to the soldiers' camp, nobody called her back.

It took a few months for her body to show its first thickening. She didn't know herself what it was, thinking perhaps of a rabbit leaping inside her. After a while it was obvious to everyone that her buttons were straining, her skirt was pulled taut by her growing belly. Her mother could not bear the thought of another mouth, another hungry body crowding into the ragged house.

"Out!" she screamed, shoving Perla into the street. *"Puta de chanchos!"*

My mother walked the dusty streets for the last month of her first pregnancy, begging for tortillas, sleeping in barns and underneath trees. She continued to visit the soldiers, walking for hours into the jungle to find them, their improbable fires in the midst of the damp growth, crouching around a tin cooking pot of monkey stew. Their eyes glittered with tears when they saw her, these men with false names who had not made love with a woman in months. They lined up to stroke her hair and never minded about her belly. In fact, there were those who were uncontrollably aroused by the huge glimmering globe of it, who swooned to touch it as if it were a giant breast. It was under the plastic shelter of one of the soldiers that her labor began, a sudden flood of water that drenched his bedroll. Two *compañeros* rushed her to the village, risking their lives as they hauled her, sobbing, in a crude stretcher, to the midwife Doña Mercedes' house. "It's not mine," they both said with certainty, although they had both been with her countless times during the previous year. It was impossible to know. She had been with a dozen of them.

Nothing had prepared Perla for the surges of pain that bombarded her body. Her eyes rolled up to the ceiling as she chewed a rag in her teeth and clung to Doña Mercedes' hand. She screamed and cried for her mother, and the midwife said that she had sent a girl to retrieve her, but Perla's mother stayed away. My oldest sister, a girl with no name, was born that day. They spent a week at the midwife's house, and Doña Mercedes tried to teach my mother how to care for the baby. But one day she returned home to find Perla squatting on the floor, trying to pour a cup of cold coffee into the squalling infant's mouth. The midwife had grabbed the coffee and flung it into the sink, exclaiming, "No, no, you idiot! Haven't I told you what your breasts are for?"

Astonished, my mother had hugged her arms protectively around her chest. "No," she said firmly. "These are for the compañeros."

"But your child will die without milk."

"Coca-Cola then. It is my favorite. Surely she will like that."

The midwife went out then, and returned with a can of powdered formula and a cracked glass bottle. "If you will not give her your milk, then for the love of the saints give her this."

When Doña Mercedes saw my mother spooning dried powder into the mouth of the infant, she picked up the baby and shook her head. "You refuse to be a proper mother, you fool. I will find a better place for her." The midwife was busy wrapping the child in a blanket of rough fabric. "You need to go now. I will take care of the child. Forget her."

Perla cried for an hour, rocking herself back and forth, squeezing her swollen breasts, a rain of tears and milk falling onto her lap. But she let herself quietly out of Mercedes' house and combed her hair with her fingers as she climbed the hill, stumbling barefoot back to the place where the tents lay like green turtles.

It continued like that for years. She wandered the village like a lost animal, and her feet grew hard on the bottom, tough like shoes. People shook their heads when she passed by, for she was as crazy as she was beautiful. Her clothes thinned into rags, and her hands were cracked and bleeding, but her hair was always shining, long, and elegant like a black cape. Every night, she washed her hair in the river by moonlight, massaging the heavy wet ropes with slivers of soap left on the rocks by women doing their laundry. She walked the rubbled streets alone, softly singing the chicken song, and at night she visited the guerrillas. Every year she bore another child, and every year the midwife spirited the child away within a week of its birth.

Seven children gone, disappeared into the landscape like wisps of flying seeds. She bore children through the bloodiest days of repression, when the National Guard helicopters rained fire down on the village, when the bodies of her beloved compañeros were blasted to confetti. Some of the babies were born in slim times of peace, and others during the hopeful years of the young revolution. Perla stood clapping in the outdoor ceremony when her mother received the title to her own square of land, the first landowner in her family for seven generations. But through all the changes that surged through Nicaragua, the cycle of Perla and her babies remained a constant. Her face grew more mournful as the number of lost children rose, as she tried to prove over and over to the midwife that she could do it, but each time she failed and was sent away with empty arms.

She tried her hardest with one of the boys, who had a serious, narrow face like Camilo, one of her favorite soldiers. She took him carefully in her arms, stepping delicately down the bank of the river, in the hot afternoon following his birth. She would give him a thorough bath, like a good mother. But the women pounding laundry on the rocks saw her lift the child by his feet, and let his small head and shoulders sink into the green water. They shouted and splashed over to her, waving their arms. One of them grabbed the child and wrapped it in her apron, scolding Perla, telling her to stay away from the men. She never saw her son again.

She thought she recognized them at times, small images of her face, a little girl with thick black hair, or the skinny-faced boy, but those children were always yanked away by someone, their faces turned away before she could get a second look. And so when I was born, she did not go to Doña Mercedes' house. For the first time she swore that it would be she who decided. It would be she who would choose my home.

She had watched the gringo for a long time, the blue-eyed man with the honey colored beard. He was the first man she had ever seen with eyes that color. The way he spoke Spanish was strange, like a child, sometimes turning words upside down, although it was clear he was very intelligent. He had arrived in Chilagalpa in a white Land Rover, with a picture of a dove stenciled on its door, and the word "Solidaridad" printed above. People said that he was from los Estados Unidos, a *yanqui,* that he had been a kind of doctor there. With him was a woman with a head full of short, springy dark curls and lipstick the color of watermelon flesh. This was his wife, Ana Paula, who had grown up in the city of Estelí. Perla watched with fascination as Ana Paula sat on a rock by the river, soaping her legs and scraping them smooth with a razor. It was strange what city women did. But Ana Paula had studied nursing; she wore a white dress and carried a stethoscope in her pocket. She went from door to door through the unpaved streets and muddy pathways of Chilagalpa, listening to the rasping breath in peoples' chests, mixing the precious fluid that could keep children from dying when they had dysentery.

Ana Paula knew how to hold a needle steady and draw a tubeful of blood from a person's arm, and then she would hand the vial to her husband, Ricardo Blanco, who spun it in a whirling machine on a rickety wooden table and then looked at the flattened drops through his microscope. He could read the glass slides like a fortune teller, and then give the person medicines or take him down to Jinotega, to the regional hospital, in the white ambulance. Sometimes, people would pretend to have unbearable pains in their chests or their bellies, hoping for a ride down the mountain in the shining vehicle with the bed bolted in the back. But Ricardo Blanco would know from their blood or their urine if they were trying to fool him or not.

His name wasn't really Ricardo Blanco, but that's what everyone called him. His American name, the one his mother gave him, was Richard Franklin White. People thought it was a joke, a white person named White, but he showed us his passport, the precious blue book stamped "United States of America" in gold letters. It was his real name.

My mother, Perla, watched Ricardo and Ana Paula for a long time.

She passed back and forth in front of their house, the small concrete and wood structure. She watched the glow of the kerosene light through their windows at night, and could see Ricardo bent over a book, Ana Paula writing something at the table. She saw the small deer that they kept in their yard, the way they stroked it and spoke softly to it, feeding it apples from their hands as if it were a child. She knew about the shelves of books they kept in their front room and that their door was open to all the children of Chilagalpa. Perla glanced sideways through the doorway and saw the boys and girls, piled like puppies on the floor, turning the pages of picture books, their fingerprints stabbing at pictures of snowmen and rainbows. She knew that Ana Paula combed and braided the hair of the little girls who visited her, and gave them bright ribbons that flew behind them like parrot feathers. This was the kind of mother she wanted for her child.

And so on the dawn of the day after my birth, my mother walked in the open door of Ricardo Blanco's house and set me down on their kitchen table. Ana Paula made a squealing noise when she saw us. My mother had torn the bottom half of her dress to wrap me in, and so she stood there with bare thighs and feet, stripes of dried blood swirling down her legs. Her hands were streaked red as well, and there was a flower of blood on her chin from when she'd bitten through the umbilical cord. I was a sight as well, with my red-black hair standing up stiffly. "Please take her," my mother said to Ana Paula.

Ana Paula sat down. "Perla," she said, because everyone knew the name of Perla, the crazy woman. "When was this baby born?"

"A little while ago."

"Where?" Ana Paula listened, shaking her head back and forth, as if to say no, no, to the whole thing: Perla alone in the back room of the clinic, her silent pain, her fear of the midwife. Finally she said, "But I can't, you see . . ." and she patted her own belly, which Perla hadn't noticed until that moment. It swelled out like a white moon under her nurse's uniform.

My mother knelt down then, clinging to Ana Paula's skirt, her hair tangled and matted with blood. "This baby would be the first one, understand me, the first one that doesn't become a ghost. I would know where she is. I would be able to see her grow, oh please señora, please . . ." She grasped both of Ana Paula's hands in hers, the delicate pink nails disappearing inside the roughness, and pleaded with her brown eyes.

There was a full moment of silence between them, and then I began to squirm on the hard wood of the table, to mew out in a hoarse voice. Ana Paula looked at me, and then lifted me up into her arms. She brought me back to the water trough and splashed me clean, then rubbed me with a rough towel while I screamed. Perla followed behind, leaving a trail of bright red drops on the floor. "Here," said Ana Paula, handing her a blue plastic bucket, "You wash yourself off too. I'll give you some breakfast."

She fed my mother a plateful of eggs and beans, a stack of tortillas and a cup of coffee. She let her brush her hair in a small shining mirror, and look into her own sad eyes. Ana Paula searched through a box of clothing and tied two clean dresses into a package.

It was nearly eight in the morning when Perla turned to leave. *"Ya me voy."*

"Wait," said Ana Paula. "I can't feed her."

"Doña Mercedes always uses powder milk."

"Doña Mercedes is foolish. That milk is dangerous for babies."

My mother shrugged.

"Perla," Ana Paula said, "You need to help me feed this child. If you will give her milk until this baby is born," she patted her stomach, "then I will continue from there." She held Perla by the wrist. "But you need to stay here for two more months."

"Here?"

Ana Paula nodded to a mattress rolled up in a corner. "You can sleep here. Feed the baby when she's hungry, and I'll do everything else."

Perla glanced at the pair of heavy boots by the door. "But señor Blanco, what will he say . . ."

Ana Paula shrugged. *"No se preocupes.* Don't worry. I will take care of him." He was in the mountains, tending to the compañeros, and would be gone for several weeks.

And so it came to be that Perla, *la loca,* came to live with Ana Paula and Ricardo Blanco for two months. When Blanco came back, he was startled to see me, and not a little angry with his wife for taking on such a responsibility. But Ana Paula was determined to have her way, and in the end he softened, carrying me in a large sash against his chest. She washed me, and sewed a stack of diapers, and sang me to sleep at night. When I was hungry, she carried me to Perla, who lifted her blouse and gave me, the only one of her eight children, her full and trickling breast. The four of us lived a strange and intertwined life. Between feedings, Perla circled the house, talked with the deer and brushed her hair. By the end of seven weeks though, Perla was getting anxious. She walked in larger diameters that pulled her to the edges of town, and spent her nights with the soldiers, who had been missing her. The day Ana Paula gave birth to my sister Lidia, my mother walked into the hills and did not come back.

The Adoption

FRAN CASTAN

I remember the quiet room, the dark
Green chair where we sat afternoons,
The sun—no matter how tightly shuttered out—
Coming in and curving across us
As if we were not separate, but a single body
joined in a ceremony of light.
My legs beneath you, my arms around you,
My breast under the glass bottle with rubber nipple,
I talked to you and sang to you.
No one interrupted us.
The dog sat quietly in the corner.
If I could have given birth to you,
I would have. I would have taken you
Inside me, held you
And given birth to you again.
All the hours we spent in that room. Then,
One day, with your eyes focused on mine, you
Reached up and stroked my cheek. Your touch
Was that of the inchworm on its aerial thread
Just resting on my skin, a larval curve
Alighting and lifting off, a lightness,
Practicing for the time it will have wings.
I like to think wherever you go, you will
Keep some memory of sunlight in the room
Where I first loved you, and you first loved.

The Naturalization of Anna Lee

JANET JERVE

I have my hand on my heart and say the pledge
of allegiance to the flag for her
because she is too small and doesn't talk,
but she is at the edge of her limit because
the ceremony has gone on too long.
Sixty babies being naturalized at the courthouse
on a hot day. Babies are thirsty and parents hungry
for information. When will we be done
swearing on the flag that our babies
will not pledge allegiance
to any other sovereign or potentate?
I am thinking of Korea and how close
I feel to a country that I do not pledge
allegiance to. I am thinking of a mother
far away who does not know that I am pledging
allegiance to this flag for the daughter
we both share. I am swearing under my breath
because I don't even know what a potentate is.
I am looking at my daughter's black hair
and black eyes and can't remember when
I didn't know her. I can't remember
not being her mother. I am looking
at my daughter holding a flag. She is
happy now because she likes to wave
the colors back and forth in front
of her eyes. Her black eyes that don't look
like mine, though we gaze into each other's eyes
all the time. I wasn't prepared for the ceremony.
I didn't know they would ask me to promise
that my daughter would bear arms
for this country. I look at
my arms wrapped around hers
and see this ceremony is about fear

that a baby could overthrow a country.
Don't they know when she looks at me
she sees mother? Don't they know
she shows me church steeples from her car seat?
It is because of her that I know
the location of every flag in this city.
I want to pretend I am saying these words
and instead say *weemur weemur weemur*
the way little Emily says her prayers
because the words don't mean anything to her.
I am looking at my daughter and I know
that some people will always wonder
what country she belongs to.
I close my eyes and remember the fear
in the voice of a Korean man who asked,
Will the families make citizens of these babies?
He said babies without a country become slaves.
I am holding my daughter and I know
I do not own her. And yet, as her mother,
I say these words because I want
her Korean face, body, hands, heart, mind,
to have a voice in the country where she lives,
her beautiful voice that no country will ever contain.

The Road North

ISABEL ALLENDE

It took Claveles Picero and her grandfather Jesús Dionisio Picero thirty-eight days to walk the seventy kilometers between their village and the capital. On foot they had traveled through lowlands where the vegetation simmered in an eternal broth of mud and sweat, climbed and descended hills past motionless iguanas and drooping palm trees, crossed coffee plantations while avoiding foremen, lizards, and snakes, and made their way beneath tobacco leaves among phosphorescent mosquitoes and sidereal butterflies. They had headed directly toward the city, following the highway, but once or twice had made long detours in order to avoid encampments of soldiers. Occasionally, truck-drivers slowed as they passed, drawn by the girl's mestizo-queen back-side and long black hair, but the look on the old man's face immediately dissuaded them from any thought of annoying her. The grandfather and granddaughter had no money, and did not know how to beg. When their basket of provisions was exhausted, they continued on sheer courage. At night they wrapped themselves in their rebozos and slept beneath the trees, with a prayer on their lips and their mind on the boy, to avoid thinking of pumas and venomous predators. They awakened covered with blue beetles. At the first light of dawn, when the land-scape was still wreathed in the last mists of dream and neither man nor beast had yet begun the day's tasks, they started off, taking advantage of the coolness. They entered the capital city by way of the Camino de los Españoles, asking everyone they met in the street where they might find the Department of Welfare. By that time Dionisio's bones were clicking and the colors had faded from Claveles's dress; she wore the bewitched expression of a sleepwalker, and a century of fatigue had fallen over the splendor of her youth.

Jesús Dionisio Picero was the best-known artist in the province; in a long life he had won a fame he never boasted of because he believed that his talent was a gift in God's service and that he was but the trustee. He had begun as a potter, and still made small clay animals, but the basis of his true renown were the wooden saints and small sculptures in bottles bought by *campesinos* for their home altars and by tourists in the capital. His was a slow labor, a matter of eye, time, and heart, as he would explain to the small boys who crowded round to watch as he worked. With long-necked tweezers he would insert a small painted stick into the bottle, with a dot of glue on the areas that needed bonding, and wait patiently for them to dry before adding the next piece. His specialty were the *Calvarios,* consisting of a large central cross complete with the figure of the crucified Christ, His nails, His crown of thorns, and a gold-paper aureole, and two more simple crosses for the thieves of Golgotha. On Christmas he carved crèches for the Baby Jesus, with doves representing the Holy Spirit and stars and flowers to symbolize the Glory. He did not know how to read or sign his name, because when he was a boy there had been no school, but he could copy Latin phrases from the missal to decorate the pedestals of his saints. He always said that his mother and father had taught him to respect the laws of Church and man, and that was worth more than having gone to school. He did not make enough with his carving to support his family, so he rounded out his income by breeding gamecocks. Each rooster demanded assiduous attention; he hand-fed them a pap of ground grains and fresh blood he obtained from the slaughterhouse; he groomed them for mites, ventilated their feathers, polished their spurs, and worked with them every day so they would not lack for valor when the chips were down. Sometimes he traveled to other villages to watch the birds fight, but he never bet, because in his view any money won without sweat and hard labor was the work of the devil. On Saturday night he and his granddaughter Claveles cleaned the church for Sunday service. The priest, who made the rounds of the villages on his bicycle, did not always get there, but good Christians gathered anyway to pray and sing. Jesús Dionisio was also responsible for taking and safeguarding the collection used for the upkeep of the temple and the priest.

Picero and his wife, Amparo Medina, had thirteen children, of whom five had survived the epidemics and accidents of infancy. Just when the couple thought they were through with children, because all theirs were grown and out of the house, their youngest son returned on a military pass, carrying a ragged bundle that he placed in Amparo's lap. When it was opened, they found a newborn baby girl, half dead from want of maternal milk and being bounced on the journey.

"Where did you get this, son?" asked Jesús Dionisio Picero.

"It seems she's mine," the youth replied, worrying his uniform cap with sweating fingers, not daring to meet his father's eyes.

"And, if it is not too much to ask, where is the mother?"

"I don't know. She left the baby at the barracks door with a piece of paper saying I'm the father. The sergeant told me to take her to the nuns; he says there's no way to prove she's mine. But I'd feel bad about that; I don't want her to be an orphan . . ."

"Who ever heard of a mother leaving her baby on someone's doorstep?"

"That's how they do it in the city."

"So, that's the way it is, then. And what is the little thing's name?"

"Whatever name you give her, Papa, but if you're asking me, I like Claveles; carnations were her mother's favorite flower."

Jesús Dionisio went out to find the she-goat to milk, while Amparo bathed the infant carefully with oil and prayed to the Virgin of the Grotto to give her the strength to care for another child. Once he saw that the baby was in good hands, their youngest son thanked them, said good-bye, threw his pack over his shoulder, and marched back to the barracks to serve out his sentence.

Claveles was raised by her grandparents. She was a stubborn, rebellious child impossible to discipline either with reasoning or exercise of authority, but she yielded immediately if someone played on her emotions. She got up every day at dawn and walked five miles to a shed set in the middle of some field, where a teacher assembled the local children to administer their basic schooling. Claveles helped her grandmother in the house and her grandfather in the workshop; she went to the hill to look for clay and she washed his brushes, but she was never interested in any other aspect of his art. When Claveles was nine, Amparo Medina, who had been shrinking until she was no bigger than a six-year-old, died cold in her bed, worn out by so many births and so many years of hard work. Her husband traded his best rooster for some planks and built her a coffin he decorated with Biblical scenes. Her granddaughter dressed her for her burial in the white tunic and celestial blue cord of Saint Bernadette, the one she herself had worn for First Communion and which fit perfectly her grandmother's emaciated body. Jesús Dionisio and Claveles set out for the cemetery pulling a small cart carrying the paper-flower-decorated pine box. Along the way they were joined by friends, men and shawl-draped women who walked beside them in silence.

Then the elderly wood-carver and his granddaughter were alone in the house. As a sign of mourning they painted a large cross on the door and for years both wore a black ribbon sewed to their sleeve. The grandfather tried to replace his wife in the practical details around the house, but nothing was ever again the same. The absence of Amparo Medina pervaded him like a malignant illness; he felt that his blood was turning to water, his bones to cotton, his memories fading, his mind swimming with doubts. For the first time in his life he rebelled against fate, asking himself why Amparo had been taken without him. After her death he was unable to carve manger scenes; from his hands came only *Calvarios* and martyred saints, all in mourning, to which Claveles pasted legends bearing pathetic messages to Divine Providence her grandfather dictated to her. Those figures did not sell well among the city tourists, who preferred the riotous colors they erroneously attributed to the Indian temperament, nor were they popular among the *campesinos,* who needed to adore joyful deities, because the only consolation for the sorrows of this world was to imagine that in heaven there was eternal celebration. It became almost impossible for Jesús Dionisio Picero to sell his crafts, but he continued to carve them, because in that occupation the hours passed effortlessly, as if it were always early morning. Even so, neither his work nor the company of his granddaughter could console him, and he began to drink, secretly, so that no one would be aware of his shame. Drunk, he would call out to his wife, and sometimes he would see her beside the kitchen hearth. Without Amparo Medina's diligent care, the house deteriorated, the hens stopped laying, he had to sell the she-goat, he neglected the garden, and soon they were the poorest family in the region. Not long thereafter, Claveles left to get a job in town. At fourteen she had reached her full growth, and as she did not have the coppery skin or prominent cheeks of the rest of the family, Jesús Dionisio Picero concluded that her mother must have been white—which would explain the inconceivable act of having left her baby at the barracks door.

A year and a half later, Claveles Picero returned home with a blemished face and prominent belly. She found her grandfather with no company but a pack of hungry dogs and a couple of bedraggled roosters in the patio. He was talking to himself, empty-eyed, and he showed signs of not having bathed for quite some time. He was surrounded by chaos. He had given up on his little bit of land and spent his days carving saints with demented haste, but with little of his former talent. His sculptures were deformed, lugubrious creatures unfit for either devotions or sale that had piled up in the corners of the house like stacks of firewood. Jesús Dionisio Picero had changed so much that he did not even favor his granddaughter with a diatribe on the evils of bringing children into the world without a father; in fact, he seemed unmindful of the signs of her pregnancy. He merely hugged her, trembling, calling her Amparo.

"Look at me, Grandfather, look carefully," the girl said. "I am Claveles, and I've come home to stay, because there's a lot to be done around here." And she went inside to light the kitchen fire to boil some potatoes and heat water to bathe the old man.

During the course of the following months, the old man seemed to come back to life; he stopped drinking, he began working his small garden, busying himself with his gamecocks, and cleaning the church. He still talked to the shade of his wife, and sometimes confused granddaughter for grandmother, but he recovered the gift of laughter. The companionship of Claveles and the hope that soon there would be another living creature in the house renewed his love of color, and gradually he stopped painting his saints pitch-black and arrayed them in robes more appropriate for an altar. Claveles's baby emerged from his mother's belly one evening at six and was received into the calloused hands of his great-grandfather, who had long experience in such matters, having assisted at the birth of his thirteen children.

"We'll call him Juan," the makeshift midwife declared as soon as he had cut the cord and wrapped his descendant in a clean swaddling cloth.

"Why Juan? There's no Juan in our family, Grandfather."

"Well, because Juan was Jesús' best friend, and this boy will be mine. And what was his father's name?"

"You can see he doesn't have a father."

"Picero, then. Juan Picero."

Two weeks after the birth of his great-grandson, Jesús Dionisio began to carve the pieces for a creche, the first he had made since the death of Amparo Medina.

Claveles and her grandfather soon realized that the boy was not normal. He was alert, and he kicked and waved his arms like any baby, but he did not react when they spoke to him, and would lie awake for hours, not fussing. They took the infant to the hospital, and there the doctor confirmed that he was deaf and, because he was deaf, that he would also be mute. The doctor added that there was not much hope for him unless they were lucky enough to place him in an institution in the city, where he would be taught good behavior and, later, trained for a trade that would enable him to earn a decent living and not always be a burden for others.

"Never. Juan stays with us," Jesús Dionisio Picero replied, without even glancing at Claveles, who was weeping in a corner, her head covered with her shawl.

"What are we going to do, Grandfather?" she asked as they left.

"Why, bring him up."

"How?"

"With patience, the way you train fighting cocks, or build *Calvarios* in bottles. It's a thing of eye, time, and heart."

And that was what they did. Ignoring the fact that the baby could not hear them, they spoke to him constantly, sang to him, and placed him beside a radio turned to full volume. The great-grandfather would take the baby's hand and press it firmly to his chest, so the boy would feel the vibration of his voice when he spoke; he made him make sounds and then celebrated his grunts with exaggerated reactions. As soon as the boy could sit up, Jesús Dionisio installed him in a box by his side; he gave him sticks, nuts, bones, bits of cloth, and small stones to play with, and as soon as the child learned not to put it in his mouth, he would hand him a ball of clay to model. Each time she got work, Claveles went into town, leaving her son with Jesús Dionisio. Wherever the old man went, the baby followed like a shadow; they were rarely apart. A camaraderie developed between the two that obliterated the vast difference in ages and the obstacle of silence. By watching his great-grandfather's gestures and expressions, Juan learned to decipher his intentions, with such good results that by the time he had learned to walk he could read his great-grandfather's thoughts. For his part, Jesús Dionisio looked after Juan like a mother. While his hands were occupied in their painstaking work, he instinctively followed the boy's footsteps, attentive to any danger, but he intervened only in extreme cases. He did not run to console him when he fell, or help him out of difficult situations; he trained him to look out for himself. At an age when other boys were still staggering around like puppies, Juan Picero could dress, wash, and eat by himself, feed the chickens, and go to the well for water; he knew how to carve the most elementary parts of the saints, mix colors, and prepare the bottles for the *Calvarios*.

"We'll have to send the boy to school so he doesn't end up ignorant like me," said Jesús Dionisio Picero as the boy's seventh birthday approached.

Claveles made some inquiries, but she was told that her son could not attend a normal class, because no teacher was prepared to venture into the abyss of solitude in which he had settled.

"It doesn't matter, Grandfather; he can earn a living carving saints, like you."

"Carving won't put food on the table."

"Not everyone can go to school, Grandfather."

"Juan can't talk, but he's not stupid. He's bright. He can get away from here; life in the country is too hard for him."

Claveles was convinced that her grandfather had lost his reason, or that his love for the boy was blinding him to his limitations. She bought a primer and tried to pass on her meager knowledge, but she could not make her son understand that those squiggles represented sounds, and she finally lost patience.

It was at that juncture that *señora* Dermoth's volunteers appeared. They were young men from the city who were traveling through the most remote regions of the country on behalf of a humanitarian project aimed at helping the poor. They explained how in some places too many children are born and their parents cannot feed them, while in others there are couples who have no children. Their organization was intent on alleviating that imbalance. They showed the Piceros a map of North America and color brochures containing photographs of dark-skinned children with blond parents, in luxurious surroundings of blazing fireplaces, huge, woolly dogs, pine trees decorated with silvery frost and Christmas ornaments. After making a rapid inventory of the Piceros' property, they told them all about *señora* Dermoth's charitable mission: locating the most neglected and afflicted children and then placing them for adoption by wealthy families, to rescue them from a life of misery. Unlike similar institutions, this good lady was interested only in children with birth defects or those handicapped through accident or illness. Up North there were couples—good Catholics, it went without saying—waiting to adopt these children. And they had the resources to take care of them. There in the North there were clinics and schools where they worked miracles for deaf-mutes; for example, they taught them to lip-read and talk, and then they sent them to special schools where they received a thorough education, and some went on to the university and graduated as lawyers, or doctors. The organization had aided many children; the Piceros had only to look at the photographs. See how happy they look, how healthy; see all those toys, and the expensive houses. The volunteers could not promise anything, but they would do everything they could to arrange for one of those couples to take Juan and give him all the opportunities his mother could not provide for him.

"You never give up your children, no matter what," said Jesús Dionisio Picero, clasping the boy's head to his chest so he would not see the visitors' faces and understand the subject of their conversation.

"Don't be selfish now, Grandfather; think of what's best for the boy. Don't you see that he would have everything up there? You don't have the money to pay for his treatment; you can't send him to school. What will become of him? The poor kid doesn't even have a father."

"But he has a mother and a great-grandfather!" was the old man's rejoinder.

The visitors departed, leaving *señora* Dermoth's brochures on the table. In the days that followed, Claveles often found herself looking at them and comparing those large, well-decorated homes with her own bare boards, straw roof, and tamped-down dirt floor; those pleasant, well-dressed parents with herself, dog-weary and barefoot; those children surrounded by toys and her own playing with clay dirt.

A week later Claveles ran into one of the volunteers in the market where she had gone to sell some of her grandfather's sculptures, and again she listened to the same arguments: that an opportunity like this would not come a second time, that people adopt healthy offspring, not those with defects; that those people up North had noble sentiments, and she should think it over carefully, because for the rest of her life she would regret having denied her son such advantages and having condemned him to a life of suffering and poverty.

"But why do they want only sick children?" Claveles asked.

"Because these gringos are near saints. Our organization is concerned only with the most distressing cases. It would be easy for us to place normal children, but we're trying to help the ones who most need assistance."

Claveles Picero kept seeing the volunteers. They showed up whenever her grandfather was out of the house. Toward the end of November they showed her a picture of a middle-aged couple standing before the door of a white house set in the middle of a park, and told her that *señora* Dermoth had found the ideal parents for her son. They pointed out to her on the map the precise spot the couple lived; they explained that there was snow in the winter and that children built big dolls from the snow and ice-skated and skied, and that in the autumn the woods looked like gold and in the summertime you could swim in the lake. The couple was so thrilled at the possibility of adopting the young lad that they had already bought him a bicycle. They also showed her the picture of the bicycle. And also this did not even take into account the fact they were offering two hundred and fifty dollars to Claveles; she could live for a year on that money, until she married again and had healthy children. It would be madness to miss this opportunity.

Two days later, when Jesús Dionisio had gone to clean the church, Claveles Picero dressed her son in his best pants, put his saint's medal around his neck, and explained in the sign language his great-grandfather had invented for him that they would not see each other for a long time, maybe never, but it was all for his good; he was going to a place where he would have plenty to eat every day, and presents on his birthday. She took him to the location the volunteers had indicated, signed a paper transferring custody of Juan to *señora* Dermoth, and quickly ran away so her son would not see her tears and begin crying, too.

When Jesús Dionisio Picero learned what she had done he was struck speechless and breathless; he flailed about wildly, destroying everything in reach, including the saints in bottles, and then set upon Claveles, punching her with a strength unexpected in someone as old and mild-mannered as he. When he could speak, he accused her of being just like her mother, a woman capable of giving away her own son, something not even beasts in the wild do, and he called on the ghost of Amparo Medina to wreak vengeance on her depraved granddaughter. In the following months he refused to speak a word to Claveles; he opened his mouth only to eat and to mutter curses all the while his hands were busy with his carving tools. Grandfather and granddaughter grew used to living in stony silence, each absorbed in his or her own tasks. She cooked and set his plate on the table; he ate with eyes fixed on the food. Together they tended the garden and animals, each going through the motions of the daily routine in perfect coordination with the other, but never touching. On local fair days, Claveles collected the bottles and wooden saints, took them to market to sell, returned with provisions, and put any remaining coins in a tin can. On Sundays they went to church, separately, like strangers.

They might have spent the rest of their lives without speaking if sometime in mid-February *señora* Dermoth's name had not been in the news. The grandfather heard about it on the radio, while Claveles was washing clothes in the patio: first the announcer's commentary and then a personal confirmation by the Department of Welfare. With his heart in his mouth, Jesús Dionisio ran to the door and shouted for Claveles. She turned, and when she saw his distorted face she ran to catch him, thinking he was dying.

"They've killed him," the old man moaned, dropping to his knees. "Oh, God, I know they've killed him!"

"Killed who, Grandfather?"

"Juan," and through his sobs he repeated the words of the Secretary of Welfare: a criminal organization headed by a *señora* Dermoth had been discovered selling Indian children. They chose children who were ill or from very poor families, with the promise that they would be put up for adoption. They kept the children for a while to fatten them, and when they were in better shape took them to a secret clinic where they performed operations on them. Dozens of innocents had been sacrificed like living organ banks, their eyes, kidneys, liver, and other body parts removed and sent to be used as transplants in the North. He added that in one of these fattening houses they had found twenty-eight youngsters waiting their turn. The police had intervened, and the government was continuing its investigations in order to exterminate such an abominable trafficking.

Thus had begun the long journey of Claveles and Jesús Dionisio Picero to the capital to talk with the Secretary of Welfare. They wanted to ask him, with all due deference, whether their boy was among the children rescued, and whether possibly they could have him back. There was very little left of the money they had been given, but they would work like slaves for this *señora* Dermoth however long it took to pay her back the last cent of her two hundred and fifty dollars.

Standing in the Shadows

ELIZA MONROE

Dirt under my nails, my truck double-parked outside, I'm halfway through the As of which list, I won't say. A woman in Los Angeles told me over the phone how to find my son, but she made me promise to keep her method to myself. There are groups, she said, who don't believe that birth mothers should have access to their children, and are working to cut off all sources of information.

I can't think of Kyle without crying. And I think of him almost every day. I picture him at each stage of growth, even as an adult, though he just turned ten, but mostly I miss not holding him enough as a baby, soft skin against my arms, a giggle surfacing and rising like a bubble from his mouth to mine.

I wasn't always a farmer. Martin and I were living in a condo in Stockton the day John Lennon was shot. We were depressed, and broke our pact of seven years to never bring children into this world. All at once, it seemed that maybe the earth needed our child, and though Martin had a violent temper and no job, two characteristics which seemed to feed off each other, we believed that a baby could change him. Conceiving Kyle was no accident. It was a last-ditch effort to save Martin, if not the universe.

The lab called me at work with the results a week later. At first, I felt awe at carrying life, then fear of bringing up my child in conditions less than ideal. I stood in the salmon-colored bathroom stall in the basement of my office building, the only place on earth I had privacy, and apologized in advance. I was the only one working, and role reversals were frowned upon in the Mormon Church. We were still struggling to keep our membership. I don't know if Martin still struggles.

I can't blame the Church entirely. Martin was already twisted when he was converted, fresh out of juvenile hall, at a fireside where he ate cookies baked by fiercely optimistic virgins. And if it hadn't been for my meeting him at that fireside, I'd probably still be one of those virgins. But Martin and I married, outside the Temple. Gradually, I lost the ability to think positively. Eventually, the ability to feel pain left me.

By the time we gave Kyle up for adoption, all I knew was that we were going straight to hell, a place in which Mormons didn't even believe.

But before we gave him away, I was pregnant. I felt responsible for maintaining a buffer between the world and my amniotic fluid. I didn't want to scare the fetus off before it gave us a chance to be parents, and Kyle grew inside me, on the slow side, as if he knew what he was getting into, but was coming anyway.

Too nervous to go to school or get a job, one of Martin's short-range goals became overseeing the production of the world's most perfect baby. Martin spent his days preparing sushi, the perfect food, and after work, I swallowed big chunks of raw squid and tuna piled on rice or wrapped with seaweed.

Martin's other short-range goal became coaching the world's smoothest delivery. He said that a woman's pregnant state was just an extension of her non-pregnant state. The vast majority of pregnancy-related problems were psychosomatic. I tried to be living confirmation of his statement, too scared to make him a liar. Besides, I still expected childbirth to be easy. My mother had given birth eight times easily. My sisters had all had numerous and effortless deliveries, some so fast that more than one of my thirty-odd nieces and nephews had been born without any labor at all. I had no reason to believe I would be any different. I had come from good childbearing stock. It was my heritage, if not my religion.

Martin's only long-range goal was to stay home and care for the baby while I worked. We'd considered going on welfare, another un-Mormony concept, but I said I'd rather take the salary and benefits that came along with keeping my job. I wouldn't mind leaving the baby with Martin. He hadn't hit me in two years, and he seemed satisfied with the househusbanding most of the time. The baby and I both needed Martin to decide on something, and if househusbanding was it, Kyle and I would work around it.

I was content to come home, round and waddling, to Martin on each of his good days. After all the times I'd seen him fail, it was refreshing to see him do something well, safe inside our immaculate refuge, which he referred to as his "cell." Sometimes he seemed able to accept his role wholeheartedly, and I thought courageously. Stockton was a conservative town, and role reversal was hard to swallow. But I was proud of Martin. He was finally looking at what he could do instead of what he couldn't do. He was beginning to sound like a liberated, sophisticated, educated American male, but not all the time. Sometimes he looked up from the kitchen sink or above a pile of clothes he was folding, still warm from the dryer, and came up with ideas on how he could become the breadwinner.

The due date came. They gave me a baby shower at work on September seventeenth, then sent me home. I sat and waited. There was no money coming in, so we had garage sales. I sold the tiny lavender earrings my father had brought me back from Cincinnati when I was a child. I sold the turquoise ring that had belonged to my great-grandmother. I even sold the baby presents from my shower.

I'd been working Monday through Friday, nine-to-five, ever since Martin and I had met, and for the first time, we spent an entire month together. In between garage sales, we went to our Lamaze class and to movies, but all we talked about was money. He took me for brisk walks and bumpy rides to induce labor, so my disability checks would come in, but the baby wouldn't budge.

I didn't know how long my pregnancy would last. Every day went by in hot slow motion. After carrying the baby a full ten months, the first contractions came almost anti-climactically.

During the evening of October eighteenth, I realized I was in labor. By eleven, the contractions gnawed three minutes apart. I felt uneasy, and exhaled, "He-he-he," hoping the worst was almost over.

Everyone at work had said that since my pregnancy was so easy, my labor and delivery would be, too, and I believed them. Martin just plain demanded it. In our Lamaze class, we'd heard stories of women cussing out their coaches, and Martin warned me to control my tongue, mind over body. "Remember," he said, "there is no excuse for lashing out, regardless of your physical condition."

At one in the morning, he drove me to the hospital. My contractions gripped, then released. The doctor on staff told me to go home because I had not dilated yet and he doubted I really was in labor. But even Martin was convinced that I was, which made me feel good, and he didn't take me home. We walked up and down the dark halls of the hospital, careful not to slip on the freshly mopped tile floors, which smelled of sickness and antiseptic. I couldn't walk through the contractions anymore, but with Martin's help, I hobbled between them. I still showed no signs of dilation, but I was finally admitted to the labor and delivery department.

Martin held my hand and blew with me. If blowing and preparedness meant anything, we'd have been in and out in forty-five minutes, but after twenty-four hours, natural childbirth was no longer an option. My eyes met Martin's. I hadn't even wanted to scream at him. I'd expected him to get irate long before and demand forceps, surgery, drugs—but he just stood by me, a quiet, olive blur of patience and understanding.

He didn't even put up a fuss when we parted at the elevator, and at first I didn't want to be separated from him. I contracted and exhaled in the operating room as I waited alone for the anesthesiologist. Even then, what saved me was the image of Martin blowing in my face. But after the anesthesia entered my body, relief registered in my brain, and I was glad to be without him.

I felt no more contractions. At first, I felt nothing at all, only heard the doctors bang my body against the table. Then, over the next seven minutes, I felt slight pressure as they unjammed my son's head from between my bones and pulled him out through an incision in my belly. He let out a low bellow for a cry. From a distance I could see his long, lean, healthy body, and tears came to the anesthesiologist's eyes as she blotted my brow.

It was a boy. I envisioned a companion for Martin, a kitchen helper, standing on a wooden stool, chopping celery while I worked, and I began to cry. But when someone held him up close to me and I saw nothing but myself in him, I was glad that Martin hadn't been included, not in that moment.

I was out of the hospital in five days and back on my feet in ten. My doctor had given me an extra couple of weeks of disability because of the surgery, and though the checks started coming in again, Martin asked me to go back to work early. I didn't want to stay home unwanted, but I certainly wasn't going back to work sooner than I had to, and I had no place else to go. So I stayed onstage without a role to play. Martin took over caring for the baby and the house, and I could see what a good father he wanted to be, how he needed me to stand in the shadows.

I was scared of what would happen to his soul if he failed one more time, but not scared of my own self-denial. I took a deep breath and garnered a strange brand of courage, not the down-and-dirty, stand-up-and-fight, recognizable-as-such brand that heroes are made of, but the brand that resembles cowardice to me now. Other than pumping my breasts and freezing bottles of milk, I seemed to do nothing but crowd Martin's cell, and as crowded as we were, I was lonely for the light.

I rarely held or suckled the baby, and when I did, it felt like from a distance, as if I didn't have the right. I bathed or changed him only if Martin needed a break. Martin said that since he was going to be the househusband, we may as well practice our roles now to make it easier for him and Kyle when I finally did go back to work. "It will be easier on you, too, Sonja. Then you won't get used to being home and taking over the mothering role. I'm already afraid of being an inadequate father. I don't need you around to steal any rewards that should be coming to me."

I'd been as little of a bother as I could be. All through the pregnancy, I'd never been sick. I never got grouchy, or deprived Martin of his sexual release. I never really lost my figure, and I never got stretch marks. And Kyle did his part, too. He was an easy, quiet baby. He never fussed, and he slept all night.

I still had to get up and pump at one o'clock every morning, but breastfeeding was the one thing I wouldn't give up, and I didn't always have enough energy to make love to Martin when he wanted it. One night, after I'd been back to work two or three weeks, I was so tired I fell asleep right next to him, knowing he was horny and uptight and his reaction would be so far from favorable. I woke up in the living room with the wind knocked out of me.

"Oh, I'm sorry, Sonja. I meant to just tap you on the thigh. It's dark in here. I didn't mean to get you in the solar plexus."

I was so tired, I just climbed back into bed and fell asleep again. Now that we had a baby watching, I figured Martin wouldn't do anything, but just as I was dozing off, he threw me out of bed, along with a pillow and blanket. Was he just too mad to sleep with me? I put my head on my pillow on the floor and curled up to go to sleep again. Pow! I woke up to punches against my thigh and back. I was still curled up, and coiled tighter while he hit me. I accidentally jerked my knee into my own eye. Martin had finally gotten my attention. I was wide awake. He went for ice.

"Oh, shit, now you're going to have a black eye tomorrow at work." He applied the ice pack, trying to get the swelling down before it even started. "They're going to think I hit you in the eye, and I didn't."

I spent the rest of the night listening to Martin devise an excuse to tell my co-workers the next day. By morning, my eye was quite bruised, but I had my story straight. We were playing softball with another couple in the parking lot. I missed the catch and got it in the eye with the ball.

When I came home that evening, he said I wasn't producing enough milk, but I knew I was. I figured that his real objection was not having my breasts attached to his body. He suggested that we start using formula, but when I said no, he dropped it, and I was surprised.

A few days later, Martin was bathing the baby. He raised his hand to slap Kyle for crying and I lurched forward.

"Don't you ever come between me and the baby," he said.

I backed off. After that, I sat helplessly on my hands on the living room couch and listened to Kyle scream. But eventually, he slept. Martin and I made love quietly in the darkness with the window open, a winter chill soothing our hollow bodies. After he came, he let me hold him the way I wish I could have held Kyle, completely and all night long. And then he said, "I can't trust myself around the baby anymore." His teardrops, large and hot, rolled down my forearm as I wiped his eyes.

In the morning, he asked me to find a babysitter, and I looked, but I couldn't find one. During the next two weeks, he started leaving the baby alone for a few minutes here and there, then half-an-hour, then an hour. Once, he left the baby unattended in his truck. Then he called me at work.

"I can't handle this fucking baby, Sonja."

I rushed home and when I got there, he said, "No violence ever happens when you're away. I want you to know that, Sonja. It only happens when you're home, because if I know you're watching, I'll do less."

The following Monday night, he yelled at Kyle again. I sat on my hands in the living room, and grieved. Martin came out of the bedroom.

"Sonja, I like the idea of having a son, but I'm not ready to be a father. And I won't allow you to raise him without me. We can't keep Kyle. I'm sorry."

I didn't whine or cry or patronize him. I didn't try to talk him out of it. I just grabbed up his offer to let the baby go, hoping Kyle would be out of danger before Martin changed his mind again.

The next morning I called L.D.S. Social Services, the Mormon adoption agency, and stated my case without mentioning violence. I talked only about Martin "not being mature enough" to care for the baby and my "wanting the baby out of our house immediately." The agency was booked up for interviews, but when I said that the safety of the baby was at stake, the social worker agreed to stay late and interview us that night. He gave us the option of putting Kyle in a foster home for six or nine months until Martin got a job and therapy, but Martin said, "No. I don't want my son bounced around from foster home to foster home waiting for his father to get his act together. I want to break the chain right now."

I wanted the baby gone, safe, permanently away from his father, and my inability to protect. That evening, Martin and I signed relinquishment papers, the R word, the thing that makes birth parents inhuman, incomprehensible, separate from the rest of society, and rightly so. How could we give up our own flesh and blood?

I stopped breastfeeding cold turkey. I slithered in pain, applied ice, and pushed the hard, round orbs under warm bath water, but nothing helped.

The agency didn't have any trouble finding a permanent home for Kyle. They chose a Mormon family in northern California with coloring, body types, and genealogy that matched us perfectly. The father was an upper-middle-class, twenty-nine-year-old architect in business for himself and made good money even in the middle of the recession. The mother was also twenty-nine, an artsy-craftsy homemaker. They couldn't have children of their own, and had adopted an infant girl five years earlier. For two and a half years, they'd been calling the agency every week, asking for a boy, and now their prayer had been answered. Their family was complete.

Martin and I said we felt happiness for Kyle and his new parents. We said we were also happy for ourselves, to be rid of the child that perhaps we never should have had.

Martin was so sure that no one would accept what we'd done, he told the neighbors the baby was in L.A. with his grandmother. The people I worked with assumed he was still at home with Martin and asked questions accordingly until I finally broke down and said, "He's no longer with us." Word got around that the baby was dead, and they stopped asking questions.

The social worker said that a change of scene might help, so I put in a transfer to Sacramento and took the rest of February off to wait for it. Martin sold our furniture so it would be easier to move, and we spent three weeks together in our empty condo, too ashamed to come out in daylight, and waited for a transfer that never came.

In March, I went back to work. Life went on. The pressure was off. But by the first of April, Martin wanted the baby back. I felt as though I were living in a recurring nightmare. I'd given up everything for that man. The baby was gone. We'd let him go to a better life. And now, Martin wanted him back. I stood by Martin, hating myself as I lied to the attorney. The truth was that I no longer wanted the baby. He belonged to some other people now. He had a different name, a different home, a big sister. I didn't want more problems. It was time to get on with life.

The attorney compared us with the adoptive parents and told us that it would be up to the jury, but the adoptive parents looked awfully good and would probably win. So we didn't pursue it. Martin finally realized he had to let go. I was tired and disgusted with myself, then relieved, because I knew it was getting late, and we couldn't very well try again to get him back.

By summer, it seemed as though we would finally start living again. A lot of the stress, like a poisonous cloud, had blown over. We were stuck in Stockton and had decided to buy all new furniture. Martin signed up for a full class-load, and I enrolled in a management training program at work and enjoyed the recognition. I'd toned up, and was starting to be noticed—I could feel it—by other men. I cried behind my new sunglasses during my long bus ride home every night, wishing Martin would die, hating myself for not having the guts to leave him. But when I'd get home, he was always there, perfectly healthy. Then I'd have to get into it. When we made love, I covered the reality of him with an opaque sheet of fantasy. I made up old boyfriends that I never had, let them stroke my arm tenderly, and I could feel that, too. It's not like I would leave him, I thought, but I did leave. That was nine and a half years ago, and though I've remarried, I have no other children. I knew they couldn't replace Kyle.

As I stand here, the motor running, checking names, I know that I could have left with the baby, but I didn't know it then. I could have escaped, changed our names, managed as a single parent until I found Wiley and his farm. I could have kept my baby.

With creases in my brow from standing in the sun, I've wondered if I'm healed enough to care for another child. I've considered adopting a baby and naming it, boy or girl, black or white, whole or cracked, "Joaquin," after this valley that has given my life back to me. But adopted babies don't come from agencies. They come from their real mothers, and I would always wonder about Joaquin's. I also wonder about the woman who is raising my son, but it doesn't stop me from continuing my search. Even on the most dismal days, when I have nothing to look forward to, I have the hope that I will find him, and that he will accept me, not for who I was, but for who I am now.

(III)

GROWING

It

JOHN HILDEBIDLE

They walked for what seemed hours, until Frank's fingers were half numb from It's tight sticky grip. Once they reached the clearing, a place known only to a few clever children, Frank pried loose his hand and distracted It by piling up acorns; It loved to sort. Frank tied It's blanket tightly to a heavy fallen branch and then more comfortably to It's right leg. Not wishing to be cruel, he found three or four deadfall apples that were not too wormy, and left them within It's easy reach. Then Frank crept quietly away. He could hear small coos of discovery and accomplishment even after the thick undergrowth cut It off from view. The walk back home was surprisingly quick; his mother was just coming out of the kitchen, her face full of the smile that only a clean house could cause, her arms red from the washtub. She looked around the yard, and her smile disappeared.

"Where's Rachel?" she asked, in a very odd tone of voice.

"Gone," Frank said, climbing the porch steps.

The first true warning sign was her shriek; the second was the grip of her hands on his shoulders as she shook him, all the time shouting, "Gone? Gone? Gone? Gone?" at a pitch and volume he did not remember ever hearing before.

If even a few weeks before, you'd pressed him for an informed opinion, Frank would have said that he had, all in all, quite a well-ordered home. And not by accident, either. Nearly seven years' work had gone into making things run smoothly—months and months, for instance, habituating his parents to a reasonable bedtime; months more training his mother to fry eggs so the yolk was just right and the white did not look or taste like white India rubber; week upon week upon week teaching his father to stop at Bouchard's on his way home from work and pick up several of those marvelous half-moon cookies that could redeem even a supper of liver and butter beans. There was, Frank felt certain, reason to take pride; and never more so than during long pleasant autumn evenings full of the sound of his parents' voices reading aloud while Frank lay wrapped in a patchwork quilt on the sofa, pretending to be getting sleepy.

All that was before It arrived (his mother and father persisted in calling It "she" or even "Rachel," but Frank saw no reason to dabble in such words). It came, apparently, with a story attached—some cock-and-bull yarn about a poor foundling child whom someone had left in the care of the minister, a clumsy man of nearly sixty who had cold hands and a tendency to mumble. Frank was offered an explanation of the path It took out of the minister's parlor (a room, Frank had to admit, that anyone, even a foundling, would have done anything to leave) and into his own (and as he had once thought, safe) house. But Frank did not listen. He had long ago lost his taste for fairy tales.

And in any case *how* It got there was beside the point; for there It was, noisy and intrusive, hardly a child at all, more like a mobile principle of disorder. It had a nose that ran constantly, hands that itched for Frank's most fragile possessions, legs that hardly seemed sufficient to hold It up but could work up astonishing speed when an opportunity for trouble offered, and eyes—oh my, eyes that were impossible! To look at they were nothing much, neither blue nor brown nor any color, really; but turned on any adult they seemed all powerful. Even the minister gawked and cooed.

And now what of those long autumn evenings? Instead of reading, his mother made strange inarticulate noises and his father sang—very badly—an endless song about a yellow duckie. Left unexpectedly to himself, Frank had nearly too much time to consider what to do. This much was certain: steps needed taking, careful, effective, firm steps. And most important of all *rapid*—here it was, mid-November, and Frank did not propose to have his Christmas bollixed.

The autumn had been unusually wet, but now the days turned sunny and very nearly hot. Astoundingly, It was, by all adult authorities, granted the credit for that. When Frank first heard his mother announce, over the counter to the butcher, that "our little Rachel brought the sun with her," he assumed it was only one of those odd, silly remarks with which, as he had observed, adults tended to clutter up their conversation. But when she repeated it over the side fence to Old Lady Ryan, and then again to Limping Danny, the odd job man at St. Brigid's Church who hired out on weekends to sweep up the last of the fallen leaves, and then once more to Frank's father, who smiled and nodded and added an entire verse about sunshine to the song about the yellow duckie, Frank knew that his parents, at least, believed that this smelly little creature had some sort of magical power.

But the warm weather gave him his first great opportunity and one of Frank's axioms was "Let opportunity do the hard work." His father was away on business for a day or so, off to Boston on the train. Frank's mother was working on the laundry and told Frank to let It run about the backyard under his watchful eye. Run It certainly did, off to the fence as if It were discovering Peru, then back to the porch, clutching Its blanket in one hand and in the other a few dead flowers, then off careening again—a born wanderer, obviously. Surely, Frank thought, something so mobile and once so lost and then "found," could be lost again.

Frank swallowed his pride for the moment and held out a hand; It grasped his fingers and looked up with those insufferable eyes. The back gate never stayed securely shut anyway, and the path ran deep into the woods. Probably, Frank decided, It thought It was on an outing.

Even safely inside his own room, with the door closed and barricaded with two ladder-back chairs, Frank could hear the commotion downstairs. His mother's voice rose every so often into the horrifying wail he had first heard on the porch. Underneath that sound ran the raspy murmur of Old Lady Ryan's voice; she had arrived within minutes, laden, as she always was when any crisis offered itself, with food. Then there was the rumble and tramp of the men—every single male in town over seventeen, as far as Frank could tell. They were arguing over who would look where and whether there were enough lanterns and how long it had actually been since the last wolf was seen anywhere nearby. When, well past dark, the search at last got under way, Frank could see out his bedroom window the winking of the lanterns in the woods, like stars behind thin clouds.

By then it was clear to him that his plan simply would not work; although *why* the newly arrived annoyance should provoke all this much ruckus was not entirely clear. The strange sound of his mother's cries proved one thing at least: until It came back, more or less safe and sound, there would be no peace at all, and perhaps not even any chance for Frank to leave this one room. He had no faith whatever in the search; as far as he knew, no living adult soul had ever found that particular clearing, and the late autumn dark was hardly the best time for looking. No. Things were once again up to him.

He climbed out his window and over the shed roof and then slid down a drainpipe; he remembered how from his father's reading *Tom Sawyer* to him, back when things were still on a normal footing. The dark woods kept him hidden from the noisy searchers; he needed no light, and made his way by memory and touch. When he reached the clearing, the searchers were far, far behind, and It lay placidly asleep, the core of an apple clutched in one hand. Frank woke It, reached out a hand, felt the sticky grip take hold, untied the blanket, and walked back toward home.

"Walk?" It kept saying—in amazement? in pride? "Walk? Walk? Walk!"

A little over halfway home they met a pair of searchers, who crowed the news out through the dark forest. Clapping Frank heartily on the back, they picked up his quarry and hurried It back to a kitchen full of half-eaten pies. "That little Frank," they said to his mother, "He's a goddamned hero!" Frank tried to look modest; and when somebody finally got around to asking how he'd known where to look, he yawned as if exhaustion was only inches away and said, "Luck, I guess," and let himself be grandly escorted up to bed.

There was, in his mother's eyes the next morning, and in his father's eyes two days later when he got back from Boston, a wariness Frank knew would take time and effort to erase. But the town was unanimous: Frank was the hero of the hour, and his path was strewn, not with laurel wreathes but with free cookies from Bouchard's and handsful of penny candy from Cloutier's five-and-dime, and a brand new red wool scarf, courtesy of Old Lady Ryan. But then there was the dark side: now he could go nowhere without a tiny hand clutching his, and two adoring eyes following his every gesture, and his mother's voice trailing along somewhere behind: "This time you keep an eye on her, hear?"

It would have been easy to lose hope altogether, but Frank did not. Losing It had proved impossible; but since everyone agreed that It had, only a few weeks before, been desperately in need of a home, surely he could now find It one, somewhere where It might be doted upon, blessedly outside his sight and hearing. Walking the afternoon streets with

It in tow, he ran over the list of possibilities, which proved distressingly short. The minister had more than enough room and surely a duty to offer refuge, but he had already passed up the opportunity. There were the Donelans, who had a huge house and so many children already that one more would barely be noticed. But when, one Tuesday, he managed to leave It behind on their porch, happily playing with various toddling Donelans, Mr. Donelan was unexpectedly quick to bring It back to Frank's house. There was Old Lady Ryan, who always insisted she knew how to raise everyone's children better than they did, but she kept cooing about how perfectly "Darling Little Rachel" fit into Frank's household. And anyway, what good would it do to have the little nuisance living right next door?

It all boiled down to one chance: the Bouchards. They were a little old, perhaps, but experienced. They had a daughter, whom Frank could just barely remember, a tall, silent young woman who had disappeared one summer and about whom, nowadays, nothing was ever said, beyond a widespread clucking of adult tongues when her name came up and a few enigmatic phrases like "A traveling salesman, for Pete's sake!" accompanied by lifted eyebrows. The Bouchards must, in some attic or other, have all the necessary tools and toys stored away, Frank decided. And what a kindness he would be doing It to let It become the child of the best cake baker in the state!

At first Frank thought that the idea would dawn on them, too, if only he took It into the bakeshop often enough: which was hardly a burden on him, especially since Mr. Bouchard had long since proven susceptible to a certain mildly hungry look in Frank's eyes. "What you need," he would announce, bending over to look into the showcase, his round belly looming against his white baker's coat, "is a jelly cruller. *Two* of them—one for the little one, eh?" And then he would smile as Frank ate.

But never more than that; and time was running short. Mid-December had arrived and the gray cold of early winter had set in firmly. Frank could see how accustomed everyone was getting to the two of them walking here and there: he in his red scarf and the lovely knitted wool hat that had once been his mother's, It wrapped in a coat Old Lady Ryan had found in her attic, like a beef roast on legs. Bad habits were being formed, all around. One afternoon, barely a week before Christmas, Frank took the final and, as he hoped, determining step. Nodding his thanks for the cream puff Mr. Bouchard had picked out for him, he said, "And what you need, Mr. Bouchard, is a nice daughter."

The baker stopped with his hand halfway toward the second cream puff "for the little one." "A daughter?" he said.

"You know, instead of the one you . . . used to have. A daughter like this one, maybe."

Bouchard looked at the two of them, his face going blank and then twitching oddly. "What a little jokester," he said, his voice thick.

"It's not a joke. You see, we're really awfully crowded and you've got a nice house and maybe even the crib you used before, and . . ." Frank stopped when he realized Mr. Bouchard was crying, great sobs heaving his bulky body, tears running down his face.

"A daughter. A daughter," the baker said. "Oh, just go away now." And he pushed the two of them out of the store, not quite gently, and slammed the door and flipped the sign in the window from Open to Closed.

By Christmas Eve Frank had, at long last, given in to despair. He sat all through the Christmas Eve church service nearly in tears; not even the carols could raise his spirits or make him forget the squirming shape that insisted on sitting next to him. The minister's sermon was full of hope and joy and that just made Frank feel all the worse. "Tonight comes the answer to all our prayers," the minister said; and Frank found himself earnestly, silently praying: "Make It go away. Please. Please. Please."

All the way home and up to bed he kept at it: "Please. Please." He did not bargain or promise; he merely pleaded. He fell asleep praying the same prayer and woke up, at the first gray light, with the word "Please" on his lips. He listened; there was silence. He crept out of his bed and down the stairs to the parlor, where the Christmas tree stood surrounded by presents; and he listened again, for any sound of small, interfering life. He heard only his father's snore, then the creak of the bed as his mother got out, then the swish of her nightdress and the thump of his father's feet as the two of them came downstairs too. Alone! A miracle!

And then the miracle shattered into the sound of a child's wailing: It was still there, and awake, and before long with them in the parlor, huddling on Frank's mother's knees. A vast, dismal sense of failure came over Frank, made his hands stiff and clumsy as he opened gifts, made him almost crush between his fists the package marked "To My Brother, From Rachel." Inside, nestled in tissue paper, was the carved wooden railway set he had wanted for months, right out of Cloutier's store window.

"Now then, what do you think of this fine new sister you've gotten?" his father asked.

"She's . . . something," Frank said.

Rachel climbed down and walked over to him and grabbed his fingers in the usual way and said, "Frank. Walk?"

His parents beamed. Perhaps, he decided, It was not so much a curse as a challenge; could she not be trained, too? He sighed; a life's work stretched before him. "Come on, then, Rachel," he said. "We'll go see how this train goes." And holding the box under one arm, he led her up the stairs to his room.

The Telling Part

JACKIE KAY

Roman typeface: adopted daughter
San serif typeface: adoptive mother

Ma mammy bot me oot a shop
Ma mammy says I was a luvly baby

Ma mammy picked me (I wiz the best)
Your mammy had to take you (she'd no choice)

Ma mammy says she's no really ma mammy
(just kid on)

It's a bit like a part you've rehearsed so well
you can't play it on the opening night
She says my real mammy is away far away
Mammy why aren't you and me the same colour
But I love my mammy whether she's real or no
My heart started rat tat tat like a tin drum
all the words took off to another planet
Why

But I love ma mammy whether she's real or no

I could hear the upset in her voice
I says *I'm not your real mother,*
though Christ knows why I said that,
If I'm not who is, but all my planned speech
went out the window

She took me when I'd nowhere to go
my mammy is the best mammy in the world OK.

After mammy telt me she wisnae my real mammy
I was scared to death she was gonnie melt
or something or mibbe disappear in the dead
of night and somebody would say she wis a fairy
godmother. So the next morning I felt her skin

to check it was flesh, but mibbe it was just
a good imitation. How could I tell if my mammy
was a dummy with a voice spoken by someone else?
So I searches the whole house for clues
but I never found nothing. Anyhow a day after
I got my guinea pig and forgot all about it.

I always believed in the telling anyhow.
You can't keep something like that secret
I wanted her to think of her other mother
out there, thinking that child I had will be
seven today eight today all the way up to
god knows when. I told my daughter—
I bet your mother's never missed your birthday,
how could she?

Mammy's face is cherries.
She is stirring the big pot of mutton soup
singing *I gave my love a cherry*
it had no stone.
I am up to her apron.
I jump onto her feet and grab her legs
like a huge pair of trousers,
she walks round the kitchen lifting me up.

Suddenly I fall off her feet.
And mammy falls to the floor.
She won't stop the song
I gave my love a chicken it had no bone.
I run next door for help.
When me and Uncle Alec come back
Mammy's skin is toffee stuck to the floor.
And her bones are all scattered like toys.

Now when people say 'ah but
it's not like having your own child though is it',
I say of course it is, what else is it?
she's my child, I have told her stories
wept at her losses, laughed at her pleasures,
she is mine.

I was always the first to hear her in the night
all this umbilical knot business is nonsense
—the men can afford deeper sleeps that's all.
I listened to hear her talk,
and when she did I heard my voice under hers
and now some of her mannerisms crack me up

Me and my best pal
don't have Donny Osmond or David Cassidy
on our walls and we don't wear Starsky and Hutch
jumpers either. Round at her house we put on
the old record player and mime to Pearl Bailey
Tired of the life I lead, tired of the blues I breed
and Bessie Smith I can't do without my kitchen man.
Then we practise ballroom dancing giggling,
everyone thinks we're dead old-fashioned.

The Boy Arden

BERNICE RENDRICK

Father of many lives, in this
picture you had not met Mother.
A young widower, you stand
against a wall, your hands cupping
the shoulders of a son, about seven,
in a smaller version
of your floppy cap. How could you
farm out the boy to his grandparents
in Washington? Across impossible miles?
As if we could not learn to love him?
Always I wanted a brother.
For years you carried his picture
in your pocket until
a network of fine lines
crazed the corners, and your tobacco
stained the child who smiled back.

When I inquired of my brother,
Mother always corrected me:
Your half brother, she'd say,
Snapping string beans in two,
Splitting the heart of the cabbage
Through the middle, reducing
The pale green leaves
To shreds on the board.

I only know half of the boy Arden's
story. But there he was in 1925,
his cap askew, his head pressed
against your belly, your hands
holding the son you let go.

Just for the Time Being

MARIAN MATHEWS CLARK

The fourth day after I move into my Twin Falls home (just for the time being, Mama promised), I hear Mrs. Reynolds talking about me on the phone. "Poor little Ruth," she says. "Do you know all she brought was a tiny bag and the clothes on her back?"

I'd crept downstairs from my room where I've been tucked in bed with a stomachache. "A case of the flu," the doctor told Mrs. Reynolds, but it's really knots in my stomach. I've had them before.

"She's the most fragile eight-year-old I've seen and so quiet," Mrs. Reynolds says to whoever's on the phone.

I can't help but smile, as I crouch behind the door leading into the kitchen. Mama told me once, "You're a shy little mouse until you get to know people, and then a whole bedspread stuffed in your mouth couldn't shut you up." I thought of Julia Finch, the neighbor I run to with the twins when Carson drinks too much, and the big bedspread on Julia's king-sized bed. "Julia's would fill up my whole belly," I told Mama, and we'd laughed for a long time. Carson wasn't around for a few days, so we didn't have to watch the noise.

Behind the door, I don't move a muscle even though I'm getting a leg cramp. I've been in tighter spots. In Pocatello I kept an eye on the twins, especially Rusty. He freezes sometimes when he's scared.

Once when Carson got drunk, I came out of the bathroom just in time to see him roar like a grizzly, then chase Rusty out of the apartment and down the hallway of our building. I took off after Carson and grabbed his shirt. He stumbled, fell flat, and stayed sprawled out, but Rusty kept moving and didn't come back. Rachel and Mama and I looked everywhere—in the laundry mat, in Doc's Grocery next door and at Julia Finch's just in case he'd circled back. After two hours, Mama said we'd better call the cops, but I said, "Let's take one more look."

I was just heading down the alley one last time when here came Doc, dragging Rusty behind him. Rusty stunk of rotten lettuce and cabbage and bad meat. Doc said he accidentally came across him in the dumpster behind the store and that was only because he'd seen red hair sticking up among the boxes. "He's a strange kid," Doc said. "He didn't move a muscle even with rotten food pouring down on him." Then he handed him over to me.

"Just having a game of hide-and-seek," I told Doc. "Rusty can hide really good."

"Yeah, sure," Doc said.

I rub my leg when Mrs. Reynolds lowers her voice, and lean closer to the back of the door. "The social worker said Ruth can't be bounced from pillar to post much more, so if the mother and her man friend don't straighten up . . . Well, it's hard to tell what will happen. We're trying not to get our hopes up, but it sure would be nice for Shirley if something permanent would work out. We're so far from town and she wants a sister so badly. And Shirley's only eight months older than Ruth."

I don't know why she's saying it could be permanent. I'm at the Reynoldses just for the time being. Mama promised. That's what I promised the twins, too, when we dropped them off at a foster home in Burley on the way to the Reynoldses. I don't like to think about Rachel, clinging onto me so tight the social worker had to pry her hands loose. Rusty stood on the porch like a corpse, not even waving good-bye and looking as white as Julia Finch's doilies.

"You should have heard what happened to her just before she came," Mrs. Reynolds says.

I hold my breath, waiting for her to mention the ax cut Carson put over Mama's eye, the reason I'm here in the first place. After we knew we had to leave I told Mama, "We should take the twins and hide and not tell anybody where we are, especially Carson."

But that made her cry. "The better we are," she said, "the quicker we'll all be together again."

"What're you doing?" a voice says from behind me. I nearly jump out of my skin. It's Shirley, the one who told me the first twenty minutes I got here that she was my new sister.

"Nothing," I tell her.

"Are you hiding?"

I shrug. In my first letter home, I told Mama, "The Reynoldses are all right, but their girl doesn't know straight up sometimes." I told her Shirley wanted to play pretend and paper dolls and talked about being sisters. I said, "I don't want to be her sister. Love, Ruth. P.S. I don't have to, do I, Mama?"

"What are you girls doing?" Mrs. Reynolds says. "Playing hide-and-seek?" She smiles at us.

Shirley shakes her head and looks at me. I shrug again. Then she says, "I think Ruth was listening to your phone conversation."

She doesn't know when to keep her mouth shut. I wait for Mrs. Reynolds to holler. It'll be the first time I'm in trouble in this new place. Instead she laughs in a nervous way, and her face turns red. "I was just talking to my sister," she says. "Did you hear anything, Ruth?"

"Unh unh," I say and stare at the floor.

Shirley frowns at me. "But you were . . ."

"That's all right," Mrs. Reynolds says, then straightens my collar. "Why don't you girls run upstairs and play? Supper will be ready in about an hour."

I climb the stairs. This place is confusing. If I've just gotten in trouble, it doesn't seem like it, but my heart's still pounding. Shirley's right on my heels. I wish I knew a place to hide.

"Want to play something?" she says, and before I can tell her I don't play with tattlers, she says, "Let's play rhymes."

"What?"

"You know," she says. "Like 'What are little girls made of? What are little girls made of? Sugar and spice and everything nice, that's what little girls are made of.'"

"Little girls are made of what?" I say. It's the silliest thing I've ever heard.

"You can rhyme anything." She picks up this big Raggedy Ann doll sitting next to her and hugs her tight. "What is Squishy made of? Buttons and strings and lots of things.' Like that," she says. She looks at Squishy. "You're made of other things, too," she says and hugs her tighter.

I stare at her, talking to a doll the way I would talk to the twins. Maybe before I came, she used Squishy for a sister.

"Now you try it," she says.

I shake my head.

"Why not?"

I crawl under the covers and turn away from her.

"You want to play something else then?"

I don't answer. She finally lets out a big sigh and drags herself out of the room. I think of following her, to see if she'll tattle. But I'm too tired.

All I'm thinking about these days are Rusty and Rachel and Mama and Julia Finch. I even think about Carson once when I hear Mr. Reynolds singing in the bathroom. Carson sang Happy Birthday to me last year when I was eight. He sings pretty. Mama says his voice is magnificent. But I haven't missed him.

I've been watching Mr. Reynolds every night at supper. He seems quiet, which might be a bad sign. It was just after Carson hadn't said a word for a week that he went on the fritz with his ax.

"Sometimes when people are quiet you have to watch out," Mama told me in the hospital, after Carson chopped up the kitchen table and made a hole in the apartment wall right through to the Logans' bedroom. Mr. Logan came bursting over with the ax that had crashed into Mrs. Logan's "Flow Gently Sweet Afton" antique music box. Mr. Logan grabbed Carson, who was leaning against the wall, dizzy, and shoved him into a chair. Julia Finch called the doctor, then wiped the blood off Mama's head. Mrs. Logan just kept moaning, "My God! My God!" through the hole.

After two weeks, I get my first letter from Mama. "I miss you so much," she says, but then she says that Carson loves everybody but gets upset because he's been out of work. She might be right. When Carson first came to live with us in Boise, he was working for Ore-Ida. We ate lots of free French fries, and he used to bring Mama bottles of Charley. That's her favorite. Once he brought the twins squirt guns and me a slingshot, but he hasn't done anything like that for months. Before I left, he only brought home Millers. Mama likes Coors. In the P.S. part of her letter, Mama says, "Carson thinks he's onto a job managing a Wendy's. Things are looking up. We'll be back together before you know it. I love you more than anything."

My stomach loosens up for the first time since I've been here. I tuck the letter in the corner of the top drawer of my chest of drawers. When I moved into Shirley's room, Mrs. Reynolds said, "Ruth, this is your bed. And that's your chest of drawers over there. We'll put all your underwear in one drawer and pajamas in another and shorts in another."

I didn't have pajamas and only two pair of underpants and no shorts to my name. At Mama's, all of us, even Carson, put our things together in boxes. Once Rusty dropped his paint box into our clothes without putting the lid on it. Carson's work shirt looked like a rainbow, which got him real mad. But most of the time, putting things together worked fine.

At the Reynoldses, people have drawers and closets and shelves full of all kinds of things. "We have a place for everything and try to keep everything in its place, honey," Mrs. Reynolds said, the day I unpacked.

"That way you can find something when you want it," Shirley said, pulling my top drawer open and moving closer to look into my bag.

"We need to step back to give Ruth room to unpack, honey," Mrs. Reynolds said to her.

I stuck my winter jacket in one drawer, my underpants and jeans in the next, and my tennis shoes in the third. I was wearing my dress and good shoes. "I'll use the last drawer for the twins when they come," I said.

"Shoes don't go in the drawer," Shirley said.

"We'll put them in the closet," Mrs. Reynolds said and lifted them out. "Moving into a new place just takes getting used to." She gave me a hug, the first one since I'd left Mama and the twins, and I wasn't sure what to do.

Shirley looked real startled, too. She followed Mr. and Mrs. Reynolds around the rest of the night asking if there was anything she could do to help, the way Mama does with Carson after they've had a fight.

I've just finished tucking Mama's letter beneath my underpants.

"What are you putting in there?" Shirley says and scares the wits out of me again. She sneaks up on you kind of like Carson does. Except he's trying to catch you doing something wrong. Shirley just wants to play.

Ever since I told her two days ago I wasn't here permanent and was heading back to Mama and the twins as soon as the social worker gives me the go-ahead, she quit kissing up to the Reynoldses. Now she hardly lets me out of her sight. Sometimes I wonder what she did before I came. When she isn't upstairs, I sneak over and hold Squishy. She has red hair like me except mine frizzes out when it's humid. Shirley's got nice brown hair that lays down flat. Some people don't know when they've got it good.

I make sure I only touch her things when she's not in the room. After all, Mama said to be good, and Carson didn't like us kids sitting in his chair or looking at his magazines. The Reynoldses might be like that. Except Shirley let me use her green sweater when we all went out one night to look at a wild duck that landed on the creek. And Mrs. Reynolds's sister borrowed the lawnmower and a black dress. Still you have to be careful.

"Huh?" Shirley says. "What are you hiding in the drawer?"

"Let's play something," I say, and close the drawer fast.

She lights up like a Christmas tree. "We can give the rubber dolls a bath and play a pretend and maybe even rhymes," she says, and runs to a little cupboard, grabbing two dolls off the shelf. "Come on," she says and almost leaps down the stairs.

In the bathroom, she runs a tub of soapy water and shoves a doll with black hair and a sad smile into my hands. "You'll be Sook Kim's mother," she says. Then she picks up the blond-headed doll with great big blue eyes. "And I'm Bridget's mother. I'm bringing her over from Sweden to visit you in your palace in China and . . ."

"China?" I say. It's bad enough having to come to Twin Falls. "Who's Sook Kim?"

"I named her after a girl in a book. She just turned eight last May. She's our age."

The twins will be six their next birthday. For their last birthday, Mama made two cakes. She carried one and I carried one and the twins' eyes got big as Carson's when the sheriff came to haul him off after the ax thing. Except the twins were excited, and Carson looked like he wanted to put his fist through something else. "I don't want to play pretend," I tell her.

She frowns, then says real fast, "Okay, then let's do rhymes." She points to my doll. 'Where does China Doll come from? The land of kites and. . . .'" She stops and thinks a minute.

"Palaces," I say.

"It has to rhyme, though. Something with kites. Maybe 'the land of kites and stormy nights.' That's a good one," she says.

"How do you know there are storms in China?"

"It's a pretend. It doesn't have to be true," she says. "It just has to rhyme."

"You mean like lying?"

"I'm not lying," she says. "China has kites, and it could have storms. It doesn't matter. It's just made up," she says again. "Now you do one."

"I can't."

"It's easy. Do 'What are bathrooms made of?'"

"Toilets," I say.

She shakes her head. "That'll be awful hard to rhyme." She starts scrubbing Bridget.

I think of our bathroom in the apartment with Carson pounding on the door yelling, "Hurry the hell up." Mama's taking a bath and I'm brushing my teeth and Rachel's sitting on the can. "I know," I say. "Bathrooms are made of tubs and spit and lots of shit."

Shirley lets out a funny squeak. "You can't say that," she says.

"It rhymes."

"Mother won't let us say it," she says. "It's a dirty word."

"It's not that bad," I tell her. "Fuck's a bad word. Shit's all right."

Her face turns white and her mouth falls open. She dunks Bridget, head and all, under the water and holds her there while she stares at me.

"Bridget's drowning," I tell her.

"Oh," she says and pulls her head up but keeps looking at me. Then she stands. "I have to tell Mother."

"Why?"

"I'm supposed to tell her when I hear bad words, so she can talk to who's saying them."

"That's tattling," I tell her.

"It's telling the truth."

"You don't tell the truth if it's walking you into a snake pit," I say, and I sit Sook Kim on the edge of the tub. "I'm not playing with you anymore."

"Well . . . well . . ." she says and sits back down. "Okay. But you can't say those words anymore. If you do I'll have to tell Mother."

I dunk Sook Kim into the water again but I can't wait to get home where people know what's a bad word what's not so bad and what's telling the truth and what's being stupid. I'm glad this is only my home for the time being. Mama promised.

The first time Shirley shows me how to catch crawdads is the day Miss Cline, the social worker, comes for her six-month visit. "Didn't the twins come?" I ask her before she sits down.

"They couldn't come this time, honey," she says. "But they're just fine. Rachel lost a tooth, and the tooth fairy left a quarter under her pillow."

"The what?"

"It's a game," she says. "When people lose a tooth, sometimes they find money under their pillow the next morning, and people say the tooth fairy left it."

Miss Cline and Shirley should get together on this pretend stuff. A tooth could fall out of Sook Kim's mouth and some fairy could drop off money for her so she could buy a kite and fly to China.

The only time I got money for a tooth was once when Carson was hitting Mama. I yelled at him to stop, and he said he would smack me good if I didn't shut the hell up. I said, "Go ahead, you bastard," which is when he grabbed me, but I bit his arm. When I unsunk my teeth, one stayed behind. It was my first loose one. Mama told Carson if he didn't straighten up, he'd have to get out. After that, he gave me a quarter if I'd calm down and not tell Julia, and he even gave me my tooth back. It sounds like Miss Cline's tooth fairy keeps the teeth.

Mom Reynolds tells us to run outside and play while she and Miss Cline talk. She says, "When the cookies are ready I'll call you."

"Come on," Shirley says. "Let's go hunt crawdads."

I follow her to the creek. It's pretty down here with a little bridge you can walk over. When you're halfway across, you can look into the water that's so clean you can watch a rock sink to the bottom. I wish Rusty could see it. That kid loves water so much he crouched under a drainpipe with his head sideways after a big rain to see if he could get some of that gush to run straight through his head. "There's things in your head that water'll run into," I told him when I dragged him out from under there looking half drowned.

I rushed him in the house and dried him off before Carson got home. Once before when Rusty tried that, Carson had slapped him and said,

"I'm surprised the water didn't run through your head. It's for sure there's no brains getting in the way."

That second time, I never let on where Rusty got an earache that hung on for a week. Usually I can tell Mama things. But every once in a while when Carson goes on the wagon for a few days and treats us nice, Mama tells him things she shouldn't. So when Mama said, "I don't see where Rusty could have picked up such a bad ear infection in the summer," I said, "Must be those darned neighbor kids."

I don't know if she believed me, but she didn't push it.

Shirley's at the creek bank with a stick, poking around in the water. "I got one," she says and drags this orange, crusty crawdad out on the bank. He staggers around, like Carson when he's had more than a twelve pack. She sticks him in her bucket she's scooped some water into. "Ruth, there's another one," she says, pointing to a spot in the water. "Quick, hold him down right where he's curling his tail under."

I grab a stick and watch this huge, ugly thing backing away fast.

"Hurry, we're going to lose him."

"He doesn't want to get caught," I tell her. "Maybe he has babies under the bank."

Shirley takes the stick from me. "He doesn't have babies," she says, and keeps poking at him until she scrapes him onto the bank. "They don't care if you catch them." She takes hold of him right behind his front legs that reach up trying to grab her fingers.

"He's mad as a wet hen," I tell her.

"I'm not hurting him," she says. "I always put them back."

I look in the bucket and see the little one is walking on the big one's head, and his long whiskers are flopping around. "I don't think they like each other," I tell her. "You better dump them out before that big one bites the little one's arm off."

"They're pincers. They don't bite each other. Besides, we haven't caught four yet. When we do, we'll pretend we're pioneers fishing for food. And we're having company for dinner."

"The twins?" I say.

"No," she says. "Squishy and China Doll."

"Eating crawdads would make me sick," I tell her and think of their whiskers wiggling all the way down to my stomach. Then I climb the creek bank and run toward the house.

"Wait. I'll dump them out," she hollers after me. "Come on back."

"I have to do something," I yell and walk into the living room where Miss Cline and Mom Reynolds are talking in quiet, secret voices. I stand smack in front of Miss Cline and don't budge.

"What's the matter, honey?" she says.

"The twins' birthday is coming up, and we've always been together for it. That would be a good time to move home to Mama's."

She smiles. "You can't go home yet, Ruth, but maybe we could find a way for you to be with the twins on their birthday. If it's all right with Mrs. Reynolds."

Mom Reynolds blinks and her face turns red. "Well, I guess that's fine," she says.

Shirley walks in then, but I run upstairs fast as I can to write Mama a letter. "With Miss Cline letting the twins and me get together, that must mean we're being good," I tell her. "It won't be long now till we're back together."

It's a week before the twins' visit when Shirley scares the wits out of me again. We've just been to the creek for another crawdad hunt. We're pioneer women in China, and the crawdads are giants who are trying to get our kids.

"Let's pretend we have eighteen babies and every time we catch a crawdad, two babies get away," I tell her.

"Okay," she says and pokes around in the bucket, counting. "That means we have five more to catch."

We hunt and jab and scrape at crawdads for another hour, but only catch three.

"Let's play something like Annie Over," Shirley says. "I don't think any more crawdads are coming out today."

"We haven't saved all the babies yet," I tell her. "The giants are waiting for us to leave."

"My feet are getting wet," she says. "Let's say the giants go to Australia for a convention and won't be back until tomorrow."

"What if it rains tomorrow and we can't come out?"

"Then they'll stay away longer," she says.

I think about it a minute then tell her okay, that I'm going to the house to talk to Mom Reynolds about the twins' birthday party again.

"Oh, don't leave," Shirley says, and looks around like she's trying to find something. Then she grins. "I know. I have a secret to show you. It's in Daddy's shop."

"I thought we weren't supposed to go in there."

"Well . . . well, just this once won't hurt."

"Are you sure?"

She nods, and we run across the back lawn, sneak into the shop, and shut the door. "Daddy's making me this in his spare time," she says and points to a large cedar chest. "He's been working on it for three years, and he says there's not another one like it."

I rub my hand over the wood. It smells sweet. Shirley says cedar makes the best hope chests. "It's real pretty," I tell her.

"I bet when he gets this done, he'll make one for you, too."

"Three years?" I say and shake my head. "I won't be here that long."

She frowns. "Why not? Don't you like it here?" She starts tapping her fingers on the top of the hope chest, then rubbing the handle.

I don't know what to say. She keeps tapping, then picks up this thin strip of wood lying on the top. It has a tiny sliver hanging off it—like a hangnail. She starts peeling it. "Huh?" she says. "Don't you like it here?"

"It's not that," I tell her. "I'm just here for the time being."

"But I want you to stay," she says, still pulling that hangnail which gets bigger and bigger.

"You'd better not . . ." I start to say, then see the whole board has cracked in half. She gasps like she just woke up. "Oh no," she says, and runs her hand along the top ridge of the lid. "I wrecked it. I think that board was the last one Daddy needed, and it went right here."

I look where she's pointing and sure enough there's one missing board. "It looked real smooth," I tell her. "Like he's been working on it awhile. Grab it quick, and we'll hide it in this place I found under the shop." It slipped out before I could think about it. I didn't plan to tell her about the secret places I'd come across—for hide-and-seek or bad times, just in case.

"We can't do that," she says. "Daddy won't know where it went."

"Exactly," I say, "and we won't get belted."

"What?" she says and makes her way to the house with her head hanging and her hands in her pockets.

I run straight for our room and crawl in bed.

Shirley comes upstairs in a few minutes. "What are you doing?"

"I'm getting a stomachache."

"Well, it's time for dinner," she says. "Mother says to come down. Daddy won't be home for a while, but we'll go ahead anyway."

At the table, I reach for the burgers, but Mom Reynolds says, "Ruth, honey, remember the blessing."

My heart pounds, hoping she won't go on and on. The Reynoldses pray for every meal and everybody. It's not that Mama never says prayers. When Carson goes haywire, she says, "Lord help us." But no matter how many times I've asked God to change things, we still have to stand in line in front of the nasty lady who hands out food stamps, and Carson still blows up like dynamite.

"Thank you God for what we are about to receive," Mom Reynolds says, then moves into blessing the sick and the suffering. Shirley and I will be the suffering as soon as Dad Reynolds goes to his shop. As soon as I hear "Amen," I start choking down the burgers and corn on the cob.

"Slow down. Slow down," Mom Reynolds says.

Halfway through my burger, Dad Reynolds walks in looking very tired. Shirley starts squirming and looking guilty, a face I've learned to get rid of on a moment's notice. I'm taking my last bite when she says, "Daddy, I have something bad to tell you."

I don't move.

"What, honey?" he says.

"Well," she starts out, "Ruth and I were in the shop today."

"Oh my God," I'm thinking. "She's going to get me in trouble, too, even though I didn't do a thing." I'm looking at the door.

"I thought we had a rule about the shop," Dad Reynolds says, but he's holding his burger in his hitting hand, and Shirley is sitting closest to him. "We've talked about that band saw being real sharp. You're only supposed to go in the shop when I'm there."

"I know," Shirley says, "but I wanted to show Ruth my hope chest."

"Well, no harm done this time," he says. "Just remember the rule from now on."

"But something happened with the hope chest," Shirley says and if she doesn't blab out the whole story.

I keep my eye on Dad Reynolds's face. He stops eating and gets real quiet, that scary kind of quiet, and then I hear Shirley sniffing. I'm cringing. Like I've always told the twins, "When you're on the spot, no crying and keep lying."

Dad Reynolds sighs big and looks even more tired. "Well, I can't say I'm not disappointed. But it's just a board. I'll pick up another one at the lumberyard tomorrow. But you girls might have to help me sand it. I was hoping to finish that up this week." Shirley quits crying and says she won't go in the shop again, and Dad Reynolds gives her a hug. I wait until bedtime for something bad to happen, but it never does. I can't remember my dad, but I wonder if dads who work all the time are too tired to throw things and yell and chase after you.

The morning the twins come, I wake up early to check the weather. There are a couple clouds in the sky but not enough to worry about. Shirley's still sleeping. Most mornings when I open my eyes she's grinning at me, wanting to play something.

I gulp my breakfast, then sit in front of the living room window.

When Miss Cline pulls in, I yell upstairs, "Hurry Shirley, they're here." She acts like she doesn't want to come down, and I'm wondering if she's sick. Mom Reynolds says when things settle down, I can ask her to show the twins the crawdads and the ant beetle traps in the garden.

I run out to hug the twins who've grown six feet apiece. They have new matching blue shirts, and Rusty's nose isn't running for a change. Rachel's hair is way too short, up to her shoulders. But at least it isn't tangled up and Carson will have a harder time getting his hands around it when he's mad. It isn't easy for him anyway. "Rachel's faster than greased lightning when she wants to be," Mama says.

After I've hugged the twins and fluffed up the tops of their heads like old times, Shirley comes out. But she's real quiet.

I say, "Shirley, these are the twins, and twins, this is Shirley." Mom Reynolds has been teaching me how to introduce people.

Rachel says to Shirley, "You're the one with that big old Squishy doll with orange hair and thread for a nose."

Shirley smiles a little, and I say to her, "Could you show us that ant beetle's trap? Rusty would like to see how that beetle fools other little bugs so they slide right onto his dinner table."

Shirley nods, and Rusty says, "How can a little bug make a trap like that?"

"I don't know," I say. "Do you, Shirley?"

She shakes her head and doesn't say a thing the whole time we're looking at the garden and then the creek. I try to wait for her, but she stays behind. The twins and I talk about Mama and Carson and Julia Finch.

Once Rusty says, "Who's looking out for Mama now, Ruth?"

"She can handle things and if Carson gets mean again, Julia Finch's Lucky will sink his teeth in where it hurts." The twins laugh and hang onto my hands tighter. Nobody mentions axes. I glance back at Shirley, but she's frowning.

When we get to the creek, she sits on the bank for a while, then gets up like she's going to leave.

Rusty says, "Where are those orange crawdads?"

"Shirley's the one who can catch them," I say.

"I want to see those dolls," Rachel says.

"As soon as Rusty sees the crawdads," I tell her.

"Then come on, Shirley," Rachel says, runs over and grabs her arm. "You have to show us all this stuff before Miss Cline gets back."

Shirley looks nervous, like she's never had a kid pull on her, but holds Rachel's hand till we get to the place with the crawdads. After that, she pulls a crawdad out for Rusty and lets Rachel hug Squishy. She helps Mom Reynolds blow up balloons and even laughs a couple times.

Miss Cline comes at 5:00 to haul the twins off with "all their loot," as Mama used to say when we got presents from her and Julia Finch. Shirley heads for the house while I'm hugging Rusty and Rachel ten times apiece.

They don't want to get in the car, but Miss Cline says we'll do this again. I whisper to them, "It won't be long now," and wave till they're out of sight.

Mom Reynolds puts her arm around me and walks me back to the house. "You got something in the mail today," she says and hands me a letter from Mama. I read it on the way to the bedroom. "Dear Ruth," Mama says. "Carson's had a little setback. His Wendy's job didn't work out and he's feeling depressed again. But don't give up. Things will work out soon. I love you more than anything. Mama. P.S. Julia Finch says 'Hi.'" I climb onto the bed with my back against the headboard and pull the pink quilt under my chin.

In about five minutes, I hear Shirley coming up the stairs.

She stares at me from the foot of the bed. "Why are you sitting in the dark?"

"I don't know."

"You can't see anything."

"I don't care."

"Mother says you miss the twins."

I nod.

"Don't you like it here?"

"I'm used to watching out for them."

She rocks from one foot to the other while she stares at me. Then she walks to the cupboard, takes out Squishy and Sook Kim and brings them back to the bed. She holds Sook Kim out for me.

I shake my head.

"Just hold her for a minute," she says, and sits next to me.

"Unh unh."

She props her up against my arm. "Squishy and Sook Kim are the twins and we're taking care of them."

"They're not here."

"I know, but close your eyes, and we'll think of something we're all doing together."

"I don't want to think of anything."

"Then I will," she says. "Okay, we're all in Disneyland. We're . . ."

"I've never been to Disneyland, and neither have Rachel and Rusty."

"Shh," she says. "I'll tell you what happens. We're in this little boat, going on the jungle ride. You and I are holding the twins real tight, and they're licking on chocolate ice-cream cones. We're riding along looking at the grass and daffodils on the riverbank when all at once we hear a big roar. Rachel jumps up and points behind a tree. 'It's a tiger,' she yells. 'He's got spots.' Rusty's sitting real still, smiling."

"He wouldn't do that. He'd be scared out of his wits."

"Not on this ride," she says. "The riverboat captain told us before we left, anybody sitting on somebody's lap and eating chocolate ice cream is safe. Now we just passed the tiger," she says. "Rusty's leaning over the side to see the green and purple and red agates at the bottom of the river. And you're holding on to him. Now he's dragging his hand in the water, trying to grab a big, shiny goldfish."

"That sounds more like him," I say, and pick up Sook Kim. "But I don't want to talk anymore."

"Oh all right," she says. Then we sit there for a while, holding Squishy and Sook Kim, just floating along in the boat.

I haven't heard from Mama for a few months, but I've seen the twins three times. They're still growing like weeds. The social worker says Carson's got a job as a night watchman and things look good. I nod, and want to ask her, "How long now?" but I know she won't be able to tell me. It's been two years I've been with Mom and Dad and Shirley, and Carson's jobs come and go.

In May when fifth grade gets out, Mom and Dad tell us we're going to Disneyland in June. "It'll be someplace special," Mom says, and she pulls out maps of Frontierland and Adventureland and Fantasyland.

"I think Adventureland will be the best," I say, "riding down that river with all those animals roaring and growling and hissing." Shirley says Fantasyland was her favorite, which doesn't surprise me. It sounds like one big pretend.

Mom buys me a sleeping bag and Shirley and me shorts and shirts and new tennis shoes. And Dad gets the car tuned up and buys a new spare tire and cleans out the trunk. There's a lot of work for a trip.

One morning, two weeks before we're supposed to leave, Mom walks in our room, looking real serious. Shirley and I are figuring out if we want to start with Adventureland or Fantasyland, but Mom says to put the materials away because she needs to talk to us. She sits on my bed and has this awful look on her face.

"Something happened to the twins or Mama, didn't it," I say.

"No, no," Mom says and lets out a big sigh. "It's just that . . ." She can't talk for a minute. Then she says, "Miss Cline called this morning, and says Ruth will be going back to her family next Saturday."

"The twins, too?" I ask her.

"Yes, honey."

"But why?" Shirley says and looks back and forth from Mom to me.

"Ruth's Mama and the twins want her to live with them."

"But she lives here."

Mom puts her arm around Shirley. "Sometimes things don't work out the way we plan, honey."

"But I don't want her to go," she says to Mom. "And what about

Disneyland?" Then she looks at me. "I thought you liked it here," she says and starts to cry.

I try to say something, but all I can do is shrug at her and swallow hard. My throat aches.

"It's not Ruth's decision," Mom says, but Shirley grabs Squishy and heads for the door. "We're going to the creek . . . by ourselves," she mumbles on the way out.

Mom looks at me. "She's just upset," she says. "It's not your fault."

I nod. Then she hugs me a long time.

When she lets go, I tell her we'd better get some orange crates. "There won't be room for a chest of drawers where I'm going."

"Okay," she says, and blows her nose. "And we can't forget your new sleeping bag."

"There won't be any camping out in Pocatello."

"It might come in handy sometime."

"Okay," I say, but know the only one it'll be handy for is Carson if he needs something to hock. He pawned off Mama's old diamond once, which raised a stink that didn't settle down for months.

"Everything will be all right. Don't worry," Mom says, then gives me another hug and leaves the room.

I nod, but she doesn't know Carson or apartments in Pocatello. I'm feeling tired and my stomach's starting to ache. For just a minute I think about hiding under the house when Miss Cline comes, but people always find you. Besides, the twins will need watching. I look around the room—at the chest of drawers and the closet where my Disneyland clothes are hanging beside Shirley's. And then I spot Sook Kim.

I close my eyes and think of Miss Cline hurrying up the driveway. "Ruth, Ruth," she yells. "Where are you? We have to go. Where are you, Ruth? Can you hear me?" But I don't answer. Because I'm not here. I'm standing in a field in China with Mom and Dad and Shirley and Rusty and Rachel and Mama and Julia Finch.

And what's the field made of?
Crawdads and daisies and one little cow pie,
All of us running and reaching to the sky,
Catching the butterfly kites that fly by,
That's what the field is made of.

Then I hug Sook Kim tight, open my new suitcase, and start packing.

Shelter

LOUISE ERDRICH

My four adopted sons in photographs
wear solemn black. Their faces comprehend
their mother's death, an absence in a well
of empty noise, and Otto strange and lost.
Her name was Mary also, Mary Kröger.
Two of us have lived and one is gone.
Her hair was blond; it floated back in wings,
and still you see her traces in the boys:
bright hair and long, thin, knotted woman's hands.
I knew her, Mary Kröger, and we were bosom friends.
All graves are shelters for our mislaid twins.

Otto was for many years her husband,
and that's the way I always thought of him.
I nursed her when she sickened and the cure
fell through at Rochester. The healing bath
that dropped her temperature, I think, too fast.
I was in attendance at her death:
She sent the others out. She rose and gripped my arm
and tried to make me promise that I'd care
for Otto and the boys. I had to turn away
as my own mother had when her time came.
How few do not return in memory
and make us act in ways we can't explain.
I could not lie to ease her, living, dying.
All graves are full of such accumulation.
And yet, the boys were waiting in New York
to take the first boat back to Otto's folks
in Germany, prewar, dark powers were at work,
and Otto asked me on the westbound bus
to marry him. I could not tell him no—
We help our neighbors out. I loved him though

It took me several years to know I did
from that first time he walked in to deliver

winter food. Through Father Adler's kitchen,
he shouldered half an ox like it was bread
and looked at me too long for simple greeting.
This is how our lives complete themselves,
as effortless as weather, circles blaze
in ordinary days, and through our waking selves
they reach, to touch our true and sleeping speech.

So I took up with Otto, took the boys
and watched for them, and made their daily bread
from what the grocer gave them in exchange
for helping him. It's hard to tell you how
they soon became so precious I got sick
from worry, and woke up for two months straight
and had to check them, sleeping, in their beds,
and had to watch and see each breathe or move
before I could regain my sleep again.
All graves are pregnant with our nearest kin.

Mileva

SUSAN ITO

Einstein: the world's wild-haired darling, the genius clown, wobbling
in the rain on his bicycle, his raincoat billowing, a charcoal sail.
We all loved him, love him still, but not like you did;
it was you who stroked that cloud of electric hair, strange and wild
like a windblown tree; your eyes who held his own,
heavy with memory, their creases holding sad secrets.

Mileva, your mind, too, was strung with brilliant lights,
your footsteps light and confident,
the girl who threw down her embroidery
and took up physics, the molecules spinning their own bright cloth.

Oh Mileva, those letters he wrote you, *Tell me what you think
of this theory?*
And amidst the scribbled numbers and equations, arrows arcing the
page, were circled endearments, the carbon smudged by his
trembling finger—
he loved you Leva, the scientist, the woman.

That day in 1902: a hot white morning when you told him
of the child.
the atoms stopped their spinning, leaned in to listen close,
to learn of their own folding away, how he promised
to forsake even them
for you, for the daughter quick inside your belly. You said no.
Albert, you said, *don't throw away your talent.*

The girl, Lieserl, born in the new year, was taken by nuns
to city parents
who promised picture books and pony rides, hot chocolate
in porcelain cups,
who braided her pale frizzled hair so tightly her ears ached.
You and Albert married; there were sons. He rose,
dazzling the world
yet with a strange earthy sadness like Chaplin's little tramp.

While his theories exploded under shattering bits of chalk,
you grew quiet, your bowed head shadowing your lap.

He still brought you his papers, although not as often.
He explained the qualities of energy behind your back
as you stirred pots of soup, buttoned the smallest one's sweater.
You said, *yes, yes,* while you thought of her,
eleven years old that month.
In the fluorescent auditorium, Albert's soft voice
fanned out through loudspeakers.
Relativity, he said. The room thundered with the striking of hands
as you whispered the word: *Relativity.*

You closed your eyes and saw her, standing between two strangers.
She was moving her lips saying, *This is my mother. This is my father.*
The people were all on their feet then, Albert nodding and beaming,
gesturing with his hands while you went to stand by him,
tear-streaked.
You wept into his collar, *She's gone forever—Lieserl, our little star.*

In the end you grew too dark, Mileva, a storm raging around him,
the hole inside you echoing *mama,*
her voice louder at times than even the boys' as they
pulled at your skirt, their high voices sternly telling you,
Smile Mother, for the newspaper people. You couldn't smile.
Albert, tired of nudging the edges of your mouth upward,
took his fingers away, slipped away from your home.

Photos from *LIFE* magazine, the *New York Times*
loved his ragged form.
You clipped them out, laid them down tenderly with crumbs of paste.
Sat alone at the dusky kitchen table drinking pale green wine,
after several hours slipping down
onto your knees and gently, gently unbraided
the woven rug, smoothed its rippled skeins under your palms.

Einstein Thinks about the Daughter He Put Up for Adoption and Then Could Never Find

JENNIFER CLEMENT

Perhaps
She uses her fingers
like a compass
making circles in the dirt.

Perhaps
she cuts her hand
in the dark day, splitting an atom
in the middle of her palm.

Particles of light curve
through glass-empty windows.

Numbers tattooed on her wrist
are blue equations,
and the knots in the barbed wire
look like stars.

He hugs his violin—
small body of wood.

A Perfect Life

CHITRA DIVAKARUNI

Before the boy came, I had a good life. A beautiful apartment in the foothills with a view of the Golden Gate Bridge, an interesting job at the bank with colleagues I mostly liked, and, of course, my boyfriend Richard.

Richard was exactly the kind of man I'd dreamed about during my teenage years in Calcutta, all those moist, sticky evenings that I spent at the Empire Cinema House under a rickety ceiling fan that revolved tiredly, eating melted mango-pista ice cream and watching Gregory Peck and Warren Beatty and Clint Eastwood. Tall and lean and sophisticated, he was very different from the Indian men I'd known back home, and even the work he did as a marketing manager for a publishing company seemed unbelievably glamorous. When I was with Richard I felt like a true American. We'd go jogging every morning and hiking on the weekends, and in the evenings we'd take in an art film, or go out to a favorite restaurant, or discuss a recent novel as we sat out on my balcony and drank chilled wine and watched the sunset. And in bed we tried wild and wonderful things that would have left me speechless with shock in India had I been able to imagine them.

What I liked most about Richard was that he gave me *space*. I'd been afraid that after we slept together he'd either lose interest in me or start pressuring me to marry him. Or else I'd get pregnant. That was what always happened in India. (My knowledge of such things, of course, was limited to the romantic Hindi movies I'd seen. At home, we never discussed such things, and though my girlfriends in college gossiped avidly about them, they were just as protected as I from what our parents considered sordid reality.) But Richard continued to be passionate without getting possessive. He didn't mind if I went out with my other friends, or if work pressures kept us from seeing each other for days; when we met again, we slipped into our usual comfortable groove, as though we hadn't been apart at all. Thanks to the Pill and his easygoing attitude (it was a California thing, he told me once), for the first time in my life I felt free. It was an exhilarating sensation, once I got used to it. It made me giddy and weightless, like I could float away at any moment.

Eventually Richard and I planned to get married and have children, but neither of us was in a hurry. The households of friends who had babies seemed to me a constant flurry of crying and feeding and burping and throwing up, quilts taped over fireplace bricks for padding, and knickknacks crammed onto top shelves out of the reach of destructive little hands. And over everything hung the oppressive stench (there was no other word for it) of baby wipes and Lysol spray and soiled diapers.

I guessed, of course, that there was more to child-rearing than that. Mother-love, for instance. I'd felt the flaming rush of it when I'd gone to the maternity ward to visit Sharmila, who'd been my best friend at work before she quit (abandoned me, I claimed) to have a baby.

Sharmila had pressed her cheek to the baby's wrinkled one, to that skin translucent and delicate like expensive onion-skin paper, and looked at me with eyes that shone in spite of the hollows gouged under them. "I'd never have thought I could love anyone so much, so instantly, Meera," she'd whispered. And this from a woman who'd always agreed that the world already had too many people in it for us to add to the problem! So I knew mother-love was real. Real and primitive and dangerous, lurking somewhere in the female genes—especially our Indian ones—waiting to attack. I was determined to watch out for it.

Many of my women friends considered me strange. The Americans were more circumspect, but the Indian women came right out and asked. *Don't you mind not being married? Don't you miss having a little one to scramble onto your lap when you come home at the end of the day?* I'd look at their limp hair pulled into an unattractive bun, their crumpled saris sporting stains of a suspicious nature, the bulge of love handles that hung below the edges of their blouses. (Even the ones who made an effort to hang on to their looks seemed intellectually diminished, their conversations limited to discussions of colic and teething pains and Dr. Spock's views on bed-wetting.) They looked just like my cousins back home who were already on their second and third and sometimes fourth babies. They might as well not have come to America.

"No," I would tell them, smoothing my silk Yves St. Laurent jersey over my own gratifyingly slim hips. "Most emphatically no."

But I could see they didn't believe me.

Nor did my mother, who for years had been trying to arrange my marriage with a nice Indian boy. Every month she sent me photos of eligible young men, nephews and second cousins of friends and neighbors, earnest, mustachioed men in stiff-collared shirts with slicked-back Brylcreem hair. She accompanied these photographs with warnings (I wasn't getting any younger; soon I'd be thirty and then who would want me?) and laments (Look at Roma-auntie, her daughter was expecting her third, while thanks to me, *she* remained deprived of grandchildren). When I wrote back that I wasn't ready to settle down (I didn't say anything about Richard, which would have upset her even more), she decried my crazy Western notions. "I should *never* have given in and allowed you to go to America," she wrote, underlining the "never" in emphatic red.

In spite of the brief twinge of guilt I felt when yet another fat packet with a Calcutta postmark arrived from my mother, I knew I was right. Because in Indian marriages becoming a wife was only the prelude to that all-important, all-consuming event—becoming a mother. That wasn't why I'd fought so hard with my mother to leave India; with my professors to make it through graduate school; with my bosses to establish my career. Not that I was against marriage—or even against having a child. I just wanted to make sure that when it happened, it would be on my own terms, because I wanted it.

Meanwhile, I heaved a sigh of relief whenever I came away from the baby-houses (that's how I thought of them, homes ruled by tiny red-faced tyrants with enormous lung power). Back in my own cool, clean living room I would put on a Ravi Shankar record or maybe a Chopin nocturne, change into the blue silk kimono that Richard had given me, and curl up on my fawn, buffed-leather sofa. As the soothing strains of sitar or piano washed over me, I would close my eyes and think of what we'd planned for that evening, Richard and I. And I would thank God for my life, which was as civilized, as much in control as *perfect,* as a life could ever be.

The boy changed all that.

He was crouched under the stairwell when I found him, on my way out of the building for my regular 6 A.M. jog around the rose gardens with Richard. I would have missed him completely had he not coughed just as I reached the door. He had wedged himself into the far end of the dark triangular recess, so that all I saw at first was a small, huddled shape and the glint of terrified eyes. And thought, *Wild animal.* Later I would wonder how I must have appeared to him, a large, loud, bent-over figure in pink sweats with hair swinging wildly about her face, ordering him to *come out of there right now,* demanding *where did you come from* and *how did you get past the security door.* Only probably he didn't understand a word.

By the time I got him out, my Liz Claiborne suit was ruined, my cheek stung where he had scratched me, and my watch said 6:20. *Richard,* I thought with dismay, because he didn't like to be kept waiting. Then the boy claimed my attention again.

He looked about seven, though he could have been older. He was so thin it was hard to tell. His collarbones stuck out from under his filthy shirt, and in the hollow between them I could see a pulse beating frantically. Ragged black hair fell into eyes that stared at me unblinkingly. He didn't seem to comprehend anything I said, not even when I switched to halting Spanish, and when I leaned forward, he flinched and flung up a thin brown arm to protect his face.

What am I going to do with him, I wondered desperately. It was getting late. I'd already missed my morning jog, and if I didn't get back to my apartment pretty soon, I wouldn't have time for my sit-ups either. Then I had to wash my hair—there was a big meeting at the bank, and I was scheduled to make the opening presentation. I hadn't figured out what kind of power-outfit to wear, either. I closed my eyes and hoped the boy would just disappear the way he had appeared, but when I opened them, he was there still, watching me warily.

I unlocked my apartment door but didn't enter right away. I was afraid of what I might find. Then I said to myself, *How could it be any worse?* I'd been late to work (a first). I'd run into the meeting room, out of breath, my unwashed hair falling into my eyes, my spreadsheets all out of order. My presentation had been second-rate at best (another first), and when Dan Luftner, Head of Loans, who'd been waiting for years to catch me out, asked me for an update on the monthly statements software the bank had purchased a while back, I'd been unable to give him an adequate answer. "Why, Meera," he'd said, raising his eyebrows in mock surprise, "I thought you knew *everything!*" I smarted all morning at the memory of the triumph in his eyes, and when a customer asked a particularly stupid question, I snapped at him. "Are you feeling all right, Meera?" said my supervisor, who had overheard. "Maybe you should take the rest of the day off." So here I was in the middle of the afternoon, with the mother of all headaches pounding its way across my skull.

I'm going to spend the rest of the day in bed, I decided, with the curtains drawn, the phone off the hook, a handkerchief soaked in eau de cologne on my forehead, and strict instructions to the boy to not disturb me. When my headache gets better, I'm going to listen to the new Dvorak record which Richard gave me for Valentine's day. Everything else—including calling Richard to explain why I hadn't shown up—I'll handle later.

As soon as I opened the door I was struck by the smell. It was worse than ten baby-houses put together. I followed my nose to the bathroom. There was pee all over the floor, a big yellow puddle, with blobs of brown floating in it.

I went into the kitchen, took two aspirin, then another one. I grabbed the mop and bucket and a bottle of Pine Sol and went looking for the boy, rehearsing all the things I was going to tell him. *You little savage, didn't I explain to you how to use the toilet before I left, at least ten times, in clear sign language? That's what made me late this morning, messed up my presentation. If I don't get chosen as employee of the month like I was the last three times, it's going to be all your fault.* I was going to make him clean up the bathroom was well. But first I was going to shake him until his teeth rattled in his stupid head.

"You should have turned him over to the super that same morning," Richard would tell me later. "You should never have brought him into your apartment at all. I can't figure out why you did it—it isn't like you at all."

Richard was right, of course, on both counts. I've never been given to the easy sentimentality of taking in strays—I know my own fastidiousness, the limits to my patience. The first thought I'd had when I saw the boy was that I should call the super. Mr. Leroy, a large, not unkind man with children of his own, would have known what to do with the boy. Better than I did, certainly.

So why didn't I make that call? Did my decision have something to do with the boy's enormous eyes, the way he fixed them on my face? The way his thin shoulders had trembled, there, under the staircase, when I touched them? Did a part of me, that treacherous Indian side that believed in the workings of karma, feel that the universe had brought him to my door for a special reason? I'm not sure. But even now, as I searched the apartment angrily, I knew I couldn't send him away.

I finally found him behind the drapes in the bedroom. He shrank against the wall when he saw me. I could hear the hiss of his indrawn breath, see his shoulders stiffen. He made a small moaning sound that seemed to go on and on.

"Oh shit." I gave a short laugh as the appropriateness of my expression struck me. "Don't look so scared, for God's sake. Just don't do it again, OK? And now I guess you'd better take a bath."

"Sharmila," I said on the phone, "what's a good place to buy clothes for kids?"

"Why'd you want to know? You planning to have one?"

"Very funny. Actually, my brother's son is visiting, and . . ." My voice trailed away guiltily. I'd never lied to Sharmila before. But the boy was my special secret. I wasn't ready to share him with anyone yet.

"Your brother! Didn't you tell me once you were an only child?"

"Did I? Maybe I'd just had a fight with him or something."

"Hmm," said Sharmila, obviously unconvinced. "Well, how old is the boy? Some stores are better for babies, and others . . ."

"He looks like he's about seven . . ."

"Looks like? You don't know your own nephew's age?"

"So I'm not as close to my family as you are, Madam Perfect," I shouted. "I'm sorry I asked." I slammed down the phone, then took it off the hook. Sharmila would surely call back to find out why I—who never got upset, not even the time when the bank computer suddenly swallowed the information on 563 accounts—was behaving so strangely. She might even decide to drive over. And I was afraid of what she would say when she found out about the boy.

I looked over to the kitchen table and met the boy's worried eyes. "It's OK," I said. "I'm not mad at you." I smiled at him until the frown line between his brows faded. I was pleased to see that he'd eaten most of the large egg sandwich I'd fixed him and that he'd drunk all his milk. He looked a lot better after his bath, with his hair all shiny and his face clean, and weren't the circles under his eyes a little lighter?

The bath had been difficult. He wouldn't go into the tub by himself, so I had to make him. "I'm not going to hurt you," I kept saying. Still, when I took off his shirt, he struggled and trembled, with that same moaning sound, holding on to his tattered pants until I said, "OK, OK, keep them on." I put him in the tub and started soaping him, and that's when I felt them, the puckers of old burns along his back. *Cigarettes? Who?* I tried to imagine someone—a man? a *woman?*—holding him down, his body trembling like a caught bird's under the enormous press of that adult arm, the burning butt jabbed into his back over and over until he stopped making even that thin, whimpering sound. Then I was crying, holding him tight and crying, the lukewarm sudsy water soaking my white Givenchy blouse that I'd forgotten to change out of, and I didn't even care.

We'd made it through the bath somehow, and now he was dressed in a pair of my cutoffs tied around his middle with my kimono belt and an aquamarine Moschino shirt that hung almost to his knees. On his feet he wore my old Hawaiian sandals.

"What the heck," I said, forcing a smile onto my face. "There's a lot of folks out there dressed more weirdly than you. Let's go shopping. Ever heard of Macy's, kid?"

But all the while I was thinking, *Could it have been someone in his family? Could it have been his father? Could it—God help us all—have been his mother?*

When the doorbell rang with the two impatient double buzzes I knew to be Sharmila's, I was fixing lunch: peanut butter and jelly sandwiches and alphabet soup. I didn't know if the boy knew his ABCs yet, or if he cared for peanut butter, but generations of children on TV shows seemed to thrive on them, so they couldn't be too bad. I wondered if I could get away with not answering, but now Sharmila was pounding on the door.

"Nothing to worry," I told the boy, who'd jumped up from his chair and backed into the corner by the refrigerator. "You get started on the soup while it's hot."

"Knew you were in here," said Sharmila, pushing past me. She seemed to be carrying an entire household on her back, but on a closer look I saw it was only the baby, wrapped in a quilt and positioned inside some kind of sack that seemed to double as a diaper bag as well. "I knew something was really wrong when I called the bank and they said you'd taken a day off. You *never* take a day off."

I mumbled something about having accumulated a lot of vacation time.

"Right," said Sharmila. "And I was born yesterday. Here, help me get this damn thing off. I swear it weighs a ton. No, Mummy's not complaining about you, *raja beta,* just your baggage." This last was to the baby, who looked like he was getting ready to scream. But before he could, Sharmila adroitly popped a pacifier into his mouth and turned toward the kitchen. "So this is the young man," she said.

"His name is Krishna," I said, struck by a happy inspiration. I needed to give him a name anyway (he didn't seem to have one), and that of a demon-destroying god who was raised by a foster mother seemed a good choice. This way, his friends at school could call him Kris.

"For heaven's sake, Meera, the boy doesn't even look Indian. Now tell me the whole story and don't you dare leave anything out."

By the time I finished, the shadows from the pepper tree outside slanted across the room. Sharmila wiped at her eyes. She picked up her baby and held him close for a long moment. The baby gurgled with laughter and Krishna, who'd been hovering around him all afternoon, reached out to touch his chubby hand. The baby grabbed his finger. Krishna, too, was laughing now—for the first time, I told Sharmila.

"Maybe he used to have a little brother or sister, poor kid," said Sharmila, watching him play with her son. Then she turned to me. "I know how you feel, Meera, but you can't just *keep* him . . ."

"Why not?" I said, talking fast. I didn't want to hear what was coming next. I was afraid her words would echo the objections I'd kept pushing to the back of my own mind. "I can give him a good home. I can . . ."

"What if he's lost? Maybe his family's looking for him right now . . ."

I felt a pang of guilt. Then I shrugged it off resolutely. Angrily. *So what if they were,* I thought, remembering the burn marks. But I only said, "He looked like he'd been on his own a long time."

"Even then, sooner or later he'll have to go to school, and then you'll need a birth certificate, a social security number, something to show that you're his guardian . . ."

"What if I move someplace where no one knows us? What if I say I lost all our papers in a fire?"

"Meera," Sharmila said patiently, "you know that won't work. Maybe it would have in India, but not here, where everyone keeps records—hospitals, doctors. No, you've got to do it the legal way."

"Adoption! That's out of the question!" exclaimed Richard, so sharply that heads turned toward our table.

I pushed away my half-eaten dinner, although it was grilled salmon with a light almond sauce on the side, which I particularly like.

"Why? Why is it out of the question?" My voice was sharp, too—mostly to hide my dismay. There was a cold, leaden heaviness in the pit of my stomach. I'd expected some arguments, but I hadn't thought Richard would be so strongly opposed to my plan. In fact, I'd hoped he'd help me iron out the details, once we'd talked things over. I was shaken by how disapproving his voice sounded, how final and filled with distaste. And he hadn't even met Krishna.

We were dining at Le Gourmand, which is a bit too fancy for me with its French menu (they'll give you one in English if you ask, but grudgingly), its napkins edged with real lace (Belgian, Richard tells me), and an intimidating array of monogrammed silverware (there were four forks by my plate, not to count knives and spoons). But Richard really enjoys this kind of thing. And since I wanted to put him in a good mood, I'd invited him here.

So far the evening wasn't going well at all.

"Stupid. You did a stupid thing, Meera, bringing him into the apartment," Richard had said when I told him about Krishna. His tone made me bristle right away. No man was going to call me stupid and get away with it. And he sounded so *avuncular*, so I-know-it-all. So unlike himself. *Or was this,* an insidious voice inside me asked, *the real Richard?*

"Stupid and dangerous," he was saying now. "I can't believe you've kept him for over week. You could get into a lot of trouble with the law. They could bring all kinds of charges against you—kidnapping, child abuse . . ."

"And since when do you know so much about the law, Mr. Perry

Mason?" I broke in. The bit about child abuse had brought back too vividly the feel of those puckered scars under my fingers. I made my voice hard because I didn't want to cry in front of Richard. "Or have you had personal experience with the charges you just mentioned?"

I guess I didn't sound like myself either, because Richard's mouth opened in a brief O that made him look astonished and indignant at the same time. I could feel hysterical laughter gathering itself inside me. We were about to have our first fight. I was surprised to find that I was almost looking forward to it.

But of course Richard is too civilized to fight. After a moment he said, his voice carefully controlled, "I can see you're too emotional to think clearly. But this can't go on. For one thing, how long can you keep him holed up in your apartment?"

I thought about it. Krishna and I had established a good routine. We ate breakfast together in the mornings and watched the news. While I was at work, he amused himself by looking through the pictures in the books I brought for him from the library. When I got back from work, we usually went to the park (we'd bought ourselves a kite) or the library, or sometimes rented a video—he liked movies about animals. After dinner we'd sit together on the couch and watch it and talk about the more exciting scenes. Actually, I was the one who did all the talking. I still hadn't got him to say anything. He wouldn't even nod or shake his head in a yes or no. But I was sure he understood everything I said. He knew the house rules and followed them carefully: no going out on the balcony where someone could see him, no opening drawers in my bedroom, no answering the door. He had learned to use the microwave oven and the bathroom, and to make himself (and me, whenever I managed to rush home for a quick lunch) sandwiches slathered with peanut butter and jelly. And at night when I fixed dinner he liked to be near me, doing little things: breaking up the spaghetti, washing the spinach leaves, slicing the salad tomatoes into neat rounds that hinted at previous experience. Perhaps he had been used to helping his mother.

His mother.

I'd made myself decide he didn't have a mother, for surely she would have stood between him and that burning cigarette, as mothers are supposed to. But she appeared in my dreams almost every night, weeping as she looked around, bewildered, for her son. Sometimes her eyes would meet mine, accusing. I would stare back defiantly. *You should have been more careful,* I'd tell her. *You shouldn't have lost him.*

"I can keep him holed up for a long time if I need to," I told Richard, though even then I must have known it wasn't possible. I lifted my chin. "And now I'd like to go home. I don't like to leave Krishna alone this late at night."

I heard the patter of his feet even before I turned the key, and when I opened the apartment door, he was waiting. He took my hand and pulled me to the couch and put into my hands the book we'd been reading earlier. When I'd picked up the book, a simple story about a mouse family that lived in a vegetable garden, I'd been afraid it would be too childish for Krishna, but he loved it. He'd sit for long minutes tracing the bright vegetables with his finger—eggplant, zucchini, beans, lettuce—as though he knew the feel of them intimately. And when we came to the part where Baby Mouse wanders off and gets lost and doesn't hear her parents calling for her, his entire body would grow still with tense attention.

We settled ourselves on the couch, Krishna leaning over the book so he could turn the pages for me. (Somehow he knew just when to do it, though I was pretty sure he couldn't read.) Usually I enjoyed reading to him, but tonight I found it hard to concentrate. I kept thinking of what Richard had said when he dropped me off.

He'd offered to accompany me upstairs, and when I'd refused (somehow I couldn't stand the thought of his eyes, cool and critical, traveling up and down Krishna), he'd gripped my shoulders and pulled me to face him. "You're obsessed with this boy, Meera," he'd said. In the flickering light of the street lamp I could see the lines around his mouth, sharp and deep like cracks in porcelain, before he bent to kiss me hard on the lips. The violent press of his mouth against mine, so unlike his usual suave embraces, startled me. Was he jealous? Was he, perhaps, not that different after all from the heroes of the Hindi screen whom I'd left behind in Calcutta?

"Maybe what you need is a child of your own," he said, trying to kiss me again.

I thought of Krishna waiting upstairs. The way a faint line would appear between his brows when he concentrated on something I was saying. "Maybe what I need is to not see you for a while," I'd snapped, pushing Richard away.

But what he said had struck deep.

Sitting on the sofa now, I tried to imagine it. My child—and Richard's, for that was what he meant. But somehow I just couldn't picture it. The details confused me. Would the baby have a thick dark mop of hair, like Indian babies do? Or would it be pink and bald, like American babies? What color would its eyes be? I couldn't picture Richard in the role of father either, hitching up his Armani pants to kneel on the floor and change diapers, walking up and down at 2 A.M. trying to quieten a colicky baby who burped all over his satin Bill Blass dressing gown.

It was much easier to picture Krishna. He is running in the park. While I cheer, he pulls the kite up in a tight purple arc until it hangs high above his head, as graceful as any bird. On the first day of school, I drop him off at the gate, hand him his lunch money with a kiss, watch him follow the other kids in. He turns at the door to offer me a tremulous smile and a wave, scared but determined to be brave. At Disneyland, we scream with delicious terror as the roller-coaster car plunges down, down, down, faster than we ever imagined anything could ever be. At baseball games I clap for him till my palms are sore. I take him to buy his first car. I help him to fill out his college applications. Late in the night we sit as we're doing right now and talk about life and death and girls and rock music or whatever else it is that mothers and sons talk about. There is no Richard in these pictures, and (I feel only a moment's guilt as I think this) no need of him.

Krishna was looking at me inquiringly. Glancing down, I saw we'd reached the end of the book—probably several minutes back.

"It's time for bed, young man," I said. When I leaned over to give him a hug, his skin smelled of my jasmine soap. It pleased me that he no longer flinched away from me, not even when, after his bath every morning, I rubbed face cream on his scars. (They were probably too old for it to do any good, but it made me feel better.) And now, though he didn't hug me back, he did tilt his cheek toward me for his customary goodnight kiss.

As I watched him bring over his sheets and blankets (all carefully folded—he was a neat boy) to the sofa where he slept, I noticed that he'd put on a few pounds. It made me ridiculously happy, more than the time, even, when I straightened out the Von Hausen account, which had been missing several million dollars. He was getting taller, too. Or maybe it was just the way he walked nowadays, shoulders pushed back, head up high.

Tomorrow, I promised myself as I helped him with the sheets. Tomorrow I would start making discreet inquiries into the California adoption laws.

Sitting across the desk from Ms. Mayhew while she went through my papers one more time, I was struck again by how cheerful the Foster Homes office was. I'd expected something drab and regulation gray, with lots of metal furniture. Instead, the room was bright with hangings and rugs, and through the big window, the afternoon sun lit up the play corner, which was comfortably crowded with stuffed animals and bean bags and big, colorful blocks. They had books too, even the one about the mouse family that Krishna loved. I wondered if I could take that to be a good omen.

Mrs. Mayhew herself was quite different from the witch-like figure I'd conjured up—complete with horn-rimmed glasses, a thin pointy nose, and gray hair pulled into a tight, unforgiving bun. She did wear glasses, but they had thin gold rims that gave her a rather thoughtful look, and her short, fashionably bobbed hair curled attractively around her face. She was pleasant in a businesslike way—no wasting time or getting around rules with her—which I appreciated because that's how I too was at the bank. When the county office I'd called referred me to her, she had explained that adoption was a lengthy and complicated process, but the State of California was always looking for responsible foster parents. It would be a good thing for me to try while I figured out if adoption was really for me.

Though I had no doubts about that issue, I agreed. It was the best way of keeping Krishna with me legally until the adoption could be arranged.

Surprisingly, Richard too liked the idea. I suspected that deep down he was hoping that the novelty of having a child in the house would wear out for me long before the adoption papers came through. I knew better, of course, but I didn't want to argue. Richard had been making a real effort to be nice. When I finally invited him over to meet Krishna (I was still reluctant, but I figured I had to do it some time), he'd brought him a baseball and a catcher's mitt. When Krishna refused to come out from behind the curtain where he'd hidden himself at the first sound of a male voice, Richard said he understood. He even offered to take him to the park to practice, "once we get a bit more used to each other." I appreciated that. It didn't make me change the pictures in my head, which were still just of me and Krishna, but I started going out with Richard again.

"Well, Ms. Bose"—Ms. Mayhew was looking up with a smile—"your papers look good so far. The recommendation letters are all very positive, your fingerprints indicate you've lived a crime-free life, and I see from the social worker's home visit that you've child-proofed your apartment as required and are changing the study into an extra bedroom. Just one more week of the parenting class you're attending, and you'll be ready to be a foster mother. So now it's time for us to discuss further the kind of child you want to take in."

This part was going to be tricky. I had to say it just right.

"In your papers," Ms. Mayhew continued, "you mentioned that you wanted a boy of about seven or eight—which is a good idea since you have a full-time job. But you didn't mention ethnicity—or doesn't it matter?"

"Actually, you don't need to look for a child for me. I have one in mind already."

Ms. Mayhew's brows drew together. I'd deviated from regulations. "Where is he staying now? With relatives?"

I swallowed. "He's staying with me."

"And are you related to him?"

"No." Seeing the look on her face, I hurried to explain Krishna's situation. "I knew I probably should have turned him in," I ended, "but he was so small and so scared. . . ." Even to my own ears, my reasoning sounded weak and sentimental.

"Where was he when the social worker came to check your apartment?"

"With friends," I said guiltily. I'd deposited him at Sharmila's early that morning, not wanting to take a chance.

Ms. Mayhew was shaking her head. "What you've done is quite illegal, Ms. Bose, even though your motives may have been altruistic. I'm afraid we must ask you to bring the child in at once. We need to make every effort to locate his parents. . . ."

I wanted to tell her about the burns, but I didn't. *Later,* I thought. It would be my weapon if she really did find them.

"If they can be located, we'll try to place him with you once you become a registered foster parent. But for now he must stay with someone else."

"It's just a week." I leaned forward, gripping the edge of her desk. "Can't you make an exception, please, just for one week? He's doing so well with me. He'll be terrified if he's moved to a strange place . . ."

"I'm sorry. I have to follow certain rules, and this is a very important one. Actually, what you've done is quite serious. It could even prevent you from becoming a foster parent."

The edges of the room turned black.

But I'll put a note into your file saying that you acted out of ignorance and in good faith," said Ms. Mayhew, not unkindly. "That's the best I can do."

I knew it was no use arguing any further. I answered the questions she asked me about Krishna's background the best I could, and then I said, "I'll bring him in tomorrow." I looked at her and added, "Please?"

For a moment I was afraid that Ms. Mayhew was going to insist that I bring Krishna in that very afternoon. Then she glanced at her watch and gave a sigh. "Oh, OK," she said, "since it's after three already. But mind you, be here at 9 A.M. sharp tomorrow, as soon as the office opens.

"Sharmila, what am I going to *do?*" I tried to keep my voice calm and low, not wanting to frighten Krishna, who was building a Lego tower in the corner. But his head jerked up sharply.

"I don't see that you have a choice. You've got to take him in tomorrow." Sharmila's voice over the phone line was sympathetic but firm. "You'll get in a lot more trouble if you don't."

"I shouldn't even have started this whole process. I should have just taken Krishna and gone back to India. . . ."

"Meera!"

"I was a fool to tell her about him! I should have just pretended I wanted them to find me a child, at least until I got the license. . . ."

"And then what? Call and say, 'Oh, by the way, guess who turned up in my apartment yesterday?' That would never have worked, Meera. They would have seen through it right away. I think telling the truth was for the best. And this Mayhew woman seems quite positively inclined toward you. . . ."

"How can you *say* that? She's the one who insists that I have to turn him over. . . ." Though I'd avoided using Krishna's name, he made a sudden movement. The Lego tower fell over with a crash. On Sharmila's end I could hear her baby crying, and I wondered if he had picked up on the tension as well.

"She's just doing her job. If you were in her place, you'd probably have done the same."

"Never," I said hotly, but I knew Sharmila was right.

"I'm sorry, Meera, I've got to go. Baby's screaming his head off in his crib. He's been real cranky all day. I don't know what's wrong." Sharmila sounded anxious.

I felt guilty. I'd heaped all my troubles on her without even asking about her son. "You go take care of him. I'll be all right."

"Don't worry too much. It's only a week, after all. Explain to Krishna—he's a smart boy, he'll understand. Listen, I'll come with you tomorrow if you want."

"Would you?" I said gratefully. "That would make me feel so much better." I dreaded, most of all, the ride back alone, the stepping into my empty apartment.

The crying in the background had given place to angry shrieks. "Sure thing!" said Sharmila hurriedly as she hung up. "See you in the morning!"

That night I cooked Krishna's favorite dish, spicy fried chicken served over hot rice. It was one of my favorites, too, but I couldn't eat more than a few mouthfuls. A feeling of dread pressed down on me, and though I told myself I was being foolish, I couldn't shake it off.

After dinner was our regular reading time. But when Krishna brought the mouse book over to the sofa, I took a deep breath and shook my head.

"I have to tell you something first," I said.

When I explained to him where we had to go in the morning, and why, the blank expression on his face didn't change. When I told him that he must have faith in me, that I'd do my best to get him back as soon as I could, he waited politely, and when he was sure that I was done, he put the book in my lap.

As I read to him about how Baby Mouse's parents find her again, I wasn't sure what I felt more deeply, relief or hurt. Had Krishna not understood me? Was he autistic? (Richard had suggested that once, and I had denied it hotly.) Or did he just not care?

That night I couldn't sleep. I lay there watching the shadows thrown onto my wall by the street lamp outside, thinking how strange the nature of love is and how strangely it transforms people. The street noises quietened. The shadows shivered on the wall and across the vast white expanse of my bed, making me shiver too. Then I noticed that another shadow had joined them.

It was Krishna, his pillow tucked under his arm, his face as unreadable as ever.

"Can't you sleep either?" I asked.

He said nothing, of course.

"Oh well," I said, raising the corner of my blanket even though I knew that this was probably the number one taboo in Ms. Mayhew's book, "climb in."

He settled himself with his back toward me, the mattress hardly dimpling under him, he was still that thin. I touched his hair with a light finger and tried to think of something that would comfort him, maybe one of the lullabies that my mother had sung for me when I was little, an impossibly long time ago. But I had forgotten them all. The only thing I remembered was how my mother had held me. And so I tried to do the same for Krishna, looping an arm over his body, not with my mother's easy confidence but hesitantly, fearfully, as though he might break. That's how I lay all night as his breathing deepened and his body slumped against mine in trustful sleep, his scarred spine pressed to my chest, his skin giving off the mingled odor of jasmine and spicy chicken.

The phone jangled me out of a sleep I must have just fallen into. My eyes burned with tiredness, and my body ached as though I were coming down with something. Still, as I groped for the phone, I noticed how in his sleep Krishna had moved until his head was snuggled under my chin, and how right it felt.

"Meera." Sharmila's voice sounded like she too hadn't had much sleep. "It's my baby. He cried all night. I've given him his gas medicine and his gripe water and even some baby Tylenol, but none of it seems to do any good. And now he's throwing up. I've got to rush him to the clinic."

I wanted to say something to express my concern, but all I could manage was a "Yes, of course you must."

"Meera, wake up! This means I can't go with you to the Foster Homes office."

Remembrance struck like a stone between my eyes.

"Oh God," I said. I wanted to crawl back into bed and pull the covers up over myself and Krishna. Forever.

"I'm really sorry to let you down," said Sharmila. "But I have no choice."

I wanted to tell her that I understood perfectly. The needs of children came before the needs of adults, I had learned that already. Mother-love, that tidal wave, swept everything else away. Friendship. Romantic fulfillment. Even the need for sex.

"Meera, are you listening? I don't want you to have to go there alone. Will you call Richard, please? See if he can go with you."

"OK," I said, partly because Sharmila sounded so distressed, and partly because I was still dazed. When she hung up after having made me promise once again, I obediently dialed Richard's number.

"In a few minutes I'd like to introduce you to Mrs. Amelia Ortiz," said Ms. Mayhew, smiling. In a warm brown skirt and matching jacket, she looked both efficient and charming. I felt neither and didn't smile back. But Richard, who was sitting next to me holding my hand, did.

"We tried to find someone quickly so that the child wouldn't have to go into the Children's Shelter, which isn't the most pleasant experience, and she was kind enough to agree at such short notice."

"I'm sure Meera and little Krishna appreciate that," said Richard, squeezing my hand.

I wanted to snatch my hand away and inform him that I was capable of voicing my own opinions, thank you. But I knew I needed to save all my emotional energy. At the sound of his name, Krishna had looked up, his eyes moving from face to adult face till they came to rest on mine. He didn't look particularly anxious, but he clutched tightly at my other hand and pushed in closer to my chair.

"I can tell the little boy is very attached to you," said Ms. Mayhew. "I'll make every attempt to place him back with you as soon as it's legally possible. Meanwhile Mrs. Ortiz—here she is—will take good care of him."

I swung around to face Mrs. Amelia Ortiz, a plump middle-aged woman in a floral print dress who was dabbing at her face with a handkerchief. "Sorry to be late. The traffic was worse than I expected," she said in a pleasant, slightly out-of-breath voice and held out her hand to me with a smile. She looked kind and wholesome and motherly, and I hated her.

"I think the boy will feel quite at home with Mrs. Ortiz, who has two children herself. However, I must ask you not to contact him while he is with her—it'll only agitate him. By the way, Mrs. Ortiz speaks Spanish, which I thought would help in case that is his native language."

"Isn't that nice," said Richard.

"*Hola, mi pequenito,*" said Mrs. Ortiz, bending down to Krishna. But when he shrank toward me, she moved back right away. "No rush," she said.

My antagonism lessened a little. "His name is Krishna," I told her. "You can call him Kris."

Mrs. Ortiz nodded at me. "I will."

"He likes books, especially that one there about the mouse family."

Mrs. Ortiz picked up the book and held it out. "Chris, would you like me to read you this book?"

Krishna looked uncertain.

I gave him a little push. "Go on," I said, and he moved hesitantly toward her.

"Well!" Richard stood up. "It looks like everything is settled for now. Meera and I had better get back to our work. . . ."

He held out his hand to me. I had to stand up too, although I wasn't quite ready to leave.

"His clothes are in this bag—I packed enough for the week. His favorite T-shirt is the red Mickey Mouse one. And for dinner he likes to eat . . ." My voice wobbled.

"Don't worry about Chris," said Mrs. Ortiz with a sympathetic smile. "He'll be OK."

I picked up my purse. There seemed nothing left for me to do. "Good-bye, Krishna," I said and started toward the door. "I'll see you soon."

Krishna pushed past Mrs. Ortiz and launched himself at my knees. He grabbed them and held on tight.

"This is often the hardest part," said Ms. Mayhew as she and Mrs. Ortiz tried to pull him loose. "You probably won't believe it, but they often calm down right after you leave."

Krishna clung to me with unexpected tenacity. I knew I should be trying to help the women, at least by saying the right things—*Be a good boy and go with the nice lady, it's only for a little while*—but it was as though my tongue were frozen right down to its root. It was all I could do not to cling on to him too.

"This is ridiculous," Richard said after he had watched us for a few minutes. Bending, he pried Krishna's fingers loose. Ignoring the kicks Krishna aimed at his shins and deftly avoiding his bared teeth, he handed him over to the two women. While he struggled fiercely—like he had with me that first day which seemed so long ago now—Richard grabbed my elbow and pulled me toward the door.

"Mama!" Krishna cried out then. "Mama!"

I whirled around. Tears were streaming down his face. "Mama-mama-mama," he called, his voice as high and sweet as I had imagined it would be, the words pouring out as though a stopper had been removed from his throat.

"He's never spoken before," I said. No one seemed to have heard me.

"Ms. Bose, you're making things harder by staying," said Ms. Mayhew, her glasses accusingly askew.

"Please, yes, do leave," said Mrs. Ortiz, red-faced and breathing hard.

"I've got to go to Krishna one last time," I said, trying to pull away from Richard. I don't know what I had in mind—a last hug, a final kiss, some word of reassurance that would keep him safe till I saw him again. But Richard wouldn't let go.

"Take him away," he shouted to the women, and as they dragged Krishna, crying and kicking, into another room, he pushed me—also struggling—out the door and into his car.

"Phew," he said once we were in the car. "That kid's worse than a wild animal!" He fingered the torn cuff of his shirt and shook his head in a way that made me want to rip the entire sleeve off.

"I'll never forgive you for this," I said. I clenched my hands but the trembling in them wouldn't stop. "You kept me from going to my baby when he needed me most."

"For heaven's sake, Meera, don't exaggerate. He's not your baby. And besides, it's better for him that we cut the parting short."

"You don't know anything," I said. Suddenly I felt very tired. Old. An old woman. Unmarried, childless, a failure. There was a name for such women in India, *banja,* empty. I put my face in my hands and let the sounds of Richard's voice flow over me until they faded away.

For the next three days, carefully, correctly, I did all the things I was supposed to. I went to the bank, where I completed installing a new software program on the teller machines. In the study, now converted into a boy's bedroom, I arranged Krishna's books on the shelves and put up posters of animals. (There were no mouse posters available, so I had to make do with wide-eyed puppies and cats peeping from baskets.) I went to visit Sharmila, whose baby was now doing much better, though she was still too exhausted to ask me her usual sharp questions. I attended my last parenting class and received my certificate from the smiling instructor, who congratulated me on a job well done. I didn't call Amelia Ortiz, not even once, though several times each day I looked at her number in the phone book.

On the fourth day when I came back from my solitary morning jog, the red Cyclops eye on the answering machine was blinking ominously. I turned the machine on with unsteady fingers, telling myself that it was stupid to get so nervous, it could be anyone, Sharmila, or perhaps Richard—he'd been leaving a lot of messages on my machine lately. But of course it wasn't.

"Please come over to the office at 9 A.M.," said the message. I replayed it several times, trying to read the terse inflections of Ms. Mayhew's voice. Her tone didn't give much away, but I knew it was bad news, something really serious.

"Krishna," I whispered. The word was a dull, dead sound in my mouth.

"I just went in for a moment," Amelia Ortiz was telling us, "just for a moment to answer the phone, and when I came back out into the backyard where he'd been helping me with the weeding, he was gone." She wiped at her tear-streaked face with a balled-up Kleenex. "At first I thought he must be in the house—the gate was still latched. But he wasn't. He must have climbed over the wall or something."

I sat in front of Ms. Mayhew's meticulous desk, stupidly silent. I kept waiting for the anger to hit me, but I felt nothing.

"Of course Mrs. Ortiz called the police right away, but they couldn't find him. They're going to keep searching for the next few days." Behind her glasses, Ms. Mayhew's eyes looked tired. "I thought I should let you know."

"Six years I've been a foster mother, this never happened to me," said Mrs. Ortiz. "And he was so good too, so quiet and neat and obedient, who would have thought . . ."

From outside the window, a eucalyptus tree that surely hadn't been there the last time was throwing an intricate pattern of light and shadow onto Ms. Mayhew's desk, onto the solid brass plaque bearing her name. The plaque, I noticed, sat at a crooked angle. I felt a crazy impulse to reach out and straighten it.

"Ms. Bose, are you feeling OK?" Ms. Mayhew leaned across the desk to touch my hand.

The feel of her fingers, warm and moist on my cold, cold hand, shattered the numbness inside me. I snatched my arm back and sprang up so fast that my chair toppled to the carpeted floor with a thud.

"Don't touch me, you bitch," I heard myself say, low and furious, in a stranger's voice. "None of this would have happened if you'd let him stay with me for a week—just one more week—instead of sending him off with this—this cow. But no, you had to be legal. *Legal!*"

"Ms. Bose." Ms. Mayhew spoke calmly enough, but her face was white. Mrs. Ortiz had clapped a shocked hand over her mouth. "I realize you're upset, but it doesn't help to point the finger at other people or call them names. Mrs. Ortiz did the best she could—she's not a jailer, after all. And though you seem to have such little regard for the laws of the State of California, I *am* obliged to follow them."

I was already at the door.

"I'm going to go look for my little boy," I shouted over my shoulder, "and if I find him, this time sure as hell I'm not going to hand him over to you." I slammed the door hard behind me and was pleased to feel the walls shake. But it was a small, hollow pleasure.

I searched for Krishna all that day, and the next, and the next. All week I drove up and down the streets of Mrs. Ortiz's neighborhood, stopping passersby to ask if they had seen him. I even went up into the foothills which were several miles from her house. I struggled through groves of eucalyptus and thorny thickets of scrub oak, calling Krishna's name. At night I ignored the stares of the other tenants and sat for hours on the front steps of my building, my legs aching, my arms stinging from the thorns, waiting and hoping.

But I didn't really expect him to turn up. I wouldn't have come back either to someone who'd taken me in only to give me up, who had loved me briefly only to betray me forever.

It's been more than a year since then, a time in which my life has returned pretty much to normal. As Richard says, you can only mourn so long. I guess he's right.

For a while though, it was touch and go. I wouldn't answer the anxious messages Richard left on my answering machine, and when he showed up at the apartment I threatened to call the police if he didn't leave me alone. Even with Sharmila I refused to discuss Krishna. I considered quitting my job—I was doing so badly I was close to being fired anyway—and returning to India. I spent a lot of time going through the photos of the Brylcreemed men my mother had sent me. At one point I wrote her a letter saying that I would consider an arranged marriage if she could find me a widower with a little boy of about seven. Such a man, I reasoned, would understand about mother-love far more than Richard—or any other American male, for that matter—ever could. But I never posted the letter. Even then, crazy as I was with anger and sorrow and guilt, I knew that would have been a bigger mistake than the ones I'd made already.

And I was right. Things are good again. Recently I received a promotion at work for debugging a data-entry program that was driving everyone crazy. Even Dan Luftner stopped by my office to say thank you. I've moved to a bigger, better apartment up near Grizzly Peak, with all white carpeting and bleached Scandinavian furniture to match. From the front window I can see the entire San Francisco Bay spread out at my feet. When I get together with Sharmila—though not as often as before because she's really busy with her little boy—we have a good time, talking only about happy things.

Richard and I are back together, and last month when I finally wrote to my mother about him, she surprised me by being far less upset than I'd feared. Maybe she figured that even a foreign husband—a *firingi*— is better than no husband at all. At any rate, she's planning to attend our wedding, which is to be this June, followed by a honeymoon in the south of France. I haven't yet told her that I agreed to the marriage only on condition that we don't have children. But no doubt she'll get used to that as well. For a while Ms. Mayhew would leave messages on my machine about boys I might like to take in, now that I was an eligible foster parent. I would erase the messages right away (though her voice continued to travel through my body, insidious, deadly, like a piece of shrapnel the surgeon had missed), and after some time she stopped calling.

Only sometimes, once in a while, I take a day off from work. I go back to Mrs. Ortiz's neighborhood—nobody knows this—and drive through all the streets, slowly, carefully, peering at passing faces. I hike up into the eucalyptus and scrub oak, the dead bark crumbling under my feet like sloughed-off snakeskin, the thorny branches catching in my clothes, and call a name until the shadows congeal deep and cold around me. And when I come back to my apartment, I close my eyes before the last bend of the stairs that lead to my door. I hold my breath and imagine a boy in a red Mickey Mouse T-shirt sitting on the top-most step. *If I can count to twenty, thirty, forty, without letting go,* I say to myself, *he'll be there. He'll hold out his arms, and in his high, clear voice he'll call to me.* I stand there halfway up the darkening staircase feeling the emptiness swirl around me, my lungs burning, my eyes shut tight as though in prayer.

Valentine's Day

JUDITH W. STEINBERGH

We step out of the plane that delivers us from winter
and the humid Florida air wraps its arms around us like
overzealous relatives and by 2, we are on the beach, barefoot
and leaping ecstatically toward the jetty which starts solid
but dissipates into an expansive sea. Already my bones
soften, my wrinkles smooth out a bit, my mind rigid with
January ice stops fending things off and my son who is
eleven says thank you for bringing us here, thank you
for taking us to beautiful places, for bringing us to see
Grandpa and Florence, thank you for this bathing suit
and this shell, for caring about nature and teaching us
to care, for writing poems and making me proud of you,
for loving your work and for loving us; he is chanting
in the rhythm of our walking, sinking in a bit with each step
and glancing over at me to see the effect, as if he were
casting for my heart and knew exactly where it lurked,
so I smile, I am cautious and say thank you for thanking me,
and my son says thank you for being Jewish and thank you
for not being too Jewish, and for being a Democrat
and believing what I believe, and for helping your friends
when they need it. Our hands bump and grip, he is grinning
because he knows he has got the perfect line, the exact fly
for this fish, we both know it and leap over the blue balloons
of Portuguese men-of-war, fallen domes of the sky,
and thank you, my son says, for knowing jellyfish and stars,
relativity and the names of quarks, we are swinging our
hands wildly, flying now towards the jetty which comes
too quickly towards us, which stops the motion of sand
and waves, and thank you for being my mother and marrying
dad and getting divorced so I can see each of you alone,
and thank you for picking me when you couldn't have
your own, he says. Thank you for picking *me* when you

couldn't have *your* own, I say as he reels in my heart, that
fat red catch which for all its battles and scars heals instantly
as it soars out of my chest through the tropic sky.

Life Underground

LISA K. BUCHANAN

We have never spoken, but I know that it must be my daughter who calls every day just after three o'clock. I imagine her coming home from school, throwing her red sneakers in the corner, shoving a chocolate brownie into her mouth, sitting down at the phone in her sister's room, and dialing my number. She must wonder who I am and how I could have given her up; she must dream of the person I might be. She longs to hear my voice—then hangs up when I answer. It's her turn to reject.

The ring seems to get longer each time, eleven, twelve, thirteen rings. I try to resist, but finally I give in, jump up from the garden, bolt into the house, lunge for the phone. Hello, hello! Silence, click, the dreaded dial tone, the subsequent recording that says to please hang up and try again. She must be like me: curious, persistent, terrified, hopeful; trying to make sense out of the strange arrangement by which she, my only child, is being raised by a couple I met the day before she was born.

I stand on the deck for a moment, descend the cedar stairs back to the garden. It is February and I've switched to working evening shifts at Potter's Nursery so I can spend the days landscaping the yard that the previous tenants used for trash burial. My husband thinks I'm pleasantly insane to build a garden here in the gritty, forgotten dirt between urban houses. I find plastic bags of dirty dishes that someone couldn't face, piles of rotting newspaper along with Styrofoam take-out containers that will never decompose, scraped-up shoes, an unopened bag of kitty litter, some wadded up T-shirts. But amid the mess, I like the shaping of a landscape over months of hard labor. I like the sifting of soil with manure and the aching exhilaration of having unearthed discarded elements all morning. I'm mud-caked and sweaty, and today is one of the many in which I can't stop thinking about my daughter.

I use tricks to try to get her to speak. I say, "Hello, this is Anna," so she'll know she got the right person. I say, "Hello, The Ice Cream Store," so she'll stammer and maybe ask if we have Bananamellow today. This, to hear her precious voice, to know some small detail, such as the ice cream she likes. Once I tried pretending I was an answering machine: "Hello, you've reached Anna Pasciano and I can't come to the phone right now but please leave a message. . . ." I heard her soft, shallow, third-grade breathing. I begged silently for the sound of her voice. But she hung up.

Once I even picked up the phone and answered, "Hello, Kathleen?" That's what they said they were going to name her, and I thought that if I could just catch her off guard . . . But it was my husband calling home from work. "Anna," he said, "you need to let go."

Ross is patient and loving, but he can't feel my pain. I used to recite to him my series of if-onlys: if only there had been money, or a place to go; if only they could have predicted that she was the sole child I would conceive; if only they had let me hold her just once. But we exhausted the topic of children years ago, during long afternoons of working in each others' yards, digging, potting, talking, making love outside, and contemplating a life together. In our eight years of marriage we have incurred nieces and nephews, numerous godchildren, and countless neighbor kids. And I rarely speak of Kathleen.

According to the social worker who handled the adoption, I would have other children; I would forget the pain; I should be proud to have provided a childless couple with the gift of a daughter. But I find little satisfaction in these heroic gestures. There is no resolve to having relinquished my only child. I think I will mourn her forever.

I have started many gardens in many backyards and it's a different process each time. Here the soil is grainy and full of tiny pebbles. The bay fog is moist and salty. The sun warms the ground in the morning, then once again by late afternoon in our sunken yard among the tall Victorians. Impatiens will flourish near the house and basil will go to seed with summer's last gasp. White lilies abound, but the delphiniums that towered over me in my childhood will not grow here. I remember summer mornings helping my mother water her garden; I remember lying in bed at night, while the loud Montana winds ripped through the yard; I remember waking up one November morning to a frost that had crushed every delphinium in the garden. My mother laughed gently at my tear-streaked face and explained that frost and wind were as much a part of the earth as the sunshine and delphiniums, and that each would have its season.

"But Mom," I moaned, "we made them grow."

"They grew from seeds," she said, "we only nourish their environment."

I stared at my mother. She and God had conspired, casually, in the sad fate of the delphiniums. "They'll be back in spring," she promised, then lit the wood stove and started breakfast.

Sometimes I think of Kathleen when I read the newspaper: New Jersey Youths Carry Out Suicide Pact in Garage. Man Picks Up Hitchhiker, Age 10, Hacks Off Her Left Leg Below the Knee. Adopted Child Found Alive. Parents Murdered by Housekeeper. Mother Kills Porn-Star Daughter. I grab at the small things I remember: the Irish surname, the father's optometry practice in Pleasant Creek. I sift out the parts that can't be my daughter: Asian facial features, the November birthday, the identical twin. Hideous as it is—the momentary thought that any of these victims could be Kathleen—the morbidity comforts me somehow, as if imagining the worst could prevent it from occurring. Or because the fantasy is something; and the void is nothing.

It will be nice in April to paint the trellises and flower boxes, to have hoed and sifted and planted seeds. I will water twice a day, nourishing life I can't see. I will worry that the seeds may be poor, or the soil too sandy, or that the neighbor kids will play war games in the yard while I'm at work. The beauty shop downstairs might dump strange chemicals by the fence. Where I see fertility and life, others see dirt.

But my affair with life underground will pass, and by March, my daffodils will sprout, the first vital sign poking quietly through the dirt in the northeast corner of our yard. I will water them, talk to them, play music on the patio for them, and everyone will think I am insane. The tiny dark leaves will be pliable and vulnerable in this harsh environment, but they will survive. Other sprouts will follow; it will be a triumph.

I never saw Kathleen in the hospital, but I did see her once when she was about five, in a restaurant in San Francisco. I had ordered a sandwich to go and was standing by the cash register when I felt someone staring at me, from a booth. It was my daughter's adoptive mother and I knew her immediately, though she looked older and not so glamorous as when I had met her at the hospital. Her lips had been bright red then; she had been a proud, beautiful woman of thirty-eight, with an Anne Bancroft-ness about her. She had sat next to my bed and shown me pictures of the little girl she and her husband had adopted the year before, pictures of toys and rooms and the backyard of the house my daughter would live in. The husband had paced nervously around the room, while his wife held my pale hand and massaged my knuckles.

But in the restaurant, the woman was alone in her terror, being the only one who recognized me. She went white and damp, and her mouth fell open. When our eyes met, she turned quickly to her older daughter, helped her with the complicated task of getting the bite of rhubarb from plate to mouth. The woman was hoping she had imagined me, that her eyes had been mistaken, that the next time she looked up I would be gone forever, as planned from the beginning. My daughter sat next to her, slurping soup from a big spoon, her hair dark and unruly like mine; her skin, fair and Irish like her father. She looked like I did at five, dressed dorkish and square, in clothes chosen by her mother, who is twenty years older than I am, the same age as my own mother.

Kathleen's father laid his finger gently on my daughter's fat elbow and gave her a quiet-the-slurping look. I left the sandwich on the counter and ran, sprinted across the parking lot, threw the car in gear and barreled into the alley. I didn't stop driving till I got home, the blades having dutifully wiped the dry windshield for six miles. All I could think of was that I wouldn't have dressed her that way.

I consider the horrors Kathleen must have about me, that I died from giving her birth, that I didn't want her or try very hard to keep her, that there was something about the way she felt inside my body that made me decide to relinquish her, or that I was stupid or careless or promiscuous, and that those traits are genetically ingrained in her character. Or that I never think of her now. Her parents said they planned to tell her from the beginning that she was adopted, and that they would answer her questions but not encourage her to dwell on it. What if she's too shy to ask? Did they tell her the truth, or that I had been killed in a car wreck with her father?

The social worker from the county said that when Kathleen is eighteen, she can request background information based on interviews with me when I was pregnant. The social workers will tell her that I made my unselfish choice with her best interests in mind, that her adopted parents wanted her more than anything else in the entire world and could give her a better home. They might tell her that musical talent and hay fever run in the family, that I am of Italian descent, that I sew, garden, and sing in a choir. They will say that I was seventeen; that I had planned to go to college and that her father played banjo and was not ready for marriage. They will tell her that by now I probably have children of my own, that to contact me could disrupt my family, that I have probably put my painful past behind me, and that they have no current address for me. They will probably not tell her that tetracycline may give her a throat rash. And I doubt they will tell her that tailbones run long in the Pasciano line and that surgery is futile because the bone grows back later. And they probably will not tell her that her mother and one of her aunts have endometriosis, and that losing a child is not a pain you forget.

It would be easy enough for me to find my daughter, and I may try in a few years when she is older, though I have promised in writing and in spirit to stay away. I want to know that she has a good life; I want her to know she was loved. I want us both to have the peace of mind that could come only from looking into each other's faces.

But for now, I imagine her sitting by her sister's teal-colored phone, her long legs in some gawky position, brownie consumed. I see her living in a big house at the end of a cul-de-sac in the suburban hills. She has her own room, full of pretty things, clothes and books, maybe a flute. She has a peach tree outside her window. She is physically stunning with thick Italian curls and dark, brooding, liquid eyes like mine; she has the narrow family feet; and a tailbone just long enough to make one hour of math in a wooden chair almost impossible. She has her father's milky skin and his fine neck and jawbone; she is immune to the Pasciano double chin.

There are times when my garden is a burden: mornings when I don't feel like watering, afternoons when I get tired of screaming at the neighbor kids every time they hop the fence and land on my begonias. Sometimes the worms get the tomatoes before I do; and when the beets I have grown, picked, and washed go moldy in the refrigerator, I bemoan the waste of my efforts, swear off forever this need to cultivate botanical life.

Then I will pinch back the fuchsias and make pesto sauce from the basil, plant spinach, carrots, and brussels sprouts for fall. We'll serve fresh strawberries and drink wine with friends and neighbors, and people from work. The garden will be lush with petunias and foxglove, and my husband will take his annual snapshot of me among them. And some afternoon when I'm sitting on the patio with a cup of coffee, my daughter will call. I will answer; her heart will pound as she speaks. She will not hang up.

Personal Testimony

LYNNA WILLIAMS

The last night of church camp, 1963, and I am sitting in the front row of the junior mixed-voice choir looking out on the crowd in the big sanctuary tent. The tent glows, green and white and unexpected, in the Oklahoma night; our choir director, Dr. Bledsoe, has schooled us in the sudden crescendos needed to compete with the sounds cars make when their drivers cut the corner after a night at the bars on Highway 10 and see the tent rising out of the plain for the first time. The tent is new to Faith Camp this year, a gift to God and the Southern Baptist Convention from the owner of a small circus who repented, and then retired, in nearby Oklahoma City. It is widely rumored among the campers that Mr. Talliferro came to Jesus late in life, after having what my mother would call Life Experiences. Now he walks through camp with the unfailing good humor of a man who, after years of begging hardscrabble farmers to forsake their fields for an afternoon of elephants and acrobats, has finally found a real draw: His weekly talks to the senior boys on "Sin and the Circus?" incorporate a standing-room-only question-and-answer period, and no one ever leaves early.

Although I know I will never be allowed in the tent to hear one of Mr. Talliferro's talks—I will not be twelve forever, but I will always be a girl—I am encouraged by his late arrival into our Fellowship of Believers. I will take my time, too, I think: first I will go to high school, to college, to bed with a boy, to New York. (I think of those last two items as one since, as little as I know about sex, I do know it is not something I will ever be able to do in the same time zone as my mother.) Then when I'm fifty-two or so and have had, like Mr. Talliferro, sufficient Life Experiences, I'll move back to west Texas and repent.

Normally, thoughts of that touching—and distant—scene of repentance are how I entertain myself during evening worship service. But tonight I am unable to work up any enthusiasm for the vision of myself sweeping into my hometown to Be Forgiven. For once my thoughts are entirely on the worship service ahead.

My place in the choir is in the middle of six other girls from my father's church in Fort Worth; we are dressed alike in white lace-trimmed wash-and-wear blouses from J.C. Penney and modest navy pedal pushers that stop exactly three inches from our white socks and tennis shoes. We are also alike in having mothers who regard travel irons as an essential accessory to Christian Young Womanhood; our matching outfits are, therefore, neatly ironed.

At least their outfits are. I have been coming to this camp in the southwestern equivalent of the Sahara Desert for six years now, and I know that when it is a hundred degrees at sunset, cotton wilts. When I used my iron I did the front of my blouse and the pants, so I wouldn't stand out, and trusted that anyone standing behind me would think I was wrinkled from the heat.

Last summer, or the summer before, when I was still riding the line that separates good girls from bad, this small deception would have bothered me. This year I am twelve and a criminal. Moral niceties are lost on me. I am singing "Just As I Am" with the choir and I have three hundred dollars in my white Bible, folded and taped over John 3:16.

Since camp started three weeks ago, I have operated a business in the arts and crafts cabin in the break between afternoon Bible study and segregated (boys only/girls only) swimming. The senior boys, the same ones who are learning critical information from Mr. Talliferro every week, are paying me to write the personal testimonies we are all expected to give at evening worship service.

We do not do well on personal motivation in my family. When my brother, David, and I sin, it is the deed my parents talk about, not mitigating circumstances, and the deed they punish. This careful emphasis on what we do, never on why we do it, has affected David and me differently. He is a good boy, endlessly kind and cheerful and responsible, but his heroes are not the men my father followed into the ministry. David gives God and our father every outward sign of respect, but he worships Clarence Darrow and the law. At fifteen, he has been my defense lawyer for years.

While David wants to defend the world, I am only interested in defending myself. I know exactly why I have started the testimony business: I am doing it to get back at my father. I am doing it because I am adopted.

Even though I assure my customers with every sale that we will not get caught, I never write a testimony without imagining public exposure of my wrongdoing. The scene is so familiar to me that I do not have to close my eyes to see it: the summons to the camp director's office and the door closing behind me; the shocked faces of other campers when the news leaks out to the Baptist Academy girls, who comb their hair and go in pairs, bravely, to offer my brother comfort; the automatic rotation of my name to the top of everyone's prayer list. I spend hours imagining the small details of my shame, always leading to the moment when my father, called from Fort Worth to take me home, arrives at camp.

That will be my moment. I have done something so terrible that even my father will not be able to keep it a secret. I am doing this because of my father's secrets.

We had only been home from church for a few minutes; it was my ninth birthday, and when my father called me to come downstairs to his study, I was still wearing the dress my mother had made for the occasion, pink dotted Swiss with a white satin sash. David came out of his room to ask me what I had done this time—he likes to be prepared for court—but I told him not to worry, that I was wholly innocent of any crime in the weeks just before my birthday. At the bottom of the stairs I saw my mother walk out of the study and knew I was right not to be concerned: in matters of discipline my mother and father never work alone. At the door it came to me: my father was going to tell me I was old enough to go with him now and then to churches in other cities. David had been to Atlanta and New Orleans and a dozen little Texas towns; my turn had finally come.

My father was standing by the window. At the sound of my patent leather shoes sliding across the hardwood floor, he turned and motioned for me to sit on the sofa. He cleared his throat; it was a sermon noise I had heard hundreds of times, and I knew that he had prepared whatever he was going to say.

All thoughts of ordering room-service hamburgers in an Atlanta hotel left me—prepared remarks meant we were dealing with life or death or salvation—and I wished for my mother and David. My father said, "This is hard for your mother; she wanted to be here, but it upsets her so, we thought I should talk to you alone." We had left any territory I knew, and I sat up straight to listen, as though I were still in church.

My father, still talking, took my hands in his; after a moment I recognized the weight of his Baylor ring against my skin as something from my old life, the one in which I had woken up that morning a nine-year-old, dressed for church in my birthday dress, and come home.

My father talked and talked and talked; I stopped listening. I had grown up singing about the power of blood. I required no lengthy explanation of what it meant to be adopted. It meant I was not my father's child. It meant I was a secret, even from myself.

In the three years since that day in my father's study, I have realized, of course, that I am not my mother's child, either. But I have never believed that she was responsible for the lie about my birth. It is my father I blame. I am not allowed to talk about my adoption outside my family ("It would only hurt your mother," my father says. "Do you want to hurt your mother?"). Although I am universally regarded by the women of our church as a Child Who Wouldn't Know a Rule If One Reached Up and Bit Her in the Face, I do keep this one. My stomach hurts when I even think about telling anyone, but it hurts, too, when I think about having another mother and father somewhere. When the pain is enough to make me cry, I try to talk to my parents about it, but my mother's face changes even before I can get the first question out, and my father always follows her out of the room. "You're our child," he says when he returns. "We love you, and you're ours."

I let him hug me, but I am thinking that I have never heard my father tell a lie before. I am not his child. Not in the way David is, not in the way I believed I was. Later I remember that lie and decide that all the secrecy is for my father's benefit, that he is ashamed to tell the world that I am not his child because he is ashamed of me. I think about the Ford my father bought in Dallas three years ago; it has never run right, but he will not take it back. I think about that when I am sitting in my bunk with a flashlight, writing testimonies to the power of God's love.

My father is one reason I am handcrafting Christian testimonies while my bunkmates are making place mats from Popsicle sticks. There is another reason: I'm good at it.

Nothing else has changed. I remain Right Fielder for Life in the daily softball games. The sincerity of my belief in Jesus is perennially suspect among the most pious, and most popular, campers. And I am still the only girl who, in six years of regular attendance, has failed to advance even one step in Girl's Auxiliary. (Other, younger girls have made it all the way to Queen Regent with Scepter, while I remain a perpetual Lady-in-Waiting.) Until this year, only the strength of my family connections kept me from sinking as low in the camp hierarchy as Cassie Mosley, who lisps and wears colorful native costumes that her missionary parents send from Africa.

I arrived at camp this summer as I do every year, resigned and braced to endure but buoyed by a fantasy life that I believe is unrivaled among twelve-year-old Baptist girls. But on our second night here, the promise of fish sticks and carrot salad hanging in the air, Bobby Dunn came and stood behind me in the cafeteria line.

Bobby Dunn, blond, ambitious, and in love with Jesus, is Faith Camp's standard for male perfection. He is David's friend, but he has spoken to me only once, on the baseball field last year, when he suggested that my unhealthy fear of the ball was really a failure to trust God's plan for my life. Since that day I have taken some comfort in noticing that Bobby Dunn follows the Scripture reading by moving his finger along the text.

Feeling him next to me, I took a breath, wondering if Bobby, like other campers in other years, had decided to attempt to bring me to a better understanding of what it means to serve Jesus. But he was already talking, congratulating me on my testimony at evening worship service the night before. (I speak publicly at camp twice every summer, the exact number required by some mysterious formula that allows me to be left alone the rest of the time.)

"You put it just right," he said. "Now me, I know what I want to say, but it comes out all wrong. I've prayed about it, and it seems to me God wants me to do better."

He looked at me hard, and I realized it was my turn to say something. Nothing came to me, though, since I agreed with him completely. He does suffer from what my saintly brother, after one particularly gruesome revival meeting, took to calling "Jesus Jaw," a malady that makes it impossible for the devoted to say what they mean and sit down. Finally I said what my mother says to the ladies seeking comfort in the Dorcas Bible class: "Can I help?" Before I could take it back, Bobby Dunn had me by the hand and was pulling me across the cafeteria to a table in the far corner.

The idea of my writing testimonies for other campers—a sort of ghostwriting service for Jesus, as Bobby Dunn saw it—was Bobby's, but before we got up from the table, I had refined it and made it mine. The next afternoon in the arts and crafts cabin I made my first sale: five dollars for a two-minute testimony detailing how God gave Michael Bush the strength to stop swearing. Bobby was shocked when the money changed hands—I could see him thinking, Temple. Moneylenders. Jee-sus!—but Michael Bush is the son of an Austin car dealer, and he quoted his earthly father's scripture: "You get what you pay for."

Michael, who made me a professional writer with money he earned polishing used station wagons, is a sweet, slow-talking athlete from Bishop Military School. He'd been dateless for months and was convinced it was because the Baptist Academy girls had heard that he has a tendency to take the Lord's name in vain on difficult fourth downs. After his testimony that night, Michael left the tent with Patsy Lewis, but he waved good night to me.

For an underground business, I have as much word-of-mouth trade from the senior boys as I can handle. I estimate that my volume is second only to that of the snack stand that sells snow cones. Like the snow-cone stand, I have high prices and limited hours of operation. I arrive at the arts and crafts cabin every day at 2:00 P.M., carrying half-finished pot holders from the day before, and senior boys drift in and out for the next twenty minutes, I talk to each customer, take notes, and deliver the finished product by 5:00 P.M. the next day. My prices start at five dollars for words only and go up to twenty dollars for words and concept.

Bobby Dunn has appointed himself my sales force; he recruits customers who he thinks need my services and gives each one a talk about the need for secrecy. Bobby will not accept money from me as payment—he reminds me hourly that he is doing this for Jesus—but he is glad to be thanked in testimonies.

By the beginning of the second week of camp, our director, the Reverend Stewart, and the camp counselors are openly rejoicing about the power of the Spirit at work, as reflected in the moving personal testimonies being given night after night. Bobby Dunn has been testifying every other night and smiling at me at breakfast every morning. Patsy Lewis has taught me how to set my hair on big rollers, and I let it dry while I sit up writing testimonies. I have a perfect pageboy, a white Bible bulging with five-dollar bills, and I am popular. There are times when I forget my father.

On this last night of camp I am still at large. But although I have not been caught, I have decided I am not cut out to be a small business. There is the question of good help, for one thing. Bobby Dunn is no good for detail work—clearly, the less he knows about how my mind works, the better—and so I have turned to Missy Tucker. Missy loves Jesus and her father and disapproves of everything about me. I love her because she truly believes I can be saved and, until that happens, is willing to get into almost any trouble I can think of, provided I do not try to stop her from quoting the appropriate Scripture. Even so, she resisted being drawn into the testimony business for more than a week, giving in only after I sank low enough to introduce her to Bobby Dunn and point out that she would be able to apply her cut to the high cost of braces.

The truth is, the business needs Missy. I am no better a disciple of the Palmer Handwriting Method than I am of Christ or of my mother's standards of behavior. No one can read my writing. Missy has won the penmanship medal at E.M. Morrow Elementary School so many times there is talk that it will be retired when we go off to junior high in the fall. When she's done writing, my testimonies look like poems.

The value of Missy's cursive writing skills, however, is offset by the ways in which she manifests herself as a True Believer. I can tolerate the Scripture quoting, but her fears are something else. I am afraid of snakes and of not being asked to pledge my mother's sorority at Baylor, both standard fears in Cabin A. Missy is terrified of Eastern religions.

Her father, a religion professor at a small Baptist college, has two passions: world religions and big-game hunting. In our neighborhood, where not rotating the tires on the family Ford on a schedule is considered eccentric, Dr. Tucker wears a safari jacket to class and greets everyone the same way: "Hi, wallaby." Missy is not allowed to be afraid of the dead animals in her father's den, but a pronounced sensitivity to Oriental mysticism is thought to be acceptable in a young girl.

Unless I watch her, Missy cannot be trusted to resist inserting a paragraph into every testimony in which the speaker thanks the Lord Jesus for not having allowed him or her to be born a Buddhist. I tell Missy repeatedly that if every member of the camp baseball team suddenly begins to compare and contrast Zen and the tenets of Southern Baptist fundamentalism in this three-minute testimony, someone—even in this trusting place—is going to start to wonder.

She says she sees my point but keeps arguing for more "spiritual" content in the testimonies, a position in which she is enthusiastically supported by Bobby Dunn. Missy and Bobby have fallen in love; Bobby asked her to wear his friendship ring two nights ago, using his own words. What is art to me is faith—and now love—to Missy, and we are not as close as we were three weeks ago.

I am a success, but a lonely one, since there is no one I can talk to about either my success or my feelings. My brother, David, who normally can be counted on to protect me from myself and others, has only vague, Christian concern for me these days. He has fallen in love with Denise Meeker, universally regarded as the most spiritually developed girl in camp history, and he is talking about following my father into the ministry. I believe that when Denise goes home to Corpus Christi, David will remember law school, but in the meantime he is no comfort to me.

Now, from my place in the front row of the choir, I know that I will not have to worry about a going-out-of-business sale. What I have secretly wished for all summer is about to happen. I am going to get caught.

Ten minutes ago, during Reverend Stewart's introduction of visitors from the pulpit, I looked out at the crowd in the tent and saw my father walking down the center aisle. As I watched, he stopped every few rows to shake hands and say hello, as casual and full of good humor as if this were his church on a Sunday morning. He is a handsome man, and when he stopped at the pew near the front where David is sitting, I was struck by how much my father and brother look alike, their dark heads together as they smiled and hugged. I think of David as belonging to me, not to my father, but there was an unmistakable sameness in their movements that caught me by surprise, and my eyes filled with tears. Suddenly David pointed toward the choir, at me, and my father nodded his head and continued walking toward the front of the tent. I knew he had seen me, and I concentrated on looking straight ahead as he mounted the stairs to the stage and took a seat to the left of the altar. Reverend Stewart introduced him as the special guest preacher for the last night of camp, and for an instant I let myself believe that was the only reason he had come. He would preach and we would go home together tomorrow. Everything would be all right.

I hear a choked-off sound from my left and know without turning to look that it is Missy, about to cry. She has seen my father, too, and I touch her hand to remind her that no one will believe she was at fault. Because of me, teachers have been patiently writing "easily led" and "cries often" on Missy's report cards for years, and she is still considered a good girl. She won't get braces this year, I think, but she will be all right.

In the next moment two things happen at once. Missy starts to cry, really cry, and my father turns in his seat, looks at me, and then away. It is then that I realize that Missy has decided, without telling me, that straight teeth are not worth eternal damnation. She and Bobby Dunn have confessed, and my father has been called. Now, as he sits with his Bible in his hands and his head bowed, his profile shows none of the cheer of a moment before, and none of the successful-Baptist-preacher expressions I can identify. He does not look spiritual or joyful or weighted down by the burden of God's expectations. He looks furious.

There are more announcements than I ever remember hearing on the last night of camp: prayer lists, final volleyball standings, bus departure times, a Lottie Moon Stewardship Award for Denise Meeker. After each item, I forget I have no reason to expect Jesus to help me and I pray for one more; I know that as soon as the last announcement is read, Reverend Stewart will call for a time of personal testimonies before my father's sermon.

Even with my head down I can see Bobby Dunn sinking lower into a center pew and, next to him, Tim Bailey leaning forward, wanting to be first at the microphone. Tim is another of the Bishop School jocks, and he has combed his hair and put on Sunday clothes. In his left hand he is holding my masterwork, reproduced on three-by-five cards. He paid me twenty-five dollars for it—the most I have ever charged—and it is the best piece of my career. The script calls for Tim to talk movingly about meeting God in a car-truck accident near Galveston, when he was ten. In a dramatic touch of which I am especially proud, he seems to imply that God was driving the truck.

Tim, I know, is doing this to impress a Baptist Academy girl who has told him she will go to her cotillion alone before she goes with a boy who doesn't know Jesus as his personal Lord and Savior. He is gripping the notecards as if they were Did Thorton, and for the first time in a lifetime full of Bible verses, I see an application to my daily living. I truly am about to reap what I have sown.

The announcements end, and Reverend Stewart calls for testimonies. As Tim Bailey rises, so does my father. As he straightens up, he turns again to look at me, and this time he makes a gesture toward the pulpit. It is a mock-gallant motion, the kind I have seen him make to let my mother go first at miniature golf. For an instant that simple reminder that I am not an evil mutant—I have a family that plays miniature golf—makes me think again that everything will be all right. Then I realize what my father is telling me. Tim Bailey will never get to the pulpit to give my testimony. My father will get there first, will tell the worshippers in the packed tent his sorrow and regret over the misdeeds of his little girl. *His little girl.* He is going to do what I have never imagined in all my fantasies about this moment. He is going to forgive me.

Without knowing exactly how it has happened, I am standing up, running from the choir seats to the pulpit. I get there first, before either my father or Tim, and before Reverend Stewart can even say my name, I give my personal testimony.

I begin by admitting what I have been doing for the past three weeks. I talk about being gripped by hate, unable to appreciate the love of my wonderful parents or of Jesus. I talk about making money from other campers who, in their honest desire to honor the Lord, became trapped in my web of wrongdoing.

Bobby Dunn is crying. To his left I can see Mr. Talliferro; something in his face, intent and unsmiling, makes me relax: I am a Draw. Everyone is with me now. I can hear Missy behind me, still sobbing into her hymnal, and to prove I can make it work, I talk about realizing how blessed I am to have been born within easy reach of God's healing love. I could have been born a Buddhist, I say, and the gratifying gasps from the audience make me certain I can say anything I want now.

For an instant I lose control and begin quoting poetry instead of Scripture. There is a shaky moment when all I can remember is bits of "Stopping by Woods on a Snowy Evening," but I manage to tie the verses back to a point about Christian choices. The puzzled looks on some faces give way to shouts of "Amen!" and as I look out at the rows of people in the green-and-white striped tent I know I have won. I have written the best testimony anyone at camp has ever given.

I feel, rather than see, my father come to stand beside me, but I do not stop. As I have heard him do hundreds of times, I ask the choir to sing an invitational hymn and begin singing with them, "Softly and tenderly, Jesus is calling, calling to you and to me. Come home, come home. Ye who are weary, come home."

My father never does give a sermon.

While the hymn is still being sung, Bobby Dunn moves from his pew to the stage, and others follow. They hug me; they say they understand; they say they forgive me. As each one moves on to my father, I can hear him thanking them for their concern and saying, yes, he knows they will be praying for the family.

By ten o'clock, the last knot of worshippers has left the tent, and my father and I are alone on the stage. He is looking at me without speaking; there is no expression on his face that I have seen before. "Daddy," I surprise myself by saying. "Daddy" is a baby name that I have not used since my ninth birthday. My father raises his left hand and slaps me, hard, on my right cheek. He catches me as I start to fall, and we sit down together on the steps leading from the altar. He uses his handkerchief to clean blood from underneath my eye, where his Baylor ring has opened the skin. As he works the white square of cloth carefully around my face, I hear a sound I have never heard before, and I realize my father is crying. I am crying, too, and the mixture of tears and blood on my face makes it impossible to see him clearly. I reach for him anyway and am only a little surprised when he is there.

Summer of My Korean Soldier

MARIE G. LEE

Being back in Korea, the land where I was born, was, in a word, sucky.

I had come here with this idea to learn Korean and, in my off hours, search for my birth parents, who were waiting for me somewhere in Seoul.

So far, though, all I'd met were a bunch of spoiled Korean Americans, *chae-mi kyopo,* who were spending their parents' money like it was water.

Korean classes weren't all that bad. But it was hard to be in a room full of kids who looked just like you, and have the teacher ask, "What's wrong with *you?* Why can't you learn this? You never heard it before?"

"Actually, no," I said, and then the teacher, a well-meaning lady who sometimes got a little too excitable, looked really confused.

"Don't your parents speak Korean at home?"

"No," I said. "My parents are white. I am adopted."

And then she looked shocked and speechless. It was like all of a sudden she'd forgotten that she was in the classroom to teach, to pound Korean into our brains.

"Do you consider these Americans to be *your parents?*" she asked in amazement.

"Hey, I didn't know you're adopted," said Lee Jae-Kwan, otherwise known as Bernie Lee. "No wonder your accent is so fucked up. That must be so weird coming back here."

"Yeah, it is," I said, and then I gave him a look that meant that I was through talking about this subject.

Even in the beginners' class, Korean rolled off the tongues of the students so easily. There was only one other person who sounded like me; she was a nun. And from France. And had blue eyes. She had a visible excuse. Our teacher would often sigh impatiently, make that woeful "haa" sound at both of us; but at me, I saw her snatching secret looks, like you do through your fingers at gory scenes in *Texas Chainsaw Massacre IV,* or something like that.

It bothered me that people like Bernie Lee, who never did his homework, couldn't read or write Korean for beans, thought that the most important part of college was "the opportunity to party," would always speak Korean better than me, and would always, while we were here in Korea, feel superior because he was more Korean than me, whatever that meant.

The only Korean word I remembered from my childhood was *ddong,* the word for crap, merde, excrement. When I heard myself say it, it was the one word for which I had the perfect, clear, ringing pronunciation. Needless to say, I never had a chance to use it.

There was a time when I spoke better than everyone in the whole class. But those days are gone, and here I am marooned into this life, trying to make the best of it.

I can't blame Mom and Dad for adopting me—they wanted a kid. And wouldn't it be nice if Mr. and Mrs. Jaspers took a kid out of some poor Third World country? We'll name her Sarah, which means "God's precious treasure," they said.

Ever since I came over here, I've had what's been labeled as a "bonding problem." It makes it sound like there's something wrong with my dental work. But what it really means is that I didn't bond with my parents the way I was "supposed" to. I found this out when I turned eighteen and could finally access my file in the social worker's office.

Frankly, I wasn't surprised. My earliest memories are of Mom and Dad asking me if I loved them, and of me wondering what I should answer. And then they became panicky and, eventually, sent me to therapists and counselors all over town.

Why do they call this a bonding *problem?* Maybe I'd already bonded with my folks in Korea, and once was enough.

I like my adoptive parents, though. I called them Mom and Dad, but I'm sorry, that's the best I could do for them. The best they could do for me was to live in an Edina neighborhood with only white people and their children, who would later go to school with me and call me things like "chink" and "gook" and not include me in their games, their parties, their groups, their proms. Could anybody really blame me when I started staying in my room a lot, wearing black, getting my nose pierced at a head shop on Hennepin Avenue just because the spirit moved me?

I'm a virgin, though. Ha, gotcha.

God, I've got to find my real parents. They're waiting for me, and I know they feel as gut-wrenched about this as I do.

"You know what you need," my teacher said to me, "is to do a language exchange with someone—an hour of English, an hour of Korean a few times a week. It would improve your conversation."

I looked at her and felt very sore. Every night, from the dorm's study room, I could see Bernie and the other kids going out, dressed to the teeth and jolly. Sometimes when I woke at five to start studying, from my window I could see them getting out of elegant black taxis, stumbling to the door, then yelling in guttural Korean for the old *ajushee* to let them in, even though they'd broken curfew by a good six hours.

I wanted to be able to answer her in Korean, to say, "I'll think about it," in polite, precise Korean. But of course, I couldn't.

"I know a person named Kim Jun Ho, a friend of my younger brother's. He's at the university, although right now he's completing his time in the army. He wants to practice his English, and he would probably be a good teacher."

"Fine, fine, *gwenchana*," I said, more to get her off my back than anything. My eyelids felt sandy from staying up so late studying and, for the first time, I thought of quitting. Maybe after I found my parents I would.

You don't need a language exchange," I said to Jun Ho Kim, who sat across from me and drank celery juice, while I sipped at a ginseng tea that I'd tried in vain to sweeten with three packets of sugar.

We were at the Balzac Café. The neighborhood near school was full of these trendy coffee/juice bars that had the names of dead French authors: Flaubert, Rousseau, and around the corner, Proust.

Jun Ho seemed nice enough. He was tall, had short hair (because of the army, he said). His English was perfect. He spoke with better grammar than half the kids I went to junior college with.

"No, no," he said modestly, "I want to improve my conversation, I want to speak like an American."

So in English, we talked about nuclear plants in North Korea, dead French writers, and stories he'd read about in some old American *Newsweeks* (for instance, he wanted to know how to pronounce "Hillary" and "Chelsea").

When it came time to switch to Korean, we talked about the weather and studying. I ran out of words in about twelve minutes. He then asked me about my family: Did I have brothers and sisters? What were my parents like? Even though he spoke wholly in Korean, I somehow recognized—but did not know—the words connected to family.

I answered, substituting the English word for every Korean word I did not know and basically ended up speaking in English. I told him how I was born in Korea but hadn't ever been back—until now.

"Are you sad?" he asked.

I shook my head. "No, because my family is somewhere in Seoul, and I'm going to find them."

He nodded thoughtfully. "I will help you, if you want."

"Thank you," I said. "I'll keep it in mind."

Jun Ho's face then folded in on itself, like origami.

"It isn't 'I'll keep it in *my* mind'?" he asked.

"No, it's not," I said. "I don't know why, but the expression is 'I'll keep it in mind.'"

He laughed good-naturedly. "I'll never learn English, it's too hard." He got up and paid the bill.

The first time I called the orphanage, the person who answered the phone hung up on me. The second time, too. It wasn't necessarily that they were being rude, but they spoke in Korean to me, I spoke in English to them, and this went on for a number of minutes, until the person at the orphanage hung up. It seemed to be a gentle, almost apologetic hanging up though, as far as I could hear.

When I saw Jun Ho again, we went to the other side of the neighborhood to the Kafka Coffee House. He asked me, in English, about our Secretary of State, Warren Christopher (it was lucky that I even recognized his name, much less knew anything about him). In the Korean hour, we talked about food (I had learned to order at restaurants) and studying. Then he asked me how my search had been going. I asked him if he'd help me, and he said he would.

We went to the closest pay phone, and he dialed the number. Soon he was talking in a continuous Korean, from which I couldn't pick out any words. He looked at the piece of paper on which I'd scribbled my full name, as well as the Korean one that had been given to me at the orphanage: Lee Soon-Min.

He talked and talked. The longer he talked, the more hopeful I became—obviously the key to everything must be at the orphanage. Finally, he hung up.

"What happened?" Excitement was flowing out of every pore.

"They cannot tell me anything over the phone."

"Huh?" I said. "What'd you talk about?"

"How to get to the orphanage, that kind of thing," he said.

"Can we go now?"

"I made an appointment for two weeks. That is the soonest someone can see you."

I sighed. My family was going to have to wait, again. It seemed unfair, but after waiting so long already, I guessed I'd have to do it. I'd also have to tough out at least another two weeks of this stupid Korean language school, when what I really wanted to do was just take off, live with them, eat Korean food, and sleep in a Korean bed, and I'm sure my Korean would come back to me naturally. I admit I was starting to feel impatient.

The next time I met Jun Ho, he had his army uniform on, and he was also driving a car.

"How about if we do something different?" he asked, opening the door. I slid in. He grinned at me. Unlike the poker-faced seriousness of a lot of Korean men I'd seen, Jun had a dash of mischievousness, a kind of sparkle that flashed at you like summer lightning, where you can't quite tell if you've actually seen it, or if you've just blinked or something.

He pulled into the vortex of Seoul traffic as he explained that he'd borrowed a car from his friend so he could show me around a little bit. I was suddenly aware that I'd seen very little of Seoul besides the immediate neighborhood of the school, so I sat back, pleased.

"Next week is the orphanage," I said. "You'll come with me, right?"

He cracked another grin at me. "Right now, we will have fun," he said. "We will talk only about fun things."

"OK, later," I said agreeably. I wonder if things would be different when I could speak Korean. Would there be things I could say that I couldn't before?

We went to the Sixty-three Building. It's called that because it has sixty-three floors, or it's supposed to—I didn't count. The top floor has an observation tower. We got lucky, because during the humid summer, the city is pretty much always obscured by industrial smog; it had been raining the last few days, and today the air was mountain-clear.

The observatory was a whole floor, and you could walk all around it. Having been mostly on the ground between tall buildings, I'd forgotten about the mountains rising along the sides of the city. Now they loomed in all their majesty, forming a ring around the city. When I'd flown in and seen those mountains—so familiar, somehow, so much like home—I'd started crying.

I leaned and looked out for a long time. Somewhere out there was my family. On what side of the Han River would they live? Would they be rich? Poor? I thought of how each ticking of the clock brought me closer to them, and I felt happy.

At the souvenir shop there, Jun Ho bought me a pair of figures that looked like warped, demented totem poles. At the top, each one had a monster head. It was not pretty to look at. Jun Ho said that these were miniature versions of ones people used to erect outside their villages to scare the demons away.

"Will they scare my demons away?" I asked.

"They might," he said.

We stepped into the elevator, where a young woman bowed mechanically to us before pressing a white-gloved hand to the button for the lobby. You couldn't feel any motion in the elevator as it descended. When the doors opened and the familiar lobby scene appeared, I felt like I'd been beamed in from another planet.

The day for my appointment came, but before we went, Jun Ho sat us down at Kafka.

The orphanage had very little information, he warned me. They wouldn't be able to help me find my family.

I jumped up, wanting to hit him. What nonsense was he talking about? He'd talked so long on the phone, made an appointment for me.

"Sarah," he said. There was no news. He'd made the appointment for two weeks hence hoping that perhaps I'd give up on my own.

"It's better this way," he said. "Perhaps better for your family."

"How could that be?" I yelled. "My family is waiting for me. You're just like all the rest—keeping me from them."

I think that's when I collapsed back into my chair, sobbing. I think I might have knocked over the sugar bowl, too. Koreans don't show their emotions, especially not in public. *What a crazy foreigner,* they were probably thinking.

"We'll go," Jun Ho said. He took my hand, and we caught a taxi.

The orphanage was filled with babies. There were loud, shrill cries, the smell of unwashed baby bottoms. The heat pressed down on my shoulders almost unbearably.

But this was my last hope; I had to push on.

A woman in a severely tailored Western-style suit met us. Jun Ho told her who I was and handed her my letter of introduction from the social services agency in the States. She stared at me hard, as if trying to make the connection between me and those squalling babies.

"I told her you want to see your file," Jun Ho explained. I leaned into him gratefully. There was always that hope, I was thinking. Something undiscovered in that file.

She brought out a file folder that had a few sheets of paper filled with single-spaced Korean writing. My heart jumped. There had to be something in there . . .

"Please read it to me, Jun Ho," I said. "Read every word."

Jun Ho scanned the page, then looked up.

"Sarah," he said. "It doesn't say much. It just says about your eating habits and so forth."

"Read it to me," I said, desperation beginning to crawl up my back. "Promise me you won't leave anything out." My whole Korean life lay among those spidery interlocking symbols.

Jun Ho looked at me again. His eyes were so black, they were liquid. He lowered his head and began to read.

"'A newborn baby girl was found on the steps of the Hoei Dong fire station on July 12, 1974. There was no note attached or any other kind of correspondence indicating any relatives.'"

Jun Ho paused, but I urged him on.

"'The baby was found covered with feces . . .'"

Ddong, I was thinking. I know that word. The baby. I was that baby.

"'The baby appears to have been born in a toilet, or some kind of commode . . .'

"'. . . cleaned her up. A name of Lee, Soon-Min was given . . .'

"'. . . was placed in foster care . . .'"

"'. . . was adopted by an American couple, Sue and Ken Jaspers.'"

I couldn't see any more. It was like the day I stood behind a waterfall and tried to look out at the lake. Minnesota has more than ten thousand lakes.

Today was July 12. "It's, like, my birthday," I mumbled.

Jun Ho took my hand. He was leading me back to a cab. He barked directions to the driver, a large oily man who looked back at me, my tears and some stray hairs clogging my mouth. Jun Ho barked something else, and the man started the car.

"Where are we going?" I surprised myself by speaking in Korean.

Jun-Ho only smiled and gave my hand a squeeze.

"Home," he said.

Out the window, the rows of tiny stores were pressed together so tightly that they looked like one continuous, rickety storefront, save for the different signs in Korean writing each had in front of it. As the taxi picked up speed, the signs began to blur.

(IV)

IDENTITY

Black Bottom

JACKIE KAY

San serif typeface: adoptive mother
Roman typeface: adopted daughter
Serif italic typeface: birth mother

Maybe that's why I don't like
all this talk about her being black,
I brought her up as my own
as I would any other child
colour matters to the nutters;
but she says my daughter says
it matters to her

I suppose there would have been things
I couldn't understand with any child,
we knew she was colored.
They told us they had no babies at first
and I chanced it didn't matter what colour it was
and they said *oh well are you sure*
in that case we have a baby for you—
to think she wasn't even thought of as a baby,
my baby, my baby

I chase his *Sambo Sambo* all the way from the school gate.
A fistful of anorak—What did you call me? Say that again.
Sam-bo. He plays the word like a bouncing ball
but his eyes move fast as ping pong.
I shove him up against the wall,
say that again you wee shite. *Sambo, sambo,* he's crying now

I knee him in the balls. What was that?
My fist is steel; I punch and punch his gut.
Sorry I didn't hear you? His tears drip like wax.
Nothing he heaves *I didn't say nothing.*
I let him go. He is a rat running. He turns
and shouts *Dirty Darkie* I chase him again.

Blonde hairs in my hand. Excuse me!
This teacher from primary 7 stops us.
Names? I'll report you to the headmaster tomorrow.
But Miss. Save it for Mr Thompson she says

My teacher's face cracks into a thin smile
Her long nails scratch the note well well
I see you were fighting yesterday, again.
In a few years time you'll be a juvenile delinquent.
Do you know what that is? Look it up in the dictionary.
She spells each letter with slow pleasure.
Read it out to the class.
Thug. Vandal. Hooligan. Speak up. Have you lost your tongue?

To be honest I hardly ever think about it
except if something happens, you know
daft talk about darkies. Racialism.
Mothers ringing my bell with their kids
Crying *You tell. You tell. You tell.*
—*No.* You tell your little girl to stop calling
my little girl names and I'll tell my little girl
to stop giving your little a girl a doing.

We're practising for the school show
I'm trying to do the Cha Cha and the Black Bottom
but I can't get the steps right
my right foot's left and my left foot's right
my teacher shouts from the bottom
of the class Come on, show

us what you can do I thought
you people had it in your blood.
My skin is hot as burning coal
like that time she said Darkies are like coal
in front of the whole class—my blood
what does she mean? I thought

she'd stopped all that after the last time
my dad talked to her on parents' night
the other kids are all right till she starts;
my feet step out of time, my heart starts

to miss beats like when I can't sleep at night—
What Is In My Blood? The bell rings, it is time.

Sometimes it is hard to know what to say
that will comfort. Us two in the armchair;
me holding her breath, 'they're ignorant
let's have some tea and cake, forget them.'

Maybe it's really Bette Davis I want
to be the good twin or even better the bad
one or a nanny who drowns a baby in a bath.
I'm not sure maybe I'd prefer Katherine
Hepburn tossing my red hair, having a hot
temper. I says to my teacher Can't I be
Elizabeth Taylor, drunk and fat and she
just laughed, not much chance of that.
I went for an audition for *The Prime
of Miss Jean Brodie*. I didn't get a part
even though I've been acting longer
than Beverley Innes. So I have. Honest.

*Olubayo was the color of peat
when we walked out heads turned
like horses, folk stood like trees
their eyes fixed on us—it made me
burn, that hot glare; my hand
would sweat down to his bone.
Finally, alone, we'd melt
nothing, nothing would matter*

*He never saw her. I looked for him in her;
for a second it was as if he was there
in that glass cot looking back through her.*

On my bedroom wall is a big poster
of Angela Davis who is in prison
right now for nothing at all
except she wouldn't put up with stuff.
My mum says she is *only* 26
which seems really old to me
but my mum says it is young

just imagine, she says, being on
America's Ten Most Wanted People's List at 26!
I can't.
Angela Davis is the only female person
I've seen (except for a nurse on TV)
who looks like me. She had big hair like mine
that grows out instead of down.
My mum says it's called an *Afro*.
If I could be as brave as her when I get older
I'll be OK.
Last night I kissed her goodnight again
and wondered if she could feel the kisses
in prison all the way from Scotland.
Her skin is the same too you know.
I can see my skin is that colour
but most of the time I forget,
so sometimes when I look in the mirror
I give myself a bit of a shock
and say to myself *Do you really look like this?*
as if I'm somebody else. I wonder if she does that.

I don't believe she killed anybody.
It is all a load of phoney lies.
My dad says it's a set up.
I asked him if she'll get the electric chair
like them Roseberries he was telling me about.
No he says the world is on her side.
Well how come she's in there then I thinks.
I worry she's going to get the chair.
I worry she's worrying about the chair.
My dad says she'll be putting on a brave face.
He brought me a badge home which I wore
to school. It says FREE ANGELA DAVIS
And all my pals says 'Who's she?'

They Said

MI OK SONG BRUINING

They said
Smile for the camera
Open your eyes, they are squinting
But my eyes weren't squinting.

They said
Stop crying, stop feeling bad.
Those kids who call you "Chink"
And "Flat Face"
Don't know anything
Besides, you probably provoked them.

They said
Feel lucky
You were "chosen"
Really meaning
I was also given up.

They said
We are offended,
You have everything, so be happy.
Be appreciative, and
Never let the tears show.

They said
You don't belong here.
Where do you come from?
Do you speak English?
Do you like America?
As if I just landed
From a distant galaxy.

They said
Everything I hoped and dreamed
And prayed they wouldn't.
They still do.

In the Blood

LEANNA JAMES

Grandfather Henry looks at me from a framed black-and-white photograph on the living room wall. Thinning black hair, reserved smile, and eyes with a dark glow of kindness in them, eyes that say, *Talk to me, my little dear. Come, tell me your secrets.*

But it is your secrets, Grandfather, that I want to know. I know you only from your pictures, and the stories my mother and Grandmother Henry used to tell. Baby-in-a-Basket Grandfather. Orphanage Grandfather. Esteemed Doctor Grandfather. Clarence Henry, beloved of Violet Henry. You died in a hospital in Mexico, surrounded by wilting tropical bouquets and "Feel Better Soon!" greeting cards, a pack of Lucky Strikes under your pillow that the night nurse had sneaked in for you.

You were fifty-two years old. Your heart attack on that family vacation stunned my grandmother and left her stunned for the next thirty years. And then at last she joined you, reunited with the husband who had left her so quickly, "just up and died, no thank you or good-bye."

August 1952, Mexico City. What did it feel like to spend your last days among strangers in a strange place? Was it a fitting end, after all, for someone whose first days began on the doorstep of an orphanage? You left a blank page where our ancestors' names should have been written, but you tried to find these names, I know. My mother told me: You waited forty-six years, until both your adopted parents had died, and then you took the leap. You wrote letters, you made phone calls, you hired a private detective. There had to be a birth certificate somewhere, no matter what the Henrys had told you; there must be some kind of record, a scrawled note in a log at the orphanage, anything. But the detective came back empty-handed. The orphanage you remembered? It was burned to the ground in the San Francisco earthquake and fire of 1906. All the records were destroyed. The names of your parents, if they existed at all, curled upward in orange wisps into a burning sky.

I have only a few bits and pieces of family lore: In 1899 a young woman knocked on the door of St. Vincent's, thrust a basket containing a tiny blanketed form into the hands of the astonished nun, and fled. The nun lifted the blanket with trembling old fingers and there was your small red face, your eyes tightly shut as if protecting yourself from what you might see. But did the woman tell her name or your father's, your place of birth, anything at all?

Around you the neighborhood swarmed with sailors home from ships docked in the San Francisco harbor, ruddy-skinned women washing clothes in the street, shouting barefoot children. There were fish markets, pubs and bars, tobacco and newsstands selling papers from Ireland, Italy, Portugal, the Philippines. Your father may have read one of these newspapers, sitting at a rough wooden table with a cup of thick black coffee and a slice of sweet pannetone, worrying about his starving relatives back home in Liguria. My grandmother favored this idea. You looked "swarthy," she said, with your olive skin and dark eyes, your ink-black hair that began thinning, to your dismay, at the age of twenty-five.

You inherited other things too, I am told. Hidden things that swam eagerly to the surface as soon as you left your adopted home with the Henrys. (They brought you home when you were five years old, to a place of good manners and silent prayers, a place where you grew up safely but never learned to breathe.)

The Henrys did not understand their grown-up son: your taste for the horse track, for gambling and bridge, for gin and rare steaks and fine Cuban cigars. Mr. Henry stopped speaking. Mrs. Henry wept on the telephone. What was wrong with you? Where did you learn to love these wicked things? You wept also, afraid to lose these two people who had loved you. But you didn't stop loving what you loved, the mud-pounding storm of horses out of the starting gate at Bay Meadows, the sharp slap of cards on a polished table, the first tang of Beefeater's on your tongue after a long day at the hospital.

"If it's in the blood, it's in the blood, and no amount of upbringing or book-learning can alter that fact," my grandmother said.

In the blood. Whose voice spoke to you through this blood? The salted growl of an Italian fisherman? The lilt of an Irish miner who spent his gold on horses and opera? But the rules for living that pumped from your orphan heart didn't come from your father alone. Your mother's blood was in you, too. It is her voice that answers me when I close my eyes and ask: Who was my grandfather? Who am I?

This is the story my dreams have told me: Your mother was no cast-off waif, stumbling pregnant through the city streets. Too melodramatic, too predictable. A Lillian Gish movie. No, your father loved your mother. He was the one who wanted to marry, but she chose against a life of cooking and laundry, crying babies and fish on Fridays. She played piano at the Barbary Auditorium, entertaining the miners who poured into town from the Gold Country, looking for whiskey and lush women in red lace. Your mother pushed them off her piano bench, laughing, and played them shanties and ballads, rags and dances all night long.

Your father was the first and last man your mother allowed to sit with her on the piano bench. It was too easy, over time, to move from bench to the bar, from the bar to her suite of rooms down the street. The night he placed the green velvet box from the jeweler's on her pillow, she made up her mind. Can you see me, she asked him, halfway between a sob and a laugh, on my knees scrubbing your skivvies? Frying your trout in an old iron skillet?

Thank you kindly, but no, dear me, no.

Your father disappeared after she refused him, boarded a train home to Virginia City and didn't look back. He kept the ring in his pocket should he meet another nice lady someday (but the only lady he met after your mother was the elderly nurse at his bedside, where he lay dying of tuberculosis one year later). He never knew anything about you.

Your mother didn't grieve when your father left. She had her piano, her cozy rooms, her twenty-three silk dresses, her deck of hand-painted playing cards from India. She played her favorite music in the evenings for singing, boisterous crowds; went home alone at dawn and had sausage and eggs for breakfast, and then slept contentedly all afternoon, the fog drifting in through her window. And every Sunday afternoon (until she grew too big with you) she headed out to the stables to ride her mare, Picardy Rose, on Sutro Beach.

When you came she knew what she had to do. Your mother kissed you hard, told you she loved you, wrapped you up, and boarded the streetcar to St. Vincent's. She knew the sisters would care for you as they had once cared for her, in another orphanage on the other side of the world in Ireland.

She had lived at St. Brigid's until age fifteen, when the good sisters raised the money for her passage to America. And now ten years later here she stood ringing the bell, waiting to give her baby back to the Church. A kind of offering, perhaps. A kind of thanks.

She had planned what she would say. But when the door opened, your mother couldn't speak. She turned and ran, the hem of her dress dragging in the dirt, her crumpled face not quite hidden by her velvet hat. Sister Agnes gathered you up, took you inside, and your new life began among the other orphaned babies. You were tended to in rickety cribs by the soft hands of old women who murmured prayers over your baby head, washed your face in holy water, and held bottles of warm milk to your mouth. You were christened Christopher. You grew healthy and strong. Your world for five years was made of ringing bells and women in white, rows of tiny beds and fog dreaming outside the windows of your sleeping room. You played marbles and stickball in the concrete courtyard behind the church. You had no one to call "Mama" but many you called "Sister," and for a father you had the big picture of Jesus in his red robes, smiling down at you in the cloister.

And so you grew, happy in a way, under the loving care of Sister Agnes and Sister Maria, Sister Patricia Ann and Sister Bernadette. You washed vegetables in the big kitchen; you helped scrub the windows and sweep the floors of the rectory. You learned your prayers in English and Spanish (Sister Maria, breaking the rules). You learned to read by the age of five, sounding out the words in the little brown speller Sister Agnes gave you.

And then one afternoon, the Henrys came.

Mr. and Mrs. Orville Henry had driven down from their cottage in Calistoga after reading newspaper stories about the multitudes of motherless children bursting the seams of the city's orphanages. Beds, clothes, and medicine were in short supply. Children could no longer be fed. The Henrys had never had children; now here was their chance. They took a thoughtful tour of the big rooms where the children waited, scrubbed and sitting quietly on their beds—some in hope, others in dread. Will they pick me? Will they take me away?

You were torn between the two, not knowing whether to be excited or frightened. Your legs trembled as you waited. Mr. and Mrs. Henry looked carefully at each child until they came to you. You showed them your speller; you read from the little book in your hands, showing them how smart you were. What a bright child! And so well-behaved. And those pretty brown eyes—just precious. Your world turned over the day the Henrys found you. The paperwork took a long time, but finally they came to fetch you as you waited in Sister Agnes's office, dressed in the only clothes you had: a worn but clean pair of short serge pants with suspenders, a plaid wool shirt, a brown cap that perched crookedly on your head. Here's our boy, here he is!

Your boy? Am I your boy now?

August 1904. The Henrys renamed you Clarence and took you home. In Calistoga the summer brought sultry heat instead of fog, and yellow roses bloomed beneath your window. You tumbled out of the car. Oh! A grassy yard to play in! Trees to climb in! A room with only one bed in it, all yours! Christopher was left behind, a name that crawled under the bed in which you had slept for five years, and turned into dust. You were Clarence Henry now, and a Seventh-Day Adventist. A Seventh-Day what?

The Henrys explained, their voices calm and soothing as buttermilk. No meat. That wasn't hard; you never got much meat at the orphanage. No dancing. You hadn't danced much, either. No wine. Wine? Church on Saturdays. Church is church, no matter what day of the week it is. The next week, you started school. In your first grade there were lots of children with one mother and one father, and they found nothing strange about it at all.

"Call me 'Mummy,'" Mrs. Henry said. "And you can call Mr. Henry 'Daddy.'

Say it after me now: 'Mummy.' That's right. And now: 'Daddy.' Good, good! Come now, let me hold you, let me give you a kiss. My darling little boy." You snuggled in deep. This was heaven. Gradually you forgot Sister Agnes and Sister Maria, the words to "Hail Mary" in Spanish, the smell of fish and fog outside your window.

When did the blood of your birth father and mother begin speaking to you?

When did you know you were not Clarence Henry, nor the orphan Christopher, but someone else entirely? If you knew while you were growing up, you gave no sign. You were too grateful to have a home, too busy learning how to be a man. You did especially well in science. With your agile hands and your affectionate ways (nursing back to health a sick bird you found in your yard; bringing your mother glasses of ginger ale on a tray when she felt "fatigued" and took to her bed), you were marked as a future doctor. A foundling boy becoming a doctor! Mr. and Mrs. Henry saved their money, and you studied as if the secret to life lay in the pages of your schoolbooks. The day you turned eighteen your blood began talking. You packed your valise and boarded the train to Los Angeles, your veins humming over the urgent hum of the tracks. UCLA was waiting, your pre-med studies. You were alone for the first time in your life (although I think you may have always been alone in your heart) and the world opened in the palm of your hand like the proverbial oyster. Los Angeles! The Roaring Twenties were coming, and your blood began roaring in anticipation.

Now there were speakeasies and nightclubs, dark smoky places where men and women drank gin straight and danced close together to a new music called jazz. You ate your first steak in a clubhouse with your new roommate, taking rapid guilty bites and glancing over your shoulder as if a shadowy, Seventh-Day Adventist cop were waiting to arrest you. No one arrested you or even noticed you. You finished your steak in a burst of relief and bliss—"Say, Pete, this is awfully good!"—and soon you were joining your roommate in a round of drinks. At the dances there were women with bobbed blonde hair and dresses that showed bare arms and calves, women who smoked and smiled right at you, whose painted eyes spoke of a world that Mrs. Henry or Sister Agnes could never imagine.

You had been told all your life that too much pleasure was wrong. But your blood told you otherwise. You turned away from morning services, nut loaf and water for lunch, a passage from Matthew or John before bed. When you started your internship at the hospital, you took your new identity with you: Clarence Henry, bright young doctor and man-about-town. Your smile was wide. Your hair and shoes shone. When you smoked on your breaks, the nurses thought it was glamorous.

You didn't know when you walked among the hospital beds that you had, in fact, returned to the orphanage. Your "identity" was not so new, after all. The same rows of white beds, the same pinched faces of children in pain. Women in white rustled quietly down the halls. You had gone home again, but you thought you had found a new place. When you touched a sick child, you didn't realize you touched your own face, the face of the motherless boy twenty-five years before. Your hands had not forgotten what your thoughts had erased. And when you looked into the eyes of my grandmother for the first time, the soft blue eyes of a young nurse named Violet, your orphan heart whispered: home. Home. And then: "Sister? Is that you?"

You listened to your heart without quite hearing the words. The hat-check girl at the club was miffed when you canceled your date that night, but you didn't care. My grandmother had said, "Why, yes," when you asked her to tea, changing in two syllables the course of your life.

Violet McCall, fresh off the train from a small mining town in Virginia, her hair pinned primly under her white cap, her arms smelling of soap and starch (a strangely familiar, reassuring smell), was the right kind of woman to marry. A gentleman might dally with a bob-haired dolly, but he would never walk her down the aisle. In the spring of 1925, after a courtship of three months, you stood in a rented wedding suit under an arbor of oleanders, and slid a plain gold band on your bride's pale finger. That night, the new Mrs. Henry undressed, trembling in the closet, and approached the bed in a gown that covered every inch of her skin. And if the consummation was a little disappointing, if in fact it failed to happen at all ("I'm sorry, my dearest Vi. No, there's nothing wrong, darling, I'm just a bit tired, don't cry now, don't cry, you're lovely . . ."), you didn't worry at first. This was a holy union, you argued with yourself. It would take time.

In time, you would forget Dottie's hat-check hands on your back, Sally's arms around your waist, the feel of your mouth against Gloria's perfumed neck. You would get over this damnable shyness with Violet.

And so you began a new life: A bright young doctor starting a practice, your nurse and still-virgin wife at your side. Delivering babies on Indian reservations, you pulled the wet newborns from between their mothers' heaving thighs; you smacked their bottoms and heard their first startled cries. Again your secret heart rose up, this time crying: "Mother!" But it was not Mrs. Henry's face who answered the call. It was no face at all, just a bright glowing blur. You shook your head, banished the blur, handed the infants to Violet to be washed. Nonsense, you thought. This sudden sentimentality: simply nonsense! But you always waited around, sharing a cigar with the fathers or fussing with your bag, secretly waiting for the moment when the breast would come out, when the baby's tiny mouth would close around the dark nipple and begin, ecstatically, to suck.

It was after one of these births, back home in the little cottage near the San Jacinto mountains, that my mother was finally conceived.

Your relief knew no bounds. At last, a proper husband. And now a father! But the second man who lived within you, the man who listened to your blood's yearnings, was the man my mother loved most of all. It is this man I am talking to now. Did you really take my mother in a pink ruffled dress to the race track and teach her how to bet? Did you really show her how to fix your martinis, shuffle a deck of cards like a dealer, light your cigar? Was it you who told her that fairies danced in the smoke rings you made? And you, I'm sure, who took her riding without a saddle, let her sleep with her dog, taught her to drive a car at fourteen.

I'm angry with you. Why did you have to die before I was born? Why couldn't you have waited for me? I would have gone to the track with you. I would have shared your cigar.

And I would have forgiven you for the other woman. Don't protest, I know all about her, my grandmother told me. She called your mistress "a little nurse with a loose cap," and thirty years later still thought of her as a dangerous tart, although the woman must have been close to sixty by then.

"You can't trust women like that," Grandma would say in a whisper, "they'll wreck a home with the blink of a lash." But this one didn't wreck your home, as it turned out. She left town after the apartment you shared was discovered, hopped on a bus with a trunkful of the dresses you bought and a pocketbook stuffed with good-bye cash. She didn't get much. But she had one thing my grandmother said you never gave her, and that was the memory of a happily shared bed.

Or maybe there was one other thing she got. While you were on vacation with Violet in Mexico, on the grand "I'll make it up to you darling" trip, was the little nurse lunging out of her rooming-house bed every morning, running down the hall to the bathroom with the taste of soda crackers rising in her throat? Did the blood that talked to you flow into the blood of an unwanted son? (It is always a son, in my mind.) I might have an uncle somewhere, an uncle about ten years older than I am, who doesn't know his name or where he comes from.

Or maybe this is just a romantic notion. I will never know, just as I will never know what blood runs in my own veins. I don't know the meaning, finally, of "family," if there is such a thing. Who makes your family? The people who gave birth to you? Who raised you? The friends who have known you and loved you? The people who share your bed? Who share your secret heart?

I think I am like you, Grandfather. I have had to forge an identity out of yearning and imagination, scraps of a vision that came from I don't know where, obedience to an inner prompting (of the blood, of the spirit) that took me from my family into an unknown world. I imagine you dying in your hospital bed in Mexico, preparing to meet your people at last. I hear you asking them: Mother and Father, why did you leave me? Was it you who made me what I am? Was it you who told me to do the things I did?

This time when I close my eyes I hear no answer. There is only the silence of my own mind, unbroken silence and a still image from a dream I once had in which I died (I hear you're not supposed to dream of your own death, but I did). In the dream I returned, died and returned over and over again. Each time I returned, I looked like someone else; when I woke up, I could not remember my own face. And yet I knew I was alive.

After death, what does it matter if you are Portuguese or Irish, the son of a fisherman or the son of a poet? Your atoms fall to earth and become flowers, stones, water. Your children and grandchildren, who walk about with your blood pumping through their legs, your blood rushing to their brains, will become these things too.

I used to play a game when I lived in San Francisco. I would search out men who looked like you, who resembled your photographs, and I would pretend these men were my cousins or uncles. In cafés, laundromats, in lines at the bank, on the bus, would scan the faces with dark eyes and strong noses, black hair and olive skin, and imagine a kinship with them, imagine that the faces' owners felt something as they passed by me. Perhaps we would both feel a tiny electrical charge, a sympathetic quickening in the veins; we would look at each other and our atoms would say "kin."

After I "met" hundreds of relatives this way, I stumbled on a new idea. One day, browsing among lettuces at a produce market where all the employees looked like you—the cashier, the men unloading trucks, the woman spraying the vegetables with water—I realized how big my family had become. Anyone who might be, is.

But then why stop there? Why stop with people who share a jaw-line, a nose, a way of walking? I don't know who your people are, Grandfather. I can't draw boundaries with any certainty, saying to one person: "You are my brother," and to another, "You are not."

There is no one to claim as my own. And there is no one to turn away.

Is this, then, the lesson of your blood?

Word Problem

AMY JANE CHENEY

If you are 26 years old
and had 1 mother who gave
birth to you but then
was taken away and
married someone else and had
1 daughter and 1 son
plus you had 1 father who
married 1 woman who was
pregnant with 1 child that
was not his,
but then had 2
daughters after that
who were and then got
divorced in 1977 and
married another woman
and had 1
son—
if all that happened,
plus, additionally
you had another
mother and father
who you knew and who
lived in a house that
you lived in also and who
then had 2 sons;
how many mothers, fathers,
brothers, sisters, half
brothers, half sisters,
stepmothers, stepfathers,
aunts and uncles do you
have including the ones
you haven't met yet?

My Stone Is Sardonyx

KATHARYN HOWD MACHAN

I search for you
through half-hidden stories,
his blank pauses,
her lowered lids

the night I began,
near Hallow's Eve,
you were seventeen—did you
dress as a gypsy that year?

I see you holding
your boyfriend's hand,
his eyes brown and steady
as mine in the mirror

will the smell of leaves
stay with you forever?
pumpkins grinning
as his hands held your hips?

twenty years now
I have lived with others,
your unknown name
like a ghost at heart's edge

I call you She-
Who-Once-Touched-the-Moon
and I wake aching
in October light

Unborn Song

SIU WAI STROSHANE

She comes to me at night, unbidden, as I lie on the border of sleep. I think I am still awake. I can clearly see the streetlight shining through the blinds, the dresser with its red-fringed shawl hanging like limp, lifeless fingers. I can still feel the wrinkled sheets under my hip, and the vast ache in my womb.

When I see her, she is next to my music stand, as if she is about to sing one of my arias—"un bel di" perhaps, or "Morte Di Butterfly," the only classical role that I as a Chinese American have managed to land.

Her hair is streaked with gray, her hands thick and swollen. She is short and very stout. If I were to get out of bed and stand next to her, no doubt I would tower over her, even in my woolly socks. My milk-fed bones and broad shoulders would dwarf her Chinese frame, though I once was destined to become as malnourished as she. Because of her sacrifice, I grew up instead on hamburgers and mashed potatoes.

"It's what you wanted for me, isn't it, Ma?" I long to shout into the winter stillness, but all that comes out is a strangled groan. Besides, I haven't a scrap of Cantonese at my command, and I don't know if she would understand English or not. What do I owe her, anyway?

She doesn't speak—she never does. Only stares at me with her sad dark eyes, her hands clasped low on her belly, shaping an empty womb. Twice bereft—first a daughter, now a granddaughter, for I have no doubt that it was a girl—and now she has come to collect her debt.

What do I owe her? Life itself? It was not my doing. The lost grand-child—well, that was my doing.

"What do you want from me, Ma?" Again my strangled groan. "I had to. I had to. I couldn't go through what you went through." Nine months of stretching and swelling and bulging, the nausea, the move-ments, the kicking, the dreams—and then the pain of separation. A life torn from within, gone before the breasts have even begun to fill with milk. And the eternal wondering—What would become of the child, my own flesh? No, I couldn't endure that.

"Ma, when I'm on the street sometimes, I think I see your face. Did you follow me to America?"

She cannot read my thoughts. My heart is pounding with anger and I sit up in bed.

"Did you steal my voice, Ma? Is this your revenge?" This time I manage a hoarse croak.

She looks at the music stand and smiles for the first time. I see her missing front teeth—What has her life been like? Grinding toil, no doubt, perhaps hunched over miles of blue denim, or mountains of tiny toy parts in some factory. Pink doll legs moving past her on a conveyor belt, and her eyes have grown blurry as she seizes them and joins them to fat pink plastic bodies, then jams on sightless heads with stiff blonde hair—a she-god creating endless identical Eves. At the shrilling of the six o'clock bell, she takes off her smock and plods down smelly steps onto even smellier streets, picking her way through the garbage and the gaping tourists. Rice vendors shout, taxis honk, neon signs blind her tired eyes. She purchases fish and rice, trudges home to a fifth-floor walk-up. Are there clamoring children, a silent sullen husband? I always picture her alone, maybe because I cannot conceive of having actual brothers and sisters. Then I would have to wonder, why did she give me away?

In my mind's eye, I see her huffing up the stairs through a labyrinth of dimly lit hallways, to a many-bolted red metal door. The paint is cracked and peeling, and the air is thick with her neighbors' cooking smells. Her arthritic fingers fumble with the keys—so many of them— and the handle of her string bag cuts into her flesh. At last she is inside. If she lives alone, she has only one room. A pile of dusty oranges decorates the mantle, with its shrine and faded photographs of faces I do not recognize.

My mother, the one I've never known, wearily unloads her bag and sets out the fish, the bok choy, the ginger root. She lights the flame under the battered wok and sets the oil to sizzling. Perhaps she sits down to eat with the company of a tinny radio pouring its staticky Hong Kong pop tunes into the air. She leans back on her dingy red kitchen chair, kicks off her slippers, and drifts back to the days when she could still hope and dream—before my time.

While six thousand miles away, I dash into the donut shop for a Styrofoam cup of bitter black coffee, then back into the freezing rain to a crowded subway train that will take me to endless rehearsals and voice lessons.

My mother and I were once one flesh. Now we struggle separately through our days. It's only at night that she torments me with her silent reproach. If she has stolen my voice, I must turn to pen and paper. But creation is beyond me right now, and so I go backwards, reliving all that has gone before, in hopes of finding reasons, answers, and dreams for the future. In so many ways I am still an unborn song.

Mothers

SUSAN VOLCHOK

And just in case you're sick of talking about the whole thing, there's Miss Marion Pincus, M.S.W., to the rescue. Also known as Miss Pinch Us, Pink Ass, or plain Pinky, she's scared shitless of silence, I think. All she does is talk. And talk. Then, she tries to get you to talk, and when she's supposed to be listening, you can see she's squinting to catch that little voice in her own head, which must be whispering the next brilliant remark. The sickest part of the joke is she really does seem to think she's brilliant.

"You don't look very comfortable." That's the first thing she says to me, our first appointment, after she closes the door of the little office and turns to look me over. It isn't exactly an earth-shattering intuition; I'm standing in the middle of the room with my arms folded, standing as still as I can, staring at her. "Why don't you sit down in one of the chairs, or on the couch?" They don't call this Therapy, and I don't know about couches yet, or about how she's probably going to take notes on which chair I choose. "Make yourself comfortable. Please." I don't want to get too comfortable, or have to stay too long.

"I'm fine."

Maybe she's the uncomfortable one?

"Let's sit down and get to know one another a little better," she says, and she sits facing me in one of a pair of low, dark cushiony chairs you sort of sink into—and can't get up out of so easy, either. At least, I can't. She opens a file folder full of papers on her lap: My official story, I guess. But she asks me to "tell something" about myself. So much for that getting-to-know-you crap.

"Well, you have all of that on me already, and I don't know anything about you. Why don't *you* tell *me* about yourself?" I'll give her this: She doesn't say "no way;" she tells me her name, where she's from (Long Island), where she went to school (somewhere on Long Island), how long she's been working here (less than a year.) She isn't married . . . "yet." Of course, she has no kids. I don't know how old she is. Not old, maybe ten years older than I am. But she's the one with the chart and the pen and the questions.

"You were sixteen in October. So now, it's March, you're almost sixteen and a half, right?"

I nod, Right.

"And . . . how many months along?"

"Almost six."

"Hmmm." Of course she doesn't know about the accidental sweet sixteen celebration where everything started, and she isn't going to, not if I have anything to do with it. "How are you feeling?" Her brown eyes are big with something—sympathy, maybe.

"I'm fine."

"Good, good." She shakes her head, sighs. "It's not an easy situation for a girl to find herself in." Uh huh. Like she knows the first thing about it. "Tell me how your parents have reacted." She must have his letters and the other stuff right there, where her eyes are wandering. But she has to keep the chat going, and, I guess, she doesn't want to clue me right off that she knows everything there is to know about me. Thinks she knows, I mean.

"I'm here." They dumped me here, I want to say. But I don't have to hand her anything extra just yet.

"Well . . . Maybe they felt they had no choice; it can't be easy for them either." It doesn't surprise me that she isn't really on my side. It's actually another of those uncanny, homey touches, as if she's another stand-in for Them. I like to know what's what. "It's a difficult situation all around, don't you think?"

"I guess so." But I'm the one who's gone, kicked out, stuck here, waiting.

She lets herself frown a little bit. It isn't going the way she wants. I'm not opening up fast enough for her. She moves right in.

"You don't get along with them very well . . . ?"

Nice of her to make it a question. "I guess not."

"Even before the . . . before you were pregnant?" She isn't the only one who doesn't like to call the baby a baby just yet. Meanwhile, I have this condition, this situation, this problem, some trouble: I'm pregnant, which is like, such a dumb doctor word. Say it a few times and it starts to sound like some old bug you get and eventually get over. Like measles or mumps. Pregnant: Oh, yeah, yeah. No big deal. What does she really want to talk about, anyway?

"Before? Things were all right."

"But not great."

I just shrug. *What do you think?*

"You're adopted," she tells me, her voice a little softer, like she's worried she might be breaking the news for the first time. Like it isn't the main fact of my life, always something to remind me, every day of the sixteen-and-a-half years I've spent with them. But I have to admit, it's been a long time since anyone has actually talked about it, or expected me to want to. Everyone I know just *knows,* and that's that. I've never been particularly sensitive about the subject, not as long as you stick to the straight stuff: Who, when, where, even why. But I probably sound sensitive and sore to her. Because I still don't know what she's after.

"So?" My mother's right about one thing; I don't care enough about what kind of impression I make, first, last, or otherwise.

"Well . . . Do you think being adopted has made a difference; I mean, has it made getting along harder? You're smiling; did I say something funny? Is that such a funny question?"

Funny? In one way, the answer is screamingly obvious. But in another, it's such a Big Question, so out of the blue, that my sixteen-year-old mind can't grasp how anyone could put it to me and expect an instant answer. And I can't begin to imagine what the real answer is. I've never spent a whole lot of time thinking about what might have been. Not to say I don't think a lot about the way things are and feel pretty miserable and wish, and wish . . .

"Sometimes adopted children feel they're very different from their adoptive parents, from their brothers and . . ."

"I'm very close to my brother," I say. "And he's crazy about me." Just ask them. It drives them crazy, their own little boy, following me around like a stray puppy. When I'm supposed to be the stray.

"That's good, that's very good, to have someone at home you feel that way about." If I didn't want her to nod and smile, why mention Toddy just now? But somehow, the stamp of approval makes me sorry I've said anything. "Is there anyone else you're close to, comfortable with, someone who really loves you?" She hesitates, and adds, "Besides your brother, and your parents of course."

"Of course."

"You don't think they love you?" She purses her lips, gets a grip on her pen, like, maybe we're gonna get to the good shit.

"They say they do. And everyone knows how much they've done for me." It's their favorite theme, in public and private. "So I guess they must love me. I mean, of course they do." I'm not half as sarcastic a kid as they make me out to be; but it's true I can take a Tone when I want to.

"I see." She does scratch out a few notes then. "You sound angry." I don't even bother shrugging or shaking my head. I can see she's got her teeth into this now. "Because they sent you away?"

Or because they took me in the first place, and have never in all these years had the first clue about me, just seemed to be waiting, always, for this chance, the perfect excuse, to cut me loose? "You tell me," I invite Miss Pink Ass.

Patient social-working smile. "You're getting angry at me now, I think."

That makes me smile too, in spite of myself. "I'm not big on talking these days."

"Which is not like you, you mean?" she asks.

"I don't know what's 'like me,' anymore," I allow.

"Everything's different, all of a sudden," she says. "And difficult." That sad, sympathetic refrain again. But the truth is, I'm the only thing that's different. And they've fixed it so it won't be difficult for anyone but me. It won't take too much effort, or too much time, before they can almost forget all about me and the whole . . . situation.

"Talking can make things easier," she adds hopefully. "That's why I'm here."

"Uh huh." What a job. And she takes it seriously. That's enough to shut me up.

"And why I wondered if there isn't anyone else you felt close enough to talk to at home, someone you trusted and . . ." Her phone rings, as loud as an ambulance crashing through the quiet office.

Granny. For a moment, in the jangling confusion, I suddenly imagine it might actually be Granny on the phone, because I've thought of her, because I need her, yes. I need one of her fairy godmother appearances, the kind that worked little miracles for me when I was little. Long, long ago. But I remember; I won't ever forget. Always loved me for no good reason. Took me as I was, right from the beginning, I believe. Whoever I was. I mean, I'm not hers, not by blood. And the one I belong to, who couldn't spare the smallest part of that feeling Granny has for me, not in a lifetime. I think she can hardly stand it, really. It doesn't make sense to Mother; I don't deserve it, do I? After what I've done . . .

". . . sorry, someone needed to speak to me right away," she's saying. Like maybe she saved someone's life, phone-to-phone resuscitation. She's about the last person in the world I'd dial in an emergency, but I guess she's all some people have.

"Where were we?" She has a habit of staring straight into your eyes, with hers wide open, a tight smile stretching her thin lips. It wouldn't have looked sincere to a trusting tyke like Toddy; and of course I like to think I'm ahead of myself, at sixteen, sniffing out phonies.

"I think you want to know why I don't trust you." I figured she must have heard something like it a million times, so I'm kind of surprised to see her redden up and rake her hands through her cute bubble cut, like a cat whose feelings have been ruffled by a fall off the mantel. It almost makes me feel sorry for her.

"Oh. Is that what you thought we were getting to?" she says, breezy, feeling better about herself already, it seems. "Well, I imagine it *is* hard for you to trust people," she proposes, instantly losing herself in the whole crowd of unreliable people in my life. "Being put up for adoption is a very unsettling primary experience for a child."

It will take me awhile to realize how carefully cruel the fancy words are. Now, they sting without my knowing exactly why. And all I care about is not letting her think that words can hurt me.

"I don't remember anything about it," I laugh, shrugging.

"No, of course not," she clucks. She leans toward me. "But I'm sure you've thought about it, all the same. You've thought about it and wondered."

"Wondered what?"

"Wondered . . . wondered, *What happened?*" Her eyes narrow.

"What happened?" I repeat as innocently as I can.

"Yes, that's what I said: What happened?"

"What happened?" I ask again. It's so interesting to me to watch her face sort of fracture into small twitches.

She puts down her pen, and folds her hands over the Stella files.

"What's the matter with you?" she asks.

"With me?" I shake my head. "I thought you knew."

"What would I know? Why would I know?" she sputters.

"Don't ask me," I protest, then motion toward her paperwork. "I figured you could at least tell me What Happened." Her face tells me I better not try that on her again. OK. "Like, maybe you know something I don't. Because I don't know anything about it. And I don't care." *OK?*

But you don't shut up a Pinch Us that easy.

"Not knowing and not caring are two very different things."

"Yeah? So?"

"So I find it hard to believe that you never think about where you came from, or wonder . . ."

We're back to the wondering. "What? *What?*" I demand.

"Just wonder why your mother decided . . ." For a moment, I'm not sure who she means, or which decision, ". . . that you would be better off with another family."

My first thought is: *She never decided that, she didn't know, she couldn't have known them. That wasn't her idea at all! That wasn't part of her choice.* But this isn't exactly what's on Miss Marion Pincus's tiny mind, anyway.

"Don't you ever think about her, your real mother? Haven't you ever tried to imagine how she felt, how she faced . . ."

What I'm facing, I think. And for a moment, I'm sitting all alone on that bench in Central Park again, officially (the clinic having confirmed what I already knew) one hour into the nine months, and two hours to go before I have to board a bus back to Blanding, New Jersey, and the beginning of the end. Will anything ever be the same again? *My mother; my mother would know.* The thought literally took my breath away; never in my life had I thought of that mystery woman as Mother. My mother.

And my mind had raced on. Knocked up. Always, before, that was some other girl's bad break, or dumb mistake. I hadn't ever pictured the woman who birthed me as one of those girls—a real, regular girl, one of the ones who gets caught. Like me. Sometimes it works out that way, doesn't it, and you have no say about it; it's just tough luck. *But she was tough enough to take it,* I thought. *And I'm tough enough too.* I didn't know what I meant yet, but I liked the sound of it very much.

Here, now, feeling some of that giddiness again, I wonder: *Did she ever in a million years think this could happen to her?* I didn't; how could she? Was she sad about it right off? Or was she glad, even a little bit glad? It would be nice to think that, but it doesn't make sense. She was scared, scared stiff; she wished it was all a bad dream. But the next day, when she woke up, it was the same. Her life. And she knew she was going to have to go through with it. But that's what she could tell me: how it's going to be, tomorrow and the day after that. *I'm living her life, my mother's life; it's my life now.* I'm closer to her than I've ever been since I was inside her. It's like I'm moving into her story, the part of it that connects us. Would she laugh or cry to find out that her baby girl is following in her exact footsteps? Maybe, like the family she gave that baby to for keeps, she just wouldn't be very surprised. Like mother, like . . .

Mother. This was my *mother,* damn it. *Not just some girl. My mother. Why couldn't she have done what a mother is supposed to do?* If she were here, we could talk now; I never asked her for anything before. But it's so stupid to wish, to want—as stupid as praying to God. She was a good person, she loved me, she wanted the best, she couldn't help it, I know; I know she couldn't. She was tough, she must have been tough, and I'm tough like her. Only, *couldn't she have been a little tougher? I belonged to her. Did she have to let them take me away?*

If I thought about her all the time, or *ever,* recalling my long-lost, mostly made-up mother wouldn't hurt like this. It hurts like hell. Or maybe it's finding myself back in the headshrinker's office of this girl's home, and knowing that daughter will follow mother to the bitter end.

"What are you thinking about?" asks Pinky, not unkindly. Maybe she really wants to know, among her other possible reasons for asking pointed, painful questions.

"Nothing," I say, sounding a little less sure of myself than I want to.

"Not about your mother?"

"Nah." I won't anymore, after this.

It's not a bluff. Having those thoughts, feeling sorry for myself in *that* way is definitely not my style. It's funny, isn't it, how people always want to make sure you're feeling the way they think you're supposed to. Like, every so often someone will want to know how come I'm not more curious about my Real Parents? It isn't right, they feel, their being more curious than me. With the persistent types, it doesn't work, saying what's true; that I've always been too busy living my life to spend a lot of time wishing for another one. Never mind trying to track down the couple who dropped me off here in this weird world and disappeared forever.

Not to say I never thought about them when I was a kid. Of course I did. I mean, the story I got when I was three or four about how a couple of teenagers no one had ever met had given me to Todd and Lucille Moore for safekeeping; well, it was pretty hard to swallow. For awhile, I just didn't believe it. I had never been one of those kids who dreams she's really somebody else, a baby princess (or witchling) found in the woods, to be raised by regular people until her rightful family comes to claim her. Actually, it was pretty unsettling to have to *start* to think of myself as a sort of visitor. Maybe it came too close to the truth of how things were going to be for me, with the Moores. Maybe I already had a feeling. And it didn't help to hear how very, very much I was wanted, because until that moment, it had never entered my mind that I wasn't. Now I knew there was such a thing as being unwanted.

And unlucky. Because of course they made just as much noise about what a lucky, lucky little girl I was, about my incredible good luck, being claimed by them. At the time, of course, I was too young; nothing to compare my life or my luck with. I listened, I looked at the "certificate" they showed me, a folded-up piece of paper covered with typewriting my mother kept in the bureau drawer under her white gloves, and I told them I understood what they were saying. But it wasn't a kid's kind of story at all.

First of all, there was nothing to it, besides some names and dates. It didn't have anything in it to make me believe, no real characters, no color, nothing but a few, bare facts: On October 13, 1945, Miss Margot Millet, seventeen years of age, had given birth to a girl baby at a Sisters of Charity Hospital outside New York City. The father was a Mr. Gregory Ellison, age nineteen. There were no addresses, no other particulars, nothing personal at all. There was nothing about what Miss Millet said when I was born, or when I was taken away.

It was only when I discovered, later on, that I could tell myself a lot of the stuff that their short, short story didn't. When I discovered Margot and Gregory in my daydreams and invented and reinvented them, I found the whole thing 1) possible (it was just like in fairy tales); 2) probable (didn't it explain my suspicion that I was someone they could send back somewhere, wherever that was?); and finally 3) just a fact of life. My life.

But even at the height of my storymaking, which took me through grade school, I hardly ever imagined that Margot and Gregory (nurse and doctor, star ballet dancers, pianist and composer, lovers ad nauseam) thought about me. Or (too wild to put into so many words) would actually come get me some fine day. The stories were about making sense, figuring out *why it all had to be*. Face it: no one's coming for you, kid.

Meanwhile, making up stories, especially lost-parent stories, wasn't exactly an approved activity around our house. I made the mistake of sharing some early efforts, before I was old enough to be a little smarter about stuff like that. They were outraged, of course. "It's all lies!!" And why would I want to dream up such "outlandish" characters for parents? Why not? I thought. Not much point in making Margot and Gregory as real, as pathetically ordinary, as the parents I knew. (Maybe, after all, that's what they really resented.)

Needless to say, the idea of scandalizing them only made the game more interesting, a slick secret pastime. And they had nothing to worry about anyway. I didn't believe in my own "lies" any longer than I had to understand how I came to be. And where. We Moores are raised to be realists. I didn't seriously play around with the past anymore by the time I turned twelve or thirteen.

So when I spun one last story, the longest one ever, and actually wrote it down, just like the truth, and handed it in to my tenth grade English teacher, it was, like, meant to be a joke. She'd asked for an essay on Family History. That's what I gave her.

"Margot Millet should have married Gregory Ellison before he got himself shipped overseas. They were really, really in love. They had been like husband and wife for over a year. But he wasn't ready to take the plunge. And besides, suppose something happened to him and she became a widow at her age? For there was a big, nasty fight ahead in Europe. He didn't think how foolish it was to leave her like this, not married and a damaged piece of goods (as some people might put it). But that was him. She said she'd wait and she was so stirred up by his patriotism that she went to work herself, in a factory where they made bombs. She spent ten hours a day tightening bolts on something she hoped they would drop on Germany or Japan. Maybe Greg would be the one who did it!

"Thinking like that made her the best worker in the plant, and it made her tough. Even though she faithfully wrote him, she never told

Gregory she was carrying his child. She figured he had enough problems of his own. Next to fighting a war, having a baby wasn't so much. There were plenty of pregnant girls working right up until the day in the plant. She could do that and by then, Gregory would be back and everything would be OK.

"But Gregory wasn't coming back. A few days before they called a truce, he parachuted from a burning plane into enemy territory and was never heard from again. Missing, presumed dead.

"Margot's toughness had all been a brave front and she crumbled. No way she could keep that baby now. She couldn't have cared less about the shame of it, her family was all gone and no one in town knew or cared what she did. But she was afraid it would look like Gregory and that would be too much to take. And it was a terrible burden on a baby, too, to come into the world without a father. Life was hard enough. She stopped wishing she had gotten a ring so she could be a real war widow, and started wishing she was dead too.

"But she wasn't, and the baby was about to be born, and then it was here. She didn't know what else to do, so she took it home with her. But that night when it started crying, she knew she had to do something already. She wrapped it in a blanket and tucked it into a picnic basket, along with a little note about who it was and some little clothes she had been collecting before the news about Gregory came. And she went and left it on the steps of a church. From there, it found its way to an adoption agency, which gladly gave the adorable baby girl to the first family that came along. Which was mine.

"Meanwhile, a few months later, Gregory turned up. Alive, I mean. There was a lot he didn't remember, and his eyes looked kind of funny. But he remembered Margot, and this time he was ready to marry her and settle down.

"By now, she wanted a family of her own as soon as possible. Deep down, she knew she loved children. She didn't tell Gregory about the first one, because she wasn't sure he could take it. Though she was sure she had done the right thing, and that if he'd been there he would've told her the same. No use crying over spilt milk, let bygones be bygones. She was so happy to be married to Gregory and working on a family. But nothing happened for such a long time that she got very down in the mouth and then the whole story came out, about their lost little daughter and all. And then, Gregory went berserk and blew the house up with a hand grenade he had brought back from the war as a souvenir."

Reading this epic, my teacher was not amused. First and foremost, it didn't fulfill the assignment, because it wasn't true, was it? I guess I just shrugged. It could be. I had no idea. I didn't really care; it made a good story, it made sense, as much sense as anything else I could say about life did. And I didn't care that the teacher thought the ending was "awful"; though I did care enough to talk her out of arranging a special conference with Todd and Lucille. I also promised to write an account of my adoption by, my growing up with the Moores, that would stick to the meager facts. That's what the teacher wanted, that's the way the world looked at things. And I mostly did too, by then.

But I always had a soft spot for my stories, especially for the way they ended. (M. and G. were nearly always killed off, though not always so gruesomely.) Pinky would've had a field day with them. But I really didn't feel much of anything about my main characters. Setting them up for a fall, then making them dead (which they were to me): that was just the way the thing had to go. It made the kind of sense I needed to make of the bits and pieces of family history I'd been handed.

Could I have really given them a different fate? Even if I made them special, really romantic, even if I made them crazy in love, I couldn't give them a choice about what to do to get themselves out of trouble. If there was one thing I was supposed to understand, it was that there was only one way.

"They were just too young to take care of a child properly; she wasn't much more than a child herself," Mother always maintained. "It's a darn shame they didn't think of that first, but they were weak. Not bad, mind you, just very, very weak. In a way, letting you go on to something better was the one strong, decent thing they did."

It wasn't their fault, was it, if letting me go turned out to be no guarantee of my happiness. Or if it sometimes seemed that my happiness wasn't exactly their main concern, and that it was maybe a little too easy an out. I wanted to believe what Mother said, that they couldn't help themselves. Which is why I couldn't help making life hard for them in the stories. And then, just for good measure, making their end even harder. If I was left with nowhere else to go at the finish, so were they. Blown up by a grenade. Lost at sea. Speeding off a cliff in a racy sports car. It was all sewed up neatly and (I realized when I got old enough to appreciate these things) satisfyingly tragic.

Hunger

JULIA SUDBURY

I was born on the day Biafra declared independence. Pushed out in a bloody mass, pathetic vulnerability crying out in pain, shaking in impotent anger at the severance from all that was warm and safe. Tiny hands clenched in an agony of loss. Eyes screwed up against the inevitable betrayal. I trembled when brisk pink hands wrapped me in towels turned rough with too many washes. Coarse whiteness, hostile to my soft brown body. Then a moment of respite, returned to the familiar rhythms of breath, heartbeat, blood that is my blood. I hunger for the I-we, the never-ending I that was also my universe. Pressing my-child flesh to my-mother flesh, desperate to be as one again. But then the pink hands grasp, tear me away, and terror invades me. For worse than the shock of this harsh white world is the severance, this emptiness where I-she should be. Her smell on the towel already fading.

I am hungry. I-she withholds the rich milk that fills my dreams. I am being punished. I don't know my crime or how to ask for forgiveness. She pulls her nightgown closer as the thin liquid drips relentlessly down her front, staining the embroidered cloth. Her breasts ache. I yearn for her warm softness. I want her to surrender herself to my hunger, to become nothing but the extension of my desire. I scream my frustration, but she does not hear. They feed me formula from a bottle, mouth full of rubber I reject time and time again. I vomit, coughing, turning pale. I cannot drink their formula, I am sickening. They think that I do not feel the rejection or know that I-she is not here. They think that I am not in trauma and so diagnose an allergy to egg. They change the formula. I drink, gagging. Still the milk stains her gown.

She believes she exists outside of my need. Believes that eighteen years passed before her belly swelled with this bitter fruit. She imagines that she was a student of medicine, with a career and dreams waiting. She visualises herself marrying, moving to the city paved with gold, becoming a mother to his children, children of his seed. To me she has no name. To me she is all names. Mother, milk, food, love, blood, myself. Starved, my need swells. If allowed, my need would devour her. Her milk, her blood, her spirit. She does not exist outside of I-we. I don't want her to live without me.

Obinwa. Lovechild. Conceived in the passion of idealism. Dreamed into being in a moment of imaginary freedom.

Connected still, I invade her dreams. Lie on her belly as she sleeps, feeling the in-out of her breath, blending with her rhythm. Pressing my tiny hand to the vast expanse of soft pale skin, I suckle her breast. Her nipple is dark and infinite, its contours tell me obscure secrets. She is drawing me back inside her as I suck, breathless. Milk foams into my mouth, filling me up. Satiated, I drink still. My mouth joined to her in endless passion. Waking, her gown flooded, she wails. The anguish of loss tears at the sensible rationality that guards her sanity. Worried, the night nurse rushes to the bedside, cautioning her to stay calm, not to make a scene. But her womb is throbbing, her breasts burn with my absence. She demands my return. Just this once, to feed my baby, feel her need, shield her vulnerability. Just this once so that she can know that she was loved. Just this once to still the pain in my breasts, this endless outpouring of motherlove.

The nurse's lip curls, images of strong black hands grasping pale flesh, dark penis pushing into pink seashell softness. Have some shame, she says. That creature is no part of you. Fruit of the devil, be grateful that you don't have to see his work again. Then, pity rising. Sleep now, child, nobody blames you. It wasna your fault that beast forced himself on you.

Nwagha. Child of war. Rage rises within me bitter as bile. Hatred is toxic on my tongue. Hating her absence, hating her, I hate myself.

Double Lifeline

SASHA GABRIELLE HOM

Where It Begins

My name is Wol Soon Ann. I was born somewhere in the south of Korea in a place called Anyang, a place that did not approve of bastard children. It is a place I was in only once, when I was first born. Though later I returned in my dreams. I know Anyang through these dreams and the stories I make up.

My name is bastard child. I was born in the winter. The snow blanketed the soil in a thick crunchy layer muffling the sounds of my mother's labor so that I could slip out like a wet secret. On the third day after my birth, my mother wrapped me in blankets and a woolen knit hat. She placed me in a basket and left me on the doorstep of a wealthy man's house. I imagine her heaving a big brass knocker and then disappearing into the snow like a fleeing rabbit. Perhaps she was crying, perhaps relieved. She left a note on the basket with my birthdate. Just like in the cartoons, I thought. The orphanage named me Wol Soon Ann, a common name like Mary Smith. Maybe I had other names before that—baby names like Sweetie, Pumpkin, Muffin. I do not know.

My name is Sophia Lee. My adopted parents couldn't decide what to name me. My mother wanted to name me Fanny or Lulu, impractical names for a round Korean baby. She settled on "Sophia," because my mother had heard someone calling their child, Sophia, in an empty museum. She said it sounded like the wind echoing off the cement walls.

My name is Li So Lan, because the child must have a Chinese name, even if she is Korean living like a Chinese American. My grandmother named me before she and my grandfather passed away, before I even knew what it meant to be a Chinaman's Korean baby in a country that belonged to neither one. The Chinese believe that when you are troubled, or grieving, or dying, if your "personal" name is spoken it will draw out the sorrow and the pain. My grandfather's name was Richard, my grandmother's name was Doris. I do not know either of their personal Chinese names. I wonder what was whispered into their ears as they slipped away.

My name is Sophia Lee. My uncle tells me I should reclaim my "original" name. I don't know what he's talking about.

My name is Sophia Lee. It has been on many mailboxes, school rosters, checks, bills, invitations. It has been written on love letters, hate mail, recommendations, eviction notices, airplane tickets, and veterinary bills. My name is Sophia Lee, but I imagine that when I die many names will be whispered into my ear from loved ones and ghosts I never knew.

My Hands

I have many lines on my palms. It's like a spiderweb except there are no circular designs or any meaning to the violent intersecting patterns running toward the edges of my palms. Some people can understand the lines. I do not. My mother says I have a double lifeline. Perhaps that means I have two lives. She says it is good luck, like having a high forehead and nose, or long earlobes like Buddha.

The Chinese believe a high bridge means you have expensive taste. My grandfather used to tease me when I was little. He'd say I should wear a clothespin on my nose at night to make it stand up higher, as if I were sniffing the air for the finer things in life. I don't know what he's talking about. No Chinese person I know has a high bridge. We have snub noses that spread gently across our faces, or pug noses, or flat noses, but not high sculpted noses like the white people who peer down their ski slope noses at us, and then sniff the air and show us their nostrils.

My mother says I have thick eyebrows. It's a sign of intelligence if they meet in the middle, and it's a sign of good *chi* if they're really bushy. She says my face is in harmony with itself. She once said that I had a face like Buddha, but I got offended because all I could think of was Buddha's big belly.

My mother says I have a double lifeline. Perhaps, she says, you have two lifelines because you are like a cat jumping off a roof who lands softly only because of the luck drawn from that other lifeline. If one lifeline fails the other can sustain you. But the way your luck has been going, she says, I wonder if a double lifeline really does mean you have two lives. She thinks one lifeline is my life now in America. The other one is the life that could have been—the life that began twenty-three years ago in a place called Anyang, the life that could have been if she had not rescued me from hunger and adopted me from a dying family now slowly fading from my memory, their mouths forming the words, "I love you," like fish gasping for air on a village dock. But I'm not sure if these are memories, or dreams, or images that I've made up to build myself a beginning.

My hands are small and slender. They do not look like they belong to me. This is the story they tell: "Once there was a young mother, small and beautiful, with slim hands and round little feet. She combs ribbons into her hair during the moon festival and cries every year when her children are not with her. Her skin is soft and smooth like the inside of a raw oyster, and her bones are fine porcelain."

This is the story I hear at night when my eyes are closed lightly, and I cannot tell if the story is memory whispered into a baby's ear or a dream that comes only at night. This is the story that begins my double lifeline:

"You are a child of warriors," she whispered into my tiny ear. "Your father is their general. Although you have never met him, you would think him a very handsome man. He sits proudly on his horse and looks like he could slice a dozen men with one sharp look, plucking off their heads with his thumb and forefinger. But do not be fooled, at night he is soft and young. He will let me wash his feet and kiss the back of his neck, and he will cry with gratitude and sorrow. In the morning he will let his children climb onto his shoulders, hang on to his calves, and swing from his arms. He wrestles gently with his children, tickling them under the chin like little lion cubs. And in the morning they will wake him with the songs they sing while making the fire to heat his bath water, which they save to cook the rice.

"He loved you very much, and you will understand, little one, when I tell you that his horse fell, and was scavenged for meat and soup by hungry children, and your father will not return. And that we are without food for so long that the children's hair is falling out and their teeth are as brittle as limestone beneath a crashing wave.

"So you will save us, our youngest girl, and you will join a rich man's home and make him happy when you are older, and you will be proud that you saved our family and fed us with your freedom. You should hold only happiness inside your body, or else the grief will eat at your muscles and get in your bones so that you are always cold, as if sitting in the wind with wet hair."

But I do not remember brothers and sisters, or a handsome father on top of a horse. And I do not remember my father coming home or how the sun would look setting in South Korea, or the house that we lived in. I do not remember all of my father's children singing so that the entire village could hear the songs that sounded like marbles being shaken inside a glass jar, but that must be the sound that rings in my ears during nighttime, as if crickets were living in my eardrums. And I do not remember my mother. I do not remember her skin, her face, her softness, her smell, or her stories. I do not remember.

My mother tells me that before she got me she used to pray to God for a child. She says that if you ask God and the universe for something, you will almost always get it, but you have to remember to be specific. So she drew a picture of a round-faced little girl with an indent right above her lip and below her nose, just tiny enough to put a pinky in. She drew almond shaped eyes, and eyelids like half-moons on finger-nails, and she kept the picture in her dresser drawer until she adopted me. She says that when she got me she couldn't breathe, because I looked just like the picture of the little girl in her dresser drawer. And I wonder, did she know that I would come with a double lifeline, and creases in my hands running violently across my palms?

Always Coca-Cola

There is something about pain, about laughter, about blood, and about love that keeps the stories sprouting from my body, like extra legs and arms. And it does not matter whose laughter it is, or whose story, it somehow all circles around, like the path of a boomerang, and returns to me. These extra limbs, the additional arms, fingers, and toes, wrap around my body, and I sometimes call them family.

I forget to look at the faces of the family that has raised me. My father's grumpy silences, or my mother's lips that crackle when she smiles as spit bubbles form and burst at the corners. I forget that occa-sionally blood is not thicker than water, blood is also water.

For me, there is no blood. There is no one I know who shares my face, blood, or memories. My first child will be my first known blood relative. And so I grasp. I look for pains shared, similar missing parts, and call those who possess the same holes I do "family."

I search. I guess. I imagine. I lie. I hope. I make up what I do not know. But most of all, I am always searching for a piece that can make me whole.

One day I was searching from my front porch, watching the sun set, a cooling red ember disappearing behind rooftops. Making up stories about my past: "I was born in a rice field. I was born by a creek. My mother was a white tiger who melted into the snow as I was born. My mother is the sun, watching over me seasonally."

I met Salvador while I was sitting on my front porch. He was familiar. We had spoken before. He lived a few houses down and had a pit-bull named Munchie. His hair was thick and coarse, and I imagined if he were a woman it would be black waves tumbling down his back. I had watched him drive by many times, and wondered what his ethnicity was. Puerto Rican? Latino? Indian? He said he had stories to tell me, things he wished to share, and would I have dinner with him?

We had dinner at a cheap Italian restaurant with red plastic booths and candlelight. By the time we'd finished dinner and were walking back to my house, the streetlights were all winking at us knowingly, and the television screen showed only snow.

"You remind me of me," I said, once in the safety of my living room.

"I am like you," he said.

"Hmm."

"I'm also Korean. My mother is Mexican and I grew up with her."

"Really?"

"I grew up always getting into fights because kids teased me and called me Chino, half-breed, mutt. I was so busy trying to prove that I was Mexican, that I didn't stop to look in the mirror and see that I was half Korean. My mother never told me." I could smell clean laundry mixed with the scent of dog and I had to resist the urge to bury my face in his sweatshirt.

"Tell me from the beginning. I want to know the beginning."

"I grew up in Durango, Mexico, until I was six," he said as he ran his finger down my neck.

"I grew up on my uncle's ranch with my mother and six cousins." He slipped the sweater off my shoulders.

"I'd wake up every morning to the sound of our rooster, Macho, calling up the sun." Our clothes fell to the floor.

"We had seven chickens, all named—Chiquita, Palomita, Morena,

Betsy—and I'd wake up to the smell of frying eggs." I watched him bury his nose in the fuzz of hair below my belly button. His hair reminded me of aerial photographs of trampled wheat. I reached down and grabbed handfuls. "Your sex smells like warmed peppers that have been roasted and then gutted." Sweat dripped from his brown forehead onto my breasts, smooth and milky colored like the inside of an oyster.

I remember the feel of the smooth dark skin on his tight stomach. The smell of dried sweat in his armpit made me think of chorizo cooked in butter, and rice that is washed fifty times before being cooked. He told me about Durango, about dogs with mange, dust on everything, aging cows, featherless chickens, and girls in the village nearby whose feet were grey and chalky from never wearing any shoes. He told me about his uncle's horses, most whom once had been wild. He said that when he walked around the ranch doing chores their eyes would follow him. Their nostrils would flare and quiver from the scent of humans. He believed that their quivering nostrils meant they could smell his fears, and so he never dared look into their eyes, afraid of what he might see.

We lay on top of wrinkled clothes, our bodies tangled, hair stuck to sweaty backs and elbows, moisture evaporating from our bodies, giving off the odor of lust. "You know why I never looked into their eyes," he said.

"Why?"

"I was afraid to know a truth that always threatened to find me. My cousins knew about my father. They defended me when other kids called me names. They knew that my father was the Korean grocer at the cornerstore." He leaned on his side so that he could look me in the eyes. "Let me tell you how it happened. My mother wanted a child but no husband, so she made an arrangement with the grocer, whom she saw every day and trusted. For some reason, I'm not sure why." He rubbed his knuckles across his unshaven face.

"Maybe they were really in love," I said. "What if it was a clandestine affair that her family did not approve of. Maybe they snuck around, made love in the back of the store among toppled cans of soup and sacks of rice, passed love notes written on the back of grocery lists." I could feel my stomach rumbling.

"I can't imagine my father with my mother. I met my father once, at the grocery store. Uncle Armando tipped me off the last time I visited them. He hinted that he knew a family secret so intimate that he wanted to let it go. He put his hand over his heart, and pulled out a piece of paper. It was a fortune from a fortune cookie. 'Always Coca-Cola' was scratched out in pencil on the back of the fortune. On the front it said, 'Marry wisely.'"

"That makes little sense." I said.

Salvador continued. "'How does one know a country he was born in, but left as a child?' I asked myself. How else can one know that country except through stories? And so I thought about the story my mother had once told me. My mother had said that she was once in love, and that love tasted like sweet condensed milk with a quarter cup of Mexican coffee. She said that she grew up so poor that they ate beans with dust, and used flour to coat their sticky bodies so that they did not smell like poverty in Sunday church. She got pregnant before marrying and was forced to leave her family in order to save them from shame."

"Perhaps that man was the grocery clerk. Maybe she really did love the grocery clerk but her family did not believe in mixed marriages, let alone mixed children. She was forced to flee. Did your father ride a horse? Did he used to be a soldier in Korea?" I clutched his finger between my sweaty palms.

"I don't know."

"Are you sure he's not Chinese? How do you know he's Korean?"

"In Spanish, all Asians are called 'Chinos.' But my mother told me specifically that he was Korean."

"I understand Coca-Cola!" I exclaimed, half thinking about what Salvador was thinking, and more lost in my own thoughts. "They met in the cold of the desert night by a bus stop a town away. He would have kissed her passionately and she tasted hot sauce and pickled cabbage on his tongue. He tasted tears and pieces of her heart, rolled out thinly, baked, and then shattered on her chapped lips. The bus came to take her far, far away to an exotic city. The Chinaman could not imagine his Spanish lover, dark and cracked, wandering among neon lights and movie stars. The last thing he gave her was a light kiss and a cold bottle of Coca-Cola that he had grabbed before locking up the store."

Salvador smiled at me. "I imagined my mother as a young woman. I tried to put myself in her shoes. Do you believe that we can be fed memories of our country through our mother's tits? Because I felt like I knew Durango far more intimately than the extent of a six-year-old's memories of it. I knew the sidewalks as dusty packed dirt in the summer and running rivers of mud in the spring. So when I met my father it was almost like déja vu."

"It's like seeing your life beginning in a mucky river. It's like feeling death and your very own birth between the cold fingers of your lover. It's like falling asleep and dreaming only colors or hearing five generations of voices, including your own, in the song of one old man. I know. I have imagined." I was enthusiastically adding to his story.

"It was like seeing a part of myself for the very first time. I bought a Coca-Cola and waited for him to open the bottle for me. Then I went to the side of the store and drank it down in the hot sun, imagining the smell of my father's breath. I believe I tasted my father as I drank Coca-Cola." He looked through me.

"Salvador, I'm sure your father saw the resemblance to himself in you. He saw your hands and thought of your mother. Or looked at your lips and put his hand to his own. I'm sure he thought you were very handsome, almost Indian-looking, an Asian-Mexican. I'm sure he almost laughed out loud at the thought. Did he ask you if you were his son?"

"No, of course not."

"I'm sure he understands what is like to be a man who lives his life not knowing, wondering in the night, about the stars, about one's own blood, and about love. I know. Silence becomes like an eggshell, protective and brittle. So he just opened your Coke, and I'm sure he smiled slightly. Perhaps he sighed sadly as he closed the register, but also felt as if he had one less thing to wonder about." I looked through him.

"And you seem to understand what that is like so well yourself." He lit up a cigarette, eyed me almost suspiciously.

"That is what it is like to be adopted. To never know. I'm constantly searching for clues that could lead me to my parents. I mean, what if your father was *my* father? What if he met my mother when he went back to Korea to visit? What if we are related?" I placed my hand on his.

"Look at your eyes," he said. I glanced over at my reflection in the living room window. "Now look at mine. Yours are much more slanted." He snatched his hand from beneath mine.

Letter to Salvador

Let me write this to you now, Salvador, because you will not hear me speak these words aloud again. I will whisper them to you, how about that. I will whisper in your ear with hot breath, because it is dark, and the sun is on the other side of the world. So let me tell you how I feel, although it should be no big secret, but it is hard to make oneself vulnerable. I feel you in me like the burning from drinking pure grain alcohol. If I think about your heat, sweat forms on my forehead and my pores begin to open.

Have I told you how it felt to listen to your story through my body? I know how you are, such a man, that you would not talk about your feelings after lovemaking. No, you just smoke a cigarette, lie there with your chest hair plastered in swirls on your skin from dried sweat. When my questions were most urgent you held me in silence. But I'll tell you what I see during your silence, and during your grunts, and wet touches. I will describe to you the landscapes that I see. I will tell you about the smells of the Yellow Sea, of damp earth after the snow has melted, of the skin on a sweaty water buffalo in the middle of a hot day, and of all the smells that flow off your back as I hold on, as I dig my nails into your smells, and dig, and dig, and dig. When I feel your hands, rough and cracked, on the parts of my skin that always remain covered, I feel the pain my father has left me that covers my body like tiny hairs. I can feel how his unshaven face would scratch a baby's soft spot. I can feel my father's life and all his losses in the lower part of my navel, just below my belly button, towards my spine, where you touch me when we're sweating the most. I can feel my father's country like a gum ball swallowed whole that sits inside my stomach. I can know love and all its different words.

I am an animal seeing the world in black and white, but tasting more colors with my body than humans would ever be able to see.

But there is one thing that I can never picture.

When I try, it is as if I am squeezing my eyes shut too tightly, or concentrating on an object for too long, so that I see only moving spots, like oil in water. I try and try, but I will never be able to see the face of my father. And when my eyes and the back of my brain begin to hurt from trying to picture my father for too long, I open my eyes and I always see you smiling at me peacefully.

Your story is not mine. I know this. But I savor your pain, hold it tight inside of me as if I am a safety deposit box trusted to keep safe someone's story, as if it were your family's legacy. I hold onto it, memorize its textures, move it around to see how your story fits with mine. I allow it to seep into my beginnings and I lick my lips, longing for the taste of something I don't yet know.

The Letter With No Address

JUDITH W. STEINBERGH

My daughter is writing a letter:
She is moderate, she is reasonable,
she wants to meet in a place away
from her birth mother's home, no one
has to know, no one has to see,
the husband, those other children will never
have to know, no one has to watch them
in a remote town, in a highway motel
where they peer into a peeled away
mirror, staring at their fair skin, their honey hair,
their ample breasts and hips, they lean
closer, their shade and shape an echo,
all these years walking through separate
crowds where no one could compare.
Then sitting on twin beds, backs against red
plastic headboards each dragging on her cigarette,
whispering—as if the deed of reunion were sin—
finding the voice—amazed at a common turn
of phrase, a mirrored gesture, sorting the questions
like piles of socks:
what music they like—that
would be important! what food? what allergies,
what clothes gothic or punk, which holidays, rituals,
which God, men, boys babies abortions adoptions
what kind of work good with the hands, was she
ever in movies? what color eyeshadow, blush?
who is the grandma? what country? the father,
his prowess, his picture in uniform? who's died
from what? how many children? where
are the cousins and did she, the mother,
ever dream of this baby without a name or did she
name this baby, and how did she feel so young,
barely teenage herself, letting a life slip out between thighs,

between hands, a force so powerful, a tide, a tremor
that has shaken the 18 years of my daughter who has
baskets of questions, truckloads, a lifetime of blanks,
of question marks falling out of the sky like a blinding,
silencing, heartbreaking snow.

(V)

RELATIONS

My Familiar

MARY TALLMOUNTAIN

Just off
A bustling sidewalk
Tonight in Chinatown she
Appeared again
Wearing a hooded parka
Of soft grey squirrel fur
Looking at me still and straight
Above the people passing
Then was gone.

She comes every year;
Finds me. Once her
Eyes ebon-dark
In a weatherbrown face
Gave me assurance
Before I traveled alone
To a remote shadowed region.

At home I often sense her:
Feel a flash
Of motion behind my shoulder,
See an angle of light
Where was none before.
Her husky voice speaks
In the secret bones of my skull.

I know only this: she
Was there when I was born.
I know the eyes,
The deep, the timeless,
The wild eyes.

Elba

MARLY SWICK

Mother, who wanted to keep her, always thought of her as some wild little bird—a sparrow, let loose in the wide world, lost forever—but I knew she was a homing pigeon. I knew that at some point in her flight path, sooner or later, she would make a U-turn. A sort of human boomerang. So even though I had long since stopped expecting it, I was not surprised when I walked down the gravel drive to the mailbox, which I'd painted papaya yellow to attract good news, and found the flimsy envelope with the Dallas postmark. I didn't know a soul in Dallas, or Texas for that matter, but the handwriting reminded me of someone's. My own.

I walked back inside the house and hung my poncho on the peg by the door.

"Still raining?" Mother asked. She was sitting in her new electric wheelchair in front of the TV, painting her fingernails a neon violet. Mother's sense of color was pure aggression. This was one of her good days. On the bad days, her hands trembled so that she could barely hold a spoon, let alone that tiny paintbrush.

"Just let up," I said. "Sun's poking through." I handed her the new *People* magazine, which she insisted upon subscribing to. "You know anyone in Dallas, Mother?"

"Not so as I recall." She dabbed at her pinky with a cottonball. Mother was vain about her hands. I was used to how she looked now, but I noticed people staring in the doctor's waiting room. She had lost some weight and most of her hair to chemotherapy, and I guess people were startled to see these dragon-lady nails on a woman who looked as if she should be lying in satin with some flowers on her chest.

"Why do you ask?" she said.

I opened the envelope and a picture fluttered into my lap. It was a Polaroid of a sweet-faced blond holding a newborn baby in a blue blanket. Their names and ages were printed neatly on the back. Before I even read the letter I knew. I knew how those Nazis feel when suddenly, after twenty or thirty uneventful years, they are arrested walking down some sunny street in Buenos Aires. It's the shock of being found after waiting so long.

"What's that?" Mother said.

I wheeled her around to face me and handed her the Polaroid. She studied it for a minute and then looked up, speechless for once, waiting for me to set the tone.

"That's her," I said. "Her name's Linda Rose Caswell."

"Lin-da Rose." She pronounced it phonetically, as if it were some foreign gibberish.

I nodded. We looked at the picture again. The blond woman was seated on a flowered couch, her wavy hair just grazing the edge of a dime-a-dozen seascape in a cheap gilt frame. I hoped it was someone else's living room, some place she was just visiting.

Mother pointed to the envelope. "What's she say?"

I unfolded the letter, a single page neatly written.

"She says she's had my name and address for some time but wanted to wait to contact me until after the birth. The baby's name is Blake and he weighs eight pounds, eight ounces, and was born by cesarean. She says they are waiting and hoping to hear back from me soon."

"That's it?"

I nodded and handed her the letter. It was short and businesslike, but I could see the ghosts of all the long letters she must have written and crumpled into the wastebasket.

"I guess that makes you a great-grandmother," I said.

"What about you?" she snorted, pointing a Jungle Orchid fingernail at me. "You're a grandmother."

We shook our heads in disbelief. I sat silently, listening to my brain catch up with my history. Forty years old and I felt as if I had just shaken hands with Death. I suppose it's difficult for any woman to accept that she's a grandmother, but in the normal order of things, you have ample time to adjust to the idea. You don't get a snapshot in the mail one day from a baby girl you gave up twenty-four years ago saying, "Congratulations, you're a grandma!"

"It's not fair," I said. "I don't even feel like a *mother*."

"Well, here's the living proof." Mother tapped her nail against the glossy picture. "She looks just like you. Only her nose is more aristocratic."

"I'm going to work." My knees cracked when I stood up. "You be all right here?"

Mother nodded, scrutinizing the picture in her lap. "Actually, truth to tell, I think she looks like me." She held the Polaroid up next to her face. "She's got my profile."

I felt the pleasant warmth of the sun on my shoulder blades as I walked along the path paved with sodden bougainvillea blossoms to the garage I'd had converted into a studio a few years back. I'd moved my painting paraphernalia out of the house and repapered the spare bedroom. Mother sewed some bright curtains and matching pillows for the daybed. Then we were ready for guests, and I guess we enjoyed this illusion of sociability, even though the only person who ever visited us—my mother's sister—was already dead by the time we readied the guest room.

I spent hours in the studio every day, painting still lifes, and they were hours of perfect contentment. From my studio, I could hear the ocean across the highway, but couldn't see it. Sometimes when I was absorbed in my painting, in this trance of light and color, it seemed as if my brushstrokes and the rustle of the waves were one and the same.

After Mother and I moved to Florida, I developed a passion for citrus fruits. I liked to look at them, and I was always fondling them. When I was pregnant, the only food I could tolerate was oranges. I lived on oranges. One afternoon while I was wandering around Woolworth's, wasting time before returning to the motel, I bought a tin of watercolors just on impulse. That afternoon I sat down at the Formica table in our kitchenette at the motel and painted a picture of a red china dish with one lemon in it. As soon as the paint was dry, Mother said, "My, I never knew you had such an artistic bent," and taped it to the dwarf refrigerator. Even with my big belly, I felt like a proud first-grader. From then on, hardly a day's gone by that I haven't painted something.

My father back home in Baltimore made it clear he wasn't awaiting our return. Seduced by sunshine, we decided to stay in Florida after the baby was born. We moved out of the motel into a rented house on Siesta Key, and Mother enrolled me in an adult art class. The teacher, an excitable Cuban, nudged me to enter some local art shows. Now galleries as nearby as Miami and as far away as Atlanta sell my work on a regular basis. A local newspaper reporter interviewed me a few years back and quoted me as saying, "Painting is meditation on the moment, no past and no future." Mother sent my father a copy of the article, which he never acknowledged, although he continued to send us monthly checks, like clockwork, until the divorce settlement. I thought maybe the quote offended him.

The evening of the day we received the Polaroid, after the supper dishes were cleared, I spent a good long time in front of the medicine chest mirror. I felt as if I were saying goodbye to someone. Then I climbed up on the toilet seat and from there onto the rim of the sink. Using a washcloth as a pot holder, I unscrewed the lightbulb. It was one of those guaranteed-to-outlast-you 100-watters.

I carried the offending bulb into the living room. Mother was hunched underneath the pole lamp browsing through some old black-and-white snapshots, the kind with the wavy edges.

"Just hold on a sec," I said, as I unplugged the lamp and fumbled to exchange lightbulbs.

"What're you doing?" Mother said. "It was just fine the way it was."

Mother always got nervous when I tried to change anything around the place. She would have appreciated living at the scene of a murder, sealed off by the police, with no one allowed to touch a thing.

"I'm putting in a brighter bulb," I said. "You're going to ruin your eyes."

"That's too glary." She squinted up at me as soon as I plugged the lamp back in.

"It's much better." I slipped the 60-watt bulb into my pocket.

In the bright light I recognized the pictures she was looking at, and even after all that time, my stomach muscles clutched. They were snapshots we had taken on the drive down here to Florida from Maryland almost twenty-five years ago. I had a new Instamatic camera my father had given me for my birthday, before he found out, and I couldn't resist using it, even though I knew that I would never want to look at those pictures.

"Look at that." I picked up a picture of Mother holding a basket of nuts at a pecan stand in Georgia. She was wearing a patterned sundress with spaghetti straps, and she had a bird's nest of blond hair. "Imagine," I said. "You were younger there than I am now."

I handed the picture back to her and squeezed her bony shoulder. She reached up and patted my hand. It was hard to guess who felt worse.

I picked up another snapshot—Mother in her bathing cap with the rubber petals that resembled an artichoke, posed like Esther Williams in the shallow end of a swimming pool.

"I'd forgotten that bathing cap," I laughed.

"I'd forgotten that body," she sighed.

Some of the motels had small pools. Looking at the picture, I could smell the chlorine. At night, under the artificial lights, the water turned a sickly jade green. It was summer, and after a hot, sticky day in the car, nothing looked more inviting than those little concrete pools surrounded by barbed wire, but I was embarrassed to be seen in my bathing suit with my swollen breasts and swelling belly. I would post Mother in a lawn chair. Sweating, chain-smoking, she would dutifully keep watch in the steamy night. If anyone headed toward the pool, she would whisper, "Psst! Someone's coming!" and I would scramble up the chrome ladder into my terry-cloth beach robe. But more often than not, we would have the pool all to ourselves. Sometimes after I was through in the water, she would breaststroke a couple of slower, tired-looking laps before following me back into our room with its twin, chenille-covered beds.

Mother leafed through the little packet of snapshots as if she were looking for some particular picture. There were more shots of her— smiling beside the Welcome to Florida sign, clapping her sandals together in the surf, lugging a suitcase up the steps of an unprepossessing motel called the Last Resort. I was struck by how tired and young and lost she looked in those pictures. In my memory of those days she was strong and old and bossy. You could see in the pictures just how much it cost a woman like her to up and leave her husband, even if he was an inflexible, unforgiving, steel-reinforced ramrod of a man. The irony was that right up until he stopped speaking to me, and for a long time after, I loved him more than I loved her. I had always been a daddy's girl. I still dream of him occasionally, and in my dreams he always treats me tenderly.

"There!" Mother suddenly held a snapshot up to the light— triumphant. "There you are!"

There I was. Sitting behind the wheel of our '57 Buick (which we just sold ten years ago, all rusted from the salt air but still running), my telltale belly discreetly concealed by the dashboard. Trick photography. I seemed to be scowling at the gas pump. I was moody and sullen during the entire drive south. She did what she could to cheer me up— bought me fashion magazines and let me play the radio full blast. I had turned sixteen but didn't have my license yet. At night, even though all she wanted was a hot shower and a soft bed, she would give me driving lessons in the parking lots of the motels we stopped at. She would smile encouragingly while I stripped the gears and lurched in circles, barely missing the few parked cars with roof racks and out-of-state plates. She rarely mentioned my father, who had promised to teach me how to drive before he disowned me, but once I sauntered out of the ladies' room and caught her crying in a pay-phone booth at a gas station just across the Florida state line. Her tears relaxed something in me, just long enough for me to put an arm around her and say, "I'm sorry. I know it's all my fault."

"No," she hugged me and petted my hair. "It's his fault. He loved you too much. He thought you were perfect."

I jerked away. "I don't want to talk about him," I said. "Ever."

The whole time Mother and I were packing up the Buick, my father was in the backyard pruning the azalea bushes. I heard the angry little snips, like a dog snapping at my heels, as I trudged up and down the stairs with armloads of books and clothes. When the car was all packed, Mother and I sat in the driveway, warming the engine. We sat there waiting for him to stop us. Finally, Mother cleared her throat. "Well," she forced a brave smile. "I guess we're off."

I opened the car door and ran to the backyard. I threw my arms around my father's bent waist as he stooped over an unruly azalea. "I don't want to go!" I cried. "Don't make me go."

He shook me off and went on snipping.

"Don't you even love me?" I wailed and stomped the ground like a five-year-old.

"Look at you." He pointed the pruning shears. "Who could love that?" Then he grabbed a handful of the oversized man's shirt I was wearing and sheared a big, ragged hole that exposed my pale balloon belly.

I turned and ran back to the car.

Mother shuffled the pictures into a neat stack, like a deck of playing cards, to put away. She used to be a dedicated bridge player. After we moved, she tried to teach me a couple of times, but I have no head for card games, and anyway, you need more than two players.

"Wait a minute," I said. "What's that one there?" I pointed to an oversized picture on the bottom of the stack.

"I don't know if I ever showed you this," she said, "come to think of it." As if this had just now occurred to her.

The picture had its own private envelope. I slipped it out and turned it right side up. It was the kind of picture that hospitals used to give you, of a nurse wearing a surgical mask holding a sleeping, wrinkled infant.

"Where'd you get this?" I sat down on the edge of the sofa.

"I make friends," Mother said. "I talk to people."

I stared at the sleeping infant, wishing it would open its eyes.

They never showed me the baby in the hospital. Back then, they thought it would be harder on you. I suppose maybe today it's different. Most things are. They told me she was a girl, that she weighed six pounds something, and that she was perfectly normal, but that was all. I never asked to know anything more. I was just a kid myself, a schoolgirl. Since then, I have read novels and seen movies where these unwed mothers—cheerleaders and prom queens—suddenly develop superhuman maternal instincts and fight like she-cats to keep their babies. All I can say is I never felt any of that. I felt like this thing had leeched into me and I couldn't pry it loose.

Your body recovers quickly when you're that young. Sixteen. I remember walking along the beach a few days after being released from the hospital, just bouncing around in the waves and screaming. The pure relief and joy of it. Suddenly I didn't even care that my whole life had been ruined, that my parents were disgraced and now separated as a result of my wantonness, that I didn't have a high school diploma, and that I'd only received one postcard from Tommy Boyd.

I wasn't even in love with Tommy Boyd. It happened the first and only time we ever went out. My boyfriend of two years had just thrown me over because I refused to do anything below the waist. I went to a friend's party with Tommy, hoping to make my boyfriend jealous, but when we arrived, the first thing I saw was him making out with Julie Mullins on the Mullins's riding lawn mower. (It was summer and the party was in the backyard.) I was so upset, I started drinking and flirting, and somehow I ended up in the backseat of Tommy's brother's car, doing everything. I was crying before he ever touched me. It started out as comfort.

The postcard was of the Painted Desert. He and his older brother were driving cross-country that summer, disciples of Kerouac, before college started in the fall. In an exuberant scrawl he listed all the places they'd been. Then at the bottom, when he'd run out of room, he printed in letters nearly invisible to the naked human eye that he was thinking about me and hoped I was doing OK. He even called me from a pay phone once in California and held the receiver out of the booth so that I could hear the Pacific Ocean. I listened to the surf and sobbed for three minutes before the operator said our time was up. I try not to think back, but when I do, I don't blame Tommy Boyd. Never did. And I didn't blame my boyfriend because I loved him. Who I blamed was Julie Mullins. That is the way girls thought back then, before the women's movement raised their consciousness. It came too late for me. I feel closer to Tess of the D'Urbervilles than to Germaine Greer.

I handed the hospital picture back to Mother. We sat there for a minute listening to the geckos and the rain and the palm fronds scratching against the sliding glass doors. Mother picked up the remote control device and hit the "on" button. As the picture bloomed into view, I said, "Did I ever thank you for what you did? Taking me away and all?"

She just nodded and mumbled something, flipping through the channels. She settled on *Masterpiece Theater*. We had watched that episode together earlier in the week, but I didn't say anything. I picked the new *People* up off the coffee table and said I was going to read in bed. She nodded obliviously and then, just as I reached the hallway, she said, without taking her eyes off the screen, "You going to write to her?"

"Of course I am," I bristled. "I may be some things, but I am not rude."

"You going to invite them here? Her and the baby?" She swiveled her eyes sideways at me.

"I haven't thought that far," I said.

"Well, don't put it off." She slid her eyes back to the television. "She's been waiting twenty-five years."

I went to my room and changed into my nightgown. It was a hot, close night despite the rain, and I turned on the overhead fan. Mother and I dislike air-conditioning. A palmetto bug dropped off one of the blades onto the bed. I brushed him off, whacked him with my slipper, picked him up with a tissue, and carried him at arm's length to the toilet. I'd forgotten it was dark in the bathroom. I had to go back for the lightbulb, climb up on the sink again and screw in the 60-watt bulb. Crouched on the sink's rim, I caught sight of my face in the mirror and instinctively, like a baby, I reached out and touched my reflection. Then I brushed my hair and creamed my face, satisfied in the soft light that no one would ever suspect I was a grandmother.

The next morning by the time I had showered and dressed, Mother was already in the kitchen, eating her cereal. In the stark sunlight, she looked bad, worse than bad. The spoon doddered its way between her bowl and her mouth. The trembling spoon unnerved me. I feared it would not be long before I'd have to tuck a napkin under her chin and feed her like a baby. I felt my eyes swimming and stuck my head inside the refrigerator.

"You sleep?" I asked her. Mother and I are both thin sleepers.

I grabbed some oranges off the back porch and started to squeeze myself some fresh juice.

"I dreamed she came here with the baby. We were all sitting out on the lanai playing cards, even the baby. We had a special deck made up just for him. Only she . . .," Mother hesitated to invoke her name, ". . . Linda Rose looked exactly like that dark-haired receptionist in Dr. Rayburn's office with the big dimples. Isn't that weird?"

"I've heard weirder." I tossed some cheese and crackers into a Baggie. "I'll be in the studio," I said. "You want anything before I go?"

Mother shook her head, dabbing at some dribbled milk on her robe. "I thought I'd just write some letters," she said. "You got anything for the postman when he comes?"

"No, I don't." I plunked her cereal bowl in the sink and sponged off the counter.

"You worried she's going to be trouble or ask for money? For all we know, she's married to a brain surgeon with his and her Cadillacs. Dallas is full of rich people."

"She didn't mention any husband at all," I said, getting drawn into it despite myself.

"Maybe you're worried 'like mother, like daughter.'" She was leafing through a rosebush catalog now, pretending nonchalance. "It's no disgrace these days, you know. Nowadays you'd be hard-pressed to think what you could do to disgrace yourself."

I lit a cigarette. Since Mother had to quit smoking, I tried to limit my smoking to the studio, but every once in a while she got on my nerves.

"Give me one," she said.

"You know you can't." I exhaled a smoke ring, followed by another one. They floated in the air like a pair of handcuffs.

"Just a puff," she pleaded.

Mother had smoked two packs of Camels a day for over thirty years. She liked to say that nothing could be harder than quitting smoking, not even dying. I put the cigarette to her lips and held it steady while she took a couple of drags. She closed her eyes and a look of pure pleasure stole over her features. Then I felt guilty. "That's enough." I doused the cigarette under the faucet.

"Maybe you're worried she'll be disappointed in you," she said. "You know, that she'd had this big fantasy for all these years that maybe you were Grace Kelly or Margaret Mead and who could live up to that? No one. But you don't have to, Fran, that's the thing. You're her flesh-and-blood mother and that's enough. That's all it'll take."

"Could we just drop this?" I wished I hadn't doused the cigarette. When she got onto some topic, it didn't make the least bit of difference to her if you preferred not to discuss it.

"You call me if you need me," I said.

She nodded and waved me away. When I looked back at her through the screen door, she was sitting there, frail and dejected, with those watery blue eyes magnified behind her bifocals, massaging her heart.

The studio was mercifully cool and quiet. I stared back and forth between the blue bowl of oranges on the table and the blue bowl of oranges I had painted on the paper clipped to my easel. I dipped my brush in water and mixed up some brown and yellow on my palette until I got the citrusy color I was after. I wondered if she, Linda Rose— there *was* something in Mother and me that resisted naming her after all these years—had inherited my eye. Maybe she had it and didn't even know it. Maybe she had been raised all wrong. Which was entirely possible, starting out with a tacky name like Linda Rose. She probably grew up twirling a baton and never even picked up a paintbrush. I would have named her something cool and elegant like Claire, not something that sounds like what you would call a motorboat.

As I focused on my oranges, the rest of my life blurred and faded away. I didn't give Linda Rose another thought that afternoon. Then I did what I always do when I finish a painting, my ritual. I lit a cigarette and sat in a canvas director's chair against the wall, facing the easel. As I stared at the painting, I gradually became more and more attuned to my other senses: the clatter of birds in the banyan tree, the salty breeze, the ache in my lower back, the taste of smoke. When I was satisfied that I was satisfied with the painting, I reached for the blue bowl, selected the most fragrant orange, peeled it, and ate it with slow deliberation, section by section, like some animal eating its afterbirth. Then I washed my hands and headed up the path toward the house to fix mother her lunch.

Mother was crying in front of the television set when I walked in.

"What happened?" I peered at the set expecting to see more melodrama, but it was just a quiz show. The contestants looked hyper-cheerful.

"I can't get this open." She handed me her painkillers, which were in a plastic vial. "You forgot to tell them no safety caps." Her quivering lips and trembling voice were a study in reproach.

"What if I did? It's certainly nothing to cry about." I pried the cap off and handed her the pills. "Here."

"I need some water."

I brought her a glass of water with a slice of lemon, the way she liked it.

"It seems like a little thing," she said, "but it's just one little thing after another. Like an old car. This goes, that goes. Pretty soon you're just waiting for the next part to give out."

"That's no way to talk," I said. "Come on now."

A couple of times she lifted the water glass up off the table and then set it down again as if it were too heavy.

"Here." I picked the glass up and tilted it to her lips. She took a few sips and then waved it away. Water cascaded down her chin.

"I don't believe in my body anymore," she said. "It won't be long now." She closed her eyes, as if she were trying out being dead. It scared me.

"I sure as hell don't know what's got into you," I shouted. I was rummaging through the kitchen cupboard. "You want Gazpacho or Golden Mushroom?"

"Don't shout," she shouted, motoring herself into the kitchen. "I'm not hungry."

I sighed and opened a can of soup. Even in summer, Mother and I live on soup.

"We're having Gazpacho," I said. "Chilled."

I poured the soup, threw an ice cube into each bowl, and stirred it around with my finger.

"I was thinking about what you'll do once I'm gone," she said.

I pushed her up close to the table, like a baby in a high chair. She ignored the bowl of soup in front of her.

"You've never been alone before. I don't like to think of you here all by yourself," she said.

"Maybe I'll like it."

"Maybe." She picked up her spoon and pushed it around in her soup. "But I doubt it. Just close your eyes for a minute and imagine this place is empty except for you. . . . Come on now. Close them."

"Jesus Christ." I sighed and slammed my eyes shut.

"How's it feel?"

"Peaceful." I glared at her. "Very peaceful." But, in truth, this shiver of loneliness rippled along my spine.

"You write to your daughter," she said.

Then, as if she'd exhausted that subject, she nodded off to sleep, wheezing lightly. When I turned my back to wash the dishes, her spoon clattered to the floor. I wanted to stuff her nylon nightgowns into an overnight bag and drive her to the hospital where experts would monitor her vital signs and, at the first hint of failure, hook her up to some mysterious life-support system until I was ready to let her go, but I simply picked her spoon up off the floor and rinsed it under the tap.

While Mother slept, I sat out on the lanai staring at a blank sheet of stationery until sunset. I had never been a letter writer. Even thank-you notes and get-well cards seemed to call for more than I had to say. Once or twice I'd tried to write a letter to my father—in the spirit of reconciliation or revenge, depending on my mood—but the words seemed to stick in my mind. In the old days, when Mother still kept in touch with her friends up north, I used to marvel at how she could fill up page after page, her ballpoint flitting across the calm surface of the scented page like a motorboat skimming through water, her sentence trailing along in its wake like a water-skier holding on for dear life. Chatting on paper, she called it. I preferred postcards. When Mother and I took a twelve-day tour of Europe for my thirtieth birthday, I sent back El Grecos from the Prado, Turners from the Tate, Cézannes from the Jeu de Paume. I don't have many friends, and those I have wouldn't expect more than a couple of hasty lines on the back of a picture postcard. Mother didn't even bother with postcards. Over the years, her letters had shrunk to notes and then to nothing. At Gatwick Airport, going home, I bought a biography of the Duke and Duchess of Windsor to read on the plane. I have since read everything I can find about them. I understand them, but I don't pity them. Their fate was a simple equation. When someone gives up the world for you, you become their world.

I sat on the lanai for hours in the wicker rocker—the smell of oranges from a bushel basket at my feet mingling with the lilac-scented stationery—pen poised, trying to think what I could say, what she would want to hear:

> Dear Linda Rose,
>   Last night I slept with your picture under my pillow. Every year on your birthday mother and I would try to guess what you looked like and what you were doing . . .

> Dear Linda Rose,
>   What is it you want from me? Our connection was a purely physical one. I have never shed a tear on Mother's Day.

From behind me I heard the faint whir of Mother's electric wheelchair crescendoing as she steered herself down the hall and across the living room to the lanai. The blank white stationery looked gray in the dusk.

"Did you write her?" She was wheezing again.

"Yes." I shut the lid of the stationery box. "You take your medicine? You don't sound good."

"Never mind me. What'd you say? Did you ask her to come here?"

"Not exactly." It was cool on the lanai, a damp breeze from the ocean. I buttoned my cardigan. "Are you warm enough?"

Mother dogged me into the kitchen. I took a package of lamb chops from the refrigerator.

"Where's the letter?" She was sorting through some stamped envelopes, mostly bills, in a basket on the sideboard.

"I already mailed it." I stuck the chops in the toaster oven. "You want instant mashed or Minute Rice?"

"Don't lie to me." She jabbed me in the rear with her fingernail. "I'm your mother."

"Just leave me be." I turned the faucet on full blast to drown her out, muttering curses, but I knew she would wait. I shut the water off and set the pan on the burner to boil.

"Even half-dead I'm more alive than you are," she said.

In the bright overhead light she looked more than half-dead. She looked maybe sixty or seventy percent dead.

"You need a swift kick in the butt!" She wheeled her chair up behind me and tried to give me a swift one, but her toe only grazed my shin.

"Goddammit, I tried to write it," I said. "I kept getting stuck."

"I'll help you!" She stopped wheezing and something inside her rallied. Her spine snapped to attention. "I always could write a good letter."

I imagined I could hear her brain heating up, words hopping around in there like kernels in a popcorn popper.

"Get some paper and pencil!" she commanded. She was chipping nail polish off her thumbs, something she did when she got worked up.

The chops were spattering away in the broiler. The water was boiling on the stove. "After dinner," I said.

The phone rang. I hurried out of the kitchen and answered it in the hallway. "Hello?" I said. There was silence, then a click, then a buzz. I hung up.

"Who was it?" Mother asked, as I set a plate of food down in front of her.

"No one. They hung up."

"I'm not hungry," she said.

"Eat it anyway." I dissected the meat on her plate into bite-size pieces. "There."

After dinner, to make amends, I offered to paint Mother's nails for her. Mother graciously accepted. One thing about her, she can recognize an olive branch. Her chipped purple nails looked unsightly in the 100-watt glare. She closed her eyes and swayed her head in time to the music on the radio. I shook the little bottle of Peach Melba and painted away with the furious effort of a child trying to stay inside the lines of a coloring book. My breathing slowed. My hands steadied themselves. My concentration was perfect, dead on. Nothing existed except the tiny brush, the shimmer of color, and the Gothic arch of each nail.

"What's that?" Mother said. She opened her eyes.

"Schumann, I think." I started on the second coat.

"Not that. I thought I heard a car door slam."

"I didn't hear anything."

A second later there was a loud pounding on the front door. It startled me and my hand skittered across Mother's, leaving a trail of Peach Melba.

"Told you."

"Whoever it is, we don't want any." I set the brush back in the bottle. "Religion, encyclopedias, hairbrushes . . ." I stood up and patted Mother's hand. "Be right back."

"Don't unlock the screen door." She peeked through the drapes, careful not to disturb the wet nail polish. "Well, he's got himself a flashy car for a Fuller Brush man."

I put the chain on the door and opened it a crack. "Yes?" I said, peering into the darkness.

"Who is it?" Mother yelled from the living room.

"It's George Jeffries," a man's voice said.

I flicked on the porch light to get a good look at him.

"Who is it?" Mother yelled again.

I didn't answer her. A second later I heard the whir coming up behind me. She came to a stop right beside me.

"Hello Lillian. I didn't mean to scare you," he said. "I would've called. I guess I was afraid you'd hang up on me."

"You're right. We would have." She was wringing her hands, smearing the nail polish all over.

"You could still slam the door in my face," he said.

"Good idea," Mother said, but I was already unlocking the screen door and motioning him inside.

The disturbing part was we didn't shout or cry or bare our souls to one another. We drank iced tea, then brandy, and conversed like three old friends who had lost touch with each other and were trying unsuccessfully to recapture something. Mother made a few barbed comments, tossed off a few poison darts, but my father just bowed his head and said, "You're right," or "I'm ashamed of myself," or "I deserve worse," and pretty soon she gave up. I could sense his shock every time he glanced at her. He didn't look that well preserved himself, but she could have been his mother.

I was mostly quiet. I couldn't believe that this thin-haired mild-man-nered old gent was my father. The main thing I felt was gypped. He told us how he'd been married again, lasted about eight years, then she left him. He wouldn't say who it was, but once he slipped and said Genevieve, and Mother and I exchanged glances. We knew it was one of her old bridge club members, a divorcée with three kids I used to babysit for. My father went on about those kids—the drugs, the shoplifting, the wild parties, the car wrecks—and implied it was what did the marriage in. I figured it was his backhanded way of telling me he realized that I hadn't been so bad after all.

"Why now?" I said when he finished. "Why'd you come here after all these years?"

"I don't know," he said. "A while back someone named Linda Rose Caswell contacted me, said she was your . . . said you were her . . . that some agency had given her your name and wanted to know how to reach you. After that, I started thinking."

I nodded. The three of us were silent, not a comfortable silence.

"Then a couple of days ago—" he fumbled in his breast pocket "—she sent me this." He offered it hesitantly. It was another Polaroid, almost identical, except in this one the baby was crying.

I nodded and passed it back to him.

"We got one, too," Mother said, not one to be outshone.

"Then, I don't know," he shrugged. "I just packed my suitcase and started driving." He tucked the picture back inside his pocket and cleared his throat. "What about you? You haven't told me much about what you've been up to. I'm here to listen."

"We lead a quiet life," I said. "There's not really much to tell."

"It's a nice place you've got here," he said. We'd bought it with his money, mother's divorce settlement, but, to his credit, he didn't seem to be thinking about that.

"You should see Fran's paintings," Mother said. "She's famous around here."

"That so?" my father said, smiling.

"You know how she exaggerates," I said.

"Well, I'd like to see them. In the morning." He looked at his watch. "I'm beat. You gals know a reasonable motel nearby?"

I looked at Mother. She shrugged.

"We can put you in the spare room," I said.

"If you're sure it's no bother . . ." He looked at my mother, but she was busy chipping away at her thumbnails.

"It's no bother," I said. "The guest bed's all made."

That night, after they were both asleep, I sat down again with Mother's stationery and a shot of whiskey and wrote to Linda Rose. It was a short note, but this time the words just came. I told her it would mean a lot to Mother and me if they could come visit us—Mother was too sick to travel—and I offered to pay their plane fare. It wasn't much of a note really, under the circumstances, and once I sealed the envelope, I found myself adding lines to it in my mind.

It was after midnight and stone silent on the island except for the waves. My mouth felt dry, as if I'd been talking out loud for hours and hours. I chose an orange from the bushel basket sitting on the floor next to the rocker, bit into it, and spat the peel out onto the porch floor. They were runty, greenish juice oranges from the small grove out back. The trees were so old they'd sprouted dark, spiny thorns. But their fruit was sweeter than those picture-perfect oranges you see in the supermarkets. From California. Imports.

As I sucked the juice out, I closed my eyes and imagined Linda Rose sitting across from me on the wicker sofa, telling me all about herself while the baby slept contentedly in my lap. I breathed in his baby smell of powder and sour milk. I felt his soft warmth, a pleasant weight against my belly, radiating inward. I began to rock, crooning in harmony with the squeaky floorboards, and as I rocked, I began to pile oranges on my lap, one after another, hugging them to me, until my lap was full of oranges, heavy with oranges. And then, for the first time all night, I felt something. It could have been the avalanche of oranges, shifting in my lap, but it felt more like it was on the inside, more like something under the skin, something moving there inside me.

A Man and His Wife

BARBARA SPERBER

(the week before I meet her)
for Suzanne and Steven

I can't sleep nights and picture
her parents curled
inside their sheets like geese

at the water's edge. They slide
downstream on their double
mattress, as *she* floats, singly,

away. Her fingers press
against the curve of his spine.
His shoulder braces. Her knees

pulled high. Her thin, white cheek
fans his elbow. His right lid
blinks at five in the morning.

In the haze, his jaw is clenched,
but her mouth stays slightly
open. Does she see something pass—

A leaf? A stem? A face in the water?
They need *her* to want them;
want *her* to need them. I love them

for that. The current's pulling,
gathering steam. I dream
that *she* turns, swims slowly back.

Texas Mother

SUSAN BUMPS

What I don't tell:
How I drove out to the house,
cream colored with a bench out front.
How I stood outside while the neighbor dogs barked,
and looked through the kitchen window.
How she's in there, my mother, a phantom.
Looking at the glass plane, I don't see her
as much as I see me looking in, movement like water ripples—
beautiful and impossible to hold. It's the closest we've come.

To the Woman Who Gave Him Up for Adoption

SYBIL WOODS-SMITH

You never knew how red
his beard would be
in the sunlight,
or how deeply set and dark
would be his eyes.

You knew him only hidden,
swelling under your skin,
and you were hidden too
by your family,
for the shame.

Your fullness was not celebrated.
No women sat with you
to marvel at how taut
the belly gets,
trading oils and secrets.
No man put his hand
near yours on that mound
and laughed when it kicked him.
It might have been a cyst
or an infection.

You gave him twenty-three of your genes,
nine months of your living,
a warm place to lie in;
all things you had to give, but still,
he denies you gave him anything.
I know better. I know sometimes at night
when no one could see your face
you grieved for him,
thought it was his growing
that kept you out of the world
when you were sixteen
and the world meant so much.

I think you remembered
in an anesthetic dream
the brisk exam,
the footprinting,
his howling for you in that room
thin-lipped with your sin,
his little body
lost to you by birth
when it might have been finally found
in all its completeness
of tiny thumb and penis.

More happens
between a mother and a child
than they'd admit
or allow then,
and though he wasn't placed
still wet
to ride between your breasts
just once, to learn
the beat of your heart
and the scent of your effort,
both of you must have strained
for that moment.

Perhaps it was the best
hidden at the end
in the darkness of gas,
but oh, what a severing,
and let me tell you this:

even as a man
when he is sleeping
he moves his mouth
as if reaching through the years
for what didn't happen.
He doesn't remember this
when I wake him,
but it is your flesh
he finds

as he nudges
through the fluid darkness
into my arms.

Do You Know What I Mean?

DAN CHAON

O'Neil had come at last to the town where she lived. The bus rose up over the crest of a hill and Bedlow, South Dakota, appeared below him in a blur of falling snow. One of those houses, he thought: She was inside it.

But as the bus pulled into Bedlow, he just sat there, as if he might not move. They stopped in front of the bus depot, which was part of a truck stop on the edge of town. Heavy flakes of snow were falling onto the cars in the parking lot, and O'Neil was reminded of the furniture in a house that has been closed up, all draped with sheets. Everyone was silent. A few people in seats near him shifted fitfully, perhaps troubled by a dream. "Bedlow," the driver called impatiently. When the driver called again, O'Neil realized that he was the only one getting off. "Are you Bedlow?" the driver asked as he teetered to the front, and O'Neil nodded. He knew he was doing the wrong thing.

She didn't know he was coming; that was the worst part. As he stood alone in the parking lot under the high, brightly humming Shell sign in his trench coat, he imagined that he must look like an assassin in an old movie, someone who would make the music turn ominous and dissonant. He didn't like to think of it that way, to picture her unaware of the trouble that was bearing down on her—innocently going about her business, fixing her dinner, or balancing her checkbook at her kitchen table, or snug in an easy chair, placidly reading a book.

He had always tried to think of it like this: He'd come across a doe in the clearing of a forest, and it was still, its hide shivering, its ears pricked up; any sudden movement would cause it to bolt. Only the most subtle, graceful approach would allow him to step closer, to put out a hand. And then? He didn't know. It wasn't, he thought, a very accurate metaphor.

From a strategic standpoint, and from a moral one, all the books warned against surprising them. They were very pious about honesty, these books, with their talk of the evils of secrecy and closed records, with their stirring passages about the "right to know." But the truth was, the only way to get information—birth certificates, court documents, etc.—was to lie and connive, to fake everything. For a year now, O'Neil had pretended to be the father of a dying child, in urgent need of medical information. He forged letters from an invented pediatrician on stolen hospital stationery. He wept into the phone, into the embarrassed silence of some clerk or another, and after he got what he wanted he almost laughed with the exhilaration of fooling them, even while his eyes were still blurry with real tears.

He had her address for a long time before he did anything about it. Three months before, on his birthday, he sent her a rose. There was a card attached, with his name and phone number.

There was no response. He waited a month, and then he sent another note. "Did you receive my rose?" it said. He enclosed an envelope for her reply. The answer came at last, two weeks later. It was a little white card with the words "Thank You" in gold script on the front. Inside she'd printed, in careful block letters: SORRY. She underlined this three times.

Perhaps she really thought that this would be the end of it, but O'Neil had to believe that she knew better. She had to have doubts of her own, and deep down she was expecting him, he thought. For weeks now, every time her phone rang, every time she locked her door at night, a shadow of dread, anxiety, even vague eagerness, would pass over her. Or so he imagined. It might even be a relief for her to have it over with.

In the phone booth outside the truck stop cafe—EAT GAS WELCOME— he dialed information. His plan was simple: He would take a taxicab directly to her house and ring the bell. There would be no way for his uncertainty to get the best of him if he were standing there at the edge of her yard, and he found it practically unimaginable that she would close the door on him after she'd opened it and he began to speak.

But there was no taxi service in Bedlow. He knew he should have guessed as much, since it was a small place, but he had let himself become too pleased with the directness of his plan. Beyond the interstate, the town itself—the dazzles of streetlights that were beginning to glow in the dusk, among the dark treetops—looked to be several miles away. By nightfall, it would be below zero. Walking seemed out of the question.

He pressed his hand to the glass of the phone booth, watching the snow fall onto the barren lot. Once, in Chicago, he'd answered a randomly ringing pay phone and a husky male voice had said: "I can see you, Mister. I'm watching you right now." He'd looked up: rows of windows, dotting upward like endless ellipses, almost into infinity. The rest of that day, he'd found it hard to shake the sense that someone was out there, watching.

Remembering this made him edgy. Something inside his stomach shrunk a bit, and he couldn't help but think again that he was making a mistake. He stepped out of the phone booth, walked around it once, trying to consider his course. Then, feigning nonchalance, he turned and went inside the café.

For a moment, he'd let himself imagine that he might meet someone there, maybe hitch a ride into town. But it wasn't that type of place, he realized. It seemed to him that everyone looked up when he crossed the threshold, and he felt as if silence fell over the room and everyone was staring as he lurched into the unfriendly, greasy-smelling brightness. The cowboys and truck drivers threw a glance at his trench coat, the red and gold scarf tucked carefully into his collar, and he put a hand through his hair, combing out the snow with his fingers.

There was a little area by the cash register where trinkets and novelties were on display, and he walked over and looked at them, folding his hands in front of him as if he were self-possessed and untroubled, a man with a bit of free time to kill. Tiered within the glass case, jewelry and belt buckles made of Black Hills gold and turquoise were lined up; below them, metal figurines of forty-niners, cowpokes with lariats, Elvis, an Indian on a horse, his arms open wide, with the inscription: "Great Spirit/Teach me to criticize another man not/Until I have walked a mile/In his moccasins!" Staring at this, he half considered just staying, sitting down and drinking coffee until the bus back to Chicago showed up. He lingered over a revolving rack of postcards, trying to sort out his thoughts, flipping through the pictures of Mount Rushmore and Reptile Gardens and Wind Cave. He couldn't help but imagine himself and this woman, his mother, visiting these places, seeing the sights of the world she lived in. He pictured them slowly beginning to tell their stories, to become friends. It wasn't so improbable.

O'Neil had always felt sure that it wouldn't work over the phone: it was too unreal, too easy for her to simply hang up. But why not call her, he thought now, just to hear the voice, the brief, hesitant "Hello . . . hello . . . Is someone there?" Then hang up, go home.

Or say something, he thought: "You don't know me, but . . ."; or "Mother, this is your son"; or "You can't hide from me anymore"; or even "I love you." O'Neil whispered all of them under his breath, testing the feel of each on his tongue. None of them worked. None of them got past a few lines before he imagined a click, a dial tone.

When he looked up, he could see an elderly man staring at him from a table near the window. The old man's mouth was turned up in a tiny crescent smile, and O'Neil shrugged his shoulders at him, as if to say: "Well, we all talk to ourselves once in a while, don't we?" But rather than turning away, the old man began to nod his head, still smiling and watching, and O'Neil could feel the friendly expression on his face tighten into a mask.

No one in the world knew where he was. He'd managed to keep it secret, though sometimes he felt as if he could hold it back no longer. At work, poised over the blinking cursor on his computer, O'Neil would catch the girl in the next cubicle glancing at him, and he'd feel a quivering inside his stomach. For a moment, O'Neil imagined he was going to tell. And when he called his parents, his adoptive parents, he could sense it, moving beneath the talk of health and weather like a fish below ice. He spoke into the hiss of long distance, imagining that his words disintegrated to travel through the wire and then came together at the other end, but not in the same pattern. Who knew what they would hear him say?

So he told them nothing. He didn't want to hurt them. He didn't want his mother to ask, after a long pause, "What can she give you that we haven't?" or even "Why?"

O'Neil couldn't answer that. For years, he hadn't even thought about it. His parents had told him at an early age that he was adopted, and he'd grown up taking it for granted. He was his parents' son, he told those who asked, an O'Neil 100 percent. The nameless lady who had given birth to him didn't matter.

But slowly, it had crept up on him. Sometimes, it was just little things—a face seen closing a door, a certain smell of wood, a woman's laugh heard from across a restaurant. Sometimes, on a busy Chicago street, all the bodies passing around him would suddenly have histories—pasts, futures, secrets. It was a mundane realization, he knew, except that he was aware that any of them—a woman stumbling down his street at midnight, singing in a high clear voice; a lady vanishing into the doorway of an elevated train; a businessman in silver sunglasses, cruising slowly past in his convertible—any of them could belong to him. He sensed mothers, fathers, siblings in the faces that passed. Once, at a bar, O'Neil had been drawn to talk to a man who looked like him. A little drunk, O'Neil found himself pushing the conversation, asking the man about his family. "What's your mother like?" O'Neil had said, leaning forward, as the man shifted uncomfortably.

And O'Neil wondered what had happened to her. Did she look at him, after he was born? Did she cry? He couldn't picture her face, though sometimes if he concentrated he could almost catch a glimpse of some aspect—the set of the eyes, the shape of a finger. Occasionally, he would indulge himself, pretending she might be someone famous. He'd even clipped out photos that had caught his eye in newspapers and magazines, actresses or experts of some sort, society page ladies. He liked to imagine her as someone with quick things to say, a party-giver. Perhaps she was known for her moods. He tried not to construct a rape, the natural father pulling her onto the dirty ground, the heel of his hand against her mouth. He tried not to imagine her smiling as she left the hospital, free of an annoying burden and nothing else. He'd read a book about a home for unwed mothers, and this was where O'Neil most often saw her. For months, the pregnant girls lived separate from the rest of the world. Once, when the nuns took them to town for ice cream, they were given wedding bands to wear. There were white corridors, crisp pages of forms she had to sign, the movement of O'Neil's unformed limbs inside her.

He didn't know whether this would make sense to his adopted parents; probably, it wouldn't. He could see his father shaking his head, frowning, looking down at his hands. And late at night, when he was alone in the guest room, his old bedroom, his adoptive mother would come to him. Or so he imagined. She'd sit down on the edge of his bed and look at him sadly. "You're lonely," she'd say. "That's what it is, you know. You live in that big city by yourself and you're having a hard time finding a direction." She'd touch his hair, push it gently back from his brow. For a long time, they'd stay like that, in the dark, in silence.

"Whatever's missing in your life," she'd say at last, "whatever that is, you're not going to get it from her."

O'Neil wasn't sure that she would say this, of course. It was possible that his parents would be encouraging. Maybe, if he'd tried to explain his reasons to them, they would have nodded sympathetically. "Do you know what I mean?" O'Neil would ask them, and they would say, "Yes, we understand, we support you." But even then, the other conversation, the negative one he'd imagined, would be right there beneath the surface. After all, the questions he put in their mouths were the same ones he'd been asking himself all along.

He walked back out to the phone booth. None of those imaginary conversations mattered, O'Neil told himself. He was here now, there was no turning back. He was going to talk to her, see her, and after that, maybe all the answers would fall into place.

He felt light-headed. Out in the distance, semis and cars nudged toward the exit, the interstate underlined the flat stretch of horizon. For a long while he just stood there in the glass box, his hand on the phone. As he watched, the lines of wheel tracks, the dots of footprints casually disappeared in the accumulating snow. His hands felt disembodied when he dialed the number.

O'Neil had imagined that this moment would be dizzying, that the air would hum with electricity. But the phone seemed to ring and ring, and the air seemed suddenly thin, and his stomach tightened as if he'd been running a long way. At last he heard the receiver being lifted. And then her voice, tired, somewhat impatient, said, "Hello?"

"Hello," O'Neil murmured. "It's me. I'm calling to find out if you received the rose I sent you." His voice sounded as he imagined hers would, soft and sensual.

There was a long pause. All O'Neil could hear was an echoing hallway of static through the wire, muffled voices and computer sounds mumbling as if from behind shut doors. He gripped the telephone tightly, could feel his body straining forward as if he could somehow catch hold of her words and pull them to himself. "Yes," she said finally. "Yes. I received it."

"Did you like it?" he whispered. His heart was pounding. In his mind he was already rushing through the conversation, exchanging life histories and breathless, emotional phrases. He thought of her hands, shaking right now as his were.

"It was nice," she said. She cleared her throat at the same time O'Neil did, and he laughed a little, because they thought alike, they really were alike.

"Really?" O'Neil breathed. "I thought you'd like it. I knew you would." He was unrehearsed, speaking quickly, and he sensed himself picking up momentum. But before he could continue, she sighed heavily.

"Listen," she said, as if O'Neil were an eager salesman and she wished he'd come to the point. "What do you want? Why are you calling me?" She spoke stiffly, and the half-swoon he'd been in dropped away. He was intruding.

"I want to meet you," O'Neil said at last, and she nearly cut him off.

"But I don't want to meet you," she said. "I don't want to correspond with you, I don't want to know about you." Her voice sharpened and grew more deliberate as she spoke. "I'm sure you're a very fine person, very smart, very nice, very handsome. I'd be proud of you. But I don't want to know you."

O'Neil opened his mouth. "Please," he said, and his throat tightened, "I'm here. I came here to meet you." Outside, things were beginning to distort and double and he wiped his hand across his eyes. "What if we just met once? Then I'll be gone away and I won't bother you. I won't call you anymore. I just want to see you, we don't even have to talk."

"What good would that do?" she said flatly. It was what O'Neil always thought his other parents would say, and he felt the question sink heavily inside him. He sighed into the phone, the sound amplified, huge against the mouthpiece.

"I don't know," he said. He paused, but she made no sound. He thought he could hear her breathing. "I want to just because you're my mother."

"I'm not though," she said. "I'm just someone who made a mistake a long time ago. And I've been punished enough for it, I think."

O'Neil didn't say anything—he couldn't speak. And after a long silence she said: "I'm going to hang up now. I'm really very sorry."

"Wait!" O'Neil blurted out. "I've come a long way. I'm here now. Couldn't I just see you from a distance? Couldn't I maybe stand outside your house, or across the street, and then you could step outside for a minute? A minute."

"Don't come near my house," she said sharply. "You're not listening to me. No."

"Please," he said, and he could hear himself repeating, softly, anything to keep her on the line, "Please please please. I don't want to cause problems. You understand, don't you? What could it hurt?"

There was no sound coming from the phone, and for a moment O'Neil thought she'd hung up. Then he heard her sigh. "Look," he said. "What about this. I'm at the bus station now. I'll stay here, I won't come to your house if you'll promise me. If you could just walk by— walk by here and give me some sign so I know it's you. You wouldn't have to see me at all. You wouldn't even have to look at me."

"Why are you doing this," she said tiredly.

"What can it matter to you," he said; his voice had hardened. "Just to walk by? It would mean everything to me." She was silent. "Is that really too much to ask? In the next hour or so. I'll be in the window of the café. Walk by and just wave, so I know. Then I wouldn't have any reason to go to your house."

"Don't come to this house," she said.

"I won't," O'Neil said. "If you'll just do this for me, you'll never hear from me again." And then he startled himself, the coldness that crept into his own voice. "But if you won't," he whispered, "I'll have to come to you."

She was silent. Dead air.

"Will you do that?" O'Neil said. "Mother?"

That word felt poisonous as it left his mouth. There was something ugly about the way he said it, he thought, though he had once practiced whispering it, the exact right inflections, the exact right moment. It seemed to stun her.

"All right," she said. She was frightened now, O'Neil thought, and he felt her doubt in the space between words.

"All right," she said, and hung up.

He didn't know whether to trust her, but for her sake, as well as his own, he waited. He told himself that if she didn't come, he'd go straight to her house, he'd bang on the door. He'd force her to call the police. The thought surprised him a little. He hadn't realized how close he was to the bottom of his life.

Still, he couldn't believe that she really wouldn't come. She had to be curious, deep down, even if he was a "mistake." O'Neil thought of her, at twenty, at thirty, the years passing. Childless, watching toddlers in the park, their bright parkas the color of balloons, looking away as the mothers caught her staring. He pictured her, alone for years now, listening to the creak and groan of an empty house, mumbling to herself. Or flipping through an old photo album, a picture of herself as a child, her round face gazing solemnly at the photographer. She must think of that child she gave up. It would only be natural.

It stopped snowing, and the temperature began to drop. O'Neil went inside again, and took a seat near the window. The waitress came up at last.

"Help you?" she said sternly.

He looked up at her. Sometimes it seemed so attractive, that phrase—"May I help you?"—and he wondered what people would do if someone took them seriously, if someone really needed help. "Coffee, please," O'Neil said, and she wrote it glumly on her pad.

"That be all?"

"Yes." She reached down to turn over the cup on his table, and her hand brushed his. It gave him a funny feeling: Sometimes it was easy to forget that there are other people thinking thoughts, maybe off in some daydream like you. All those minds, talking in people's heads. And when you feel their skin on yours, you realize it. That was what O'Neil thought.

He waited. After a while, the waitress stopped filling his cup, and still he just sat there, his hands shaky, his mind whirring. There weren't very many people at the café by that time, and whenever someone approached, his body tensed. He waited for a sign as they rounded the corner, each one a possibility at first, not even the most unlikely could be easily discarded. He stared as an old lady in a scarf hurried past; stretched forward when a red-haired girl in a cowboy hat came sidling along, on the arm of a wiry, squinting man. O'Neil watched them take a booth at the back of the café. The girl leaned over the table to whisper things to her companion. No—too old, too young, not right in some way. In the end, O'Neil knew that when she passed, he'd be certain.

Almost two hours had gone by when he finally saw her. He was staring impatiently at the face of his watch. Outside, the red taillights of cars were tiny points.

Then he caught sight of the woman. She came around the side of the building and entered the lighted area outside the cafe, hesitantly, in a bright blue ski coat and a red stocking cap. He saw the cap first, bright and forlorn against the white and black landscape, melting out of the darkness. The figure appeared on the edge of the circle of light, stopping once, looking back, as if she'd forgotten something.

He sat up straight. As he watched, she walked toward the café, toward the window he was staring from, flirtatiously slow, as if coming into a spotlight.

When at last O'Neil could see her face, she stopped. She looked around, scanning the area, her breath coming from her mouth like smoke in the cold night air. She turned her head, gazing one direction, then another. As if hypnotized, she lifted her hand. It was long and pale in the fluorescent light. She pulled off her cap as if drawing back a veil, and the dark hair spilled out, falling over her shoulders, black hair like O'Neil's, that shiny jet color he'd always felt conscious of, adopted into a family of blonds. Perhaps she looked like him too, though in the bright light her features were cold and white as bone, a gaunt face, her lips tight and expressionless. She stared at the place where he was sitting, her eyes both tired and critical. "Careworn," was the word that came to him, a word his adoptive mother might have used. But that wasn't right, exactly—they were the kind of eyes that might stare back at you in the mirror, if you could judge yourself truly enough.

And then he realized. She saw her own reflection in the window he was staring from. She posed, unselfconsciously, brushed her hair with her fingers. It was her: He could feel a coldness rippling over him when she cocked her head and tried on a brief smile.

Then she turned away from him, spun on her heel, and began walking, trailing that electricity behind her, into the dark.

Without thinking, O'Neil ran after her. He left his coat in the booth, ignoring the waitress who yelled after him: "Hey! You haven't paid your tab!" O'Neil brushed past her as she tried to block his exit, digging a five from his pocket and pressing it into her hand. "Thanks a lot," she said, but he pushed on. He hit the door and the cold air came rushing over him like a premonition. She was already yards ahead.

"Hey!" he called, but she did not turn. "Hey!" He began to run toward her. She whirled, as if frightened, and for a moment their eyes met. She was looking at him, though there was no telling what was registering, really—His clothes? His expression? Did she see him as he appeared to himself in the mirror? Whom did she see?

She took a step backward. "Are you talking to me?" she said. Her voice was careful, uninterested.

"I love you," O'Neil said. He started to shiver, his arms cringing from the cold. "I wanted you to know that I love you." His breath came out in foggy gasps, curling out into the night air.

She seemed taken aback—her eyes slanted, and her mouth hardened as she appraised him. It was the face of a bureaucrat, he thought, someone whose job was to turn people away for eight hours a day, the kind of person he'd dealt with all the time when he was searching for her. That was what was in her face. She looked him up and down, and then abruptly gave a sort of sighing laugh, as if dismissing him.

"Oh, get lost," she said. "What are you, crazy? Get lost."

"I love you," O'Neil said again, but the words felt wrong, too small in his throat. She was backing away from him, and he put out his hand. His fingers brushed the slick material of her coat. She screamed.

The cry filled up the empty parking lot, ringing, echoing off the side of the building like a shot. She jerked away, but O'Neil's fingers held to her coat. They swayed: for a second it seemed to O'Neil as if they could have been dancing, held there in stasis. Her eyes widened, and he could sense how thin her body was beneath the heavy coat, sinew, muscle twisting. Her arms flailed, and she screamed again: "Let go! Let go!" The dark hair whipped from side to side. The streams of their breath twined together. He tried to catch at her hands as they flew.

"Hey!" he heard a man's voice shout. O'Neil turned in time to see a short wiry man striding toward him, cowboy boots crunching on the frozen gravel. O'Neil recognized him as the man he'd watched coming into the café. The man's girlfriend, the one in the cowboy hat, was standing off by the door.

"This man bothering you, Miss?" the man said loudly. He put his hand on O'Neil's shoulder, clenching, and she pulled free.

But she didn't answer him. She just nodded her head vaguely, still backing away. O'Neil didn't know what was in her expression, but she didn't blink as she looked at him, and he imagined a softness wavering there for a moment, pity or a kind of apology. He knew from the way she took him in that she wanted to remember his face.

"Son," the man said, "I think you'd better move on your way." He spoke firmly, and his hand tightened on O'Neil's shoulder. "Tell the lady you're sorry," he said. He gave O'Neil a little shake.

"I'm sorry," O'Neil said, but his voice was hoarse and barely audible. He looked down at his feet, trying to keep himself from shivering, and when he lifted his head, she was already moving away, she had turned and was walking fast, faster, almost running. And then she was gone, vanished into the darkened parking lot. He heard the slam of a car door, the grinding of a key in the ignition. Wheels turned in the slush and gravel.

The man released his grip on O'Neil's shoulder, but O'Neil didn't move. The cowboy observed him, squinting at his face, then shook his head. "You're going to catch cold, son," he said. "You better go on back inside, and don't bother people no more."

O'Neil couldn't say anything. He just stood there, staring out at the rows of snow-covered cars, the glitter of half-revealed chrome winking like eyes, glinting. His mind blurred. And then he heard his footsteps as the man, too, walked away. The tips of O'Neil's ears and his fingers ached sharply from the cold.

A little after midnight the bus came. O'Neil stood among others in the snow and waited. They were in a group, each of them facing a slightly different direction. They braced against the wind as the bus doors hissed open.

O'Neil left home on a bus, going east for the first time. For hours he could feel the place on his back where his adoptive mother had put her hand when they hugged goodbye. He'd sat there, watching cars and farmhouses pass, wondering whether the people inside them could sense him, O'Neil, out beyond the range of their living rooms and pickups. He was out there thinking of them, and they would never know the difference.

He stumbled down the aisle of the bus, holding on to the seats for balance. Searching for a seat, O'Neil hovered over the faces of old women, their coats draped like blankets over them, children curled into balls. And for a moment he paused, standing over the form of a sleeping woman, and he leaned over her, seeing how her feet were tucked under her, how her hair hung loose over her face. Slowly, he held out his hand. He could feel her breath, and for one second he just stared down at those eyes closed tight, the motionless lips; and he touched her wrist.

Meeting the Birthmother

JUDITH W. STEINBERGH

for Shauna and Valerie 7/29/92

They come toward each other from the edges
of the small park—separated by chestnut trees
and nearly twenty years—diaspora of the blood.

They walk inward, their breath short, leaning back
toward their pasts, their hearts like cliff swallows
swooping at dusk out of the dark safety of the chest.

They have imagined the other's pale face
without a name—all these years—arms—voice
breasts—a double existing in no fixed place.

Above maple leaves rustle and hush, rustle and hush.
Starlings weave part of their story in the air.
Their breathing is jagged, comes in a rush

held since the last birth breath, the cry and gasp,
the slipping out and away of the daughter, the first
suck of air into the delicate vase of the lungs.

Everything waits—the two so familiar, so strange
drawn like moths to flame—fly toward opening arms,
gathering strength to shape the other's name.

Reunion

SUSAN BUMPS

The woman who gave birth to me
invites me over to her house.
We sit on the couch, drink wine, talk about rain
how she says each drop is like another
not like snowflakes, and how I say
maybe she hasn't looked closely enough—
just last weekend I saw different ones,
some like inverted pyramids,
some like smooth flat stones.
We talk for hours but all those molecules
of shared DNA come down to this—
when we reach for our glasses,
our middle fingers touch first.
In a way it's a miracle, but also untrue—
just as the woman in the grocery store
has my voice, the woman at the Y,
with her small, naked body
just my breasts, my line of thigh.

These Things, That Others May Call Miracles
EILEEN MALONE

And here I am, trembling over white wine in a waterfront restaurant
found by this investigative angel on a mission of deliverance
I love that she is as nervous as I, doesn't ask me to explain
the wounding event, the adoption of thirty years ago, I love that

she has her father's hair, only on her it's sunlit and wheaten
and she has my deep-set eyes though burnished in gentle green
and looking at me, loving me, she says she has always loved me
even the humped and heavy memory of my bending shadow
this young lady, my daughter, has loved even my phantom

we declare each other in a claim that rises and cuts
through the immediate like the blade of an old, old dagger
that her hands lift from its self-plunge into my soul
it is her grasp that draws it forth like Excalibur from rock
carefully, as a garden rake pulled from a manatee's back
moves gently, as a bristly splinter from a lion's injured paw

she lifts it aloft, exposes it as the sharp-edged monstrance it is
and in one purge glittering motion, one solemn wave
she slashes the cataract of heaven's eye

and here I am in a swirl of released stars of white fog
that pour down, tumble down on air white wings of recognition's
first-born sensations, I remember, recognize, and it is all in this
    moment
more glistening than imagined, this moment that holds all other
    moments
on the pier in front of a waterside restaurant, it is all in this moment
that these things, that others may call miracles, fall on me
fall on me, and make me more.

My Tattooed Granddaughter

VICTOR WALTER

> *All night long I dreamed of Scorpions.*
> *They crawl under my bedclothes, they pass*
> *over my face; and I am not particularly*
> *excited, so many curious things do I see in*
> *my imagination.*
>
> —Jean-Henri Fabre

My eldest daughter, Tring, dropped out of art school, dropped out of my life, dropped out of everything. By the time they invented the term "hippie," she had done it all, lived free, soared, crashed. Now she lives a quiet life in Denver, married ten years to the same man, an insurance executive, shares a mortgage with her husband, dresses conservatively, works as supervisor of accounts for a chain of convenience stores. They have no children.

I thought I had no prospects of grandchildren, worried my kids were the end of the line. I'm not a good man, not a good father, lack patience for ordinary life. Where am I now in relation to Tring, to my son, to my youngest daughter?

Last month, a social worker phoned me here in Boston, asking for Tring's address. It astonished me. When Tring was a teenager, I expected calls from school counselors, social workers, the police, but now, what could they want from my yuppie daughter in Colorado? I phoned Tring, who replied, I know what it is. Call you back.

I waited in my studio, stretched a canvas, covered it with rich soft umber, planned to represent the story of my life, got the idea from a Japanese filmmaker who had the important scenes of his life tattooed on the skin of his back, only I would do it on canvas, not to celebrate my life, but to discover in paint exactly how I went wrong.

I met Tring's mother in a Persian bar called Mithra's Cave up near Central Park West. First time I went there was before I shipped out, went to see the mural because the technique interested me, colors laid on by a spirit fresco process. A fine skin of marble dust, previously applied to the wall, held color on the surface, kept the plaster from absorbing it. The scene on the wall fascinated me, a mythological picture of Creation, glowing like a vast jewel in the dim light—an enormous transparent bull filled with tiny plants and animals, a sheaf of grain sprouting out of its tail, a giant scorpion clinging to its genitals. The Persian bartender, observing my fascination, tested me, said, Is lot of bull, no?

Why the scorpion? I asked.

He seemed to know all about the mural and the idea behind it—the sun god in the moment of Creation killing the primeval bull to release fertility on earth. He insisted the scorpion was a symbol of fertility. I didn't believe it.

Even at sea, I thought about it, decided the scorpion embodied the force of evil, penetrated the bull's organ with its venomous spike. It represented the balance of good and evil—poison at the source of generation.

Home on leave in the summer of 1945, when the war in Europe was over and the Pacific war almost over, I returned to Mithra's Cave to look at the mural and met my first wife there. She worked in a restaurant nearby. The bartender introduced us, but the mural brought us together. I barely remember her face and wonder if I ever really looked at her, even when we lived together. I spread all over her, like paint on canvas.

Tring was conceived while I was between ships. I named her after the birthplace of Thomas Blossom, who studied engraving with William Blake and is almost forgotten—but not by me. Tring remembers him as well and mentions him whenever people ask how she got a name like that.

Tring's mother and I stayed together until I got out of the Navy, until I finished art school, until I had a son. Tring went with her mother when we split up, stayed with her until she was fourteen, ran away, disappeared, raised herself.

After speaking to the social worker, Tring phoned me back and said, Sit down, better yet, lie on the floor—so you won't fall off anything. You have a twenty-one-year-old granddaughter you never met.

Tring got pregnant at nineteen by an art student whose last name she can't remember, had the baby in one of those benevolent shelters for wayward girls, gave it over for adoption. Never told me. I can't remember what was going on that year, but she says she saw me once on the streets of Boston while she was pregnant and ducked into an alley to hide.

Tring named her Vanchatya, which means 'child of passionate yearning,' but the adoptive parents changed it to Amy. Even though the couple looked good on paper, he a Unitarian minister, she a woman of means, the adoption turned out badly. Both of them were alcoholics, which of course the agency didn't know. They got divorced when the child was twelve. She never bonded to either of them, stayed with her adoptive mother a few years, then ran away, lived on the streets, hung out with punks in Boston, got addicted to heroin, rode with a motorcycle gang in New York, worked as a stripper in Miami. Never mind, she's my granddaughter, probably inherited strong genes, a steady hand and clear eye. Since she was raised in Boston, I may have passed her in the street without knowing it.

Two years ago, she turned up in Boston again, very ill but determined to recover and to change her life. Her adoptive mother flew with her to Maryland, signed her into a rehabilitation center in Baltimore. There Amy recovered from addiction, finished high school, learned to counsel young addicts. The rehabilitation center released her when she turned twenty-one, and she returned to Boston, intending to go to college, find her birth mother, track down her blood relatives. The agency that had transacted her adoption let her read the file, except for information that would identify her biological parents. She learned she had been named Vanchatya and felt moved by what she read about Tring, who had said she loved the infant, felt tormented because she could not keep her. The biological father said he couldn't handle it, showed no interest in the baby. He didn't want me, she said, and had no interest in finding her father. My granddaughter discarded her identity as Amy, legally changed her name to Vanchatya, got a court order to make the agency identify her birth mother and grandparents. I learned all this from Tring, who spoke to the social worker as well as to her own lost Vanchatya.

So maybe it's not the end of the line, I thought, but when I tried to paint the story of my life on canvas, I saw the mural. The scorpion was my ego, I accused. Poison at the source of generation.

Never there much for my children, I had assumed they got what they needed. Tring's mother left me after my son was born. Maybe she loved him in her cold, passive way, but he never bonded to her. My second wife tried to raise him as her own, but he never trusted her. My son inherited strong genes, a steady hand, and clear eye, went to the Massachusetts College of Art, actually makes a living from his sculpture, works in bronze, carves wood. He's shy of women, probably will never marry.

My youngest daughter, child of my second marriage, studied painting with me, graduated from the Museum School, does my kind of work, which respects the forms and colors of nature. The human figure is the hardest thing to draw, but this girl knows her anatomy, modeled a skeleton bone by bone, shaped the muscles, understands the body inside out. She inherited my steady hand, clear eye, fine sense of color. She's gay, lives alone, may never have children of her own.

I don't marry any more but always get involved. Right now it's a colleague at the Museum School who works with fabrics, does batiks, traditional African designs. We have separate studios in the stable behind my home in Boston. She jokes it's the only way she can have a stable relationship with me. In my studio, having cleared a space in the sunlight, I sit at a blank canvas, waiting for the mural to quit my mind, waiting for an image to begin the story of my life.

Tring bought her daughter a ticket to Denver, where she spent a weekend with Tring and her husband. Just a weekend. No hint the girl might move out there, or even that they might get together again. On the phone to Tring, I complained, She's my granddaughter. When the hell am I going to meet her? Call her up, Tring advised. And Dad, she comes with six tattoos.

I invited her to dinner at my house, just the two of us. I cooked. I thought she looked a lot like Tring: chubby, dark hair, hazel eyes, clear skin, and an oblique way of looking at you, as if making up her mind whether to trust or to run. She wore a sleeveless blouse, and I stared at her arms. I had expected butterflies and flowers.

A pile of skulls on her right forearm, etched in black, dripped rusty blood over the words, *Death Before Dishonor*. The skulls, out of proportion, revealed ignorance of anatomy, and the lettering was unskilled. Her right upper arm showed a Maltese cross, shaded in light sepia, poorly executed. The work on her right arm was crude, but the left arm startled me, showing a large, beautiful scorpion, impeccably rendered in vivid colors, blue-black thorax, red pincers in front like claws of a lobster, yellow segmented tail ending in a green venom bullet and black sting. It crawled up toward her shoulder; the tail, dangling below the elbow, reached her forearm.

I'm not sure how I feel about these tattoos now, she said.

Why the scorpion? I asked.

It's my sign, she said. All they told me about my birth was the date, October twenty-third, day the sun passes into the house of Scorpio. I had it done in Miami.

Did Tring tell you, Vanchatya is a child of the scorpion?

She shook her head, smiled, said, She didn't tell me. But we think alike. There's a strong bond between us. She picked me out at the airport right away. She knows me. She's my mother.

I used to read Tring myths of ancient India, I said. In one of them a beautiful princess refused the man her father wanted her to marry, so her father, the king, kept her locked in a tower. She wept and prayed to Shiva, longed for a baby to comfort her, to share her solitude. Shiva, the creator-destroyer, taking the form of a scorpion with sperm in his tail, crept under a crack in the door and penetrated her with his sting. When the princess gave birth, she named the baby Vanchatya. Indeed, a child of passionate yearning.

My granddaughter rubbed the skin of her arms, as if she were stroking the scorpion, looked into my eyes. Have you ever seen a live scorpion? I asked.

In Florida, she replied. I saw them. They carry their young. One made a deep impression on me—a brown scorpion with pure white babies crammed together on its back. When they fell off it searched for them, let them climb back on. It even accepted strange young ones. The scorpion adopts them.

She noticed I was staring at her arm. I have more tattoos, she said, looking down at the table. She told me she had a panther on her back, but I didn't ask to see it, or inquire about the location of the other two. I told her I craved grandchildren, complained I had produced a generation of slow breeders. She agreed to stay in touch. I felt exhilarated, a sudden grandfather with a brand new but grown-up granddaughter. Just as suddenly I might become a great-grandfather!

She would phone about once a week. Always began by saying, Grandpa? This is Vanchatya. We got together a few times, and one afternoon I showed her around the Museum of Fine Arts. She seemed mildly interested in the exhibits, but I felt she really enjoyed having lunch in the Museum café.

When two weeks passed without a call, I felt worried, tried to reach her. Eventually, she rang and said in a faint voice, Grandpa, don't think I forgot you. I'm in the hospital.

A tubal pregnancy, she said. I visited the next day. She was recovering from surgery. It had happened to her before, on the other side. This time the doctor said it was unlikely she would be able to have children. I should have asked questions, found out who did it and if he was a steady boyfriend, but I felt I hardly knew her, and just listened.

Next day, she looked stronger, walked around the room. She wore black trousers gathered at the ankles and a black T-shirt with a message. In front a skull in a motorcycle helmet floated over huge crossed hypodermic needles. In back, large white letters warned, *Don't Start.*

I went to see her every day, and as far as I know, no one else visited her in the hospital. While I was in the room, she took a phone call from Baltimore, said irritably, Stop calling me. I did send a check. She mumbled words I could not hear, hung up. It's a kid I took care of in the rehabilitation center, she explained, I was a therapist to her. She's fifteen, her mother's an addict, her father's on death row in the state penitentiary. She has nobody, calls me Mom. We're very close. I want to adopt her.

When I left the hospital, I looked up at the half-moon and thought about prospects for the next generation, imagining an adoptive great-grandchild without my genes.

I need to see the connections, understand where we are in the scheme of things. It occurs to me the enormous skin at the back of the mind stretches as high and wide as the eye can reach. Now in my studio, I plan a scene of creation large enough to represent links between generations, deep enough to express what I learned about the process of generation, not an oil painting on canvas but a vast tattoo in the back of my mind. I sketch in Tring, my son, my youngest daughter, my granddaughter, and then a faceless child with a mother who is a drug addict, father on death row. Like the scorpion, I carry them all at the back of my mind.

This Need Called Father

TINA CERVIN

This need I have to find you, a habit and desire
Like strong coffee in the daylight.
Because mother is so pinched,
Her lips stiff as a beak when she tilts
To whisper, "Remember who raised you up,
Who is your real father after all."
Because the man I call father
Hides behind hard eyes
That are moist for his "authentic" daughters.
He chastises me and scolds.
The old wound is deep and begins
To throb like a heart out of control.
I am two years old again and you—
Are gone, with your eyes the color
Of tobacco and hair like wet tar.
Gone with your camera and beat-up valises.
Your desire to come clean out of the Depression
Unbroken. Except she broke you, Mother did,
Sent you into the dustbowl. I hope this is true.
Because if you wavered just a little
In 1937, it meant you did not walk easily,
Did not sign over your little girl to another man,
Adopt her away as simply as a young calf
To a neighboring farmer.
I lost my name.
I lost the touch
Of your skin. I used to bite
The flesh on the back of my hand
To cauterize the fear.
Hopefully, you remember the story, remember
Now that I am a woman and you—
Are old, that I am split from your cells
In fine division. And I am now breaking

Those cells, shaving them off
Into the son who will have your name
And bear forward our desire.

A Relative Stranger

CHARLES BAXTER

I was separated from my biological mother when I was four months old. Everything from that period goes through the wash of my memory and comes out clean, blank. The existing snapshots of my mother show this very young woman holding me, a baby, at arm's length, like a caught fish, outside in the blaring midday summer sunlight. She's got clothes up on the clothesline in the background, little cotton infant things. In one picture a spotted dog, a mongrel combination of Labrador and Dalmatian, is asleep beside the bassinet. I'd like to know what the dog's name was, but time has swallowed that information. In another picture, a half-empty bottle of Grain Belt beer stands on the lawn near a wading pool. My mother must have figured that if she could have me, at the age of seventeen, she could also have the beer.

My mother's face in these pictures is having a tough time with daylight. It's a struggle for her to bask in so much glare. She squints and smiles, but the smile is all on one side, the right. The left side stays level, except at the edge, where it slips down. Because of the sunlight and the black-and-white film, my mother's face in other respects is bleached, without details, like a sketch for a face. She's a kid in these pictures and she has a kid's face, with hair pulled back with bobby pins and a slight puffiness in the cheeks, which I think must be bubblegum.

She doesn't look like she's ever been used to the outdoors, the poor kid. Sunlight doesn't become her. It's true she smiled, but then she did give me up. I was too much serious work, too much of a squalling load. Her girlish smile was unsteady and finally didn't include me. She gave me away—this is historical record—to my adoptive parents, Harold and Ethel Harris, who were older and more capable of parental love. She also gave them these photographs, the old kind, with soft sawtooth borders, so I'd be sure to know how she had looked when the unfamiliar sunlight hit her in a certain way. I think her teenage boyfriend, my father, took these pictures. Harold and Ethel Harris were parents in every respect, in love and in their care for me, except for the fact of these pictures. The other children in the family, also adopted, looked at the snapshots of this backyard lady with curiosity but not much else.

My biological father was never a particle of interest to me compared to my adoptive father, Harold Harris, a man who lived a life of miraculous calm. A piano tuner and occasional jazz saxophonist, Harold liked to sit at home, humming and tapping his fingers in the midst of uproar and riot, kids shouting and plaster falling. He could not be riled; he never made a fist. He was the parental hit of any childhood group, and could drive a car competently with children sitting on his shoulders and banging their hands on the side of his head. Genetic inheritance or not, he gave us all a feeling for pitch. Ask me for an F-sharp, I'll give you one. I get the talent from Harold.

I went to high school, messed around here and there, did some time in the Navy, and when I was discharged I married my sweetheart of three years, the object of my shipboard love letters, Lynda Claire Norton. We had an apartment. I was clerking at Meijer's Thrifty Acres. I thought we were doing okay. Each night I was sleeping naked next to a sexual angel. At sunrise she would wake me with tender physical comfort, with hair and fingertips. I was working to get a degree from night school. Fourteen months after we were married, right on the day it was due, the baby came. A boy, this was. Jonathan Harold Harris. Then everything went to hell.

I was crazy. Don't ask me to account for it. I have no background or inclination to explain the human mind. Besides, I'm not proud of the way I acted. Lynda moved right out, baby and all, the way any sensible woman would have, and she left me two empty rooms in the apartment in which I could puzzle myself out.

I had turned into the damnedest thing. I was a human monster movie. I'd never seen my daddy shouting the way I had; he had never carried on or made a spectacle of himself. Where had I picked up this terrible craziness that made me yell at a woman who had taken me again and again into her arms? I wrote long letters to the world while I worked at home on my model ships, a dull expression on my face. You will say that liquor was the troublemaker here and you would be correct, but only so far. I had another bad ingredient I was trying to track down. I broke dishes. My mind, day and night, was muzzy with bad intentions. I threw a lightbulb against a wall and did not sweep up the glass for days. Food burned on the stove and then I ate it. I was committing outrageous offenses against the spirit. Never, though, did I smash one of the model ships. Give me credit for that.

I love oceans and the ships that move across them. I believe in man-made objects that take their chances on the earth's expanses of water. And so it happened that one weekday afternoon I was watching a rerun of *The Caine Mutiny,* with my workboard set up in front of me with the tiny pieces of my model Cutty Sark in separated piles, when the phone rang. For a moment I believed that my wife had had second thoughts about my behavior and was going to give me another chance. To tell the truth, whenever the phone rang, I thought it would be Lynda, announcing her terms for my parole.

"Hello? Is this Oliver Harris?" a man's voice asked.

"This is him," I said. "Who's this?"

"This is your brother." Just like that. Very matter-of-fact. This is your brother. Harold and Ethel Harris had had two other adopted sons, in addition to me, but I knew them. This voice was not them. I gripped the telephone.

Now—and I'm convinced of this—every adopted child fears and fantasizes getting a call like this announcing from out of the blue that someone in the world is a relative and has tracked you down. I know I am not alone in thinking that anyone in the world might be related to me. My biological mother and father were very busy, urgent lovers. Who knows how much procreation they were capable of, together and separately? And maybe they had brothers and sisters, too, as urgent in their own way as my mother and father had been in theirs, filling up the adoption agencies with their offspring. I could never go into a strange city without feeling that I had cousins in it.

Therefore I gripped the telephone, hoping for reason, for the every-day. "This is not my brother," I said.

"Oh yes, it is. Your mother was Alice Barton, right?"

"My mother was Ethel Harris," I said.

"Before that," the voice said, "your mother was Alice Barton. She was my mother, too. This is your brother, Kurt. I'm a couple of years younger than you." He waited. "I know this is a shock," he said.

"You can't find out about me," I said. The room wasn't spinning, but I had an idea that it might. My mouth was open halfway and I was taking short sweaty breaths through it. One shiver took its snaky way down and settled in the lumbar region. "The records are sealed. It's all private, completely secret."

"Not anymore, it isn't," he said. "Haven't you been keeping up? In this country you can find out anything. There are no secrets worth keeping anymore; nobody *wants* privacy, so there isn't any."

He was shoving this pile of ideas at me. *My* thoughts had left me in great flight, the whole sad flock of them. "Who are you?" I asked.

"Your brother Kurt," he said, repeating himself. "Listen, I won't bore you to explain what I had to do to find you. The fact is that it's possible. Easy, if you have money. You pay someone and someone pays someone and eventually you find out what you want to know. Big surprise, right?" He waited, and when I didn't agree with him, he started up again, this time with small talk. "So I hear that you're married and you have a kid yourself." He laughed. "And I'm an uncle."

"What? No. Now you're only partly right," I said, wanting very hard to correct this man who said he was my brother. "My wife left me. I'm living here alone now."

"Oh. I'm sorry about that." He offered his sympathies in a shallow, masculine way: the compassion offered by princes and salesmen. "But listen, he said, "you're not alone. It's happened before. Couples separate all the time. You'll get back. It's not the end of the world. Oliver?"

"What?"

"Would you be willing to get together and talk?"

"Talk? Talk about what?"

"Well, about being brothers. Or something else. You can talk about anything you please." He waited for me to respond, and I didn't. This was my only weapon—the terrible static of telephone silence. "Look," he said, this is tough for me. *I'm not a bad person.* I've been sitting by this phone for an hour. I don't know if I'm doing the right thing. My wife . . . you'll meet her . . . she hasn't been exactly supportive. She thinks this is a mistake. She says I've gone too far this time. I dialed your number four times before I dialed it to the end. I make hundreds of business calls but this one I could not do. It may be hard for you, also: I mean, I take a little getting used to. I can get obsessive about little things. That's how I found you."

"By being obsessive."

"Yeah. Lucille . . . that's my wife . . . she says it's one of my faults. Well, I always wanted a brother, you know, blood-related and everything, but I couldn't have one until I found you. But then I thought you might not like me. It's possible. Are you following me?"

"Yes, I am." I was thinking: here I am in my apartment, recently vacated by my wife, talking to a man who says he's my brother. Isn't there a law against this? Someone help me.

"You don't have to like me," he said, his brusque voice starting to stumble over the consonants. That made me feel better. "But that isn't the point, is it?" Another question I didn't have to answer, so I made him wait. "I can imagine what's in your head. But let's meet. Just once. Let's try it. Not at a house. I only live about twenty miles away. I can meet you in Ann Arbor. We can meet in a bar. I *know* where you live. I drove by your building. I believe I've even seen your car."

"Have you seen me?" This brother had been cruising past my house, taking an interest. Do brothers do that? What *do* they do?

"Well, no, but who cares about looks where brothers are concerned? We'll see each other. Listen, there's this place a couple of miles from you, the Wooden Keg. Could we meet there? Tomorrow at three? Are you off tomorrow?"

"That's a real problem for me," I said. "Booze is my special poison."

"Hell, that's all right," he said. "I'll watch out for you. I'm your brother. Oh. There's one other thing. I lied. I look like you. That's how you'll recognize me. I have seen you."

I held on to the telephone a long time after I hung up. I turned my eyes to the television set. José Ferrer was getting drunk and belligerent at a cocktail party. I switched off the set.

I was in that bar one hour before I said I would be, and my feelings were very grim. I wasn't humming. I didn't want him to be stationed there when I came in. I didn't want to be the one who sauntered in through the door and walked the long distance to the barstool. I didn't want some strange sibling checking out the way I close the distance or blink behind my glasses while my eyes adjust to the light. I don't like people watching me when they think they're going to get a skeleton key to my character. I'm not a door and I won't be opened that easily.

Going into a bar in the midsummer afternoon takes you out of the steel heat and air-hammer sun; it softens you up until you're all smoothed out. This was one of those wood-sidewall bars with air that hasn't recirculated for fifty years, with framed pictures of thorough-breds and cars on the walls next to the chrome decorator hubcaps. A man's bar, smelling of cigarettes and hamburger grease and beer. The brown padded light comes down on you from some recessed source, and the leather cushions on those barstools are as soft as a woman's hand, and before long the bar is one big bed, a bed on a barge eddying down a sluggish river where you've got nothing but good friends lined up on the banks. This is why I am an alcoholic. It wasn't easy drink-ing Coca-Cola in that place, that dim halfway house between the job and home, and I was about to slide off my wagon and order my first stiff one when the door cracked open behind me, letting in a trumpet blast of light, and I saw, in the door frame outline, my brother coming toward me. He was taking his own time. He had on a hat. When the door closed and my eyes adjusted, I got a better look at him, and I saw what he said I would see: I saw instantly that this was my brother. The elves had stolen my shadow and given it to him. A version of my face was fixed on a stranger. From the outdoors came this example of me, wearing a coat and tie.

He took a barstool next to mine and held out his hand. I held out mine and we shook like old friends, which we were a long way from becoming. "Hey," we both said. He had the eyes, the cheek, and the jaw in a combination I had seen only in the mirror. "Oliver," he said, refusing to let my hand go. "Good to meet you."

"Kurt," I said. "Likewise." Brother or no brother, I wasn't giving away anything too fast. This is America, after all.

"What're you drinking?" he asked.

"Coke."

"Oh. Right." He nodded. When he nodded, the hat nodded. After he saw me looking at it, he said, "Keeps the sun out of my eyes." He took it off and tried to put it on the bar, but there wasn't enough room for it next to the uncleared beer glasses and the ashtrays, so he stood up and dropped it on a hook over by the popcorn machine. There it was, the only hat. He said, "My eyes are sensitive to light. What about yours?" I nodded. Then he laughed, hit the bar with the broad flat of his hand, and said, "Isn't this great?" I wanted to say, yes, it's great, but the true heart of the secret was that no, it was not. It was horrifyingly strange without being eventful. You can't just get a brother off the street. But before I could stop him from doing it, he leaned over and put his right arm, not a large arm but an arm all the same, over my shoulders, and he dropped his head so that it came sliding in toward my chest just under the chin. Here was a man dead set on intimacy. When he straightened up, he said, "We're going to have ourselves a day today, that's for sure." His stutter took some of the certainty out of the words. "You don't have to work this afternoon, right?"

"No," I said, "I'm not scheduled."

"Great," he said. "Let me fill you in on myself."

Instead of giving me his past, he gave me a résumé. He tried to explain his origins. My biological mother, for all the vagueness in her face, had been a demon for good times. She had been passionate and prophylactically carefree. Maybe she had had twenty kids, like old Mother Hubbard. She gave us away like presents to a world that wanted us. This one, this Kurt, she had kept for ten months before he was adopted by some people called Sykes. My brother said that he understood that we—he and I—had two other siblings in Laramie, Wyoming. There might be more he didn't know about. I had a sudden image of Alice Barton as a human stork, flying at tree level and dropping babies into the arms of waiting parents.

Did I relax as my brother's voice took me through his life? Were we related under the skin, and all the way around the block? He talked; I talked. The Sykes family had been bookish types, lawyers, both of them, and Kurt had gone to Michigan State University in East Lansing. He had had certain advantages. No falling plaster or piano tuning. By learning the mysterious dynamics of an orderly life, he had been turned out as a salesman, and now he ran a plastics factory in Southfield, north of Detroit. "A small business," he said in a friendly, smug way. "Just fifteen employees." I heard about his comfortably huge home. I heard about his children, my nephews. From the wallet thick with money and credit cards came the lineup of photos of these beautiful children.

So what was he doing, this successful man, sitting on a barstool out here, next to his brother, me, the lowly checkout clerk?

"Does anybody have enough friends?" he asked me. "Does anyone have enough *brothers*?" He asked this calmly, but the questions, as questions, were desperate. "Here's what it was," he said. "Two or three times a week I felt like checking in with someone who wasn't a wife and wasn't just a friend. Brothers are a different category, right there in the middle. It's all about *relatedness,* you know what I mean?" I must have scowled. "We can't rush this," he said. "Let's go have dinner somewhere, My treat. And then let's do something."

"Do what?" I asked.

"I've given that a lot of thought," he said. "What do you do the first time out with your brother? You can't just eat and drink. You can't shop; women do that." Then he looked me square in the eye, smiled, and said, "It's summer. Maybe we could go bowling or play some baseball." There was a wild look in his eye. He let out a quick laugh.

We went in his Pontiac Firebird to a German restaurant and loaded up on sauerbraten. I had a vague sense he was lowering himself to my level but did not say so. He ordered a chest-sized decorated stein of beer but I stayed on the cola wagon. I tried to talk about my wife, but it wouldn't come out: all I could say was that I had a problem with myself as a family man. That wasn't me. The crying babies tore me up. Feeding time gave me inexplicable jitters. I had acted like Godzilla. When I told him this, he nodded hard, like a yes man. It was all reasonable to him.

"Of course," he said. "Of course you were upset and confused." He was understanding me the way I wanted to be understood. I talked some more. Blah blah blah. Outside, it was getting dark. The bill came, and he paid it: out came the thick wallet again, and from a major-league collection of credit cards came the white bank plastic he wanted. I talked more. He agreed with everything I said. He said, "You're exactly right." Then I said something else, and he responded, "Yes, you're exactly right."

That was when I knew I was being conned. In real life people don't say that to you unless they're trying to earn your love in a hurry. But here he was, Kurt Sykes, visibly my brother, telling me I was exactly right. It was hard to resist, but I was holding on, and trying.

"Here's how," he said. He lifted his big stein of beer into the air, and I lifted my glass of Coke. Click. A big blond waitress watched us, her face disciplined into a steel-helmet smile.

After that, it was his idea to go outside and play catch. This activity had all sorts of symbolic meanings for him, but what was I going to do? Go home and watch television? I myself have participated in a few softball leagues and the jock way of life is not alien to me, but I think he believed he could open me up if we stayed at my level, throwing something back and forth, grunting and sweating. We drove across town to Buhr Park, where he unloaded his newly purchased baseball, his two brand-new gloves, and a shiny new bat. Baseball was on the agenda. We were going to play ball or die. "We don't have to do any hitting," he said. While I fitted the glove to my left hand—a perfect fit, as if he had measured me—he locked the car. I have never had a car worth locking; it was not a goal.

The sun having set, I jogged out across a field of darkening grass. The sky had that blue tablecloth color it gets at dusk just before the stars come out. I had my jeans, sweatshirt, and sneakers on, my usual day-off drag. I had not dressed up for this event. In fact, I was almost feeling comfortable, except for some growing emotional hot spot I couldn't locate that was making me feel like pushing the baseball into my brother's face. Kurt started to toss the ball toward me and then either noticed his inappropriate dress-for-success formality or felt uncomfortable. He went back to the car and changed into his sweat clothes in the half-dark. He could have been seen, but wasn't, except by me. (My brother could change his clothes out in the open, not even bothering to look around to see who would see. What did this mean?)

Now, dressed down, we started to hustle, keeping the rhythms up. He threw grounders, ineptly, his arm stiff and curious. I bent down, made the imaginary play, and pivoted. He picked up the bat and hit a few high flies toward me. Playing baseball with me was his way of claiming friendship. Fine. Stars came out. We moved across the field, closer to a floodlit tennis court, so we had a bit of light. I could see fireflies at the edge of where we were playing. On the court to my right, a high school couple was working their way through their second set. The girl let out little cries of frustration now and then. They were pleasurable to hear. Meanwhile, Kurt and I played catch in the near-dark, following the script that, I could see, he had written through one long sleepless night after another.

As we threw the ball back and forth, he talked. He continued on in his résumé. He was married but had two girlfriends. His wife knew about them both. She did not panic because she expected imperfection in men. Also, he said, he usually voted Republican. He went to parent-teacher organization meetings.

"I suppose you weren't expecting this," he said.

No, I thought, I was *not* expecting you. I glanced at the tennis court. Clouds of moths and bright bugs swarmed in insect parabolas around the high-voltage lights. The boy had a white Huron High School T-shirt on, and white shorts and tennis shoes, and a blue sweatband around his thick damp hair. The girl was dressed in an odd assortment of pink and pastel blue clothes. She was flying the colors and was the better player. He had the force, but she had the accuracy. Between his heat and her coolness, she piled up the points. I let myself watch her; I allowed myself that. I was having a harder and harder time keeping my eyes on my brother.

"You gonna play or look at them?" Kurt asked.

I glanced at him. I thought I'd ignore his question. "You got any hobbies?" I asked.

He seemed surprised. "Hobbies? No. Unless you count women and making money."

"How's your pitch?"

"You mean baseball?"

"No. Music. How's your sense of pitch?"

"Don't have one."

"I do," I said. "F-sharp." And I blew it at him.

He leaned back and grimaced. "How do you know that's F-sharp?"

"My daddy taught me," I said. "He taught me all the notes on the scale. You can live with them. You can become familiar with a note."

"I don't care for music," he said, ending that conversation. We were still both panting a bit from our exertions. The baseball idea was not quite working in the way he had planned. He seemed to be considering the possibility that he might not like me. "What the hell," he said. "Let's go back to that bar."

Why did I hit my brother in that bar? Gentlemen of the bottle, it is you I address now. You will understand when I tell you that when my brother and I entered the bar, cool and smoky and filled with midsummer ballplayers, uniformed men and women, and he thoughtlessly ordered me a scotch, you will understand that I drank it. Drank it after I saw his wad of money, his credit cards, his wallet-rubbed pictures of the children, my little nephews. He said he would save me from my alcoholism but he did not. Gentlemen, in a state of raw blank irritation

I drank down what God and nature have labeled "poison" and fixed with a secret skull and crossbones. He bought me this drink, knowing it was bad for me. My mind withdrew in a snap from my brain. The universe is vast, you cannot predict it. From the great resources of anger I pulled my fund, my honest share. But I do not remember exactly why I said something terrible, and hit my brother in the jaw with my fist. And then again, higher, a punch I had learned in the Navy.

He staggered back, and he looked at me.

His nose was bleeding and my knuckles hurt. I was sitting in the passenger side of his car. My soul ached. My soul was lying face down. He was taking me back to my apartment, and I knew that my brother would not care to see me from now on. He would reassert his right to be a stranger. I had lost my wife, and now I had lost him, too.

We stumbled into my living room. I wobbled out to the kitchen and, booze-sick, filled a dish towel with ice cubes and brought it to him. My right hand felt swollen. We were going to have ugly bruises, but his were facial and would be worse. Holding the ice to his damaged face, he looked around. Above the ice his eyes flickered on with curiosity. "Ships," he said. Then he pointed at the work table against the wall. "What's all that?"

"It's my hobby," I said. The words came slow and wormlike out of my puzzled mouth.

He squinted above the ice. "Bottles? And glue?"

"I build ships in bottles." I sounded like a balloon emptying itself of air. I pointed at the decorator shelf on the west wall, where my three-masted clipper ship, the *Thermopylae,* was on display.

"How long have you done this?" he asked.

"So long I can't remember."

"How do you do it?"

He gave me a chance. Even a bad drunk is sometimes forced to seize his life and to speak. So I went over to the worktable. "You need these." I held up the surgical forceps. I could hardly move my fingers for the pain. Alcoholic darkness sat in a corner with its black bag waiting to cover me entirely. I went on talking. "And these. Surgical scissors." Dried specks of glue were stuck to the tips. "Some people cheat and saw off the bottom of the bottle, then glue it back on once the ship is inside. I don't do it that way. It has to grow inside the bottle. You need a challenge. I build the hull inside. I have used prefab hulls. Then you've got to lay the deck down. I like to do it with deck furnishings already in place: you know, the cabin doors and hatch covers and cleats and riding bits already in place on the deck. You put the glue on and then you put the deck in, all in one piece, folded up, through the neck; then you fold it out. With all that glue on, you only have one shot. Then you do the rigging inside the bottle. See these masts? The masts are laid down inside the bottle with the bottom of the mast in a hole."

I pointed to the *Cutty Sark*, which I was working on. I did not care if my hands were broken; I would continue this, the only lecture in my head, even if I sounded like a chattering magpie.

"You see, you pull the mast up inside the bottle with a string attached to the mast, and there's a stop in the hole that'll keep the mast from going too far forward. Then you tie the lines that are already on the mast off on the belaying pins and the bits and the cleats." I stopped. "These are the best things I do. I make ships in bottles better than anything else I do in my life."

"Yes." He had been standing over my worktable, but now he was lying on the sofa again.

"I like ships," I said. "When I was growing up I had pictures on the wall of yachts. I was the only person in the Harris family who was interested in ships."

"Hmm."

"I like sailboats the most." I was talking to myself. "They're their own class."

"That's interesting," he said. "That's all very interesting, but I wonder if I could lie down here for a while."

"I think you're already doing it."

"I don't need a pillow or a blanket," Kurt said, covered with sweat. "I can lie here just as is."

"I was going to turn on the air conditioner."

"Good. Put it on low."

I went over to the rattletrap machine and turned it on. The compressor started with a mechanical complaint, a sound like *orrr orrr orrr,* and then faster, *orrorrorr.* By the time I got back into the living room, my brother's eyes were closed.

"You're asleep," I said.

"No," he said," no, I'm not. My eyes are just closed. I'm bruised and taking a rest here. Why don't you talk to me for a minute while I lie here with this ice. Say anything."

So I talked against the demons chittering in the corners of the room. I told my brother about being on a carrier in the Navy. I talked about how I watched the blue lifting swells of the Pacific even when I wasn't supposed to and would get my ass kicked for it. I was hypnotized by seawater, the crazy majesty of horizontal lines. I sleepwalked on that ship, I was so happy. I told him about the rolling progress of oceanic storms, and how the cumulonimbus clouds rose up for what looked like three or four miles into the atmosphere. Straight-edged curtains of rain followed us; near the Straits of Gibraltar it once rained for thirty minutes on the forward part of the ship, while the sun burned down on the aft.

I talked about the ship's work, the painting and repairing I did, and I told him about the constant metallic rumble vibrating below decks. I told him about the smell, which was thick with sterile grease stink that stayed in your nostrils, and the smell of working men. Men away from women, men who aren't getting any, go bad, and they start to smell like metal and fur and meat.

Then I told him about the ships I built, the models, and the originals for them, about the masts and sails, and how, in the water, they had been beautiful things.

"What if they fell?" my brother said.

I didn't understand the question, but thought I would try to answer it anyway. It was vague, but it showed he was still awake, still listening. I wanted to ask, fell from where? But I didn't. I said if a man stood on the mainmast lookout, on a whaler, for example, he could lose his balance. If he tumbled from that height, he might slap the water like he was hitting cement. He might be internally damaged, but if he did come up, they'd throw him a life buoy, the white ones made out of cork and braided with a square of rope.

I brought one of the ships toward him. "I've got one here," I said, "tiny, the size of your fingernail."

He looked at it, cleated to the ship above the deck. He studied it and then he gazed at me. "Yes," he said. It was the most painful smile I'd ever seen in an adult human being, and it reminded me of me. I thought of the ocean, which I hadn't viewed for years and might not, ever again. "Yes," my brother said from under the ice pack. "Now I get it."

Like strangers sitting randomly together in a midnight peeling-gray downtown bus depot smelling of old leather shoes, we talked until four in the morning, and he left, his face bruised dark, carrying one of my ships, *The Lightning,* under his arm. He came back a week later. We sat in the park this time, not saying much. Then I went to see him, and I met his wife. She's a pleasant woman, a tall blonde who comes fully outfitted with jewels I usually see under glass in display cases. My brother and I know each other better now; we've discovered that we have, in fact, no subjects in common. But it's love, so we have to go on talking, throwing this nonsense into the air, using up the clock. He has apologized for trying to play baseball with me; he admits now that it was a mistake.

When I was small, living with Harold and Ethel Harris and the other Harris children, I knew about my other parents, the aching lovers who had brought me into my life, but I did not miss them. They'd done me my favor and gone on to the rest of their lives. No, the only thing I missed was the world: the oceans, their huge distances, their creatures, the tides, the burning waterlight I heard you could see at the equator. I kept a globe nearby my boy's bed. Even though I live here, now, no matter where I ever was, I was always homesick for the rest of the world. My brother does not understand that. He thinks home is where he is now. I show him maps; I tell him about Turkey and the Azores; I have told him about the great variety and beauty of human pigmentation. He listens but won't take me seriously.

When my brother talks now, he fingers his nose, probably to remind me where I hit him. It's a delicate gesture, with a touch of self-pity. With this gesture he establishes a bit of history between us. He wants to look up to me. He's twenty-eight years old, hasn't ever seen Asia, and he says this to me seriously. "Have you ever heard the sound of a man's voice from a minaret?" I ask him, but he just smiles. He's already called my wife; he has a whole series of happy endings planned, scene by scene. He wants to sit in a chair and see me come into the room, perfected, thanking the past for all it has done for me.

DNA

SUKI WESSLING

Uncle Bob sits me on the vinyl couch and says, "I want to tell you about Ellen Sue." He's not spoken to me yet, so I assume this is momentous. This is his way of doing things, his ceremony. He says, "There ain't a whole lot to tell."

I think of Georgia. What am I doing in Georgia? And the smell of blossoms on the trees.

My mother was grey-haired and efficient. She worked hard at being a mother. She had wanted it for so long that it had been over-planned, executed like a business rather than a natural occurrence.

"If you eat this cookie," she'd say, "your fat intake for the day will be above the Recommended Daily Allowance.

"But if you don't eat this cookie," she'd continue, "you might suffer psychological backlash and find it necessary to sever the maternal bond, the emotional umbilical cord."

"Eat the cookie," she'd say.

She watched television with me, straight-faced, never getting any of the jokes. I had to explain to her why Bugs Bunny was funny, why I preferred the Roadrunner and the Coyote to Mr. Rogers. My six-year-old mind was already in the grips of cynicism; my mother was incapable of being cynical. I wonder if this is one of those DNA things.

"Ellen Sue," says Uncle Bob, "was one of those people who like to take life by the horns."

"I remember," he says, the "I" drawn out to "Ah," and then a pause as if he were going to sleep.

"Yes?" I find myself impatiently prompting. I bite my lip.

"I remember," he repeats, "when she was a little girl."

"Good for you," I want to reply with my best New York impatience. I bite my lip harder.

"When she was a little girl," he continues, tagging each new foray into language with the tail of the last, "people called her wild." He pauses to let that sink in. It has sunk and resurfaced by the time he gets under way.

"People called her wild," he says, losing the second half of his sentence.

I take a sip of my lemonade. He stares out the window. I shift my weight on the couch so that the vinyl goes crack, crack.

Uncle Bob returns. "But she warn't wild. She did have a temper, mind you."

I stare at the blank face of the large television in front of us. When I arrived last night before dinner, it blared sports-announcer voices into our conversation. We said our hellos, and then the whole family turned to cheer at the TV.

"I bet she's a Mets fan," said the scrawny boy cousin I later identified as Joe. I tried to remember which sport the Mets played, and smiled in acknowledgment.

"I can tell you about the time she got in trouble for eating your Uncle Ed's birthday cake," Uncle Bob offers hopefully. He's insane, I think. My Uncle Bob is insane. Georgia.

My home was in Boston. My parents were yuppies moved in from California.

"We're too old to be yuppies," my mother would remind me. "We were hippies."

"I had long hair in the sixties," my father would offer. I was sixteen. Yuppies were in the news, as were the computer chips my dad designed, and my mother's sex life.

"Feminists Find Comfort Returning to Traditional Values," headlines trumpeted. "Women who in the sixties sought the "Big O," and who in the seventies sought the Big Office, are now returning to the big M: motherhood."

My mother, in my opinion, had gone a bit daft. "Go back to work," I ordered her. But she liked to make cookies for me to eat after school. She liked to do needlepoint and talked about getting a cabin in Vermont. I liked to go clubbing with my friends and read *Playgirl* in public.

"I don't understand why you don't join the environmental debate team," my mother said. "Go back to your roots. You're a California girl at heart."

"I've only visited there," I reminded her. "And besides, I wasn't even born there, was I?"

"No, you weren't," my mother would say with shame in her voice. And I would remember. Georgia.

My cousin Jill arrives from school to save me from any further meandering conversation with Uncle Bob. "Hi, cuz," she says cheerfully, flopping onto the green carpet and grinning madly.

I like Jill. I like her wide-set front teeth and the freckles that keep her from acting like her busty, bleached sisters. Nobody wants her and she knows it. Someone will get stuck with her.

"Do you have any memories of your Aunt Ellie?" I ask her.

"Naw. I was too young," Jill answers.

"Do you remember any stories?" I ask, thinking about all the long-dead members of my childhood family who populated evenings in front of the fire.

Jill shrugs. "Her kids will be able to say something, I expect."

"I expect they'll have plenty of things to say about their mama," Uncle Bob says, lifting himself from the couch with a grunt and walking stiff-legged to a photo left on one of unmatched coffee tables shoved into the corners of the room. He brings it back and hands it to me.

"Ellen," he says. "Ellen Sue." The photograph is the only formal one I've seen. She looks like me, as I would look if I were ever possessed to wear a fuzzy pastel sleeveless sweater. She has the squinty eyes of her family, small and set wide, and the little bump at the end of her nose that all the relatives have to some degree. She has big stripes of makeup above her eyes, and though the picture is black-and-white, I assume the eye shadow is blue. Little has changed in twenty-odd years.

"Tell me about New York," Jill says with the only imaginative spark that I've seen in the dull eyes of this family. She looks defiantly at Uncle Bob, who is preparing to say something. I've already heard his wife's opinions of my adopted home.

"You might like it," I say, challenging Uncle Bob to find his words. "You'll have to come visit."

Uncle Bob takes another gulp of air as if he's going to say something, and though he doesn't, what I hear is, *Take her, please.*

When I was ten, my mother decided to test genetics versus conditioning. She was starting to wonder if I was her child. She didn't put it that way, but I knew. I looked a lot like her, same mousy hair, though hers was going grey. Same gap between my teeth, soon to be straightened out with expensive orthodontia. She liked to point these things out to me, trying to convince herself. Then she started to give me tests, and have me give them to her. Later, I identified them: Rorschach inkblots, criteria for American Psychiatry Association personality disorders, *Redbook*'s "Are You a Dependent Woman?" questionnaire. She compared our results.

"See how similar we are?" she liked to say. "See how we're two peas in a pod?"

I had to admit that the similarities were striking, even taking into account the liberal amount of help she gave me in my answers. Later, she gave that up. She started to have late night discussions with my father next to the thin bedroom wall.

"Maybe we should tell her about *it,*" she'd say.

My father's reply, too quiet to come through the wall, would have been something like, "I thought we decided on that." All decisions had been made sometime before I was born.

"I feel so deceptive," she'd continue. "What if *She* is still alive?"

"Never bothered you before," my father probably answered, and my mother broke in.

"—Yes, it did. It always did. I always thought we should tell her. Now it's too late."

One might think that a sixteen-year-old might have curiosity about these late night chats, but I had ceased having any curiosity where my parents were concerned. It was not that I didn't love them, I assured myself. We just had nothing in common. I smoked cigarettes on the front doorstep and studied myself into Columbia. My parents retired to that cabin in Vermont.

Everyone is home now and Aunt Jem is frying something smoky in the kitchen. The oldest daughter, Sue-Ellen (pronounced "Swellin"), is feeding her baby from a bottle, as if her large breasts wouldn't do the job. The boys, who eye me in a predatory way that cousins probably shouldn't, pace around the room and stuff dirty hands in their too-tight jeans. Uncle Bob has reverted to his former, shapeless self in a corner of the sofa. Jill's other sister, Deedee, is examining her voluptuous figure in the only mirror big enough to capture most of her body (an ornate, peeling gilded affair that Aunt Jem said was "probably somebody's family heirloom"). The television blasts some tabloid program that no one is paying attention to; Jill beckons me from around the corner.

I follow her down the hall, which opens into four doors, two on either side, and a linen closet at the end. Jill and her sisters share the end room, and that's where she takes me. One sagging double bed; a stiff single bed; two large dressers, unmatched, shoved next to each other; a closet spilling out pastel clothing; a small mirror where the older girls paste on their make up; posters of Elvis and a country star I can't quite name; an array of drugstore perfumes; three curling irons; two light bulbs hanging bare from a socket in the ceiling; assorted baby items that Sue-Ellen rescued from her trailer before her husband burned it; and a small pile of Jill's schoolbooks, next to her side of the double bed. Jill sits me down on the bed and kneels in front of me.

"Will you really take me to New York?" she asks. She is very sincere: her homely face, her stringy hair, her brother's cast-off jeans. I try to imagine her at school with the other kids.

"Well, you can visit," I say hesitantly.

She doesn't let me add disclaimers. "'Cause I *gotta* get out of here." Her speech is faster than her family's, insistent. I wonder if anyone in her family, besides Aunt Jem and her endless string of laments masked in shrill, demanding tones, ever insisted on anything.

"I can understand that," I answer.

"I knew you could. So I can come live with you in New York, you being family and all?"

I smile at her and feel a sickness brought on by more than the greasy food I've been eating for the last day.

"How old are you, Jill?" I ask her. "Because you have to finish school."

Jill flops backward in an expression of complete despair.

"That's *forever*," she says. "I'm only thirteen."

"You seem older," I say as a weak sort of compliment.

She sits up and looks me in the eye. "I don't belong in this family. I don't belong here," she says. "I think *I'm* the one who's adopted."

The eternal wish, I want to say, to deny bonds that we have in favor of bonds that we choose. I want to sing *Georgia on my Mind,* but I don't know the tune.

My mother never did tell me. She let it sit there and fester like some awful secret. She kept hoping I wouldn't develop any physical characteristics that couldn't be explained away with a genetic comparison to some grandmother or distant cousin. She kept hoping I wouldn't demand to see my birth certificate, or question her story: "We were just passing through Georgia on the way to Boston."

That was my birth story, the explanation for my existence. I accepted it the way I accepted that fathers lived inside computers, that mothers tested their children and worried about honey versus sugar, that all children felt like alien beings just passing through a hostile world. All my friends did, at least. Or that's what they told me.

I didn't find out until I was at college. I wanted to go abroad for a year and, not wanting my mother to get involved, I did the necessary paperwork to get a passport. I wrote to the court house in the little town in Georgia to get my birth certificate: "It was night, I wasn't due for weeks, and well, we just had to stop."

"It was a lovely town, with a pleasant little hospital. Of course," my mother added. "They were Southerners. There were Racial Divisions." She glanced at my father. "We don't believe in such things. Freedom. Peace, love, and freedom. The revolution lives in our hearts, if not in our hairstyles." My father actually smiled. "But you were born. We didn't stay there long. But I guess you can say that you have Southern roots."

Maybe she came to believe the lie as well. It was clear enough on my birth certificate. Birth mother: Ellen Sue Johnson. Birth father: . . .

By the time Ellen Sue Johnson's husband and her children arrive on Saturday, I am no longer interested. Any fascination brought on by our common thread of DNA has diminished. I think with longing of a quiet night in a pine-scented room. I remember the sweet smell of cookies baking back home. But I'm stuck until my flight tomorrow afternoon. I wonder if I can create a family emergency. Jill's freckled pixie face winks at me when their car rumbles up the gravel drive. In her room, on the sagging bed, I tell Jill about Sarah Cornwall.

"I got stuck rooming with this girl, Sarah Cornwall. She was perfect. She looked just like everyone else in her family, and they were beautiful. She talked to her mother every day on the phone. She wore her grandmother's strand of pearls and her great-aunt's diamond ring. She didn't just have a family, she *oozed* family."

Jill nodded knowingly.

"I mean, she was OK. I shouldn't dump on her, but you know, I'd always surrounded myself with other mutants. They all had 'natural' parents, so I figured it was normal to feel like an alien in your own house. But then there was Sarah Cornwall."

"She made you feel pretty bad."

I nodded. "She was there when my birth certificate arrived in the mail. I told her because she was *there,* not like she was any great friend or anything. 'I'm adopted,' I said. 'And they never told me.' And you know what she said? She said, 'How could you not know? You have to find out who you *are.*' So it's all her fault."

"Sorry," Jill said.

"It's OK," I said.

"Families are stupid," she summed up. And that's what she mouths at me when my family comes in the door. First, the man who is my stepfather, a tall man with a belly perched precariously high above his belt. He grins, shows nicotine teeth, and grasps my hand as he might have Ellen-Sue's, my mother's, his wife's. My half siblings follow, three of them, two girls and a boy whose names I cannot digest. Too many hyphenations, too many of the type of names that have graced my genetic ancestors since they left their stone house in England.

"This is Auburn," my Aunt Jem introduces me, and the relatives no doubt wonder about *my* name.

"She wants to know all about Aunt Ellie, and how she came to be born," Jill helps out. We drift in and out of conversation: the weather sparks interest; New York drops dead on the green carpet. Ellen Sue, who is my mother, their mother or sister or aunt, weaves in and out of the conversation like a recurring headache. In dribbles and innuendo my birth story is revealed.

"Near as I can figure," my stepfather says, "Ellie got herself in trouble with some stranger. Fifteen, wasn't it?"

There is a general consensus. Fifteen years old.

"Some stranger," he repeats. "Some Jew, I believe. City guy. She said she was afraid—" His lips sealed tight when he looked at me. Was I really that small bloody thing that came from her body?

"Well, she had to give it away, see what I mean." All the cousins nodded. "I was working with her daddy at the time."

"You don't look much like her," a half sibling informs me, staring at my breasts.

"Maybe you look—" one starts to say.

"Yeah . . ." another continues.

"Like him," someone finishes under his breath.

"When can I get anyone to help me with the cooking?" Aunt Jem asks.

"When you were gone a couple of years, we married," my step-father says, his mouth full of peanuts. "The kids were born. And then she died in a car accident. The cab of the truck collapsed. It just collapsed."

I went overseas, and I guess I should have told them that I knew, but I was a mutant and what more was there to say.

"Be sure to go see this, and that," my mother instructed, rattling off London districts that had been all the rage in the sixties.

"Bring an umbrella," my father said.

I didn't take an umbrella. I took a hat. I tried to hang out with punks and skinheads, and found myself a mutant again. I studied, went back to Columbia, and got a job in publishing. And that would have been the end of the story if I hadn't run into Sarah Cornwall in Macy's. What was I doing in Macy's anyway, she wanted to know. Had I found my family?

And so *this* is the end of the story. I'm in Georgia. I'm stuffing my clothes in a duffel bag, the same one I took to Europe. I'm in the room the brothers vacated for my visit. I smell oil smells and dirty laundry and the contrasting sweetness of my perfume. My devil-faced cousin appears at the door.

"So you're not going to take me with you," she says, leaning against the doorframe.

"There's nothing to say two mutants would get along," I tell her, slinging my bag over my shoulder.

"What do you mean?" she says.

"I mean, just because we're family. You get it?"

She shrugs.

"Can I give you some advice, though?"

She nods.

"Study. Get to college. Do whatever the hell you want with your life. And don't let those boys stick it in you and get you pregnant before you have a chance."

A wry smile appeared on her lips. "I got nothing they want," she-says, pulling out the front of her sweatshirt.

"Just promise me," I say.

"OK." She follows me out to the car. For some unspoken reason, my cousin Dave is designated chauffeur for the airport legs of my trip.

"Bye." She says "Bah" like a sheep.

"Bah," I say. I hesitate for a moment, because maybe there is something in her matching hair, her matching teeth, the eyes that lock perfectly into mine. No, it's nothing, I tell myself, and I get into the rumbling car so I can get out of Georgia. People are whatever they are; they become what they need to be to get by.

Pray for Angels

GAIL FORD

When my adopted son cries
my own adopted self cries,
No! Don't leave me.

Fat round tears run to his chin.
My own eyes brim.
How many times can one heart break?

He clings to me for comfort,
we are warm, we hold tight.
I wonder if the love I give him
can ever mend the hollow
of his mother's leaving?

My first high school love
disappeared—no warning—
tantalized by some other skirt,
some other sweet expression.

My body got up
went to school,
attended class.

I was curled
tight inside
not thinking,
numb to all but a need to

rock

back and forth and back and forth
and back and forth and back.

Suspended above life
and below death.
No one noticed that I was gone.
I guess they didn't miss me.

I don't know what saved me.

One day I woke,
a fever patient rising from delirium,
and noticed that the air
smelled sweet.

When my adopted son cries,
red-faced, his arms
stretched up as far
as he can reach,
I wrap him tight
hold him close.

When someday
some sweet he or she
leaves him
and the hollow
that has followed him
from birth swallows him,

who will reach down,
help him put his feet back
on the ground,
who will save him?

Wings and Seeds

SANDRA MCPHERSON

Hiking a levee through the salt marsh,
My birthmother and I. She is not teaching
Me to read and write but to believe
The hummingbird mistrusts its feet,
Weak below its feisty wings.

We trample brass buttons and chamomile,
As if to concern ourselves no more
With clothing and tea.
We twine hands, we trade heavy binoculars.
The clouds are coming from far out on the sea
Where they'd only the fetch to ruffle.

Separately our lives have passed from earthy passion
To wilder highliving creatures with wings.
With our early expectancies
Did we come to think ourselves a flight of nature?

Terns flash here, four dolled-up stilts in a pool,
Dozens of godwits a thick golden hem on the bay—
You'd think we too knew how to find
Our way back to this home ground.

I was a child of pleasure.
The strong pleasurable seeds of life
Found each other.
And I was created by passion's impatience
For the long wait till our meeting.

Sculpting the Whistle

ALBERTO RÍOS

The machine is in us,
It is what after all makes us pick up,
Make a sound like the sound
We have just heard—
Something of the animal in us,
The mynah—
      What the Japanese call *eight songs*—
The parrot, and all the zoo,
Some thing of the sculptor—
      Do you know the story of the sculptor
      Who sculpts the whistling
      Sound of the *iay Lazaro!* birds
Wanting by hands to make it better,
Or simply remembered.
Making the voice of another animal
Creates the other animal
A little. That echo
Everything gives back,
The mirror for the ears
So that in your absence since childhood
When I say your name
Aloud, a small thing happens.

There Is No Word For Goodbye

MARY TALLMOUNTAIN

Sokoya*, I said, looking through
    the net of wrinkles into
    wise black pools
    of her eyes.

What do you say in Athabaskan
    when you leave each other?
    What is the word
    for goodbye?

A shade of feeling rippled
    the wind-tanned skin.
    Ah, nothing, she said,
    watching the river flash.

She looked at me close.
    We just say, *Tlaa.* That means,
    See you.
    We never leave each other.
    When does your mouth
    say goodbye to your heart?

She touched me light
    as a bluebell.
    You forget when you leave us.
    You're so small then.
    We don't use that word.

We always think you're coming back,
    but if you don't,
    we'll see you someplace else.
    You understand.
    There is no word for goodbye.

*Sokoya: Aunt (mother's sister)

Contributors

Isabel Allende has used events of her life to create prize-winning bestsellers. She is the first Latin American woman writer to receive such international acclaim. Her books include *The House of Spirits* (1985), *Eva Luna* (1988), *The Stories of Eva Luna* (1991), *Of Love and Shadows* (1991), *The Infinite Plan* (1993), *Paula* (1995), and most recently, *Aphrodite*. She currently lives in California.

Charles Baxter is on the faculty of the University of Michigan M.F.A. program. His most recent book of fiction is *Believers,* published by Pantheon in hardback and Vintage in paperback. He has edited a collection of essays, *The Business of Memory* (1999, Graywolf) and lives in Ann Arbor, Michigan.

Mi Ok Song Bruining, MSW was born in 1960, the Year of the Rat, in Seoul, South Korea. In 1966, she became the 1,500th adopted Korean child in the United States. Mi Ok has been an activist in the international adoption movement since 1984. After thirty-six years of estrangement, Mi Ok found her birth mother in Korea. She currently lives in Cambridge, Massachusetts, after having spent two years living and working in Korea and has completed the first draft of a book, for which she is seeking an agent and publisher. She can be reached at: skidding@hotmail.com.

Lisa K. Buchanan is based in San Francisco. Her award-winning fiction has appeared in *Mademoiselle, Cosmopolitan, San Francisco Focus,* several anthologies, and magazines in Ireland, South Africa, Japan, and Canada. She is currently writing a novel. "Life Underground" was inspired by conversations with her biological mother.

Susan Bumps received her M.F.A. in creative writing from Mills College. Her poems have been published in the anthology *Bite to Eat Place,* as well as in *Art/Life* and *The Santa Barbara Review.*

Fran Castan teaches writing and literature at the School of Visual Arts college in Manhattan. Her poetry has appeared in *Ms.* and *Poetry,* as well as in the anthologies *From Both Sides Now* (Scribner), *Seasons of Women* (Norton), and *On Predjudice: A Global Perspective* (Anchor/Doubleday). Her full-length collection, *The Widow's Quilt,* was published in 1996 by Canio's Editions, New York.

Joy Castro's fiction has appeared in *Mid-American Review, Quarterly West, Chelsea,* and other journals. She teaches literature and creative writing at Wabash College in Crawfordsville, Indiana, where she lives with her husband and son. She found her biological mother in 1994.

Tina Cervin is a psychotherapist and poet. She has been published in *Alchemy* and *Kaleidoscope Kyoto.* She's currently working on a collection of poetry. She lives on a hill in San Francisco with her husband and two sons.

Dan Chaon is the author of *Fitting Ends and Other Stories,* published in 1996 by Northwestern University Press. He lives in the Cleveland area with his wife and children.

Amy Jane Cheney's "Word Problem" is a true story with evolving and mystifying answers. Based in San Francisco, she is a writer, storyteller, and counselor. Her practice focuses on assisting people in finding creative answers to their wordiest and wordless problems.

Marian Mathews Clark grew up in Mist, Oregon, attended Graceland College, and graduated from the University of Iowa Writer's Workshop in 1987. Since then, she has been an academic advisor at the university and has taught in Iowa's Summer Writing Festival. Her stories have appeared in *Story, The Sun,* and *Cottonwood Magazine.*

Jennifer Clement is the author of two books of poetry: *The Next Stranger* (1993), with a rare commendatory introduction by W.S. Merwin, and *Newton's Sailor* (1998). Her novel *Widow Basquiat* will be published by Canongate Books, ltd., (UK), and Plaza & Janez, (Spain), in the Spring of 2000. Clement is the director of the San Miguel Poetry Week.

Chitra Divakaruni's writing has won the American Book Award, a Pushcart Prize, two PEN Syndicated Fiction Awards, the C.Y. Lee Creative Writing Award, and the Allen Ginsberg Poetry Prize. Her books include *Black Candle* (Calyx Books), *Arranged Marriage, The Mistress of Spices,* and most recently, *Sister of My Heart* (all from Doubleday).

Louise Erdrich was raised in North Dakota and is German-American and French-Ojibwa. She is the author of many bestselling and award-winning novels, including *Love Medicine* and most recently *The Antelope Wife* (Harper-Flamingo). She has also written two collections of poetry, *Jacklight,* and *Baptism of Desire. The Blue Jay's Dance,* a memoir of motherhood, was her first nonfiction work. She is the mother of four children, two of whom were adopted.

Carrie Etter is a doctoral candidate in English at the University of California, Irvine, where she received her M.F.A. in 1997. Her poems have appeared in *Arshile, the Anthology of Magazine Verse, Yearbook of American Poetry, Seneca Review, Poetry Wales, West Branch,* and other journals. Potes & Poets Press published her chapbook *Subterfuge for the Unrequitable,* in 1998.

Gail Ford was born and placed for adoption in 1952. Poet, novelist, and short story writer, Gail uses her writing to try to make sense of her life. She began Broken Shadow Publications, a small literary press, in 1993. She lives happily in Oakland, California, with her husband (writer and teacher, Clive Matson) and their adopted son, Ezra. (For more about Gail and BSP-hosted events for writers, see www.matson-ford.com.)

Pamela Gross holds an M.F.A. from Florida International University. She has taught creative writing and journalism and introduced "Writing Your Autobiography" at FIU Elder Institute. Her poetry has appeared in several literary magazines and anthologies, and one of her short stories appeared in the *Alaska Review.* She is married and has five children and six grandchildren.

John Hildebidle spent an oddly peripatetic childhood before settling in New England to go to college. He has spent nearly thirty years teaching: in a public junior high school, at Harvard, and now at MIT, where he brings the light of humane letters into the darkness of the technoworld. He lives in Cambridge, Massachusetts, with his wife and children, and writes fiction, essays, and poetry. His books include *The Old Chore* (Alice James Books), *Stubbornness: A Field Guide* (SUNY Binghamton), *One Sleep, One Waking* (Wyndham Hall Press), and the forthcoming *Defining Absence* (Salmon Books), plus two "scholarly works" of the sort that earn you tenure.

Edward Hirsch has published five books of poems, including *Earthly Measures* (1994) and *On Love* (1998), and two prose books, *How to Read a Poem and Fall in Love with Poetry* (1999) and *Responsive Reading* (1999). He writes a regular column on poetry for the *American Poetry Review,* serves as the editorial advisor on poetry for *DoubleTake* magazine, and teaches in the Creative Writing Program at the University of Houston. He has received many awards and fellowships, among them a Guggenheim Fellowship, an Ingram Merrill Award, the Rome Prize, and an Award in Literature from the American Academy of Arts and Letters. He received a MacArthur Fellowship in 1998.

Sasha Gabrielle Hom was born in South Korea in 1975. She was adopted by a Chinese American family and came to live with them in Berkeley, California, as a small child. She has attended numerous colleges including Brown University, UC Berkeley, Mills, and Laney, and has yet to graduate from any of them. She is currently living in Oakland, California and working as a dog-walker/professional pet-care provider. "Double Lifeline" is excerpted from a longer piece entitled, "Impressions of Anyang."

Susan Ito, adopted years ago, lives in Oakland, California, with her husband and two daughters. She is the founder of Rice Papers, a Bay Area organization of Asian-American women writers, and currently teaches fiction writing at UC Berkeley's Extension program. Her fiction, poetry, and nonfiction have appeared in *Growing Up Asian American* (Wm. Morrow & Co.), *Making More Waves* (Beacon Press), *Two Worlds Walking* (New Rivers Press), *Hip Mama* and elsewhere.

Lori Jakiela lives in New York City and Pittsburgh, Pennsylvania. She teaches composition and creative writing at the State University of New York at Purchase. She is also a flight attendant for Delta Airlines.

Leanna James received her M.F.A. in creative writing from Mills College, and now teaches writing, literature, and performance at John F. Kennedy University. She is in the process of completing her first book, a novel about a struggling family, a grand piano, a case of bourbon, and a host of Catholic martyr saints.

Janet Jerve is a teacher and lives in Minneapolis with her husband and children. Her poems have appeared in *The Great River Review, Lake Effect* and *Hurricane Alice.* In addition, she has written stories and screenplays in collaboration with a friend. She has completed a poetry manuscript and is looking for a publisher.

Jackie Kay was born in Scotland in 1961. *The Adoption Papers,* the poetry collection from which the poems in this book were excerpted, received a Scottish Arts

Council Book Award, a Saltire First Book of the Year Award, and a Forward Prize. She is also the author of *Other Lovers* and a book of poetry for children titled *Two's Company*. Her first novel, *Trumpet,* has just been published by Random House. She lives in London.

Robert Lacy lives in Medicine Lake, Minnesota. His stories and essays have appeared in a wide range of magazines, literary journals and anthologies. His story collection, *The Natural Father,* was published in 1997 by New Rivers Press in Minneapolis.

Marie G. Lee is the author of *Necessary Roughness, If It Hadn't Been for Yoon Jun,* and *Finding My Voice,* which won the Friends of American Writers Award. Her short fiction has appeared in the *Kenyon Review* and the *American Voice.* She has recently completed her novel, *Somebody's Daughter,* which explores Korean adoptions and is based on her experiences as a Fulbright Scholar in Korea. She has also taught creative writing at Yale University and is a founder of the Asian American Writers' Workshop.

Alison Lurie is the author of nine novels, of which the most recent is *The Last Resort.* "Waiting for the Baby" is one of the stories in her collection *Women and Ghosts.* She is a professor of English at Cornell University, where she teaches courses in writing, folklore, and children's literature.

Katharyn Howd Machan grew up in Woodbury, Connecticut, and Pleasantville, N.Y. She studied creative writing and literature at the College of Saint Rose and the University of Iowa and received a Ph.D. in Interpretaton (Performance Studies) at Northwestern University. She has coordinated the Ithaca Community Poets and directed the national Feminist Women's Writing Workshops. She currently teaches in the writing program of Ithaca College. Her poems have appeared in *Yankee, Nimrod, South Coast Poetry Journal, The HollinsCritic, Seneca Review,* and collections, anthologies, and textbooks *(Early Ripening: American Women's Poetry Now, Sound and Sense, Writing Poems, the Bedford Introduction to Literature).*

Eileen Malone lives in the coastal fog of Colma at the edge of San Francisco, where she writes and teaches and does whatever she can to support other poets in her community. She recently won the Phyllis Smart Young Prize offered by the *Madison Review* and first prize in the Half Tones to Jubilee contest. "These Things, That Others May Call Miracles," was written to validate and announce the end to the secret of Joann, her lifelong friend and the mom of the poem.

Sandra McPherson is the author of many volumes of poetry, including *Edge Effect: Trails and Portrayals* and *The Spaces Between Birds: Mother/Daughter Poems 1967-1995,* both published in 1996 by Wesleyan University Press of New England. Earlier major collections include *The God of Indeterminacy* (University of Illinois,1993), *Streamers* (Ecco, 1988), and *Patron Happiness* (Ecco, 1983). Her many awards include three National Endowment for the Arts fellowships, an Award in Literature from the American Academy and Institute of Arts and Letters, and a nomination for the National Book Award. Several hundred of her poems have appeared in magazines, from *American Poetry Review, the Paris Review, TriQuarterly The New Yorker,* and *the Yale Review,* to *Zyzzyva.* She is on the faculty of the University of California at Davis.

Jacquelyn Mitchard, the author of *The Deep End of the Ocean, The Most Wanted* and *The Rest of Us: Dispatches from the Mothership* lives with her husband and six children in Wisconsin.

Joni Mitchell, a legendary singer and songwriter, is also a birth mother. She searched for and was reunited with her daughter, to whom she refers in "Little Green," in 1997.

Eliza Monroe holds a master's in creative writing from Antioch University. Her stories and novel excerpts have appeared in such literary journals as *Sonoma Mandala, Widener Review,* and *American Writing.* Her work has been anthologized in *Our Mothers, Our Selves: Writers and Poets Celebrating Motherhood.* She won third prize in Syracuse University's fiction competition, and made the finals in the Pushcart, PEN Syndicated Fiction Project, Dana Award, New Voices and New Letters competitions. Her Web page is www.parrotproductions.com/monroe.htm.

George Rabasa was born in Maine and raised in Mexico. He lived in Mexico City on and off for several years until finally settling in Minnesota in 1981. His work encompasses a variety of worlds from the changing urban landscape of the Upper Midwest to the shifting realities of the Rio Grande border and the first sparks of World War II in 1930s' Spain. His collection of short stories, *Glass Houses* (Coffee House, 1996), received the Writer's Voice Capricorn Award for Excellence in Fiction and the Minnesota Book Award for Short Stories, 1997. His novel, *Floating Kingdom,* (Coffee House, 1997) was awarded the 1998 Minnesota Book Award for Fiction.

Bernice Rendrick finds writing about family a constant source of revelation and inspiration. She works with the Santa Cruz Writers' Union and has been published in the *Santa Barbara Review, Quarry West, Coast Lines,* and Papier Mache Press anthologies. "The Boy Arden" first appeared in *Porter Gulch Review.* She's a senior citizen and spends her time doing what she loves.

Alberto Ríos is the recent recipient of the Arizona Governor's Arts Award. Other honors include fellowships from the Guggenheim Foundation and the National Endowment for the Arts, the Walt Whitman Award, the Western States Book Award for Fiction, five Pushcart Prizes in both poetry and fiction, and inclusion in the *Norton Anthology of Modern Poetry* as well as more than 150 other national and international literary anthologies. Ríos is presently the Regents' Professor of English at Arizona State University. He is the author of seven books and chapbooks of poetry and two collections of short stories. A third collection of stories, *The Curtain of Trees,* is forthcoming in 1999, along with *Capirotada,* a memoir about growing up and living on the border.

Cynthia Rylant is the acclaimed author of more than thirty books. Among them are *Appalachia: The Voices of Sleeping Birds,* a Boston Globe-Horn Book Nonfiction Award winner; *A Couple of Kooks and Other Stories about Love,* an ALA Best Book for Young Adults; and *Missing May,* winner of the 1993 John Newberry Medal. She lives in the Pacific Northwest.

Ronda Slater found her daughter Jodi in 1984. Her touching, humorous play, *A Name You Never Got,* is well-known in the adoption reform community. She and

Jodi currently do a workshop together. Called "After the Honeymoon Is Over," the workshop is a poignant, entertaining tour of the peaks and valleys of their fifteen-year reunion.

Sybil Woods Smith has had her poems have been published in many literary magazines, including the *New England Review/Bread Loaf Quarterly, Southern Poetry Review, Peregrine, The Poetry Review, The Spoon River Quarterly,* and in an anthology titled *The Breast.* Her fiction and non-fiction have appeared in *Gulfstream Magazine, Yankee Magazine, The Connecticut Review, The Sun,* and many others. She has work upcoming in *The Gun Beneath The Bed,* (an anthology edited by Kay Marie Porterfield), *The Larcom Review* and *The Sun.* A movie based on her book *(My Mother's Early Lovers)* was a finalist at the Austin Film Festival in October, and won at the New Haven Film Festival in April.

Barbara Sperber is the author of *In the Garden of Our Making* (Papier-Mache Press). It is the story of coming to terms with her mother's death and finding the daughter she gave up for adoption.

Judith W. Steinbergh, a Bunting Fellow at Radcliffe in 1996/97, has published four books of poetry, most recently *A Living Anytime.* In addition, she has written three textbooks on teaching poetry writing to children: *Beyond Words: Writing Poems with Children* (with Elizabeth McKim), *Reading and Writing Poetry, Grades K-4* (Scholastic Books), and *Reading and Writing Poetry with Teenagers* (with Frederic Lown). She has been teaching poetry to students of all ages for nearly thirty years.

Siu Wai Stroshane has written previous works which have appeared in *The Forbidden Stitch: An Asian American Women's Anthology,* and *Haciendo Caras: Making Faces, Making Selves.* Her piece, "Unborn Song" is semi-autobiographical in its reflections on an aging and bereft birth mother she has never known, but she has never had to grapple with an unwanted pregnancy. Now that she is a mother, she imagines it would be especially painful to make a decision when reflecting what her birth mother had to suffer in choosing to carry her and then let her go. The rest of her novel is still an "unborn song."

Julia Sudbury was born in Edinburgh, Scotland, of Nigerian and English parents. She was adopted into a white family at six months of age, and has reunited with her birth parents and five siblings. She is the author of *Other Kinds of Dreams: Black Women's Organisations and the Politics of Transformation* (Routledge, 1998). She is a co-founder of Sankofa: Association of Transracial Adoptees. Currently, she is an assistant professor of Ethnic Studies at Mills College in Oakland, California.

Marly Swick is the author of two novels, *Paper Wings* and most recently *Evening News.* She has also published two collections of short stories, *Monogamy* and *The Summer Before the Summer of Love.* She lives and teaches in Lincoln, Nebraska.

Mary TallMountain, an Alaskan native born in 1918, was taken from Alaska as a child by a white doctor and his wife who adopted her when her mother became fatally ill. She lost touch with her father for decades, then used writing to regain her connection to the land and her family. Her book of poetry and prose, *The Light* *on the Tent Wall: A Bridging,* was published by the UCLA American Indian Studies Center in 1990. Mary TallMountain died in 1994.

Susan Volchok is a New Yorker whose short fiction has appeared in *the Virginia Quarterly Review, the Kenyon Review, Confrontation, 13th Moon,* and *Asylum* (among others), as well as in numerous anthologies. A first collection as well as a novel are currently on offer to publishers. The story "Mothers" is a chapter from an earlier, unfinished novel.

Victor Walter is a fiction writer who previously taught sociology at several universities. His novel, *The Voice of Manush,* was published in 1996 by White Pine Press. His short stories appear in literary journals as well as popular magazines. His nonfiction books include *Placeways: A Theory of the Human Environment* and *Terror and Resistance: A Study of Political Violence.* He has six grown children and three grandchildren.

Suki Wessling is a fiction writer and poet living in coastal California. Her fiction has been published in various literary journals, and she was winner of the Hopwood Award for Fiction at the University of Michigan. She runs a graphic design business and a small poetry press, Chatoyant (www.chatoyant.com).

Lynna Williams teaches at Emory University. Her collection of stories, *Things Not Seen and Other Stories,* was published by Little, Brown. She is currently working on a new book.

About the Editors

Susan Ito lives in Oakland, California. Her short stories, poems and essays have appeared in numerous publications including the anthologies *Growing up Asian American, Two Worlds Walking, Making More Waves,* as well as in *The Santa Barbara Review* and *Hip Mama* magazine. She teaches writing at the University of California Berkeley's Extension program.

Tina Cervin, psychotherapist and poet, lives on a hill in San Francisco with her husband and two sons. Her poems have been published in *Alchemy* and *Kaleidoscope Kyoto.* She is currently working on a collection of poetry.